An Amish Christmas Love

Other Novels by the Authors

Beth Wiseman

THE AMISH SECRETS NOVELS

Her Brother's Keeper
Love Bears All Things

THE DAUGHTERS OF THE PROMISE NOVELS

Plain Perfect
Plain Pursuit
Plain Promise
Plain Paradise
Plain Proposal
Plain Peace

THE LAND OF CANAAN NOVELS

Seek Me with All Your Heart
The Wonder of Your Love
His Love Endures Forever

OTHER NOVELS

Need You Now
The House that Love Built
The Promise

NOVELLAS

Love Birds included in *An Amish Market*
Love and Buggy Rides included in *An Amish Harvest*
Home Sweet Home included in *An Amish Home*
A Spoonful of Love included in *An Amish Kitchen*
A Son for Always included in *An Amish Cradle*
Naomi's Gift included in *An Amish Christmas Gift*

YOUNG ADULT

Roadside Assistance
Destination Unknown
Miles from Nowhere
Reckless Heart

NONFICTION

A Gift of Love

Amy Clipston

THE AMISH HEIRLOOM SERIES

The Forgotten Recipe
The Courtship Basket
The Cherished Quilt
The Beloved Hope Chest

THE HEARTS OF THE LANCASTER GRAND HOTEL SERIES

A Hopeful Heart
A Mother's Secret
A Dream of Home
A Simple Prayer

THE KAUFFMAN AMISH BAKERY SERIES

A Gift of Grace
A Promise of Hope
A Place of Peace
A Life of Joy
A Season of Love
A Plain and Simple Christmas
Naomi's Gift

Kelly Irvin

THE AMISH OF BEE COUNTY NOVELS

The Beekeeper's Son
The Bishop's Son
The Saddle Maker's Son

EVERY AMISH SEASON NOVELS

Upon a Spring Breeze

Ruth Reid

THE AMISH WONDERS NOVELS

A Miracle of Hope
A Woodland Miracle
A Dream of Miracles

THE HEAVEN ON EARTH NOVELS

The Promise of an Angel
Brush of Angel's Wings
An Angel by Her Side

NOVELLAS

Always His Providence included in *An Amish Miracle*
Her Christmas Pen Pal included in *An Amish Second Christmas*
An Unexpected Joy included in *An Amish Christmas Gift*

An Amish Christmas Love

FOUR NOVELLAS

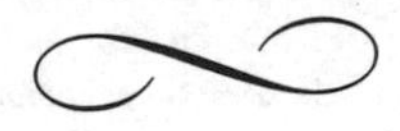

BETH WISEMAN, AMY CLIPSTON,
KELLY IRVIN, AND RUTH REID

THOMAS NELSON
Since 1798

An Amish Christmas Love

Published in Nashville, Tennessee, by Thomas Nelson. Thomas Nelson is a registered trademark of HarperCollins Christian Publishing, Inc.

Thomas Nelson titles may be purchased in bulk for educational, business, fund-raising, or sales promotional use. For information, please e-mail SpecialMarkets@ThomasNelson.com.

Library of Congress Cataloging-in-Publication Data

CIP data is available upon request.

Printed in the United States of America

17 18 19 20 21 LSC 5 4 3 2 1

Contents

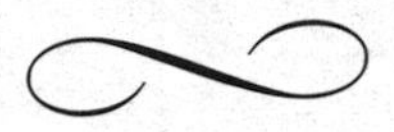

Winter Kisses

BETH WISEMAN

To: All the women who have inspired me throughout my life, especially my mother—Pat Isley—who continues to astonish and amaze me with her vitality and love of life. Happy 84th birthday this year, Mother.

Glossary

ab im kopp: off in the head, crazy
ach: oh
daadi: grandfather
daadi haus: a smaller house on the property, where older relatives might live
daed: dad
danki: thank you
dochder: daughter
Englisch: English, non-Amish
frau: wife
gut: good
haus: house
kapp: prayer cap worn by all Amish women
maedel: girl
mamm: mom, mama
mammi: grandmother
mei: my
mudder: mother
nee: no
Ordnung: the written and unwritten rules of the Amish

rumschpringe: running-around period when a teenager turns sixteen years old
sohn: son
Wie bischt?: How are you?
ya: yes

Chapter 1

Naomi Stoltzfus carried an arrangement of red roses as she crossed the living room. "*Mammi*, Mr. Cotter will be by later today to pick these up. I'm going to put them on the kitchen counter." The older *Englisch* man ordered flowers for his wife, Ann, on the first Monday of each month. The gesture was romantic, even by Amish standards, but such extravagance wasn't in Naomi's future. She'd seen what an emotional attachment could do to a person.

"*Ya, ya*. Okay." Naomi's grandmother didn't lower her binoculars as she peered out the window toward the *daadi haus*.

Naomi slowed her stride, stopped in the middle of the room, and studied the older woman. Ruth Stoltzfus was barely five feet tall, walked with a cane, and wore thick black-rimmed glasses. Pride and vanity were frowned upon, but both Naomi and her mother had tried numerous times to convince Ruth to get more delicate gold-rimmed frames that didn't take over her face. "*Mammi*, what are you looking at?"

"The renters moving into the *daadi haus* for the month of December. There are three men carting suitcases inside."

Naomi edged closer to the window until she was looking over her grandmother's shoulder across the snow-blanketed yard. A layer of white topped the silo like a winter cap, and the pond in between the main house and the *daadi haus* was partially frozen. "I thought only two people rented the *haus*," she said as she squinted to see the men.

"*Ya.* That's what your *mudder* said. But three men got out of the taxicab and are carrying suitcases up the porch steps." *Mammi's* binoculars clinked against the lenses of her glasses. "Ouch," she whispered as she lowered the binoculars, but her scowl was quickly replaced with a twinkle in her eyes. "One man looks to be about seventy, another maybe fortyish, and there's even a young lad that looks about your age."

Naomi shook her head but grinned as she walked across the wood floor to the kitchen. "That's not appropriate talk, *Mammi*," she said as she heard her grandmother's steps behind her.

"You sound like your *mudder*." *Mammi* slid into a chair at the kitchen table and reached for a biscuit left over from breakfast. "It fears me that the both of you will end up lonely old maids if you don't make an effort to find a husband."

Naomi was definitely of marrying age at twenty, but every time she saw the pain in her mother's eyes, it solidified her decision not to marry. "We are not in a hurry to find spouses."

"*Ach*, well, you should be. Almost every single fellow your age is promised for marriage, or you've already kicked the poor suitor to the curb." *Mammi* chewed on the biscuit. "And your *mudder* isn't getting any younger either. Your *daed* died three years ago, and that's more than enough time to grieve and remarry."

"Everyone's different, *Mammi*."

Naomi's grandmother began the hunt for a husband the day after they'd buried Naomi's grandfather ten years ago, even checking the obituaries in other districts so she'd know when a man lost his wife. It was a process that irritated and embarrassed Naomi's mother since *Mammi* didn't try to hide her ambitious courting attempts, often sharing her intentions and the results of her efforts with members of the community.

Mammi pushed her chair away from the table and walked to the rack by the kitchen door. She put on her black cape and bonnet and reached for a black scarf and her gloves. "I'm going to go welcome our guests."

Naomi's mother walked into the kitchen with an armful of folded kitchen towels. "You'll do no such thing." *Mamm* set the stack of towels on the table and put her hands to her hips. Naomi braced herself for the argument that was sure to come.

Barbara reminded herself that Ruth was her elder, even though most days her mother-in-law had the maturity of a teenager. "Let our guests get settled. Then we can take them a basket of baked goods and some fresh fruit." She glanced out the kitchen window. "Assuming we can make the trek to the *daadi haus* without sinking in snow or slipping on ice."

"It seems even colder than usual for December," Naomi said as she began putting the kitchen towels in the drawer.

Barbara didn't respond to her daughter as she kept her eyes on Ruth, who had tied her bonnet and was now putting on her gloves. "Are you still planning to go over there right now? Can't you wait?"

Ruth lifted her chin, a sour expression filling her features, exaggerating the spidery lines that connected across her face. "You might have been the boss of my *sohn*, but you are not the boss of me."

"*Ach*, *gut* grief, Ruth. You sound like a child. It was just a suggestion that we wait until—"

Ruth walked out the door, slamming it behind her.

Barbara shook her head. "That woman is intolerable."

Naomi walked to the kitchen window. Barbara sighed as she walked toward her daughter, stopping next to Naomi at the window. Barbara would watch Ruth all the way to the *daadi haus* and wouldn't feel settled until her mother-in-law safely returned.

"*Mammi* took off her glasses and set them on the rocking chair on the porch." Naomi leaned close to the windowpane. "She left her cane too."

"Stubborn old woman. She's blindly teetering across ice and snow to see if one of our guests would be a suitable husband for her."

Naomi giggled. "Oh, she's not just seeking a husband for herself. She's already said that there's an age-appropriate man for each of us too."

Barbara rolled her eyes before she walked to the stove to stir a pot of chicken tortilla soup she was warming for lunch. "Only two men rented the *daadi haus*." She shook her head as she clicked her tongue. "I'm grateful those two fellows don't live nearby in case your *mammi* embarrasses us. Again." She scratched her chin. "I wonder who the third man is and if he lives in this area. The two renters came from a district near Pittsburgh. A man named Wayne said they would be here for at least a month working on a construction project that they'd won the bid on."

Naomi gasped loudly. "She fell! *Mammi* fell!"

Barbara rushed back to the window. Naomi was already putting on her heavy coat and winter hat. Barbara didn't even take the time to do that. She burst out the door, hurried down the porch steps, and began trudging through the snow.

Ruth was on her side in the snow and not moving. *Oh, dear Lord, please let her be all right.*

Barbara was making slow progress and sinking in snow to her ankles. She slowed her pace when Naomi yelled at her. "Stop, *Mamm*! I have your boots and cape."

She did as her daughter instructed and slipped on the warmer clothes, though she couldn't take her eyes off her mother-in-law. Barbara felt sillier than Ruth for darting out the door without her cape and boots, but it had been an instinctive dash from the house.

I don't know what I'd do if anything happened to that crazy old woman.

Chapter 2

A woman fell down in the snow." Eli pointed out the window before he looked over his shoulder at the two men he would be working with for the next month. Or longer. The thought caused his stomach to lurch. Eli didn't mind hard work, but he didn't like the cold, and they would be outside at least eight hours a day building a large metal shop for an *Englisch* family. "Now there are two other ladies hurrying to the one who fell."

The elder of the two men, Jethro, rushed to the front door. The other fellow, Wayne, was right at Jethro's heels. Eli let out a heavy sigh, not eager to go back out in the weather, but he followed them anyway. He picked up his pace when the other two men did, even though the deep snow made walking a challenge. He was grateful he was still wearing his winter clothes.

By the time Eli, Jethro, and Wayne got to the woman, she was standing up, her black cape and bonnet caked with snow. She was a tiny lady with a lot of wrinkles, and long gray strands of hair hung loose from beneath her *kapp*. Jethro hurried out of his black coat and draped it around her.

The woman blinked her eyes several times, then smiled. "*Danki*. I'm so careless." Her voice rattled and cracked as her lips trembled.

"Ruth, are you all right?" One of the women following the eldest of the trio stepped up to her and put an arm around her shoulder.

"*Ya*, *ya*," Ruth said. "I must have lost my footing." She stared at Jethro, blinking her eyes and smiling even more. Eli wondered if she had a tic like Jacob Lapp, his friend from high school. Jacob blinked his left eye all the time, and his mother called it a tic. But Ruth blinked both eyes, so Eli wasn't sure if she suffered from the same ailment.

But everyone else faded into the white space around Eli when he laid eyes on the third woman in the group. She was tall, like Eli, with huge brown eyes and olive skin. Long eyelashes swept down onto high cheekbones, and when she smiled at Eli, he felt like a snowman melting into the white slush beneath his feet.

"Maybe we should move introductions inside," Jethro said as he motioned to the cottage. Eli breathed a frosty cloud of relief. He didn't feel very manly with his teeth chattering and his entire body shivering.

Eli waited as the women moved ahead of the men, but when the older lady—Ruth, the other woman called her—slipped, Jethro quickly reached for her and latched onto her elbow. "Careful, now."

Jethro had a deep voice and one of the longest beards Eli had ever seen, almost to the top of his pants. It was completely gray. Jethro reminded Eli of Santa Claus, even though his people didn't celebrate the icon the way the *Englisch* folks did. Jethro had a large belly, too, and the same rosy cheeks Eli had seen in pictures of Santa.

"I must have sprained my ankle when I fell." Ruth shook her head as she struggled to take steps in the snow.

"May I?" Jethro held out his arms in a position to scoop Ruth into them.

Eli turned his attention to the beautiful young woman a few feet away from him, guilt nipping at him as he sort of wished she'd trip, too, so he could take her into his arms.

"Oh my. *Danki*." Ruth began to bat her eyes again before Jethro cradled her in his arms. *Definitely a tic.*

As the six of them made their way to the *daadi haus*, Eli's eyes locked with those of the youngest of the women. He held her gaze until she smiled a little, then looked away.

Maybe this project, a penance forced upon him by his father, wouldn't be so bad after all.

Naomi was having a hard time not looking at the young man walking to her left. He was tall and straight like a towering spruce, skinny enough to still be growing into his body, but with broad and confident shoulders. His beardless face told Naomi he wasn't married, and his hair was the color of field oats. A defined, square jaw furthered his air of confidence, along with blue eyes that lent a softness to his overall appearance. The flirty glint in his eyes could surely break a girl's heart.

She'd seen that look before from suitors in her district, although those men hadn't come calling in such a perfectly put-together package. Just his looks were enough to give Naomi pause. She had spent her teenage and young adult life fending off the affections of young men who wanted to make a home with her, fearful of the emotions that went along with a relationship. But as she watched this man stroll up the porch steps, she wondered if maybe she just hadn't met anyone worth the risk.

She jumped away from her thoughts when her mother elbowed her, then whispered, "You do realize your *mammi* is faking this, *ya*?"

"Of course." Naomi grinned at her mother before letting her eyes drift to her grandmother. Her *mammi* had laid her head against the large man's shoulder. "I think it's sweet."

"How can you say that? It isn't sweet. It's embarrassing." *Mamm* rolled her eyes, something she did a lot when she referred to Naomi's grandmother. Barbara Stoltzfus was a proper woman, someone who always followed the rules and practiced perfect etiquette in everything she did. Naomi's grandmother was the exact opposite, a fun-loving bundle of energy who felt rules were in place to be broken. Naomi's father had been a glorious mix of the two personalities. *I miss you so much,* Daed.

Naomi snuck another look at the youngest man as they all moved inside the *daadi haus*. The men hadn't been there long enough to start a fire, and as all of them blew clouds of cold air, the living room reminded Naomi of the smoke-filled dance hall she'd visited once at the beginning of her *rumschpringe*, long before she'd chosen baptism. But the breaths of cold air here didn't have the horrible stench that went along with cigarettes. If there was one thing about her father Naomi would have changed, it was that he enjoyed an occasional smoke out in the barn. Sometimes it was a cigarette and sometimes it was a cigar. Naomi could recall her mother lambasting him each time, but her father would wink at Naomi and tell her, "She's the most beautiful when she's feisty. That's the only reason I smoke." Then Naomi's father would look at her mother in a way that Naomi had never seen another man look at a woman. Her parents' marriage was everything Naomi had ever longed for. Until her father died and she watched a part of her mother pass along with him. *Mamm* didn't smile anymore. Naomi missed her father, but she also missed the part of her mother that left when he did.

Barbara fought not to shake her head when Jethro set Ruth down on the couch. After he'd asked Ruth if she was okay, the older man hustled to start a fire. The youngest of the three men left the room, but not before he snuck a peek at Naomi. The young man's obvious interest in her daughter might have made Barbara hopeful, except that Naomi had turned away any boy who had come to call. She doubted this fellow would be any different. Barbara chided herself for being so cynical.

As a scowl settled into Barbara's expression, she felt eyes on her and instinctively turned to the far corner of the living room. The third man had his arms folded across his chest as he leaned against the wall gazing at Barbara. She took in his appearance the same way he seemed to be doing with her. The man was bearded, his facial hair a mix of salt and pepper, contrasting with the dark locks that framed his face beneath a black felt hat. His cropped bangs were too long and his mouth turned up slightly from one corner. Barbara raised her chin, then looked away.

When her eyes drifted back to his, he narrowed his eyebrows, squinting at her. The lines around his eyes hinted that he was older than Barbara might have thought at first glance. He was so serious-looking and solemn with deep worry lines above the bridge of his nose that he might have frightened her if she'd met up with him alone somewhere. Moreover, she was acutely aware of his height. He towered several inches over the other two men, his shoulders straining against a dark blue shirt. He'd braved the cold outside without any winter attire, and even now, in a room cold enough for human breath to cloud the space around them, he didn't so much as tremble.

Barbara quivered as her heart beat too fast for her liking. Drawing in a slow breath, she forced herself to remain calm, uncomfortable with the effect this stranger was having on her. She'd loved John with all of her heart and soul, and no man would ever take away those feelings. Not even someone who could send a shiver up her spine with barely a glance. Silly as it was, she could see why Ruth had paired them all up in her mind. Barbara's mother-in-law had used the Internet at the library to research the two men who would be staying with them—much to Barbara's disapproval—and had learned that both men were widowers. Barbara wasn't sure how the boy fit into things.

She cleared her throat as she clasped her hands together in front of her. "I'm Barbara Stoltzfus." She smiled as she addressed the men, determined not to look at the man in the corner. She motioned with her hand toward Naomi. "This is *mei dochder*, Naomi." Dropping her hands to her sides with more force than necessary, she nodded at the older woman, although she couldn't hold on to the forced smile. "And this is my mother-in-law, Ruth."

"Naomi was named after me, my middle name. And Barbara used to be married to *mei sohn*, but he passed three years ago." Ruth sat taller as she spoke. "So Barbara got stuck with me by default. I was raised on this farm."

Barbara could feel her face reddening as she took a deep breath. "I don't feel *stuck*, Ruth." She glanced at Naomi, hoping for some backup, but her daughter just grinned.

The older man added another log to the fire, and as orange sparks shimmied upward, Ruth stood and sidled up to him, reaching her palms toward the warmth. "What a lovely fire you built for us."

Barbara's face burned from embarrassment, but the older man's cheeks dimpled above his beard before he stoked the fire with one of the fireplace tools nearby.

"I see your ankle must be better," Barbara said to Ruth.

"Uh . . . *ya*." Ruth looked down and bounced up on her toes. "All *gut* now. Much better."

Barbara wondered if Ruth realized how much she was squinting. The woman surely couldn't see much past the tip of her nose without her thick glasses. On the other hand, she sure seemed spry without her cane in her hand. Barbara had always known Ruth carried the cane for other uses than merely keeping herself stable on her feet. Ruth found more uses for a cane than its maker ever could have imagined. Barbara had seen her use it to hammer in a nail, to reach things high on a shelf, and, most recently, to stave off a wild dog.

"I'm Jethro." The large man who had carried Ruth inside announced his name in a deep voice, with vigor, as if he were notifying the world of his presence. Barbara lowered her eyes, sighed, and reminded herself again: *Don't be cynical.* It was a word an *Englisch* friend had used to describe Barbara not long ago. At first, she wanted to deny the charge. But after thinking about it, Barbara supposed she had allowed herself to become this way since John's death. *I'm going to do better, Lord.*

"This is my business partner, Wayne . . ." Jethro nodded to the handsome man in the corner. Barbara allowed herself a quick peek, feeling a tiny bit disappointed that Wayne didn't look her way. "And the young lad, well . . . That's my neighbor's boy, Eli."

"I, uh, thought there would be just two of you," Barbara said as she tried to calculate if she had enough food planned for an extra person.

"*Ya, ya.* Eli's joining us was unexpected and at the last minute." Jethro stroked his long gray beard. "We'd be happy to pay for an extra renter for the month, or if you can direct us to a nearby bed-and-breakfast, we can book him a room there."

Barbara shook her head. "*Nee, nee.* It will be fine for Eli to stay on with you, although he will need to sleep on the couch since there are only two beds here."

"Very kind, Barbara. *Danki.*" Jethro nodded, smiling.

Barbara noticed the looks being exchanged between Naomi and Eli, and while their mutual interest was nice to see, Barbara remained doubtful that anything would develop. Naomi didn't talk about it much, but Barbara knew her daughter was fearful of commitment and scared someone she loved would leave her far too soon. But Naomi had to realize that with great love, there sometimes is great loss. She didn't want her daughter to miss out on what she'd had with John, even though they hadn't been able to grow old together.

"There's a sleigh out in the barn behind the cottage." Barbara held her hands in front of her again. "If it wouldn't be too much trouble, perhaps one of you men could help me get it out. I'm sure none of you want to have to carry us back to the *haus* because of a fall." She glowered at Ruth for a moment, but Ruth had her eyes on Jethro, and if not for her obvious age, Ruth could have been a schoolgirl with her first crush, batting eyes and all.

"I'll help you."

Barbara took in a sharp breath. It was the first thing she'd heard Wayne say, and his voice was as winsome as his appearance.

He ran a hand the length of his beard before he strolled toward her, studying her in a way that made her feel translucent. She raised her chin and took another deep breath. Being handsome didn't give him a right to ogle her inappropriately. Or was she misreading him?

Barbara avoided his assessing gaze, afraid he'd see the crack in her heart and the loneliness that had ensued after John died. Could he read her thoughts or see the desires of her heart?

"Very well." She started toward the front door, still dressed in her cape and bonnet. They trudged across the uneven ground between the barn and the *daadi haus*, and she didn't look back until they were in the barn and she heard the door close behind Wayne. As she turned around, the handsome stranger locked eyes with her, and Barbara thought the earth might be shifting on its axis.

Barbara was always in control of her actions and her emotions.

Until now.

Chapter 3

Wayne held Barbara's gaze, wondering if she could see the yearning in his eyes. A man who missed his wife more than words could express, but who longed for a woman's touch, even a simple kiss that could mean everything or nothing.

"There's the sleigh," she whispered, pointing over Wayne's shoulder, but their eyes stayed fused, neither drifting from the moment and the power it seemed to have over them. He wondered what it would be like to kiss her. For just a few moments, they could pretend they were in love, that they shared a life together, and that their worlds hadn't stopped spinning the moment their spouses died.

Wayne forced the inappropriate thoughts away. It was a vision he'd never act on, and he didn't want to do anything that would make her feel uncomfortable, or that might disappoint God. He cleared his throat and refocused on the task at hand.

"*Ya*, sure." Wayne pulled his eyes away from her, moved toward the sleigh, and began to prepare it for travel. But just being near Barbara caused his heart to flutter and made his cold hands clammy. He fumbled with the harness on the mule, and once the bit was in the animal's mouth, Wayne turned to her. The light from the barn window lit the space around Barbara, casting an angelic glow.

"You are . . ." He stared at her, lost in her beauty. "You are . . . ," he tried again but shook his head as he lowered his eyes for a moment. "I'm sorry," he said as he locked eyes with her once more.

Barbara moved closer to him, stepping from the light and into Wayne's shadow. She raised an eyebrow, waiting.

"I was just going to say that you are very beautiful." Soft dark waves of auburn hair framed a delicate face with rosy cheeks. She had emerald eyes that were both examining and questioning. He quickly looked away and pulled the reins over the mule's head, surprised he'd verbalized his thought. Someone as lovely as she surely remarried quickly after her husband's death. He wiped off the seat of the sleigh with his hand.

"*Danki*," she whispered.

Wayne held out his hand to her. "Shall we?"

An arm emerged from beneath her cape, and she reached for his hand. He guided her onto the seat of the sleigh, tempted not to let go of her hand, but he did.

Wayne clicked his tongue and pulled back on the reins until the mule began pulling the sleigh out of the barn. He forced himself not to look at Barbara, fearful she'd see the longing in his eyes. "*Mei frau* died two years ago. So, uh . . . I hope I wasn't being too forward, about saying how beautiful you are. I haven't told a woman that before, only my wife. I wasn't being disrespectful to a current wife. I mean, I didn't remarry." He cringed at his nervous rambling. "Did you remarry soon after your husband's death?"

"Everyone thought I should have." She raised her chin, glancing at him for only a moment. "But, *nee*, I have not remarried."

Wayne briefly turned her way as they pulled to a stop in front of the cottage. He wanted to know more about her. Was someone courting her? Why hadn't she remarried? Did she have offers? Was she attracted to him?

He'd known her less than thirty minutes, but the questions scampered about his mind like a hungry squirrel searching for nuts. Lost in a swirl of unexpected desperation to know more about this woman, he took a deep breath and tried to formulate a sentence in his mind that didn't prattle on like before. But his new acquaintance didn't wait for him to help her out of the sleigh. She was walking up the porch steps before Wayne could even tether the mule.

He recalled the way their eyes had locked in the barn, and he wanted to believe that he saw something in her gaze that matched the attraction he felt toward her. But were such thoughts right in the eyes of God? He didn't even know this woman.

Dusk was settling in as Naomi placed the platter of roast on the table that evening. Her mother had carefully surrounded the large piece of meat with potatoes cooked to a golden brown, along with carrots she'd glazed in a buttery honey sauce.

"Why so fancy?" Naomi stared at the set table. There was a tray of pickles and olives laid out in a design resembling a Christmas wreath. A plentiful tossed salad filled a crystal bowl that Naomi had never seen before, and steam rose from creamy mushroom peas. "You haven't made these peas since . . ." Naomi paused, choosing not to finish her sentence when the light clicked on in her head. "You like him."

"Like *whom*?" *Mamm* placed a plate filled with buttered bread next to the peas, but she didn't look at Naomi.

"That new man, Wayne, who is staying in the *daadi haus*." Naomi grinned as she leaned against the cabinets.

Her mother huffed as she brushed back a strand of hair from her face, then tucked it beneath her *kapp*. "I just met him earlier today. How could I possibly *like* him?"

Naomi couldn't stifle the smile on her face. "I saw him looking at you while we were all in the cottage." She chortled as she walked toward her mother. "I saw you checking him out too."

Mamm still refused to look at Naomi as she scowled and shook her head, bustling past her with a jar of raspberry jam. "'Checking him out'? That's a very *Englisch* thing to say."

Naomi touched her mother on the arm, forcing her to look at her. "It's okay to like him, *Mamm. Daed* would want you to be happy."

"I don't even know him." *Mamm* thrust her hands to her hips. "I think you need to focus on your own love life." She paused, her eyebrows knitting into a frown. "Or lack thereof."

Naomi had been hearing this for so long it didn't bother her anymore. But she couldn't deny she felt an air of excitement about seeing Eli soon. And whether her mother admitted it or not, *Mamm* was eager to see Wayne. Maybe their grandmother's matchmaking wasn't such an awful idea after all.

A bump against the wall, loud enough to rattle the china cabinet, sent Naomi and her mother hurrying to the living room.

"Ruth, what in the world . . ." Naomi's mother rushed across the room. "What happened?"

Mammi rubbed her forehead. "I turned the corner too sharply and bonked *mei* head."

"Where are your glasses? We've talked about this before." *Mamm* wagged a finger at Naomi's grandmother. "You need to wear your glasses. And if you don't like that bulky pair, we can get you some different ones." *Mamm* rolled her eyes as she sighed.

"I don't need glasses." *Mammi* stiffened before she brushed past them toward the kitchen. But both Naomi and her mother heard Ruth mumble, "You're not the boss of me."

"Ruth. We heard you. Why do you always say that, like you're a child?"

Naomi's grandmother didn't respond and kept going until she disappeared into the kitchen.

"She heard that in Walmart one day," Naomi said. "We walked through the television section on our way to pick up *Mammi's* prescription. *Mammi* stopped to watch one of those funny shows with the same people in it. Someone said that on TV."

"Was it a child who made the statement?" *Mamm* blew out a heavy breath of frustration.

Naomi nodded. "*Ya.*" She glanced around the room. Within the last hour, Christmas presents had appeared. Two were wrapped and next to the rocking chair in the corner. Three small packages were neatly stacked on the coffee table. And a large box wrapped in silver and gold with a big red ribbon was leaning against the far wall. In their Old Order district, they didn't put up a Christmas tree, but placing gifts around the house for decoration was traditional. She wondered if the gentlemen coming for supper had the same traditions since they were from Pittsburgh, not Lancaster County.

As Naomi followed her mother to the kitchen, her stomach flipped. She was looking forward to seeing Eli again, which felt strange and wonderful at the same time. But most importantly, she hoped the spark between her mother and Wayne might turn into something romantic. She even hoped that Jethro would take a liking to her grandmother. *Then there would be hope for me.*

Eli finished the last bite on his plate, his third serving. His father never prepared enough food to have more than one serving at each meal, citing the need to be frugal. Eli's father's appetite had floundered over the years, but Eli spent most days hungry, or at the least not satisfied. Barbara had supplied a plentiful meal, and he hadn't turned her down when she encouraged him to help himself to more.

"This was a very *gut* meal, Barbara." Jethro dabbed at his mouth with a napkin. Eli wondered if he knew he had a pea in his beard. He tried to lock eyes with the older man, but the elderly lady—the one named Ruth—had started talking, and Jethro's eyes were on her.

"I taught Barbara to cook when she was fifteen." Ruth squinted as she spoke. But she wasn't blinking her eyes fast like earlier. "That's when she married *mei sohn*." Ruth sat taller as her lips puckered. "I like to think I trained her up right," Ruth said.

Eli glanced at Barbara. The lady's face was turning red. But when Naomi cleared her throat, Eli stole a glance at her. What he wouldn't do to spend time with someone like Naomi. But he was no longer worthy of affection from a woman like her. His father had drilled that into his head. "You are worthless," he'd said before he shipped Eli off to work with Jethro and Wayne.

But Jethro was a kind man, so Eli welcomed the opportunity to be away from his father. And Jethro's friend Wayne was a nice fellow too. But as Eli glanced out the window, the darkness in the night matched the darkness in his heart.

The women began clearing the dishes. Jethro and Wayne stood up and thanked the ladies for the meal again. Naomi was stowing a jar of jam in the refrigerator, and when Eli turned to say good night to her, she gestured toward the living room.

Eli looked over his shoulder. Jethro and Wayne were moving toward the door in the kitchen that led to the front porch, both of them yawning. The other two women were still busy cleaning up the supper dishes. Eli casually walked into the living room, and Naomi met him there.

"Your friends look tired, so I suspect they will be off to bed early. But I was wondering if you might help me with something in the barn later. My father's workbench has been in the same spot for as long as I can remember, and I'd like to move it over a few feet." Naomi glanced around, then spoke in a whisper. "*Mei mamm* has a bad back, and *Mammi* doesn't have the strength for it."

Eli opened his mouth to speak, but his voice had forsaken him. Just the thought of spending time with Naomi sent a wave of adrenaline pulsing through his body. "Uh . . ." was all he managed to say.

Naomi reached for the string of her *kapp* and wrapped it around her finger. "It's okay if you're too tired. I have to help clean the kitchen and then we'll have devotions, so it would be a bit later this evening. I figured you would all be busy from sunup to sundown, so that's why I'm asking about this evening."

Eli struggled to find his voice.

"You said you like to read. I've read several *gut* books lately. I could bring you one." Naomi stuffed her hands in the pockets of her black apron, then shrugged. "Or it's fine if you don't want to."

Eli hated the cold, and it would be frigid in the barn. But he'd suffer through it to be with her, even if it was just for a few minutes to help her move a workbench. He couldn't court a woman like Naomi, which made him wonder right away if she had a boyfriend. *Surely she does.* "Uh, *ya*, okay," he finally managed to say.

"Meet me at nine."

Eli thought that was awfully late to meet. In his district, folks were in bed asleep by then. He figured it was only about five thirty. "Okay."

Naomi's eyes lit up before she scurried back to the kitchen.

Eli moved toward a second door that led to the front porch from the living room. Once on the porch, he hurried to catch up with Jethro and Wayne.

Excitement caused his heart to hammer in his chest as they rode in the sleigh back to the house. But the more he thought about seeing Naomi later, the more he wondered if meeting her in the barn was a good idea after all. As much as he wanted to help her with the workbench, spending time with her would only put a strain on his heart, knowing he couldn't be with someone like her.

The last time he felt this anxious, it wasn't in a good way—since he was in handcuffs and being carted off to jail.

Chapter 4

Naomi felt like a black polar bear wrapped in her father's heaviest coat, and she'd remembered to stow a book in the pocket, an *Englisch* murder mystery, but one that wasn't filled with bad language or inappropriate scenes.

Her mother hadn't gotten rid of any of Naomi's father's belongings since he died. Naomi had suggested that maybe his clothes might benefit someone in the community, and her mother had said she would get around to it soon. That was three years ago. Her father's toothbrush was still in a cup in the bathroom.

Over the past hour, snow had started falling in heavy white blankets, so much so that Naomi could barely see the barn out the window, even with the propane lamp glowing in the yard. After tiptoeing across the living room, she eased the front door open and carefully made her way down the porch steps. Her boots sank shin-high in the snow as she shined her flashlight in front of her. She used her gloved hands to dig away snow that had piled against the barn door.

Naomi pointed the light around the barn, but the two mules, three goats, and six chickens barely noticed. She sat down on a haystack in the corner, shivering and waiting for Eli. She briefly considered lighting the propane heater on her father's workbench, but the last time she'd tried to turn it on, the propane tank had been empty, and she hadn't thought to get it refilled.

As she shined her flashlight over her head, she thought about how irresponsible this was, being out in a near blizzard way past bedtime. *Irresponsible—but also silly and fun.* She and her mother weren't known for their playful spirits like her grandmother was. But lately, when Naomi looked at her mother, void of that spirit, she also saw herself, and it made her sad.

Her stomach roiled and twisted as she thought about spending a little time with Eli, maybe getting to know him a bit. It was a new way of thinking for Naomi, and it excited and scared her.

In truth, she'd wanted to move the workbench for years, but it could have waited until a better time—when it wasn't so late and cold.

But after about ten minutes, she wondered if Eli was coming.

As the wind howled, she thought maybe he couldn't get across the area separating the *daadi haus* and the barn. The *daadi haus* was closer to the barn than to the main house, but it was still a trek in this weather. And when it snowed more than a few inches, the shallow ditch between the cottage and the barn made navigating the terrain challenging in the dark. She should have considered that before she asked him to meet her.

Her teeth chattered as she thought about the boldness of her invitation. She'd spent so much time avoiding courtship of any kind that she'd surprised herself by asking Eli to meet her. She just wanted to know if there was a good personality that went along with the handsome guy she'd met earlier today. It didn't mean she was ready to open her heart to someone, but for the first time, she was willing to consider the idea.

After another thirty minutes passed, and feeling frozen to her bones, Naomi lifted herself off the bale of hay and went back to the house. She wanted to believe that Eli couldn't get to the barn because of the weather. But the snow had stopped, and when she shined her flashlight in the direction of the *daadi haus*, all was quiet. Not even the flicker of a lantern could be seen in the windows.

Eli woke the next morning, relieved that he'd heard Jethro say it was supposed to be warmer today. They'd already agreed not to start their workday until the sun was up.

He was the first one awake, so he hurried from the couch to the bathroom to get dressed. Breakfast was to be served in the main house at six o'clock. He and his coworkers were on their own for lunch, then they were to be back for supper with the ladies at five each night.

Eli was hungry, but also embarrassed that he hadn't shown up in the barn like he'd told Naomi he would. As pretty as Naomi was, and as nice as she'd seemed during supper the night before, getting to know her would only be a waste of time. Even if they hit it off, in a romantic way or as friends, Naomi would eventually find out what Eli had done and she'd want nothing to do with him. *But I could have at least helped her move the workbench.* That was all she'd proposed, so maybe Eli had overthought it.

After a quick cup of coffee with Jethro and Wayne, they all went outside. Their rental arrangements included use of a buggy or sleigh to get to their work site, which was only about a half mile down the road. Wayne had already hooked up the mule to the buggy and said they'd take it the short distance to the main house for breakfast before they went to work.

As they pulled up at the main house, Eli shivered from the cold. He was hoping to speak to Naomi privately, to apologize for not meeting her. He hadn't come up with a good reason yet, and he hoped that just saying he was sorry would be enough for them to remain polite to each other. He was sure she wouldn't ask for his help again.

Jethro knocked on the door, and Barbara opened it for them. A fire was blazing, and the aroma of bacon cooking wafted up Eli's nostrils. They followed Barbara into the kitchen, surprised to see only four plates set.

"Where is everyone?" he asked, without giving it much thought. Wayne grinned, which caused Eli to shrink into his coat a little. But Wayne couldn't say much about any interest he might suspect between Eli and Naomi. Eli had seen the way Wayne and Barbara looked at each other.

"Ruth and Naomi left early this morning to tend to a widow friend. She's a shut-in, and they wanted to take her some food and make sure she'd done all right during the snowstorm. Then they were off to the market for a few things we need. So you boys help yourselves."

Barbara set a plate of bacon on the table alongside a bowl of eggs and a basket of warm biscuits. As her eyes drifted to Wayne, they smiled at each other, but both quickly looked away. Eli wished he could steal looks with Naomi, but Naomi wasn't going to want anything to do with him, and he was relieved she wasn't here right now. He lowered his head in prayer when the others did, then decided to make the best of things by serving himself a heaping spoonful of scrambled eggs. Then he reached for two biscuits and three pieces of bacon.

He would put in a hard day's work, every day, for the entire month. Then he'd return home, to a place he despised even more than himself.

Barbara sat down to eat breakfast after the men seemed to have everything they needed. The young fellow—Eli—reminded her of her husband when he was young, with a healthy appetite that seemed insatiable. The lad had eaten four biscuits and six pieces of bacon at last count, and had finished the scrambled eggs in the bowl. Throughout the meal, the only conversation had been about the weather and how it was supposed to be warmer for the next week or so. Barbara had met eyes with Wayne one too many times, and she felt like she'd done something wrong even though nothing had happened between them. Her physical attraction to him was confusing, and guilt nipped at her.

As much as she'd loved John, loneliness had settled into Barbara's way of life and latched onto her like a one-sided friendship, taking from her and giving nothing in return. She was wise enough to recognize temptation and determined to keep it at bay, but as Wayne's soft gray eyes met hers, she wanted to throw caution to the wind, to share one kiss with this man, to feel the comfort of this stranger's strong arms.

"A fine breakfast," Jethro said, smiling as he nodded at Barbara.

"A simple meal." Barbara smiled back at him. She could feel Wayne looking at her, but she forced herself not to look his way.

Jethro's chair scraped against the wood floor as he stood up and reached for his hat and coat on the rack by the kitchen door, Eli close behind him. "I'll be on the porch, Wayne."

"You go ahead." Wayne didn't stand up but reached for another biscuit. "I'm going to stay and help Barbara clean the kitchen. I'll walk to the job site."

Barbara's chest tightened. It wasn't customary for men to help out in the kitchen, especially paying guests. "*Nee, nee*. That's not necessary." She dabbed at her mouth with her napkin, mostly to hide her trembling lip. But she noticed her hands were shaking like those of a nervous schoolgirl, as if Wayne's opting to stay signaled anything more than assisting with cleanup.

But Jethro just waved over his shoulder as he passed through the living room, closing the door behind him.

Wayne smiled at her.

Barbara swallowed hard, then coughed as she stood up and began clearing the table. But when Wayne walked toward her and leaned around her to put his plate in the sink, he smelled musky like cologne, which wasn't allowed in their district. Perhaps it was allowed where he came from. Either way, Barbara inhaled deeply before she went to gather more dishes.

"I'm sure you miss your husband this time of year." Wayne offered up a weak smile as he lifted the empty bowl previously filled with eggs. And once again, he leaned around her to submerge the dish in the soapy water, filling her senses with his savory scent.

"*Ya*, I do." She quickly maneuvered around him, even though the smell of his cologne seemed to follow her. *Or maybe it's the type of soap he uses?*

"I noticed your Christmas gifts placed throughout the living room. We always did that too, although I haven't bothered now that I'm on my own." Wayne pushed in the kitchen chairs as Barbara tried to recall if John had ever helped her in the kitchen.

"I like to make it festive for Naomi and Ruth." She tried to hold her breath since no matter where she went in the kitchen, Wayne's muskiness wrapped around her.

Wayne chuckled. "I used to wrap all of the Christmas gifts." He held up a palm in her direction, grinning. "*Ya*, I know. It's not men's work. But I enjoyed it."

Barbara dried her hands on her apron, smiling. "I don't recall my husband wrapping any gifts." She cast her eyes downward, the familiar guilt nagging at her again as she silently acknowledged her attraction to this man. "But I think it's nice you did that," she said as she looked up at him and smiled.

She felt herself in a familiar scene, like when she and Wayne had been in the barn and locked eyes for several long moments.

Barbara recalled him telling her she was beautiful, and the scene replayed even longer this time.

As the water in the sink neared its limit, neither of them made a move to turn off the faucet. They just kept looking at each other, the smells of breakfast and Wayne's musky aroma comingling in Barbara's kitchen. She wished the moment could last forever.

Naomi pushed the grocery cart through the market as her grandmother shuffled alongside her.

"What else is on your mother's list?" *Mammi* pushed her thick black glasses up on her nose.

"Just flour." Naomi glanced at the piece of paper in her hand, making sure they hadn't forgotten anything. She was glad to have missed breakfast this morning, and she was trying desperately to devise a plan so she wouldn't have to see Eli in the mornings for breakfast or in the evenings for supper, knowing that would be impossible to do for a month.

She'd finally opened the closed door where her heart had resided and decided to take a chance on a man who sparked her interest, but he'd disappointed her and made her feel silly. She wasn't going to let that happen again.

"There's Benny King." Naomi nodded down the aisle at the older man coming their way.

Mammi pushed her glasses up again and sighed. "He probably followed us here. That fellow won't give up."

Naomi stifled a grin. Benny King had been pursuing her grandmother for years. It was no secret to anyone in their district that *Mammi* wanted to be remarried. But *Mammi* always said that Benny wasn't fit for courting because he had fake teeth. Lots of older people in their district had false teeth, and Benny's display of pearly whites wasn't considered vain. Teeth were a necessity. A person couldn't eat without teeth, the bishop had said. But Naomi's grandmother had a big problem with dentures, even though *Mammi's* teeth were far from perfect. She often complained about not being able to eat a thick piece of meat without a struggle.

"I don't understand why you can't give him a chance," Naomi said in a whisper, leaning closer to her grandmother's ear. "He's been smitten with you for years."

Mammi huffed. "Stop with your nonsense." She smiled at Benny when he reached them, her glasses sliding down her nose again. "*Wie bischt*, Benny?"

Naomi echoed the sentiment as Benny tipped the rim of his straw hat at them. "*Wie bischt*, ladies? How did you fare during the snowstorm?"

Benny's long white beard was in need of grooming, but he was otherwise a nice-looking older man. Naomi glanced at her grandmother as a scowl filled the woman's face.

"We fared just fine, Benny." *Mammi* shuffled past him, so Naomi edged the grocery cart around Benny also.

"Have a *gut* day, Benny," Naomi said, feeling sorry for the man as his expression fell.

But Benny recovered quickly, turned around, and called out to Naomi's grandmother. *Mammi* spun to face him and slammed her hands to her hips. Naomi stayed where she was as Benny made his way down the aisle. She couldn't hear what Benny said to her grandmother, but she heard *Mammi's* response loud and clear.

"*Nee*, I cannot have lunch with you tomorrow. We have houseguests in the *daadi haus* that we must tend to." *Mammi* lifted her chin as she raised her eyes to his. "But *danki* for asking."

Benny's tall stance fell as his shoulders hunched over and he walked away. Naomi was grateful her grandmother had been polite, even though she could have been gentler with Benny.

"You should go to lunch with Benny. He's been pursuing you for almost a decade," Naomi said when *Mammi* returned to her side.

"I don't have romantic feelings for Benny. He knows that." *Mammi* shook her head as she grunted. "I don't know how many times I'm going to have to tell that man that I am not interested in courting."

Naomi stopped walking, and after a few moments, her grandmother did too. *Mammi* folded her arms across her chest. "Speak, child. What's on your mind?"

"I just don't understand why you won't give him a chance." Naomi glanced around, making sure no one else was in earshot. "And don't say it's about his teeth."

Mammi walked closer. "You keep saying that. Have you ever seen Benny eat?"

Naomi shook her head.

"*Ya*, well . . . it's not pleasant. Those falsies in his mouth shift all around, and once I saw a piece of food fall right out of his mouth and onto his plate." *Mammi* scrunched up her face. "I wouldn't be able to watch him eat every day." She shivered as she blew out a breath of air, then cringed. "And don't most people keep their dentures in a glass by the bed at night? I'd have nightmares if I knew those things were staring at me while I slept."

Naomi chuckled. "I don't think teeth *stare*, but I don't believe your reasons anyway." Naomi also folded her arms across her chest as she faced off with her grandmother. *Mammi* had been chasing men for almost a decade, and Naomi had laid eyes on many a man who had captured her grandmother's attention. Benny was nice-looking and kind. He should have been at the top of her grandmother's list of potential suitors.

Mammi walked closer and rolled her mouth into a pout. "Don't talk to me the way your mother does. I'm not a child. And I'm capable of choosing whom I have lunch with. If I don't want to have lunch with Benny, then that's just the way it is. You aren't the boss—"

"Stop saying that," Naomi said, louder than she meant to. "No one is the boss of you, *Mammi*. I'm just trying to understand—"

"You don't have to understand. It's my business, child." *Mammi* lightly stomped one foot and started down the aisle again.

Naomi shrugged, then pushed the basket to catch up, still wondering why her grandmother refused to consider Benny's obvious affection for her. Especially since her grandmother was desperate to remarry.

Naomi strolled down the aisle, her thoughts swirling. Then she recalled something her mother had said a long time ago, that Naomi's grandmother dated Benny when they were young. She wondered why that fact hadn't surfaced in her mind before. Pondering what might have happened between her grandmother and Benny, she slowed her step when she reached her grandmother.

"You used to date Benny when you were young. What happened between you two?" Naomi raised an eyebrow as she stared at her grandmother.

Mammi's eyebrows drew into a frown as she puckered her lips. "None of your business. And it doesn't matter. I have found the man I am interested in. He's tall, strong, handsome, and my hero. I'm going to marry Jethro when he asks me."

There'd been no mistaking the spark between Naomi's mother and Wayne, but Naomi wasn't sure she'd seen that same spark between Jethro and her grandmother. But after her grandmother stomped off, Naomi's musings shifted to Eli. She'd thought there might be something between them, but obviously she'd thought wrong.

Chapter 5

Wayne wasn't sure when his feet had moved, but he found himself facing Barbara and reaching around her to turn off the water. And now he was close enough to kiss her. He fought the growing temptation, but he was losing the battle.

She eased around him just in time, hurried across the kitchen, then spun to face him.

"I . . . I don't even know you." Her bottom lip trembled.

Wayne's heart thumped wildly at her recognition that something was happening between them.

"Then get to know me," he said softly, smiling a little.

Barbara shook her head as she stood taller, folding her hands in front of her. "*Nee*. Our behavior is inappropriate."

"We haven't done anything," he said as he walked toward her, stopping short a few feet when she took a step backward. "There's nothing to feel bad about."

But they were strangers, and Wayne knew as well as she did that any desire they might be feeling was forbidden to them, reserved for a husband and wife, and it needed to be tempered. He pulled out a chair and sat down at the table.

Barbara stared at him, then smiled as she pulled out a chair opposite from him.

"So, tell me about yourself," he said, grinning.

Barbara took a deep breath, then smiled. "Okay."

Within a few minutes, the woman across the table felt less and less like a stranger, and Wayne was surprised at how much they had in common—their love for store-bought Fig Newton cookies, their inability to sleep more than five hours per night, and a host of other random similarities. But they talked about more serious matters, too, such as their fear of growing old alone.

Wayne silently thanked the Lord for guiding him onto the path that introduced him to Barbara, and the more Barbara shared about her life, her hopes, her regrets, and her fears, the more grateful Wayne was to God.

He said another prayer . . . asking for Barbara to give him a chance.

Eli felt good about the work he'd put in so far for Jethro and Wayne, and Jethro acknowledged Eli's efforts, something his father had never done. Eli fought the urge to blame his upbringing for the mistakes he'd made, but he couldn't help but wonder if his life would be different if he'd been raised by his mother for more than six years, without only the heavy hand of his father. He was packing up his lunch box after finishing a ham sandwich and chips when he heard a buggy turning into the driveway.

Eli stood up, brought a hand to his forehead to block the sun, then saw it was Naomi and Ruth pulling in. He glanced toward the owner's house, wondering if he could bolt inside before he had to face Naomi, but he decided to face the consequences of his actions.

"*Mamm* said to bring you these snickerdoodle cookies," Naomi said when she reached them.

Jethro took the basket from her. "Wayne's favorite," he said as he unfolded a red-and-white checkered napkin from atop the basket.

Wayne's face turned red, although Eli wasn't sure why. Jethro picked up a cookie and took a large bite. Eli allowed himself a quick glance at Naomi, but she wouldn't look at him. *Can't blame her.*

The little lady—Ruth—walked up to Jethro toting a smaller basket in her left hand and pushing up her glasses with her other hand. "I brought these for you." She handed the basket to Jethro as he hurried to chew the cookie, nodding. "They're wedding cookies." She smiled broadly.

"*Ach, danki,*" Jethro said. "Are these left over from a wedding? It seems late in the year for a wedding."

Ruth chuckled. "It's never too late for a wedding."

Jethro's cheeks flushed. Eli hoped his face never turned red like Wayne's and Jethro's had today. Seemed like that would be embarrassing. But when Eli felt eyes on him and turned to see Naomi glaring at him, he feared he joined his coworkers in donning a shiny red face.

Naomi pulled her eyes away from him, then waved at Jethro and Wayne. "See you at supper," she said before she cut her eyes at Eli.

Ruth started talking to Jethro. Wayne began walking toward the house. And Eli decided to be a man and face Naomi.

"I'm sorry I didn't show up last night." He stuffed his hands in the pockets of his jacket.

Naomi raised an eyebrow. He'd never seen a person able to raise just one eyebrow as high as she did, and she was clearly waiting for Eli to give a good reason why he hadn't shown.

"Uh, anyway . . ." Eli looked down and kicked at the white fluff beneath his feet, snow that twinkled like a million stars in the afternoon sun. When he realigned his thoughts and raised his eyes to Naomi, her eyebrow was still raised. "Um. Sorry." He turned to leave, walking briskly.

"Wait."

Eli slowed his step, then slowly turned around. Naomi was walking toward him. When she got about a foot away from him, she pulled her black coat snug around her. "Did something happen last night? Was it the weather?"

The weather. Yes, it was the weather. But he decided not to lie. He kicked at the snow again, avoiding her eyes. "*Nee*, not the weather, but I'm sorry I couldn't make it. I, uh, didn't have your phone number to call you."

"I don't have a phone anyway." She raised her chin a little. "Did something happen?" she asked again.

"I thought everyone had a cell phone these days." Eli wanted to turn and leave, but maybe he did owe her an explanation.

"I know lots of our people carry a cell phone," she said, followed by a heavy sigh. "But we only have a phone in our barn, and we try to use it just for our florist business and renting the *daadi haus*."

Eli looked over his shoulder. Wayne wasn't in sight, and Ruth was still talking to Jethro. The older man was mostly nodding and looked uncomfortable. Eli turned back to Naomi. "Listen, I, uh . . . I can't really get involved with anyone."

Naomi grinned. "Get *involved*?" She put her hands on her hips. "I asked if you could help me move a workbench. What does that have to do with getting *involved*?"

For the second time in the past few minutes, Eli felt a burn creeping into his cheeks. "I just meant . . ." He shrugged. "I . . . I just think you're really pretty. But I can't date you or anything."

Naomi walked closer to him, her nostrils flared. "What makes you think I would even consider such an idea? Don't you think that's a bit presumptuous of you?"

Eli didn't even know what that word meant, but it must not be good, judging by the sound of her voice. "I'm sorry." It was all he knew to say at this point.

She didn't call after him this time when he walked away. And he didn't dare turn around to look at her. He was afraid he might tell her everything, and then he wouldn't be able to take the way she looked at him, which most likely would be with fear and disgust.

Eli slowed his pace, hoping she'd call out to him anyway. But a few moments later, Ruth scooted past him toward the buggy, and Eli heard the *clippity-clop* of hooves as the women left. *Just as well.* But he sure did wish things were different.

Wayne struggled through supper that evening, trying to keep his eyes off Barbara. Twice she'd looked his way and smiled, but then she would quickly busy herself refilling tea glasses or doing some other task that kept her from locking eyes with him. Wayne was thrilled they were getting to know each other, but he wondered if she thought about kissing him half as much as he thought about kissing her.

As Wayne plotted how he could be alone with her, he heard a loud *plop*, which brought everyone's eyes to Ruth. Her glasses had slid off her nose and were now resting in the mashed potatoes on her plate. As she fumbled around in the potatoes, she couldn't seem to keep a grasp on the glasses. Wayne was sitting next to her but resisted the urge to assist her, which would require putting his hands in her food. Finally, the poor woman dug the dark-rimmed glasses free and pushed them up on her nose, even though one lens still had potatoes on it. She pulled the glasses off and squinted.

"Here, *Mammi*." Naomi eased the glasses from her grandma, wiped them clean with her napkin, then handed them back to her, smiling. "*Gut* as new."

"*Danki*, dear." Ruth set the glasses on the table next to her plate. "I don't really need them anyway." She smiled at Jethro. The woman had been flirting with Jethro since the moment they arrived. Wayne thought it was cute, although Jethro had said the day before that it made him uncomfortable.

"I just finished a *gut* book today," Naomi said, mostly to Barbara, who smiled, which made Wayne smile too. He was trying to think of an excuse to stay longer.

Wayne grinned to himself and thought the Lord couldn't have provided a more perfect matchmaking setup. Eli and Naomi were about the same age. Wayne and Barbara were getting to know each other. And Wayne was rooting for Ruth to win over Jethro's affections. But Wayne wondered if any of the couples would carry things any further than friendship. Even with Barbara, Wayne worried that their potential relationship was being built on physical attraction alone.

He could recall not being overly attracted to Marie when he'd first met her, but once she'd opened her mouth to speak, her delicate voice spoke to his heart and he'd fallen in love with her quickly.

Supper ended too soon. Wayne had been refilling his plate, eating slowly, and drawing out the evening as much as he could, but it was coming to a close and he couldn't think of a reason to stay, which was probably good. His temptation to kiss Barbara was getting harder to ignore, but if and when that happened, he wanted them both to be comfortable with it. When he'd come close to kissing her after breakfast, he'd seen fear in her eyes, and that wasn't how he wanted a first kiss to be.

"Another fine meal," Jethro said as he stood up. Eli put his napkin on his plate and stood up also, thanking the ladies for the meal.

Wayne slowly edged his chair away from the table. "*Ya, ya.* A very *gut* meal." He glanced at Barbara, but she was stacking dishes in the sink, which brought his thoughts back to the moment he'd almost kissed her in the kitchen, followed by their long conversation. He watched her briefly before he left the kitchen, confused about where things were headed with them, if anywhere at all.

The men dressed in their winter gear and were almost out the door when Eli spoke up.

"I'll be along in a while." Then the lad walked back into the kitchen. Wayne overheard him ask Naomi if he could talk to her privately.

Wayne put on his black felt hat and smiled, remembering what it was like to be that age. Recently, he'd been feeling almost as youthful as Eli and Naomi. He hoped the two of them would hit it off. From what Jethro had told Wayne, the boy had been through a lot and made some mistakes. But overall, Jethro said, Eli was a good kid.

Wayne snuck one last look at Barbara, his temptation to stay almost overwhelming. But he needed to go, at least until he could get things right in his mind.

Eli and Naomi were walking out the door in the kitchen when Wayne left with Jethro from the living room. There was a portable heater and two rocking chairs on the porch, and he was happy to see the two young people sitting down and spending time together.

Wayne slowed his steps for a moment, then revisited his earlier thoughts and hurried to catch up with Jethro.

Chapter 6

Barbara sipped a cup of coffee at the kitchen table. Ruth was having hot tea. As much as she'd hoped Wayne might stay for a while after supper, she was sure it was best for him to go home. He'd come close to kissing her, and she'd almost allowed it to happen. As lonely as Barbara had been, she also knew that she and Wayne couldn't succumb to a physical attraction built mostly from loneliness. Their long conversation had given Barbara hope that maybe there was something more for them to explore besides the longing for a kiss. But Barbara had felt guilty all day that she hadn't even thought about John the past couple of days. Right now, however, her hopes and prayers were that Naomi would open her heart to the possibility of love.

"What do you think they're talking about?" Ruth added another spoonful of sugar to her tea. Barbara was pretty sure that was the fifth one.

"I don't know. But Eli is a handsome young man." Barbara ran her finger around the rim of her coffee cup.

"So is Wayne." Ruth reached for more sugar, and Barbara started to say something but snapped her mouth shut. Maybe she did treat Ruth like a child sometimes, and whether Barbara agreed with Ruth's choices or not, her mother-in-law was a grown woman, and she should try to respect her as such.

"I suppose he's nice-looking." Barbara raised one shoulder

and let it drop slowly, afraid Ruth would see past Barbara's words to a place Barbara wasn't willing to share with her mother-in-law.

"I think he wants to kiss you."

Barbara's eyes widened and she felt her face flush. She hoped Ruth would change the subject.

"I see the way he looks at you," Ruth said before she took a drink of her tea. "And I see the way you look at him."

Barbara avoided Ruth's scrutinizing gaze. "I don't know about that."

Ruth pushed her glasses up on her nose. Again.

"Can we please go to town next week and see about getting you some new glasses?" Barbara tried to keep the frustration out of her voice. "Those glasses are too heavy for you, and I really think you would be more comfortable with something that fit your face a little better."

Ruth frowned. "I don't really need them."

"Well, the eye doctor seems to think you do, and if you don't want them falling in your mashed potatoes again, I think we need to get you new frames."

"Jethro said he thought my glasses were just fine. I was nervous at first to wear them around him, but when I asked him about it, he said he hadn't even really noticed them."

Barbara found that hard to believe since the glasses took over Ruth's face, but she resumed running her finger around her coffee cup, thoughts of Wayne lingering in her mind.

"I asked Jethro if he would like to go to lunch tomorrow. I thought he might be tired of sandwiches for lunch."

"Ruth, don't you think that's a bit forward?" Barbara sighed.

"At my age, I don't have a choice but to be forward." She raised her chin. "Please keep your disapproval to yourself."

Barbara wasn't in the mood for a round of arguing with Ruth, so she asked, "Where are you going to lunch?"

"He can't go." Ruth slouched into her chair.

Barbara waited for her mother-in-law to elaborate, but when she didn't, she said, "Maybe another time."

"Maybe," Ruth said softly.

Barbara glanced out the kitchen window. She could just barely see Naomi and Eli in the darkness, but Barbara hoped they were having a good conversation. She was happy to see her daughter spending time with a young man who seemed to spark her interest.

Naomi crossed one leg over the other and kicked the rocking chair into motion, her teeth chattering. She wondered what kind of excuse Eli was getting ready to send her way. She prepared herself for an excuse, not a reason. Because his not showing up could only mean one thing, that he wasn't even interested in being her friend.

"I'm sorry for not showing up last night. I think you are very pretty, and I would like nothing more than to get to know you better, to help you move furniture, to talk books, and to spend time with you. But I've made some mistakes—*big* mistakes—and I'm not worthy of attention from someone as great as I think you probably are. At the time, I thought it was better not to show up, but I see that it hurt your feelings and angered you, and I am very sorry for that."

Naomi's jaw hung open. She couldn't have predicted what Eli would say if she'd been given a thousand options to choose from. She wanted to know what he felt he'd done to perceive himself as so unworthy, but she didn't want to push him. "We all make mistakes," she said softly.

He shook his head, looking down. "I know. But I made a really big mistake. One that landed me in jail."

Naomi's heart hammered against her chest. She'd never known

anyone who had been in jail, but she still didn't want to push him about something he clearly felt awful about.

"They called it domestic violence, and you don't have to say anything." Eli lifted his eyes to hers. "I know how bad it sounds, and I won't make any excuses for my actions."

Naomi wanted to hear details, but she wondered if they would haunt her in her dreams. "Who did you hurt?"

"*Mei* father. And he saw fit to call the *Englisch* police, even though such matters are normally handled by the elders." He shrugged. "It doesn't really matter. What I did was wrong, and I deserved to be in jail."

He stood up and looked down at her. "So, now you know. My choice not to meet you in the barn had nothing to do with you." He shook his head, sighing. "I have no idea why someone as beautiful as you is still single, but you deserve someone better than me, someone who hasn't lost his faith."

Naomi was stung more by Eli's last statement than by anything else. "God is always with us, through the good and the bad."

"*Nee*. He was not with me on that day. And God was not with me on a lot of other days. I clung to the hope that God would help me get out of my situation, but instead I ended up in jail. And rightly so. I raised my hand to *mei* own *daed*."

Naomi was trying to read between the lines. "Were you defending yourself?"

"It doesn't matter."

Eli was still standing. She gently touched his arm. "Sit."

Scowling, he said, "You want me to stay after you've heard what I've done?"

Naomi wasn't sure how she felt about what Eli had done. Her people didn't believe in violence, but the fact that Eli was willing to tell her something so private, just to make her understand it wasn't about her, made her want to know more. So she nodded.

He slowly sat down. They were quiet for a few moments. Naomi reached over and turned the portable heater to a higher setting. As the light in the kitchen went dim, she knew her mother and grandmother were going to bed, or at least retiring to their own rooms for the night.

Eli stared at the beautiful woman sitting next to him, her eyes glistening in the light of the lantern on the table between their rocking chairs. "I've lost my faith, Naomi. Did you hear me say that?" Belief in God and acceptance of God's will were the most important aspects of being Amish. "I haven't been baptized, and I'm not sure if I will be."

"Do you love your father?" Naomi spoke softly, her eyes locked with his.

Eli wanted to hate the man, for the beatings, for the way he'd always stripped Eli of any self-worth he tried to establish. But the man was his father. "*Ya*. I love him."

"So, you believe in love?" Naomi rested her hands in her lap.

"*Ya*, I guess I do."

"How can you believe in love and not believe in God's love for you?"

Eli couldn't come up with a good answer. He was too surprised that Naomi hadn't already asked him to leave. He changed the subject. "Why aren't you married? You're at least twenty or older."

Naomi smiled a little. "I'm twenty."

Eli waited, but she didn't elaborate on why she hadn't married. "Have you come close to getting married?" Maybe she'd had her heart broken.

She shook her head. "*Nee*."

Eli scratched his chin, not sure how hard to push her.

Finally, she sighed. "I watched my mother and grandmother suffer when my grandfather passed, and then again when my father died. It was awful for me, but their grief seemed almost unbearable, and I've been scared of that type of love."

"But if you believe in God, then you have to believe in love, just the way you told me. And to deny yourself love because you are fearful is a sin." He was sure he'd overstepped, and when she stood up, Eli did too, prepared to end the night.

But she stared at him long and hard, squinting slightly. "Do you want to go inside? I think my mother and grandmother went to bed. I can make us some coffee, and I think there's half of a pumpkin spice cake left." She paused, offering a smile. "*Mamm* only makes those at Christmastime."

She picked up the lantern, turned, and walked to the door that led to the kitchen. Smiling, she said, "You coming?"

Eli slowly followed her. She put the lantern on the kitchen table and motioned for him to sit down. A few minutes later, they each had a cup of hot coffee and a slice of pumpkin spice cake. Eli told her the cake was good, but otherwise he stayed quiet.

"Is your mother still alive?" Naomi held the cup between her hands as she barely took a sip, not taking her eyes from Eli.

"*Nee*, she died when I was six."

She nodded. "Do you want to talk about it?"

Eli sat taller. It was the last thing he wanted to talk about. "*Nee*. Mostly, I just thought I owed you an explanation for—"

She brought a finger to her lips, shushing him. "It's over, and I forgive you." She smiled, then took a bite of cake.

She's been waiting for you.

Eli heard the voice in his mind but found it hard to believe. He'd shut his heart off to God. But by the light of the lantern, Naomi's eyes twinkled, and Eli felt a flicker of hope. Maybe God hadn't forsaken him after all.

Chapter 7

Barbara and Ruth cleared the breakfast dishes, the same way they'd done the past four days, while Eli went with Naomi to feed the chickens and milk the goats. Naomi had a new bounce in her step. Barbara had prayed Naomi would open her heart to the possibility of love, but now she worried what would happen when Eli had to go back home.

Jethro and Wayne left shortly after breakfast, and each day after they were gone, Barbara felt a wave of relief meld with a surge of disappointment. When she closed her eyes at night, she could almost feel Wayne's lips on hers. But such desire was wrong, and Barbara was doing her best to forget what almost happened, even though the entire scene replayed in her mind all day long, especially during breakfasts and suppers.

Ruth stashed the jams and jellies in the refrigerator. "Jethro likes banana nut bread, so I made him a loaf early this morning." She went to the far corner of the kitchen counter and picked up a bread pan covered with foil. "I'm going to take this to him shortly."

Barbara wiped her hands on the kitchen towel, scowling. "If he likes it so much, why didn't you offer it for everyone to enjoy this morning?"

Ruth's glasses fell off as she set the bread on the kitchen table. She scooped them up and quickly put them back on her nose, the glasses promptly sliding down as usual. Barbara rolled her eyes but stayed quiet.

"I forgot about the bread." Ruth smiled as she moved toward the door.

"The poor man hasn't been gone ten minutes. Do you really need to deliver it now? You can give it to him tonight at supper if you really made it especially for him."

"Unlike you, Barbara, I'm not on a schedule. And I can come and go whenever I choose. You are not—"

"Don't say it! Do *not* tell me one more time that I'm not the boss of you! If anyone tells you what to do, you say that."

Ruth glared at Barbara. "*Nee*, I don't say that when anyone tells me what to do, only *you*." She huffed and marched out the door.

Barbara knew that wasn't true, but as she leaned against the kitchen counter, she wondered when things had become so tense between her and Ruth. They were so different, but Barbara could still see her mother-in-law's face the day Ruth's husband passed. And she saw it again the day her son left this earth. The pain wasn't something Barbara could put into words, and she didn't have to. She'd felt it, along with Ruth, both times. She'd loved her husband very much, but she'd also loved her father-in-law. It was something she and Ruth had in common—maybe the only thing—their immeasurable grief. And Naomi had picked up on the shared misery, adding her own to the mix, until they'd become three old maids living under one roof for longer than any of them expected.

Barbara was lost in her thoughts when she heard the door in the living room open and shut. Wayne walked into the kitchen and stared at her. Barbara tried to control her heart rate but ultimately put a hand on her chest. "Did you forget something?"

He took two steps toward her, then another. "*Nee*, I don't think so." He scratched his forehead as his eyebrows narrowed into a frown. "Well, maybe."

Barbara swallowed back the lump in her throat, but her feet took on a life of their own and moved toward him. "What is it?"

Within seconds, they were once again close enough that Wayne could kiss her if he chose to. The familiar looks they'd exchanged earlier closed the space between them as they lingered in the moment.

Barbara tried to corral the tornado swirling in her stomach, along with the wide range of emotions fighting for space in her mind. Wayne's finger lightly brushed against hers before he lifted his hand to tuck back a strand of hair that had fallen from beneath her *kapp.* Barbara took a deep breath and tried to prepare for the first kiss she'd had since John. He leaned down, his minty breath comingling with hers.

The front door swung wide, and Ruth stepped over the threshold.

Barbara took an instinctive step backward as Ruth's jaw dropped.

Wayne cleared his throat. "Ruth, *wie bischt*? I was just . . . just going. I'll see you at supper, Barbara." He slowly walked toward the front door, but looked over his shoulder at the last second and smiled at Barbara. She tried to smile back, but Ruth's rounded eyeballs looked larger than life staring at Barbara from behind the thick black glasses.

The front door closed, and Barbara's chest tightened as she waited for a lashing from Ruth. A lashing she deserved for almost allowing herself to fall into Wayne's arms.

Ruth took off her glasses and rubbed her eyes, then put the bulky glasses back on, giving a raspy chuckle. "I just needed to make sure I saw what I think I saw." She raised an eyebrow. Then her expression stilled. "I'm pretty sure Wayne was about to kiss you."

"I loved John." Barbara didn't realize she was on the verge of tears until she heard her voice cracking. "I loved him very much. You know that." She hung her head as a tear slipped down her cheek, followed by a steady stream of more tears. She covered her face with her hands. "I'm ashamed." After allowing herself a few good sobs, she put her hands at her sides, her lips still trembling. "I'm so lonely."

Ruth hadn't moved, and in a rare moment, Barbara couldn't read her mother-in-law's expression. Ruth's lips were pressed together, the lines on her forehead deeper than usual, and again, Barbara braced herself for a lashing from her mother-in-law. Ruth inched toward her, then put a hand on Barbara's arm.

"Shame is the devil's work, one of his trickiest ways to make us feel bad about ourselves." Ruth rubbed Barbara's arm before she lowered her hand. "You mustn't allow that to happen. You have nothing to be ashamed of."

"How can you say that? You just walked in and caught me almost in the arms of another man, a man I barely know." She shook her head so hard that more loose strands of hair fell from beneath her *kapp*.

Ruth stared at her long and hard, squinting her eyes and puckering her mouth. "Did he at least get in one good kiss before I barged in?"

"What?" Barbara brought both hands to her chest, fearing her hammering heart might crack her chest wall. "*Nee*, no kissing." She shook her head again.

Ruth let out an exasperated huff of air. "I have never understood why you can't just allow yourself to be happy. Even when you were with John, you always held back a little, striving for perfection and proper etiquette at all times. Don't you ever just want to step out of the corral a bit?"

"'Step out of the corral?'" Barbara wished the floor would open up and swallow her.

Ruth slid out of her coat, threw it on the couch, and then sat down. "You know, open the gate, get out of the corral, run free with the rest of the horses—"

"Ruth, we are not in one of those western movies that the *Englisch* watch. And our faith demands that we behave a certain way." Barbara took a tissue out of her apron pocket and blew her nose.

"Where in the *Ordnung* does it say that a man and a woman don't feel passion as part of the courting process?"

"This isn't even a conversation I should be having with you." Barbara pulled another tissue from her pocket and dabbed at her eyes. "I'm sorry you saw me with Wayne, but nothing happened."

Ruth patted the couch beside her. "Come, child, and sit."

Barbara opened her mouth to tell her that she was a woman in her forties, not a child, but instead she sat down by Ruth.

"*Mei maedel*, I'm happy that I saw you with Wayne. I've hoped and prayed for nearly three years that you would find someone. Don't you think I want you to be happy? I know you loved John. And he loved you. But he would want you to find another love."

Barbara stared at Ruth, realizing this exasperating woman was closer to her than anyone—except maybe Naomi—and as she listened to her mother-in-law, she couldn't help but think this was the most normal conversation she'd ever had with Ruth. Barbara spent most of her time correcting Ruth or feeling embarrassed about Ruth's actions. Maybe if she'd shared her feelings of loneliness, she wouldn't have been tempted by a man she barely knew.

Ruth stood up, picked up her coat, and hung it on the rack by the front door. Then she walked back to where Barbara was sitting, leaned down to the coffee table, and picked up the loaf of banana nut bread. It was the first time Barbara saw that she had returned with the gift for Jethro.

Ruth's mouth curled up slightly as she locked eyes with Barbara. "It turns out I was wrong. Jethro doesn't care for banana nut bread after all." She shuffled toward the kitchen. Barbara quickly stood up.

"Ruth?"

Her mother-in-law slowly turned around. "*Ya*. What is it, dear?"

Barbara took a few quick steps toward her. "You will find someone, you know. You will find that special someone to share the rest of your life with."

"*Nee*." Ruth barely smiled as she shook her head. "I won't. Because I'm through trying. You and Naomi will no longer have to worry about me embarrassing you by doing silly things to attract a man's love. And that's okay. I love you and Naomi enough to see me through my years." She paused, then almost smiled again. "Don't let him slip away, that Wayne fellow. I did that once a very long time ago, way before I met your father-in-law. And sometimes you just can't go backward."

Ruth turned and walked away as a tear slipped down Barbara's cheek. She wondered if Ruth was talking about Benny King.

Barbara felt shame about getting caught with Wayne, but it didn't compare to the regret she felt right now, for not seeing Ruth's pain. Her mother-in-law's need for love was as strong as Barbara's, if not stronger. Ruth had been alone much longer.

Barbara walked to the window and looked past two cardinals on the porch handrail. The winter day had turned cloudy. She eyed the brown foliage recently beaten down by the snow, struggling to hang on until the revival of spring rains and sunshine brought forth renewed life. It was a dreary scene, until she spotted Naomi and Eli outside the barn. She recognized the way they were looking at each other, and when Eli reached for Naomi's hand, Barbara turned away, not wanting to intrude on their special time.

An air of romance and thoughts of winter kisses floated on clouds of hope.

For everyone, except the one person who seemed to long for love the most. She started toward the kitchen to join Ruth.

Chapter 8

Naomi eased away from Eli, lingering in the euphoria of their first kiss. They'd been spending time together early in the mornings tending to the animals, and twice they'd snuck off for lunch.

Now, as they stood holding hands and facing each other, Naomi wanted him to know something. "That was my first kiss." Her cheeks warmed as she smiled at Eli.

"That can't be," he said as his eyebrows drew inward. "I'm sure you've had lots of guys who wanted to date you."

She nodded. "*Ya*. But none that I ever thought I could really care about." She lowered her gaze for a few moments before looking up at him again. "Um, I tried to move my father's workbench yesterday, but I could only budge it a few inches. Do you think maybe we could meet in the barn tonight and you could help me move it?"

Eli looked down for a few seconds, shaking his head. "I'm so sorry. I forgot all about that. Sure."

Naomi smiled. There was something she wanted to show Eli in the barn, but she was also hoping to share another kiss with him.

Eli pushed back a strand of hair that had blown across her face. "I could stay here all day with you." He paused. "But I have to go to work."

"I know." Naomi smiled. "See you at supper?"

Eli nodded. "And afterward in the barn?"

"*Ya.*"

Eli kissed her gently on the lips and smiled before he turned to leave, but then he stopped and faced her again. "Naomi?"

She waited.

"For the first time in a while, I feel like I might want to be baptized into our faith."

Naomi couldn't stop a smile from spreading across her face. Sometimes a person needed hope to see past prior hurts, and hearing that Eli was slowly finding his way back to God warmed Naomi's heart.

He smiled at her before he jogged toward the road where he'd have to keep running to the job site.

Naomi watched him until he was out of sight, wondering what would happen when their job was complete and Eli went back to Pittsburgh with Wayne and Jethro.

The thought caused an uneasiness to settle around her, but for now, she was going to keep hope in her heart. And keep praying that Eli would stay on the path back into God's light.

Barbara stirred a pot of red beans she had cooking on the stove, but jumped when someone knocked at the door.

"Wayne." She eased open the door and tried not to smile, forcing her lips into a thin line. "What are you doing here?" She glanced at the clock on the mantel. It was barely past the lunch hour. "Do you need something? Does one of the other men need something?"

Wayne pulled his arm out from behind him and presented her with a bouquet of roses. She fought the urge to remind him that they owned a floral shop housing dozens of roses, although this was a slow time of year and there hadn't been enough activity for anyone to really notice a business was in play.

Barbara opened the door wider, accepted the roses, and took a step backward. "*Danki*, these are lovely."

Wayne stepped over the threshold, then closed the door, grinning.

"You can't stay." Barbara took another step backward. "I'm, uh . . . cooking beans."

Wayne took a large step forward. "I think you want me to stay."

Barbara raised her chin. "*Nee*, I do not. You get me in trouble. *Mei* mother-in-law caught us behaving like teenagers instead of the responsible forty-something people we are."

"You're forty?" Wayne dropped his jaw, frowning. "*Ach*. I thought you were much younger. I'm only thirty-three."

Barbara's knees went weak. How was she going to tell him that she was forty-four? She felt the color draining from her face. *You look older than thirty-three.*

Wayne burst out laughing. "I'm thirty-three"—he cringed—"plus another twelve years."

Barbara held the flowers with one hand and rested her other hand on her hip. "Shame on you for teasing me," she said, unable to keep from smiling.

He took an exaggerated step forward. She took one backward.

"You shouldn't be here. Naomi is at the market. And Ruth is at a quilting party." She pointed a finger at him. "But you know that, because I mentioned their plans at breakfast this morning."

He stepped even closer. Barbara held her position this time.

"It's inappropriate for you to be here." She raised her chin higher, fighting the smile that threatened to overtake her. "Now, go back to your work." She gave a taut nod of her head.

Wayne's expression stilled before he smiled. "I like you,

Barbara Stoltzfus. I like you a lot. But . . ." He inched closer. "I'm not going to let anything happen that would be inappropriate or disrespectful of you in any way."

Barbara brought a hand to her chest and sighed. "I'm happy to hear that. It seems like every time we're together, we almost . . ." She cleared her throat and looked away. "You know."

Wayne grinned. "Kiss? That's what you were going to say."

She faced him and sighed again. "*Ya.* It seems to be on our minds. But we don't know each other very well." She frowned as she shook her head.

"But we are getting to know each other, and I *want* to kiss you." Wayne's smile filled his face.

Barbara raised her chin, stifling a grin. "There has to be more to our relationship than just physical attraction." She wondered if she'd overstepped by mentioning a relationship. "Or whatever it is we think we are doing . . . Not sure I'd call it a relationship." She shook her head. "I don't know what we're doing." She scrunched up her face. "What *are* we doing?"

Wayne gently eased the flowers from her hand and placed them on the coffee table. He moved toward Barbara, but she took a big step backward again.

Wayne scratched his nose, then ran his hand the length of his beard. "Like I said, we *are* getting to know each other. We like each other." He grinned. "And I think we would enjoy kissing each other. So . . ." He shrugged. "I came to kiss you."

"*Nee.* No kissing." Barbara lifted her hands, palms to Wayne. "Back to work for you."

"I'm going to kiss you."

Barbara grinned, feeling the excitement of new love. *Could it be love? Infatuation? Just loneliness?*

"I see the wheels in your head turning." Wayne made a circular motion next to his head. "So here's what I'm going to do.

I'm going to give you a running head start before I chase you and kiss you."

Barbara's eyes rounded so much she thought they might pop out. "Are you *ab im kopp*?"

"I'm going to count to three. One . . ."

She took a step backward. "Stop it, Wayne. This is silly."

"Two." He made his way to where she was standing.

Barbara laughed, then she ran toward the kitchen as footsteps hurried behind her. She wound around the kitchen table, then darted back the other way just before he reached her. She scurried back to the living room, circled around the coffee table, then braced herself behind the rocking chair.

Laughter filled the room. And her heart. She didn't even realize she was squealing until Wayne threw his arms around her, lifted her from the ground, and swung her around by the waist. He kissed her, and it was a kiss that meant everything.

When she opened her eyes, Ruth was standing just over the threshold into the living room. *How did we not hear her pull up?*

"Oh dear." Barbara covered her mouth with her hand, but her shoulders shook from laughter, and it was the kind of laughter that came from the belly, so that she couldn't control it even if she'd wanted to. It was the best feeling in the world.

Wayne tipped his hat, moved past Ruth, and then gave a quick wave to Barbara.

Ruth stomped her way to Barbara and glared up at her. Then she rolled her eyes at Barbara and said, "Intolerable. Simply intolerable." Then she grinned, cupped Barbara's cheek, and moved toward the kitchen. "You burned the beans, by the way! I can smell them."

Barbara touched a finger to her lips as she took slow steps toward the kitchen. But nothing could wipe the grin from her face. Or steal the giddiness from her heart.

Eli met Naomi in the barn after everyone had gone to bed. They'd agreed not to meet right after supper, since they both would have missed devotions at that time. Eli still wasn't sure about his relationship with God, but spending prayer time with Wayne and Jethro gave him a sense of hope.

Though the weather was a bit warmer than the day before and it wasn't snowing, there was still a noticeable nip in the air. They were protected from the biting chill of the wind, but Eli's teeth chattered just the same.

Naomi shined the flashlight across the barn. She looked at him and smiled. "Look what I found when I moved the workbench over a few inches." She nodded to where her flashlight lit a small area in the far corner of the barn, past where the goats were huddling to stay warm.

Eli tried to make out what she wanted him to see in the darkness, but he couldn't. She motioned for him to follow her, and it wasn't until he was right up on it that he saw it. His jaw dropped, and all he could say was, "That's my name carved into the wood."

"*Ya*, I know. And you can see half of a heart and part of the word *ever* at the bottom. I bet when we move the workbench, there will be another name."

Eli had seen hearts engraved into trees. There were always two names with a plus sign and equal sign. He was wishing with all his might that the other name might be Naomi. *Eli plus Naomi equals forever.* But what were the chances of that?

Eli lifted the workbench, and right away he could see why Naomi had only been able to move it a couple of inches. It was solid wood with a back that had lots of tools hanging from the pegs. It took him a couple of hard pushes to get it to slide over and reveal the rest of the carving. Disappointment filled him when he saw that there was a heart, but instead of Naomi's name, it read *BR + Eli = Forever.*

"Who is BR?" Eli raised an eyebrow as he straightened his back and hoped he hadn't overdone it.

Naomi shrugged. "I have no idea."

Eli smiled. "I was kinda hoping it said Naomi."

Even in the darkness, Eli could see Naomi blush as she grinned. "It's probably been there for years. I can't recall *mei daed* ever moving his workbench from this spot."

"Do you want the workbench moved more? Didn't you say a couple of feet?"

Cringing, she nodded. "I know it's heavy, but I'd like to have that space along the wall to keep tack and supplies closer to the mule. But I'm happy to help you push it."

Eli shook his head and waved his hand at her dismissively before throwing his weight against the bench and moving it until she said to stop. He might regret the effort tomorrow, but when Naomi smiled and thanked him with a kiss, he decided it would be worth it.

"So, how is the job going?" Naomi pulled her coat around her as they sat down on a haystack in the corner. "Will you be done on time?"

Eli suspected she wanted to know when he would have to leave. "*Ya*, I think we'll be done by the end of the month."

"Will you go home to be with your family at Christmas?"

Eli shrugged. "I don't know." Going home was the last thing he wanted to do. "Jethro and Wayne have extended families, but no one living at home with them, so I think they're planning to stay here for Christmas. I'm not sure though."

"Maybe we can all spend the holiday together. *Mamm* makes a great meal. We all help, but she does most of it."

"That sounds nice." Eli took a deep breath, savoring the vision of a festive—and normal—Christmas celebration. But he also couldn't stop thinking about the funny story Wayne had told him and Jethro. "Did you know that your mother and Wayne are spending time together?"

"By spending time together, what do you mean?" Naomi grinned. "Spending time together like we are?"

Eli chuckled as he ran a sliver of hay between his fingers, folding it over and over. "*Ya.* Your grandma walked in on them chasing each other around the house . . ." He paused, grinning as he chewed on the piece of hay. "And kissing."

Naomi's mouth fell open. "*My* mother?" As she laughed out loud, she bent over at the waist for a few seconds, then straightened. "That doesn't sound like *my* mother." Pausing, she sighed, but her smile remained. "But that makes me very happy. Although, if anyone has been searching for love, it's *mei mammi.*"

Eli avoided Naomi's eyes, afraid she'd see what he was thinking with regard to Jethro and Ruth. He wasn't sure they were a good match.

But for now, he just wanted to be with Naomi. She calmed his heart and his soul, something no one had done before.

Chapter 9

Wayne finished nailing a sidewall to the metal building, then gathered his lunch from the buggy and made his way to Jethro, who was already eating a sandwich at the picnic table. It was cold outside, but the chilly temperature was better than the smell of mothballs that overwhelmed the senses in the owner's house. "Where's the boy?" Wayne asked as he sat down and opened his lunch pail.

"Inside with the owner, Mrs. Owens. She asked Eli to help her hang a rod in her closet, and I told him that was fine if he could tolerate the smell." Jethro scratched his forehead. "I got a call from Eli's probation officer. Eli missed a meeting he was supposed to have with the *Englisch* man. The fellow was all worked up about it and said Eli also wasn't supposed to leave the county." Jethro shook his head. "His father never said anything about that when he asked me to bring Eli along on the job. I mean, I knew Eli was on probation, but no one said anything about the distance he was allowed to travel."

"What's the story with them?" Wayne bit into a ham and cheese sandwich, savoring the flavor of the homemade mayonnaise Barbara had left in the refrigerator at the cottage.

"I'm not sure I have all the facts." Jethro set his sandwich down on his paper towel, his eyebrows narrowing into a frown. "But I can speculate on some of it. Leroy hasn't been right since his wife died. He raised the boy mostly on his own. I've suspected there were things going on in that house that I didn't want to know about." He blew out a big breath, scowling. "Things the bishop should have inquired about. Eli has shown up at church with a black eye or some other ailment on more than one occasion over the years. Even if the boy is willful, that's just not our way."

Wayne hadn't asked much about Eli and why Jethro had agreed to bring the boy along when Eli's father suggested the arrangement. Wayne was happy to have another set of hands on the job, and the boy was working for free because his father had insisted on it. He'd just assumed Eli's tagging along was a punishment imposed by his father. But this sounded like more than just a lad being forced to do manual labor as a punishment.

"Eli has to go back tomorrow, back to Pittsburgh. He has to meet with the *Englisch* probation officer. The man said Eli could end up back in jail." Jethro was a big man and a big eater, but since he'd barely touched his lunch, Wayne could see the situation with Eli was bothering him. "Why would Eli's father insist he come work with us if he knew it would get the boy in trouble?" Jethro scratched his head, still wearing a scowl on his face.

"What exactly did Eli do to get himself in jail?"

Jethro shook his head, staring at his half-eaten sandwich. "He hit his father, hard enough to break the man's nose."

"Self-defense?" Wayne stuffed the last of his lunch in his mouth.

"I suspect so."

Wayne had always wanted children, but he and his wife had never been able to have a child. He couldn't imagine parents harming their offspring. It just wasn't natural.

"But I'll send him on the train for Pittsburgh tonight." Jethro took one last bite of his lunch, then stuffed the rest back in his lunch pail. "It's going to take us longer than expected to finish the job without the boy."

Wayne was in no hurry to leave, and he wondered if he and Barbara would stay in touch after he went back home. Was there really something between them, or were they two lonely people enjoying each other's company, with nothing more to it than that?

"I don't feel *gut* about sending him back." Jethro pushed back his coat and looped his hands beneath his suspenders. "Especially if he ends up in jail again. I've known Eli since he was born. His *mudder* was a *gut* woman. But it's not my place to interfere with the *Englisch* law."

"I hope it works out for the boy." Wayne stood up just as Eli came out of the house with Mrs. Owens. The woman laughed, patted Eli on the arm, and then waved at Jethro and Wayne.

Both older men waited until Eli reached the picnic table. Then Jethro said, "Eli, we have some news."

Eli's expression fell flat as he glanced back and forth between Wayne and Jethro.

"I got a call from your probation officer today. He said you missed a meeting, and it sounds serious. Did you know that you weren't supposed to leave the county?"

Eli hung his head and kicked at the ground before he looked back at Jethro. "I knew about the meeting, but *Daed* said it would be okay to miss it, that he'd take care of it. He said I needed to work off my wrongdoings."

Wayne's blood boiled as he clenched his fists at his sides. Eli's own father had set him up.

Jethro stroked his long gray beard. "Eli, you have to go back to Pittsburgh. I'll put you on a train, and—"

"*Nee!* I'm not going back." Eli stiffened, his jaw set in anger.

"I'm sorry, *sohn*. I can't keep you here working illegally. You have to face the consequences of your actions and the fact that you left when you weren't supposed to."

"But *Daed* said it was okay. He said I *had* to come with you."

Jethro opened his mouth to say something, but Eli spoke up before he could get a word out.

"I'm *not* going back. They'll put me in jail!" Eli's jaw twitched.

"*Sohn*, you have to go back." Jethro stood taller. "Tonight."

Wayne glanced back and forth between the two of them. "Eli, let's take a walk."

"I don't need a walk." Eli's voice cracked as he spoke.

Wayne glanced at Jethro, and his friend nodded. "Go take a walk with Wayne. Cool down. And then we'll finish up work early today."

Poor kid. Eli didn't seem to have any kind of advocate. Even Jethro seemed to be washing his hands of the situation.

Wayne motioned for Eli to get in step with him. After they were out of earshot, Wayne said, "Tell me about life at home. And don't leave out any details."

Eli cut his eyes at Wayne, but after a few moments of silence, the boy began to talk.

Barbara placed a chicken casserole on the table for supper, a simple recipe, but plentiful. She'd noticed that Jethro ate more than the average man his age, and Eli consumed as much as most teenage boys. It was a tossup each day as to who would reach for the last helping. Twice she'd felt they ran out of food before their guests were full. She'd even doubled the casserole recipe this time.

"Something smells *gut* in here." Jethro walked into the kitchen holding his hat, his coat over his shoulder.

Barbara had instructed the three men to just come into the house for supper without knocking. It felt like one big, happy family to Barbara. Naomi glowed as she laid out silverware, and

Barbara knew Eli got credit for that. Barbara's anticipation about seeing Wayne seemed to grow with each day as well. If anyone wasn't feeling their best lately, it was Ruth. She'd shuffled around the house aimlessly all day, and even now it seemed to take all of her mother-in-law's effort to pour iced tea for everyone.

Barbara took a loaf of bread from the oven and set it on the table. "*Danki*, Jethro. We're having a casserole that's one of my most requested meals, and I've doubled the recipe." Barbara smiled, but as Jethro scratched his forehead, she saw the worry in his eyes. "What's wrong?" She glanced over Jethro's shoulder and into the living room. "Where are the others?"

"They won't be joining us tonight."

Barbara didn't realize until that moment how much she looked forward to seeing Wayne, especially in the evenings when the meal wasn't as rushed as breakfast. "Is everything okay?" She glanced at her daughter. Naomi looked like she was holding her breath.

"*Ya*, I think everything will be all right." Jethro avoided eye contact, and Barbara wasn't sure he believed what he said. The older man glanced at Naomi, then finally looked at Barbara. "Wayne should be back in a couple of days." He cleared his throat again, glancing at Naomi only briefly before he found Barbara's eyes again. "Eli won't be coming back at all."

"Why?" Naomi took a step toward Jethro. Even Ruth had stopped pouring tea and stilled the pitcher as they all waited for Jethro to answer.

"He has business in Pittsburgh."

Barbara looked at Naomi as the room grew silent.

"Excuse me, please." Naomi pulled a kitchen towel from over her shoulder and set it on the kitchen counter, then hurriedly left the room.

This is what I get. Naomi closed the door to her bedroom, then flung herself on the bed. How could she have opened her heart to Eli? He didn't even tell her good-bye. The last couple of weeks had been the best she'd had in a long time, maybe ever. She fought the tears gathering in the corners of her eyes, angry with herself for putting her heart on a platter, only to have it sliced and diced by a guy she barely knew.

But after she'd allowed a few tears to spill, she tried to find the good in Jethro's news. At least Wayne was coming back. Their household had certainly had its share of grief and troublesome news, but Naomi thanked God that Wayne was coming back. She couldn't help but smile as she pictured her mother and Wayne chasing each other around the house, about to share a kiss in the living room, and then getting caught by *Mammi*. Each time she became sad about Eli, she was going to be happy for her mother.

Naomi sat up on her bed, dabbed at her tears with a tissue, then closed her eyes. She was going to keep her cup half full, something her father had insisted on when he was alive. Naomi was going to stay grateful for what they did have and not focus on what they didn't.

Even though Naomi's thoughts felt logical, her heart wasn't going along with the plan. She lay back on her bed and cried. She didn't even move when her bedroom door opened.

Her grandmother walked to the bed, sat down, and began to stroke Naomi's hair. No words were necessary. If anyone knew about having her heart broken over a potential suitor, it was Naomi's grandmother. Naomi had prayed that *Mammi* and Jethro would develop a relationship, since *Mammi* wanted that so badly.

"I know you're hurting, child." *Mammi* continued to run her hand over Naomi's hair. "But don't write that boy off just yet."

"You heard what Jethro said. Eli isn't coming back." Naomi sniffled. "And that's fine. I didn't even know him very long."

"You knew him long enough." *Mammi* took off her glasses and laid them on Naomi's bedside table. Then she lay on the bed with Naomi and turned on her side so they were facing each other.

"My heart hurts, *Mammi*. He's the only person I've ever really considered dating. I . . . I liked him a lot."

"I know, child." *Mammi* reached out and cupped Naomi's cheek, then sighed. "I'm going to tell you a story I've never told anyone, not even your *mudder* or father."

Naomi tucked her hands under one side of her head as a pillow. Her grandmother did the same thing. *Mammi* smiled.

"I'm going to tell you about a boy I was close to. It was long before your grandfather and I fell in love. His name was Benny King."

Naomi's ears perked up. "Our Benny King?" She'd known the older man all her life. "The one who is always wanting you to go to lunch?"

Mammi smiled. "That's him, all right. Elijah Benjamin King. Everyone back then called him Eli. I'm not sure when he started going by Benny." She shrugged. "I heard it told that his wife started calling him Benny, and it stuck."

Naomi waited, intrigued, as she thought about the carving in the barn.

"And Eli—Benny—had a nickname for me too."

Naomi gasped. "Was it BR?" Her grandmother had grown up on this farm, so maybe she was the one who had etched the heart.

Mammi touched Naomi's cheek. "You found the carving on the barn wall, *ya*?"

Naomi nodded, smiling. "What does BR stand for?"

Mammi chuckled. "Well, I'll tell you the story about me and Benny, if you'd like to hear."

Naomi nodded. She couldn't wait.

Chapter 10

Barbara readied a Christmas flower arrangement for delivery later in the afternoon. She made sure they had plenty of poinsettias during the holidays, but an *Englisch* woman from Bird-in-Hand had wanted an arrangement for her mother, and she'd been specific—red and white miniature carnations, red roses, and a red-and-white bow, all arranged in a red vase. Barbara was thankful she had all of that, since it was such short notice.

She double-checked that the timers for the watering system were set and that the batteries were charged. Then she carted the arrangement to the living room. "Ruth, do you feel up to delivering this to a woman in Bird-in-Hand?"

Barbara's mother-in-law looked up from a mobile phone in her lap. "Did you know you can send typed messages across the miles on these things?"

"Ruth, where did you get a cell phone?"

"Walmart."

Barbara set the arrangement on the coffee table and stuffed her hands in her apron pockets. She was about to reprimand Ruth about the use of cell phones, but she thought better of it. "Can you make the delivery?" Barbara glanced out the window. There wasn't a cloud in the sky. She'd already been outside to feed the chickens, and it wasn't supposed to snow again for a few days. "If you think it's too cold, I'll go."

"*Nee*. I'll go." She raised her head but kept her eyes on the phone this time. "And on these phones, you can look at the Internet." She grinned, looking up at Barbara now. "And, of course, you can make phone calls. You can also check the weather and read the newspaper."

Barbara sighed. "You know how the bishop feels about using cell phones for anything other than an emergency. And what kind of example does that set for Naomi?"

"Naomi is a grown woman. Any example that needed to be set has already been handled."

Barbara clamped her mouth shut, trying to stay true to her promise to herself that she wouldn't treat Ruth like a child.

"This arrangement must be delivered by three o'clock. Can you get it there by then?"

Ruth nodded, then jumped when the phone began to play music. "Look! My first phone call." She stared at the phone, pushing more buttons than was probably necessary, then she held the phone in front of her and yelled, "Hello!"

"Ruth, put it to your ear," Barbara said, shaking her head.

After Ruth had done as Barbara suggested, she said, "*Ya, ya*." Then she handed the phone to Barbara. "It's for you."

Barbara lifted her eyebrows. "For me? Who would be calling me on your new phone?"

Ruth smiled, then covered the phone with her hand. "It's Wayne. I saw that he and Jethro had mobile phones, so I asked if I could put their numbers in my phone." She puckered her lips into a pout and whispered, "Jethro said his was strictly for business, but Wayne and I traded numbers."

Barbara took the phone. "*Wie bischt?*"

"I've missed you."

Barbara hurried to her bedroom so she'd have some privacy. Smiling, she said, "Is that so?"

"You've missed me too, haven't you?"

Barbara couldn't have stopped smiling if she'd wanted to. "Maybe a little," she said playfully. "How are things there? Do you think you'll be back by Christmas? I was hoping we could all have Christmas supper together. And what about Eli? I know Naomi is upset that she hasn't heard from him."

"I want very much to have Christmas with you. I'm doing what I can to help Eli, but his father isn't being cooperative. I don't think Eli will be able to return."

"Oh dear." Barbara was light on her feet, walking on a cloud of hope, her feelings for Wayne stronger than she had thought. But Naomi was going to be terribly upset about Eli.

"I will try to call you again. If I'm not there for Christmas, just know that there is nowhere else I'd rather be."

Wayne didn't offer extra information about his and Eli's plans, and after she'd hung up with him, she wished she had asked more questions.

Barbara returned the phone to Ruth, happy to hear her mother-in-law humming. She was proud of Ruth for not sulking around the house, since it seemed apparent that she and Jethro had not found a spark. Barbara suspected Ruth's restored spirit might have something to do with her new cell phone. Ruth was born in the wrong era, Barbara thought, smiling, and she wondered if someday cell phones would be as commonplace for them as propane was now.

Her mother-in-law carried her new phone with her to the kitchen, and Barbara went to dust the furniture in her bedroom. She was worried about Naomi. Her daughter had finally taken a chance on someone and opened her heart, only to have him leave before they had much of a chance to explore their feelings.

But when Barbara returned to the living room, Naomi was smiling.

"*Mamm*, did you know *Mammi* has a cell phone? She's in the kitchen, and she said she's *surfing* the Internet. I'm not sure what that means."

"You should know by now that I can't control what your *mammi* does. She lives in her own world." Barbara allowed herself one eye roll since Ruth wasn't in the room. "And sometimes what the bishop doesn't know won't hurt him."

"What did you say?" Naomi grinned. "That doesn't sound like the mother I know, someone who doesn't believe in breaking the rules."

Barbara shrugged, then smiled. "People change." She started toward the kitchen, then stopped and turned around. "*Ach*, I almost forgot. Wayne called." She paused, knowing Naomi was going to be upset. "Eli probably isn't going to be able to come back, so it's doubtful he will be here for Christmas." In Barbara's attempt to soften the blow, she added, "And Wayne isn't sure if he can be here either. But that's okay. You, me, and *Mammi* have each other." She forced a smile, silently praying that both Wayne and Eli would be back.

Naomi nodded but then hurried away, afraid she might cry.

Christmas was only a few days away, and Naomi had fantasized about what it would be like to have someone special to share the holiday with. But she was happy for her mother and the possibility that Wayne might be back, so she was going to try to stay focused on that.

By the time the supper hour came around, Naomi's grandmother wasn't back from making the three o'clock delivery. Jethro arrived alone, as expected. Naomi thought maybe it was best that *Mammi* wasn't back yet, since Jethro hadn't returned her affections. But after hearing her grandmother's story about Benny King, Naomi wondered if anything really could have developed between her grandmother and Jethro anyway, or between her grandmother and anyone else—despite her *mammi's* many pursuits.

Jethro cleaned his plate, and once he was done, he thanked *Mamm* for the meal the way he always did.

"I also wanted to let you know that I've decided to go home for Christmas since I just learned that my sister will be alone otherwise. Since Wayne and Eli had to leave early and won't be coming back, I've hired someone local to finish the few small things necessary on the metal shop. I'll be leaving first thing tomorrow morning." He smiled at Naomi's mother. "*Danki* for your hospitality and the wonderful meals."

"We are sorry to see you go so soon," *Mamm* said, barely smiling.

Naomi wondered what might have changed since her mother had talked to Wayne. *Mamm* had made it sound like Wayne might be back, at least.

Then her thoughts drifted to her grandmother, and she wondered if *Mammi* would be upset that she wasn't able to say good-bye to Jethro, even though things hadn't progressed the way *Mammi* had hoped.

Naomi had also noticed the shakiness in her mother's voice. There seemed to be a certain sense of finality, and Naomi felt it too.

Jethro reached into the pocket of his jacket. He handed *Mamm* the key to the cottage. "Merry Christmas to you both, and please let Ruth know that I send holiday wishes her way as well."

After Jethro was gone, Naomi and her mother looked at each other, but no words were necessary. Things felt different. Quieter.

Eli and Wayne waited to see the probation officer in a small room with four chairs and a lady behind a frosted window. Eli wasn't sure why Wayne was with him. He didn't know the man all that well. Eli and his father lived not far away from Jethro and his wife, but Wayne had been a stranger until Eli went to work with him and Jethro. Wayne was from a neighboring church district.

"You don't have to stay." Eli mostly didn't want Wayne to hear the probation officer reprimand him for leaving the county.

Eli and Wayne had both taken the train to Pittsburgh. It had been a long ride, but it was a lot cheaper than hiring a driver. Afterward, Eli assumed they would part ways. Instead, Wayne offered to go with Eli to the meeting.

Eli had called his father to ask why he'd sent Eli away when he knew it would get him in trouble. His father hung up on him. In his heart, Eli knew why his father wanted him gone. Eli knew the man's secrets, the grief that had turned to rage and bitterness over the years—an ugly part of his father that had lashed out at his only son. But Eli still struggled to see the man his father used to be, before his mother died. He wondered if his mother had been able to see what was happening from heaven.

"I don't really have anything else to do." Wayne flipped through a farming magazine that had been on a small table between two of the chairs.

"Don't you have plans for Christmas in a few days?" Eli suspected Wayne would travel back to Lancaster County to spend the holiday with Barbara.

"I'm not sure yet." He didn't look up from the magazine.

"Don't you want to spend it with Barbara?" Eli would do anything to be with Naomi on Christmas. He didn't have anything to give her though. His family had always exchanged small gifts, like most of the community did, but Christmas with his father the past few years hadn't been a good representation of what Christmas should mean.

"*Ya*, I would like to spend it with Barbara."

Eli waited for Wayne to say more, but the door to the waiting room opened and a woman said, "Mr. Williams will see you now."

Eli stood up on shaky knees and swallowed hard. He wasn't sure how he'd missed the part of his paperwork that stated he couldn't leave the county, but he did remember the section that listed what could happen if he violated any of his probation.

Jail.

Chapter 11

Barbara, Naomi, and Ruth scurried around the kitchen as if they were preparing the Christmas meal for a large family, even though just the three of them would be in attendance. Wayne had said he might be there but had been noncommittal, which left Barbara feeling anxious. She would have thought he would commit one way or the other, especially for Christmas Day. Perhaps distance hadn't made the heart grow fonder.

Naomi hadn't heard from Eli at all in the past few days since he'd left, and Barbara could tell that her daughter was retreating back to the safe place where she guarded her heart. She was quieter, her eyes no longer glowed with anticipation like they did when Eli was around, and she'd taken to twisting her hair with her finger, something she did when she was upset.

But Ruth was a whirlwind of giddiness, laughing, shuffling about, and occasionally bumping into things since she wasn't wearing her glasses. Barbara wasn't going to say a word. Ruth was in good spirits, and Barbara hoped some of it would wear off on her and Naomi.

"*Mammi* sure is in a *gut* mood," Naomi said when Ruth went to get a jar of rhubarb jam from the basement.

"I know." Barbara looked out the window for the hundredth time, it seemed. "The Christmas spirit seems to have found your *mammi*."

"I'm sure Wayne is coming, *Mamm*." Naomi touched her mother on the arm as she stood next to her at the window.

Barbara forced a smile. "Maybe." She kissed Naomi on the cheek. "But either way, we are going to have a wonderful Christmas and thank the Lord for His many blessings." Naomi was hurting, no matter how much she tried to hide it from Barbara, and Barbara was going to do her best to be cheerful for her daughter.

"It's colder in the basement than it is outside," Ruth said as she came back into the kitchen with the jam. She put it on the table and smiled, then reached into her pocket and put on a new pair of gold-rimmed glasses. "What do you think?"

Barbara wiped her hands on the kitchen towel she had on her shoulder, then moved closer to her mother-in-law. "Ruth, I think they are lovely. And I'm sure they are much more comfortable than those other heavy frames you've worn for so long."

"I like them, *Mammi*," Naomi said, smiling.

Ruth sighed as she raised her palms up while lifting her shoulders. "What can I say? Change is in the air."

Barbara and Naomi exchanged looks but didn't say anything. Barbara opened the oven to check the turkey, and Naomi went back to making fruit salad.

After Barbara mashed the potatoes, she noticed there were four place settings at the table. "Ruth, are you expecting someone?"

"I'm not expecting anyone for Christmas dinner, but between the two of you, I figured at least one of your suitors would show up, if not both." Ruth rolled her eyes. Barbara wanted to say something, but then she thought about all the times she'd done the same thing to Ruth.

"I haven't heard a word from Eli, *Mamm*," Naomi whispered to her after Ruth had left the room. "But I'm sure Wayne will be here for Christmas."

Barbara was surprised that Eli hadn't even called Naomi, but when she'd questioned Wayne about it, he'd said the boy didn't know what his future held and didn't want to cause Naomi any more pain if he wasn't able to come back. Wayne had also told Barbara the horrific story about Eli and his father. At first, Barbara was concerned for her daughter's well-being. Jail was something none of them were familiar with. But Wayne explained the situation, assuring her Eli was a fine lad. Barbara hadn't mentioned the purpose of Eli's "business" to Naomi, but she suspected Naomi knew enough about what had happened. It was Christmas, so she'd skimmed over any conversation about it.

Barbara had never seen Naomi look at a boy the way she looked at Eli, someone who seemed to make her heart sing. But now that everyone was back in their normal routine, Barbara had her doubts that Wayne would show up either. He'd assured her that he wanted to be here and would try, but why couldn't he commit?

Naomi brought a hand to her chest when she heard a buggy coming up the driveway. "*Mamm*, someone's coming."

Naomi's mother hit the corner of one of the chairs with her knee as she hurried to the window and peered outside into a beautiful sunshiny day. She brought her hands together like she was going to pray. "He's here." She turned to Naomi. "Look. There's someone with him."

Mamm took several deep breaths and smoothed the wrinkles from her black apron, brushing off spilled flour too. "I feel like a schoolgirl," she said as she kept her eyes on the approaching buggy. She reached over and found Naomi's hand and squeezed, relieved when she saw for sure that the passenger in the buggy was Eli.

"I want to run out there and jump into Eli's arms, but that

wouldn't be appropriate." Naomi kept her feet rooted to the floor.

"Forget being appropriate."

Naomi and her mother turned at the sound of Ruth's voice.

"It's Christmas. Go greet your visitors." Ruth rolled her eyes for the second time, and Naomi wondered if her mother saw, but she didn't think so. *Mamm* was ear-to-ear smiles, and it was hard for Naomi not to smile along with her. Especially when Eli was almost running toward the house. But she forced herself to remain calm and waited for him to reach the front porch before she bolted across the living room and out the front door.

"Merry Christmas," Eli said when she stopped a few inches away. "I wasn't going to come." He looked away for a few seconds. "Actually, I didn't think I'd be able to come, but Wayne worked it out with my probation officer. He assured the man that I had a job here and that I hadn't understood I wasn't supposed to leave the county. And it turns out that Jethro bid on another job in this area, so we'll both be working here again." He cupped her cheeks. "But I also feel bad for doubting God's plans for me."

"I think we all doubt God's plans for us when things aren't going how we hoped. We're human. But we have to keep the faith that His will is being done."

"I missed you, Naomi."

"I missed you too."

Eli held a branch of green foliage above Naomi's head. "I told Wayne we didn't need any mistletoe, but he insisted on giving me some."

As Eli's lips met with hers, she felt them reconnect as if no time had passed. Even though it had only been a few days since they'd seen each other, it had seemed like an eternity to Naomi. Over her shoulder, Naomi could see Wayne holding a twig above her mother's head, and as her mother shared a kiss with Wayne,

Naomi didn't think life could be any more perfect for her and her mother. But Naomi wished *Mammi* could have someone here with her for Christmas dinner.

Naomi and Eli finally joined her mother, Wayne, and her grandmother in the kitchen.

"I'll carry in another chair," Wayne said after seeing the four place settings.

"Don't bother," *Mammi* said as she put on her black cape, then secured her bonnet. "I won't be staying."

"What?" *Mamm's* expression fell as she walked toward Ruth. "It's Christmas. You can't leave."

"*Ach*, I can, and I will." *Mammi* pointed to the stove. "The mashed potatoes need more butter. And don't forget to put out the cranberry sauce like you did last year." She pointed to the counter. "There's a fresh pitcher of iced tea."

Mammi put her hands on her hips, fully clothed in her cape and bonnet, and glanced at each one of them. "You people kiss more than anyone I know." *Mammi* took her small purse from the coatrack. "Back in my day, any type of public affection would be frowned upon, but it clearly is not a rule that you people abide by." She pointed a finger at Naomi's mother. "In all your days, did you ever see your father-in-law and me kiss? *Nee*, you didn't." She turned to Naomi and rolled her eyes. "Like mother, like daughter."

Then *Mammi* smiled broadly. "And I love you both very much. Merry Christmas." She turned to leave, then said over her shoulder, "No peeking at gifts until I return."

"*Mammi*, wait. Why are you leaving?"

Naomi's grandmother pointed out the screen door, then winked at Naomi.

"Forever arrived."

Naomi flashed her grandmother an all-knowing smile and nodded as her grandmother left the room with a twinkle in her eye, then headed down the porch steps. A buggy was coming up the driveway.

"Ruth, your cane." Naomi's mother unhooked the cane from the rack and started outside with it, but Ruth turned around and pointed to her new glasses. "One step at a time, child."

"Where are you going to eat? We have this huge meal that you helped prepare." *Mamm* put a hand to her forehead, peering into the sun's glare to see who was coming. "Who is that?"

Naomi cozied up to her mother on the porch while Wayne and Eli held back.

"It's Benny King," Naomi said to her mother, smiling.

Mamm turned to face Naomi. "What?"

"Did you know that Benny was *Mammi's* first love, the first boy she ever kissed?"

"*Nee*, I didn't. I knew they dated when *Mammi* was very young, but that's all I knew."

"It was a long time ago. And Benny was *Englisch* back then."

Mamm brought a hand to her chest.

"*Ya*, and *Mammi's* parents forbid her to see him. Years later, she found out that Benny had been baptized into the community and had come looking for her. But by then she'd already met *Daadi* and married him. Benny ended up marrying someone else, but Benny's wife died not long after *Daadi*, and Benny's been trying to court *Mammi* ever since."

As they both watched Naomi's grandmother standing outside the buggy talking to Benny, *Mamm* said, "All these years Ruth has been running around town like a lovesick teenager, pursuing any available man nearby. If she loved Benny so much back then, why didn't she ever agree to go to lunch with him? And why is she agreeing to it now?"

Naomi laughed. "Those are all the same questions I asked her. She said . . ." Naomi cleared her throat. "She said that Benny got *better teeth.*"

Mamm sat expressionless for a few seconds before she burst into laughter and shook her head.

Naomi laughed also, but once they'd caught their breath, Naomi said, "I think she was afraid of putting her heart out there again with Benny. I think she loved him very much at one time."

Mamm nodded.

"But when she saw that we were taking a chance on love, I think maybe that gave her the courage to give her first love a chance."

"Whatever the reason, I'm happy to see her spending time with Benny."

"Benny used to go by the name Eli." Naomi told her mother about the heart carved into the wood in the barn.

"I understand about Benny going by Eli back then," *Mamm* said, "but who is BR?"

Naomi laughed. "Remember how I said Benny was *Englisch* when they first met?"

Her mother nodded.

"He was also a baseball fan. Before he was born there was a baseball player named Babe Ruth. That was the nickname he had for *Mammi*."

They both chuckled, and then *Mammi* turned and faced the foursome, all on the front porch now, but quickly turned back to Benny as he pulled her into his arms and kissed her in front of all of them.

"Intolerable," Naomi's mother whispered, smiling as she kept her eyes on Naomi's grandmother. "And beautiful."

A warm glow lit Naomi's heart.

Forever had definitely arrived—hopefully, for all of them.

Discussion Questions

1. Ruth, Barbara, and Naomi are all at different stages in their lives, but each of the women would like to find love. Out of the three ladies, were you rooting for one of them more than the other? Who could you relate to the most?
2. How did relationships change throughout the story? What are some of the things that each of the women learned about the others?
3. If you could sit down for coffee with one of the women in the story, who would you choose and why?
4. What was your takeaway from the story, and were there any comparisons to the relationships in your own life?
5. Jump ahead ten years. Where do you see Ruth, Barbara, and Naomi? What obstacles might they face in the coming years?
6. Were you hoping Ruth would end up with Jethro, or did you figure out that Benny was the man for her?

Acknowledgments

I love writing stories about women—friends, mothers, daughters, sisters, and the many ways these personalities forge lifelong relationships. I've been blessed to have a group of women who inspire me personally and professionally, too many to list here, but you know who you are. Then throw in a trio of romances, and this story quickly became one of my favorite novellas to write.

Much thanks to my publishing team at HarperCollins. You all continue to rock, and are certainly included on my list of inspirational women. And that includes you, Natasha, my fabulous agent.

Reneé Griggs, thanks for not only being my BFF for forty years, but also for your willingness to always jump in at the last minute to help me with anything writing related! I love you to the moon and back—times infinity, as you always say.

Janet—my friend, my voice of reason, my marketing guru—you are at the heart of my "core" group, and you know what I mean.

Diana and Laurie, I'd be remiss not to mention the love and support you both shower on me continuously. Love you both.

To my husband, Patrick—what a ride, huh? I love you always and forever. xo

And my ultimate thanks to God, for continuing to bless me and provide me with stories to tell, tales I hope entertain and glorify You.

About the Author

Beth Wiseman is the award-winning and bestselling author of the Daughters of the Promise, Land of Canaan, and Amish Secrets series. While she is best known for her Amish novels, Beth has also written contemporary novels including *Need You Now, The House that Love Built*, and *The Promise.*

The Christmas Cat

Amy Clipston

For my loving (and purring) herd of "editors"—Jet, Lily, and Rico
And in loving memory of my sweet "editor"
Molly. We miss you every day!

Glossary

ach: oh
appeditlich: delicious
Ausbund: hymn book used in the Amish congregation
bedauerlich: sad
boppli: baby
bu: boy
buwe: boys
Christenpflict: Amish prayer book
daadi: grandpa
daadihaus: grandparents' house
danki: thank you
dat: dad
Englisch: English, non-Amish
fraa: wife
Frehlicher Grischtdaag: Merry Christmas
freind: friend
freinden: friends
froh: happy
gegisch: silly
gern gschehne: you're welcome
gut: good
gut nacht: good night
haus: house

Ich liebe dich: I love you
kaffi: coffee
kichli: cookie
kichlin: cookies
liewe: love
maed: young women, girls
maedel: young woman
mamm: mom
mammi: grandma
mei: my
naerfich: nervous
narrisch: crazy
nee: no
schee: pretty
schmaert: smart
schtupp: family room
schweschder: sister
Was iss letz?: What's wrong?
Wie geht's: How do you do? or Good day!
wunderbaar: wonderful
ya: yes

Chapter 1

A cat was sitting on her back porch.

Emma Bontrager balanced her grocery bag and a stack of mail in one hand and rubbed her tired eyes. Then she looked at the porch again. Yes, there was definitely a cat there.

Not just any cat, but a rotund orange tabby. And he—weren't most cats that large male?—seemed quite comfortable as he lifted one of his paws and licked it in the crisp late afternoon. In fact, did he look as though he'd been patiently awaiting her return?

No. Of course not.

Emma pursed her lips and studied the animal. Though he wore no collar, he looked well fed, as though he'd never had to make his own way in the world. Had someone dropped him off in the country because they didn't want him anymore? She'd heard of that happening.

Well, no matter. He didn't belong on the back porch of her house. Somebody else would have to take care of him. He'd probably try one of her neighbors next, someone who'd see to him.

As Emma's sore knees carried her up the back steps of her two-story white clapboard house, she was careful not to slip on the slick wood. A layer of ice had formed over already-packed snow. She should have shoveled the snow as soon as it fell, but her aching back had convinced her to dismiss the idea. And she should have bought another bag of salt to melt the ice, but she'd forgotten to put it on her list.

The fact was, if she hadn't needed a few food supplies, she wouldn't have ventured out at all today except to care for her mare. Her horse was the only animal left on this small farm. She didn't even keep chickens anymore.

"Shoo! Shoo!" she hissed, waving the envelopes at the cat. "Go on. Git!"

The cat blinked at her and then lazily sauntered down the steps toward the rock driveway, his belly swinging with the rhythm of his gait.

Something wet slid down Emma's nose, and she wiped it away. Glancing up, she blinked as snow flurries floated from the sky.

"*Ach*, *nee*," she whispered, shaking her head. "We don't need more snow."

The air suddenly felt colder as snowflakes peppered her hands and her coat. She shivered.

Emma pushed open the storm door, entered the mudroom, and then closed the heavy wooden door behind her. The warmth of the house began to cover her like a soft blanket. She removed her boots and hung up her coat and purse on pegs, then stepped into her spacious kitchen, placed the grocery bag and stack of mail from the last two days on the counter, and tended to the coal stove in one corner.

She knew what most of the envelopes held before she even opened them—Christmas cards. But she couldn't bring herself to read thoughtful Christmas wishes from members of her community and friends who had moved away. While they all meant well, it couldn't possibly be a merry Christmas without Henry.

With a sigh, she left the unopened cards on the counter and looked around the kitchen. It was Christmas Eve, and the house was too quiet. For the first time since this farmhouse had become her home, Emma hadn't bothered to decorate with greenery. She hadn't purchased a special candle for her shelf next to the kitchen window. And she hadn't baked cookies or bought any gifts.

She stared at the grocery bag. Every Christmas Eve since she and Henry married forty-five years ago, Emma had made him cherry bars. Inside were the ingredients she'd purchased to make them once more, and beside the bag was her favorite cookbook with the precious recipe inside.

But this was her first Christmas without Henry. He wouldn't be here to eat the special treat. Tears blurred her vision. She'd purchased the ingredients on impulse, hoping baking the bars would improve her mood. But who would eat them all?

Emma bit her lower lip as she picked up a dish towel. Making the bars was better than sitting around and feeling sorry for herself. It would not only give her something to do but fill the house with the delicious aroma she'd looked forward to every year. She'd worry about what to do with all the cherry bars later.

She found the worn, stained page with the recipe and stared at the directions. But then memories washed over her, and ambition drained from her body. Her thoughts transported her back to the day Henry Bontrager changed her life.

"Two more youth groups joined us today," Sally said as she sat down on the grass beside Emma. "One is from near Lititz, and the other is from Ronks."

"Oh, *ya*. I had forgotten about that." Emma pulled at a blade of grass and looked toward the three makeshift volleyball courts nearby. The warm June sun kissed her cheeks and warmed her back as Emma scanned the unfamiliar faces at the Fisher farm that Sunday afternoon. Her gaze fixed on a young man with the most striking blue eyes she'd ever seen. He laughed at something someone near him said, and an electric smile lit up his handsome face. He was tall—probably several inches taller than her five-foot-five frame—and had golden-brown hair, a long, thin nose, chiseled cheekbones, and a strong jaw. And, of course, a clean-shaven face.

Suddenly he looked toward Emma, and when their gazes locked he smiled at her.

Emma gaped as her cheeks heated from more than the sun's rays. She quickly looked down, averting her eyes from his compelling stare.

"What were you looking at?" Sally leaned closer to Emma. Sally Stoltzfus had been Emma's best friend since first grade, and it was hard to hide anything from her. But she had to try.

"Nothing." Emma returned her attention to pulling blades of grass. She couldn't bother wasting her emotions on any young man with Sally there, even if he was from another church district. With her hair that shone like gold, bright smile, and outgoing, friendly personality, Sally always caught the boys' attention, not Emma. She had ordinary dark-brown hair and unremarkable brown eyes. And she was shy.

"You were looking at something. Or should I say some*one*." Sally's voice was right next to Emma's ear. "Which *bu*?"

"There's *nee bu*." Emma kept her gaze focused on the grass she'd torn from the ground.

"Oh, come on. Tell me which one so I don't accidentally like the same *bu*."

Emma swallowed a sarcastic snort. "It wouldn't matter. The *buwe* notice you before they even realize I'm alive."

Sally gasped. "That's not true."

"*Ya*, it is." Emma turned toward her friend's shocked expression. "Don't you remember when we were at the gathering at

Sadie's *haus*, and Danny Esh smiled at us? When he walked over, he talked to you and not me. He completely ignored me."

"Oh *nee*. I didn't even realize that." Sally frowned. "I'm so sorry. I should have brought you into the conversation."

"It's fine." Emma touched her arm. "I didn't mean to make you feel bad. I'm not envious of you. I just know the *buwe* prefer you to me. It's okay. My time will come. It just has to be the right *bu*."

"Do you want to join my volleyball team?"

Emma glanced up toward the unfamiliar voice and squinted against the bright sun. She tented her hand over her eyes, then stifled a gasp. She blinked, half expecting the boy with the captivating smile to disappear like a figment of her imagination. But he stood there, those blue eyes searching hers as if his next words were going to change the course of his life.

"Do you like volleyball?"

Dumbfounded, Emma studied his expression. Surely he had to be asking Sally and not her.

"*Ya*, she does like volleyball." Sally nudged Emma's arm. "She was just telling me she wanted to play, but she wasn't sure which team to join."

Emma glared at Sally, who nudged her again as if urging her to go.

"Get up, Emma." Sally nodded toward the young man. "He wants you to play volleyball. You should go."

"So do you want to join my team?" the boy asked, his eyes still focused solely on Emma. "One of our players just decided to take a break, so we need someone else."

His smile was so genuine, so enticing. How could she say no?

"Okay." Emma brushed her hands together, cleaning off the stray blades of grass.

"*Wunderbaar*." He held out his hand to her.

Emma took it, and electricity seemed to spark between them

when their skin touched. He lifted her to her feet as if she weighed nothing.

"I'm Henry Bontrager. I live in Ronks." He wasn't letting go of her hand.

"I'm Emma Zook, and I live here in Bird-in-Hand."

"It's nice to meet you." He shook her hand once and then released it. "I noticed you watching the game, so I thought you might like to join us."

He noticed me? Emma's stomach did a flip-flop. *Why would this handsome man notice me with Sally sitting right there?*

"Henry!" a guy by the volleyball court called. "Are you coming?"

"*Ya!*" Henry responded before looking back at Emma. "Let's go play. Then maybe we can talk later. Does that sound *gut*?"

"*Ya.*" Emma nodded. "It does."

Henry turned toward Sally. "You're sure it's all right if I steal your *freind* for a while?"

Sally grinned as she waved them off. "*Ya*, it's fine. Go and have fun. I'll be fine here." When Henry looked away, Sally winked at Emma.

Emma and Henry played volleyball all afternoon, and later they sat by the pond on the Fisher farm and talked until it was time to head for home. Later that week Henry came to visit her at her family's house, and they sat on the front porch talking late into the evening. His visits grew more frequent, and their summer quickly filled with picnics and dinners with each other's family.

By the time the summer came to an end, Emma realized she had found the love of her life.

When a strange scratching sound filled the kitchen, Emma came back to the present. She walked through the mudroom and peered out the window, then opened the inside door to peer out. The back porch was empty, and the path leading to the rock driveway was looking whiter and whiter. The snow flurries had turned to large, fluffy flakes.

But who had scratched on her door?

She cracked open the storm door, and a slight movement made her look down to her right. The fat tabby was just sitting there, snowflakes sprinkled all over his orange fur. He was staring up at her as if to say, *What took you so long?*

"*Rrrwow.*" He blinked at her.

Emma shook her head and clicked her tongue. "You again?"

The cat took a step toward the house, and Emma pulled the storm door nearly closed.

"*Nee, nee. Nee* animals in the *haus.*" She waved the cat away with her dish towel. "Shoo! Go on. Go find another place to land."

But he didn't move, and the guilt she felt as she studied his snowy fur made her hesitate.

"All right. Go to the barn. I'm sure you'll find a way in, and you can make a bed in the hay. It's warmer in there than it is on the porch."

As she closed the door, Emma thought she saw something move in her peripheral vision. But when she glanced over her shoulder toward the kitchen, she didn't see anything.

With a shrug, Emma moved to put away her perishables, then decided to build a fire in the family room and rest. When she reached the doorway, she halted and gasped. The orange tabby was curled up in a ball in Henry's favorite chair. She marched across the room and stared down at him.

"What are you doing?" she demanded, hands on her hips.

The cat simply lifted his head, blinked at her again, and snuggled deeper into the worn and faded blue fabric of the wing chair.

"I told you to go to the barn."

The ball of fur rolled onto his back and, upside down, looked up at her. Emma didn't see any intent to obey her command in those eyes.

A smile tugged at the corners of her lips. The cat certainly was cute. Perhaps it would be nice to have someone, even if only a cat, to talk to tonight. The Blank family had invited her over for supper, but Emma couldn't imagine venturing out again today.

She never liked traveling in the snow and ice, even when Henry had been here to guide the horse. And now the streets would be dangerous. She'd heard too many stories about cars colliding with buggies on roads with treacherous conditions.

Emma lowered herself into the chair beside Henry's and touched the cat's fur. When his head shot up, she flinched and pulled her hand away. The tabby studied her, blinked, and then lowered his head again. She scratched his velvety ear, and a soft rumble sounded from deep inside his body. He was purring!

"Oh, you like that?" Emma smiled. "What should I call you?"

The cat rolled onto his side.

"Henry loved this chair as much as you seem to love it. His *freind* Urie used to call him Hank sometimes. Why don't I call you that?" When the cat didn't protest, she chuckled. "Hank it is."

Emma continued to rub his ear as he closed his eyes and purred again.

"What would Henry say if he saw you lounging in his chair?" She tilted her head as the image of her husband filled her mind. "I suppose he would ask me why I'd let a cat into the *haus*." They'd never had pets at all. Henry had been allergic to cats and dogs.

A memory flooded Emma's mind. "I remember one hot summer evening when Henry came to see me," she whispered to her new companion. He opened one eye and seemed perfectly content to listen. "He seemed so *naerfich*, but it wasn't because of a cat. It was a year after we met, and he had some exciting news."

Emma shooed one of their barn cats off the porch as Henry sneezed once more, then handed him a bottle of her father's homemade root beer before sitting beside him on her parents' front-porch swing. "How was your day?"

"It was *gut*." Henry smiled. "*Danki* for the root beer. I've been thinking about your *dat's* root beer all day." His smile waned as his voice took on a serious tone. "Actually, I was thinking about *you* all day."

Her heart felt as though it turned over in her chest as he looked down at the bottle in his hands. He moved his fingers over it, leaving rivulets in the condensation.

He suddenly looked up at her, and his expression seemed tentative, almost nervous. "*Mei dat* and I found an empty storefront in Bird-in-Hand, and he's offered to help me pay the rent to open up my feed store."

"Really?" A smile overtook her lips. "You want to open your store here in Bird-in-Hand?"

He nodded. "I've been thinking about it for a long time. *Mei dat* thinks it's a *gut* location that will stay busy."

"That's fantastic." She placed her bottle on the table beside the swing. "How soon do you think you'll open it?"

He shrugged. "I don't know. Maybe two months? Possibly three?" He paused. "There's a little farm with a big *haus* not far from the store. *Mei dat* said he'd also help me buy it. I'd like you to see it and tell me what you think."

"Oh?"

"*Ya.*" He set his bottle on the table next to his side of the swing, then turned to look into her eyes. "If you like the *haus*, then I was thinking it could be our *haus*."

Her breath caught in her throat.

"Emma," he began, taking her hands in his, "I've known you for a year now. You're my best *freind*. You're the most important person to me in this world. I'm so thankful I went to your youth group gathering last summer and had the confidence to ask you to play volleyball with me." He paused as if carefully choosing his words. "*Ich liebe dich*. I want to build a life with you here in Bird-in-Hand. I'd be so very honored to make you *mei fraa*. Will you marry me?"

"*Ya, ya.*" Her eyes misted. "Of course I will."

His hand cupped her cheek. Then, leaning down, he brushed his lips over hers, sending a shiver dancing down her spine.

"It seems like only yesterday when Henry found this *haus*," Emma told Hank as she stroked his back. "He was so excited. His dream since he'd been a teenager was to open a feed store and buy a little farm nearby. I remember the day we came to see this place. An *Englisch* couple had owned it, so we had to remove the electrical system and paint the walls before we could move in. It was a lot of work, but it was worth it for the price."

Hank lifted his head and she began to rub his chin. "You know, we heard that the *Englisch* couple who owned this big *haus* sold it because they never had any *kinner* to fill it. How strange that Henry and I never raised any *kinner* here either."

A knot swelled in Emma's throat. Oh, how she and Henry had longed to have children. When they'd purchased the four-bedroom house, she had imagined their future children would fill the spacious home with love and noise. But it wasn't to be.

And now Henry was gone, and she was alone.

"Looks like it will be just you and me this Christmas, Hank," she told the cat. He looked up at her as if to make a plea. "Oh. I suppose you'd like to have something to eat."

Emma returned to the kitchen, where she poured a bowl of milk and then searched the cabinets until she found a can of tuna. She carried the meager feast into the family room and held up two bowls. "Are you hungry?"

Hank sat up before smelling the air, his little pink nose resembling a rabbit's as it worked to identify the aroma.

"You smell the tuna, *ya*?" The cat scurried behind her as she carried the bowls back to the kitchen. When she set them on the floor, he went for the tuna first.

Glancing at the clock above the refrigerator, Emma saw it was almost five. The Blank family would be expecting her to arrive for supper in thirty minutes. She should call and leave a message on their voice mail, telling them she wasn't coming. She didn't want to worry them.

Emma moved to the back door window and looked out toward the barn, where her phone was. Even with the darkened sky she could tell the snow was coming down at a steady pace, now thoroughly covering the path leading to the barn and beginning to accumulate on the ground. She frowned as she imagined slipping on the porch steps and breaking a leg or hip, like another member of her community had a few weeks ago. With her bad knees, she couldn't risk getting injured and being stranded in the snow until someone found her.

She felt guilty about not calling the Blank family and leaving a message, but surely they would assume she'd chosen not to travel on the dangerous roads. It would be best if she stayed inside.

She sighed. The idea of being so alone, with only a cat to keep her company during her first Christmas without Henry, sent regret settling deep into her bones.

Chapter 2

On the front porch of her house, Katie Ann Blank shivered and hugged her coat closer to her body. The wind blew the ties of her prayer covering, sending them fluttering over her shoulders as she stood on her tiptoes and peered down the street. Swirling snow danced to the already-white ground.

It was six o'clock and Emma Bontrager should have arrived by now. Could the older woman have been in an accident? Or had Emma simply decided to stay home and not brave precarious road conditions? Worried, Katie Ann silently prayed it was the latter. But if Emma had decided to stay home, then why hadn't she left a voice mail message letting them know she wasn't coming for supper as she'd promised?

Concern continued to plague Katie Ann as she stepped back into the house, removed her snow boots, and crossed the family room.

"Katie Ann?" *Mamm* called from the kitchen. "Is Emma with you?"

"*Nee*, she's still not here." Katie Ann stepped into the kitchen, where her mother was bringing a chicken casserole to the table. "I wonder if she changed her mind and decided to stay home. The roads look like they could be getting bad."

"Did you check voice mail?" *Mamm* asked.

"*Ya*, I did, but she didn't leave a message." Katie Ann shucked her coat and brushed off the snow before hanging it on a peg in the mudroom. She stepped back into the kitchen and folded her arms across her black apron. "I'm worried about her. Do you think she was in an accident?"

"Who was in an accident?" Her older brother, Ephraim, appeared in the doorway. At twenty-three, two years older than Katie Ann, he stood six feet tall and had the same blond hair and honey-brown eyes she'd inherited from their mother.

"I don't know if she was in an accident, but I *am* worried about Emma Bontrager." Katie Ann gestured toward the window. "The snow is still falling, and the roads are probably already slick. She was supposed to be here thirty minutes ago. You know she lives alone now."

Ephraim leaned against the doorframe and crossed his arms. "Oh. That's not *gut*. Maybe we should go check on her."

Mamm considered that idea. "She most likely decided to stay home. Maybe she didn't even want to risk walking out to her barn to call us if her porch steps are slick. Still, I don't want her to be alone at Christmas, and I want to be certain she's safe. So, *ya*, why don't you go see her? I haven't heard any predictions that make me think this storm will get too much worse. Just be careful. And take her some of this food too."

"Food is a *gut* idea. I'll get the horse hitched up to the buggy." Ephraim retrieved his coat from the mudroom and then walked back into the kitchen as he pulled it on. "Do you have anything for me to carry out now?"

Mamm pointed to the tins of cookies on the counter. "Not yet. I'll put together a basket with some of those *kichlin* along with supper." She turned to her daughter. "Find a gift for her, Katie Ann. And take some candles too. Before she left town this week, Ella Glick told me Emma hasn't decorated at all. She's trying to keep her grief to herself, but I have a feeling she could be overcome this time of year. That's why I was so *froh* when she agreed to come for dinner tonight."

She turned back to her son. "Ephraim, why don't you cut some greenery for her mantel?"

Katie Ann nodded and smiled. "I think that's all a *wunderbaar* idea, *Mamm*. *Nee* one should be alone on Christmas Eve, and maybe we can still cheer her up."

"You're right. She must be very lonely," Ephraim said. He paused as if contemplating something. "Maybe we should take someone else with us too. We can stop at Mandy's *haus* and see if she wants to go."

Katie Ann couldn't help but gape at her brother. This was a first. Why would Ephraim want to ask her best friend to go with them to see Emma? *Does Ephraim like Mandy?*

Her brother frowned. "What?"

"Nothing. I'm just surprised you want Mandy to go with us, but I know she'd love to be a part of this."

Katie Ann let her concerns go. She couldn't wait to help Emma Bontrager have a merry Christmas. She rubbed her hands together and turned toward her mother.

"Would you and *Dat* mind if we pack up enough for us to eat supper with Emma?"

"Do you like bacon, Hank?" Emma removed two bacon strips from a frying pan and looked down at the cat as he rubbed his side on her leg. Hank had finished the tuna, and when he continued to beg, she remembered she'd bought bacon that day. "I thought you might enjoy this."

She blotted the grease off the bacon with a paper towel and

then crumbled it into small pieces onto a plate. She set the plate on the floor next to a bowl of water, and Hank dove in.

As Emma sat at the kitchen table and watched her guest happily munching away, she realized how grateful she was she'd unhitched her mare before coming inside. She'd left plenty of feed and water for her too—almost as if she'd already known she wouldn't need her again that night.

Perhaps the Lord had prompted her to do that. After all, he would have known.

Thoughts about blessings from the Lord sent her mind wandering to her wedding day. She smiled.

"Henry was so *naerfich* he looked like he was going to pass out," Emma said to Hank as she leaned back in her chair. "I actually saw beads of sweat on his brow as he sat next to me."

Emma glanced at the cat, who looked up as he licked his chops. But then she lost herself in the memory. She wanted to remember every moment.

Emma glanced over at her mother, who sniffed and wiped her eyes with the back of her hand. *Mamm* smiled, and Emma's heart fluttered with happiness. She was sitting at the front of her father's barn, and today she was marrying the love of her life, Henry Bontrager!

It was a brisk November day, but her excitement kept her warm. She and her mother had worked hard creating the matching purple dresses she and Sally wore. The preparations had taken months, but the day had finally arrived!

The service had begun with Emma and Henry meeting with the minister while the congregation sang hymns from the *Ausbund*. After the singing, Emma and Henry had returned to the congregation and sat with their attendants—Sally and Henry's best friend, Urie Glick.

Now the two women sat facing the two men, who were clad in their traditional Sunday black-and-white clothing. Though he looked nervous, Henry smiled at her, and her pulse took flight as if on the wings of a thousand hummingbirds.

Emma tried her best to concentrate as the minister delivered his first sermon, but her thoughts spun with excitement over the new life chapter she was about to begin.

Urie and his new wife, Ella, had helped them move Henry's belongings into her parents' house because the farmhouse they'd purchased with his father's help wasn't ready yet. But they hoped to move in a couple of months, when all the renovations were done. Henry had also opened his store a couple of months earlier.

Their future seemed bright, and Emma was eager to begin their marriage. She wanted to fill their home with love, laughter, and children. Neither she nor Henry had any siblings, and Emma dreamed of having as many as six children. She'd already thought of both first and middle name possibilities for the first baby who came along.

Soon it was time to kneel for the silent prayer. Emma closed her eyes and opened her heart to God as a prayer poured from the very depths of her soul.

Danki, *God, for bringing Henry into my life.* Danki *for* mei wunderbaar *family and community. Please bless our marriage, and help us to live a life together that is acceptable in your eyes. In Jesus' holy name, amen.*

After the silent prayer, everyone rose for the minister's reading of Matthew 19:1–12. Then when they returned to their seats, the bishop began the main sermon, continuing with the book of Genesis, including the story of Abraham and the other patriarchs in the book.

Emma's thoughts again wandered as she considered what her new life would be like. It seemed like only yesterday she was wondering if she would ever fall in love and get married.

She snapped to attention when she realized the bishop was instructing her and Henry on how to run a godly household. Then he moved on to a forty-five-minute sermon on the story of Sarah and Tobias from the intertestamental book of Tobit, and she did her best to stay alert.

When the sermon was over, the bishop divided his gaze between Emma and Henry. "Now here are two in one faith, Emma Mae Zook and Henry Robert Bontrager." He asked the congregation if they knew any scriptural reason for the couple not to be married. Hearing no response, he continued. "If it is your desire to be married, you may in the name of the Lord come forth."

Emma's pulse zinged as Henry took her hand in his and they stood before the bishop to take their vows.

This is really happening! I'm going to be Henry's fraa*!*

Her heart continued to thump as the bishop read "A Prayer for Those About to Be Married" from an Amish prayer book called the *Christenpflict*.

After the prayer, Emma and Henry returned to their seats, and the bishop began another sermon. Emma and Henry stole glances at each other as often as they dared, and Emma noted Henry seemed much calmer.

The sermon ended, and the congregation knelt as the bishop again read from the *Christenpflict*. After he recited the Lord's Prayer, everyone stood, and the three-hour service ended with another hymn.

Emma and Henry were immediately surrounded by friends and family who wanted to congratulate them, and Emma grinned as she shook hands and accepted hugs from the well-wishers.

Soon a flurry of activity erupted around them as the men

began rearranging furniture so the women could serve the wedding dinner. Chicken with stuffing, mashed potatoes with gravy, pepper cabbage, and creamed celery would be followed by bountiful desserts—cookies, pies, fruit, and Jell-O salad.

Henry took Emma's hands, and his blue eyes locked with hers as he pulled her to one side and leaned down to speak into her ear. "Emma, I'm not perfect," he told her. "I'm just a humble man who happened to win the most *schee* and amazing *maedel* in the community. I'm certain I'll make mistakes. But I promise you I will always work hard to be the husband you deserve."

Emma leaned back and raised one hand to stroke Henry's cheek. "You are the answer to my prayers, Henry, and I couldn't be more *froh* to be your *fraa*. I will do my best to always make you *froh* too. *Ich liebe dich*."

As he squeezed her other hand, Henry whispered, "I will love and cherish you for the rest of my life."

Emma sniffed as the memory crashed over her. She felt as though their wedding had taken place only months ago, not forty-five years.

If only their life together had lasted a little longer.

Katie Ann stuffed her hands into the pockets of her coat as she followed Ephraim, who was jogging up the front steps of Mandy Bender's house despite their being so slick. After he knocked on the front door, it soon swung open to reveal Mandy herself.

Katie Ann smiled. Mandy had been Katie Ann's best friend since they started first grade together, and she'd always been a pretty girl. Tonight she was clad in a blue dress Katie Ann always thought complemented her cornflower-blue eyes, and a matching blue scarf covered her light-blond hair. Failing to keep up with Katie Ann as they grew into young women, Mandy was petite at five foot two, five inches shorter than Katie Ann.

And, Katie Ann noted for the first time, that made her nearly a foot shorter than Ephraim.

"Hi." Mandy blinked as she looked back and forth between Ephraim and Katie Ann, then quickly invited them in out of the cold and snow.

Ephraim leaned against the closed door. "*Frehlicher Grischtdaag!*"

Mandy smiled up at him, and her cheeks flushed as she repeated the greeting. Katie Ann managed not to gape again as the question she'd had earlier echoed in her mind. Did Ephraim like Mandy? Then another thought occurred to her. Did her brother and best friend like *each other*?

Her thoughts reeled with the implications of that possibility. What if her brother started dating her best friend? How would her relationship with Mandy change if she and Ephraim became girlfriend and boyfriend?

"It's great to see you both, but it's a little unusual for you to come this late on Christmas Eve. What are you doing here?" Mandy asked, bringing Katie Ann's thoughts back to the conversation.

Katie Ann opened her mouth to respond, but Ephraim cut her off.

"We were wondering if you'd like to go with us to visit one of the older members of our church district." Ephraim jammed his thumb toward his waiting horse and buggy. "We're going to visit Emma Bontrager and take her some Christmas cheer."

"Emma Bontrager?" Mandy asked.

"*Ya*," Katie Ann chimed in. "She was supposed to join us for supper, but she didn't come. We're going to take her some food and make sure she's okay."

Mandy's pretty face contorted with a frown. "Oh, *ya*. Her husband died in July." She clicked her tongue. "I imagine she's lonely."

"We've got food, a gift, and some decorations for her too."

Mandy's face brightened. "That sounds *wunderbaar. Mei schweschder* and I made peanut-butter brownies today. We can take some of those to her too." She motioned for them to stay where they were. "Let me just tell *mei mamm* I'm leaving."

Katie Ann breathed in the air of excitement as she enjoyed the warmth of the Bender house.

"We could stop and get Wayne on our way too," Ephraim said nonchalantly as he sidled up to her.

"Okay. Why not?"

Noticing Ephraim's tone, she wondered what this was about. Wayne was her brother's best friend, and they all liked him. Normally she wouldn't think anything of Ephraim inviting him along, but . . .

Wait a minute. Did Ephraim hope Wayne would keep her busy so Mandy could focus all her attention on *him*?

Chapter 3

The sound of knocking made Emma turn toward the mudroom.

"Who could that be this time of the evening, Hank?" She glanced at the clock. She'd just begun to think she should eat something—if only to keep Hank company.

Emma yanked open the back door and took in the sight of Katie Ann and Ephraim Blank, Mandy Bender, and Wayne King standing on her porch. The girls shivered as they gave her little waves. Ephraim and Wayne each held a lantern.

Emma pushed the storm door open wide. "*Wie geht's?*" Behind the arrivals, the snow continued to fall as the wind whipped over the open porch. No wonder she hadn't heard a horse and buggy arrive.

"What are you all doing out in this weather?"

"*Frehlicher Grischtdaag!*" they shouted in unison.

"We were worried about you when you didn't come for supper, so we decided to check on you." Katie Ann held out a large picnic basket. "We brought food too, and we have enough for all of us, if it's okay for us to stay awhile."

"Oh my goodness." Emma gasped and tears filled her eyes as she took the basket from Katie Ann. "You didn't need to do that." She beckoned them to step into the house. "Please come in and get warm. It's so cold out."

"We'll be in as soon as we put our horse in your barn, if that's okay. It's pretty bad out here," Ephraim said.

"Of course. I'll make some hot chocolate while you're gone."

Katie Ann stepped into the mudroom and hung her coat on a peg before taking off her boots. Mandy followed her lead.

Emma headed into the kitchen with the young women trailing close behind. She set the basket on the longest counter.

"Hot chocolate sounds *wunderbaar*." Mandy set a covered container and red gift bag on the counter as well. Katie Ann stared down at Hank, who sat by his empty plate and looked entirely disinterested in her company. *He's pretending no one's come to compete for my attention*, Emma thought.

"Is that your cat?"

"*Ya*, I suppose he is." Emma turned toward her and shrugged with a smile. "He showed up earlier, and I couldn't convince him to leave. I decided he's going to be my guest for Christmas."

Katie Ann laughed and bent to pet him. "He's a big *bu*."

"*Ya*. I call him Hank." Emma began filling her kettle with water.

"Hank." Katie Ann smiled, but then her smile quickly faded. "After your husband, Henry."

"That's right. Henry's *freind* Urie used to call him Hank," Emma said as she set the kettle on a burner.

The boys made it back in record time, and Katie Ann turned toward her brother as he walked into the kitchen. "Why don't you and Wayne go ahead and decorate Emma's *schtupp* for her?"

"You're going to decorate for me?" Emma asked.

"*Ya*, we brought greenery." Wayne walked in behind Ephraim and held up the pine branches in his arms. *He must be around twenty or twenty-one*, Emma thought. With that dark hair and those dark-blue eyes, he was the spitting image of his father at that age.

"We also brought a few candles," Ephraim said as he retrieved them from the picnic basket. "We can put it all on your mantel if you'd like."

"That would be perfect. *Danki*." Emma pointed toward the doorway leading to the family room. "It's right through there. Would you please add a log to the fire if it needs it?"

"*Ya*, of course," Ephraim said. Emma was so grateful Urie had seen to it she had plenty of wood for the winter. He and Ella would have spent some time with her this Christmas, but their youngest lived in Ohio now, and of course they wanted to see their latest grandchild. She'd assured them she'd be fine. These precious friends grieved Henry just as she did, and they needed some time away.

Once the young men left, Emma turned toward Katie Ann and Mandy. "I'm so sorry for worrying you. I was going to call, but I was concerned about slipping on the snow and ice."

"I understand," Katie Ann said. "But we didn't want you to spend your first Christmas Eve without Henry alone."

"That's so thoughtful." Emma's voice quavered as tears threatened. "But don't your families mind your leaving them on this special night?"

"They were *froh* for us to come. They care about you, Emma," Katie Ann said. "We all do."

Mandy touched her arm. "How are you doing?"

Emma wiped her eyes with the back of her hand. "I'm all right, I guess." She glanced at the calendar on the wall. "Sometimes I wake up and think Henry's still here, but then I roll over in bed and remember he passed away. Some days it feels as if it's been only a few weeks, and other days it feels like years."

"I'm sorry." Katie Ann glanced toward the counter where the ingredients for the cherry bars sat. "Have you been baking?"

"I was going to, but then I decided I wouldn't." Emma shook her head as a lump swelled in her throat.

"What were you going to make?" Mandy peered down at the open cookbook.

"Cherry bars. That was our tradition for Christmas Eve. I would make Henry a pan of them. They were his favorite." Emma touched the recipe.

"Would you like us to help you make them?" Katie Ann offered.

"Do you like to bake?" Emma asked.

They both grinned and nodded.

"We love to bake," Mandy responded.

"Why don't we eat the food you brought, and then if you have the time, we'll make the cherry bars," Emma suggested.

"That's a great idea." Katie started pulling containers out of the picnic basket. "We brought chicken casserole and rolls."

The kettle whistled, and Mandy jumped with a start. "I'll get mugs."

"The hot chocolate mix is in the cabinet over there." Emma pointed. "I'll get plates and utensils."

Soon the table was set with the hot chocolate and all the food they'd brought.

"Okay," Katie Ann said. "Let's eat."

"I'll get the *buwe*." Emma started toward the family room.

When she stepped through the doorway, she sucked in her breath in surprise. The mantel was beautifully decorated with the pine branches and several small white votive candles. Hank sat in the middle of the room, watching the young men with interest. Apparently, Emma thought, he'd decided to be sociable after all.

"Do you like it?" Ephraim asked, his expression hopeful.

"Is it too much?" Wayne added.

"It's perfect." Emma smiled as warmth flooded her soul. "*Danki*." She pointed toward the kitchen. "We have the food set out. Are you hungry?"

"*Ya*." Wayne rubbed his hands together. "I worked up an appetite when we cut these branches down."

"*Gut*. Let's eat." Emma motioned for them to follow her back to the kitchen, and they all sat down at the table. After a silent prayer, they filled their plates.

"I'm so glad *Mamm* packed enough food for all of us." Katie Ann buttered a roll and then passed the butter to Wayne beside her.

"The casserole is *appeditlich*." Mandy forked more of the chicken. "You have to give me the recipe."

"I agree." Emma cradled her warm mug in her hands. "I'd like to have the recipe too."

"*Danki*." Katie Ann lifted her roll. "I will ask *mei mamm* for it."

"Please thank her for me. Do you like to bake with your *mamm*?" Emma asked, and Katie Ann nodded. "What are your favorite things to bake together?"

Katie Ann took a sip of hot chocolate before answering. "*Kichlin*."

"What are your favorite kinds of *kichlin* to bake?"

"Oh, let's see." Katie Ann tapped her chin as she thought. "I think cinnamon roll *kichlin* are probably my favorite."

"Oh *ya*?" Emma raised her eyebrows. "I've never made those." She turned to Mandy. "Have you?"

Mandy nodded, her blue eyes sparkling. "Oh *ya*, I have made those. *Mei schweschder* and I made cake mix *kichlin* the other day. Oh, they were so *gut*." She turned to Ephraim. "You liked them, didn't you?"

"Of course I did. She makes the best *kichlin*." Ephraim smiled at Mandy.

Emma's chest tightened at the sight of the sweet expression Ephraim sent toward Mandy. Henry used to look at her with similar admiration in his eyes, especially when they were first married. Oh, how she missed her husband!

A fresh wave of grief trapped Emma's words in her throat.

"Emma?"

Emma turned toward Katie Ann, who had placed her hand on Emma's arm.

"*Was iss letz?*" Katie Ann's brown eyes shined with concern.

"Nothing. I was just lost in thought." Emma cleared her throat against the knot of emotion. "What's your favorite recipe for *kichlin*, Mandy?"

As they continued talking around her table, warmth flooded Emma's soul. She was pleased that Hank—her Christmas cat—had arrived and made himself at home. And now these young people were here too. They were so kind to take her mind off her first lonely Christmas without Henry.

Soon their plates were scraped clean and Mandy stood to gather the dishes.

"Could we make those cherry bars now?" she asked.

Emma picked up a drinking glass. "That sounds *gut* to me."

Katie Ann set a platter in the sink and began to fill it with hot, frothy water. "This will be fun. I'll wash the dishes while you and Mandy start on the cherry bars."

"Can we eat Mandy's peanut-butter brownies while you ladies bake?" Ephraim tossed the used paper napkins into the trash and then opened the container of brownies.

"I think that's a great idea." Wayne moved beside him. "Those smell great, Mandy."

"Let me put *kaffi* on for you." Emma stepped forward to fill the percolator.

"*Danki*," Ephraim said as he and Wayne sat down at the table with the container of brownies and fresh napkins.

"Don't eat them all," Katie Ann warned over her shoulder as she washed the first of the dishes. "Save room for the cherry bars."

"I think your cat wants a brownie," Ephraim said to Emma.

She turned to find Hank sitting on the chair beside Ephraim. His front paws were resting on the table as he leaned over and smelled the container of brownies.

"Don't give him one," Mandy warned. "I think chocolate is dangerous for cats."

"I actually think it's dangerous for dogs to eat chocolate, but I still wouldn't give him any." Ephraim touched Hank's back. "I think you need to get down."

Hank meowed as he sat back down on the chair and stared at Ephraim.

"I think he wants to be part of the family." Wayne chuckled.

Emma laughed and then looked down at the recipe. "Let's see . . ."

"What temperature should I preheat the oven?" Mandy asked, moving to the stove.

"Three fifty." Emma took a mixing bowl from a cabinet.

"May I help you?" Mandy pointed to the recipe.

"I'd love that." Emma smiled and explained what to do next.

After they'd mixed the filling and spread it over the crust, Emma sprinkled the crumbs and walnuts over the filling, slid the pan of cherry bars into the oven, and set the timer for fifteen minutes.

"I'll wash up the mixing bowl and utensils," Katie Ann offered as she scrubbed the last supper dish.

"I'll dry," Mandy said.

"I'll put everything away," Emma chimed in.

Soon all the dishes were put away and the warm, rich aroma of coffee had filled the kitchen. Emma poured five mugs of the strong brew and the women joined the men at the table.

"I can't wait to try one of those cherry bars." Ephraim added sugar to his coffee.

"Do you have any room for them?" Mandy pointed to the

half-empty container of brownies. "You and Wayne ate nearly half my brownies."

"We couldn't help ourselves." Ephraim gave her an apologetic expression. "They were amazing."

Mandy poked him in the arm, and he laughed.

"He's telling the truth," Wayne added, lifting his mug toward Mandy. "They were fantastic. And, *ya*, we still have room for the cherry bars."

"We always have room for your *appeditlich* baked goods." Ephraim touched her arm. "I promise, Mandy."

Emma chuckled as memories of time spent with her youth group filled her mind. How she had loved joking with Henry and their friends.

"Katie Ann," Ephraim said, "did *Mamm* pack that tin of *kichlin*?"

"*Ya*." She looked toward the counter and then suddenly popped up from her chair. She retrieved a tin from the picnic basket and said, "Emma, I almost forgot. We have something else for you." She set the tin of cookies in front of the boys and the red gift bag in front of Emma. "This is from all of us."

Emma studied the bag, running her fingers over the cool paper. She hadn't expected to receive any gifts this Christmas, although Urie and Ella insisted they'd bring something for her from their trip.

"You didn't need to do this."

"We wanted to." Katie Ann touched Emma's arm. "Please open it."

Emma dug into the gift bag, moving the tissue paper aside until she found a jar candle with a lid. She pulled it out and smiled when she read the scent—apple pie. She removed the lid and inhaled the sweet smell.

But then Emma's vision clouded with a sudden sheen of tears. "*Danki*."

"Don't you like it?" Katie Ann bit her lip as if worried Emma would say no.

"I love it." She sniffed as more memories flooded her mind. "Henry loved my apple pie."

"Oh *ya*?" Mandy took a brownie from the container and broke it in half. "Did you make it often?"

Emma nodded as she set down the candle and lifted her mug. "I used to make pies every fall for *mei freind* Sally's bake stand. I'd get the apples from the market and then bake all day until I had enough to sell."

"Where does Sally live?" Katie Ann asked.

"She lived in Ronks back then, but now she lives in Indiana. She wanted to be closer to her grandchildren." Emma ran her fingers over the warm mug. "I not only baked pies and *kichlin* but also made little crafts and quilts to sell. That was early in our marriage. Business at Henry's store was too slow for the whole first year, and the rent for the storefront was a little higher than we could really afford. His father had been helping with the rent, but he had some tough times and had to stop. And by then Henry also had an employee to pay, his best *friend*, Urie Glick. He'd realized it wasn't possible to run the business alone."

"Really?" Ephraim's golden eyebrows lifted. "I thought Lancaster Farm Supply had always had a steady stream of customers."

"*Nee*, not in the beginning." Emma frowned as some of the most difficult memories returned. "With Henry's *dat's* help, we'd also bought this *haus*. Neither of our parents' homes had a *daadihaus*, and they weren't ready to retire anyway. Then, as I said, his parents fell on some hard times. And my parents never were able to help us. We struggled for a while, and it was stressful for us and our marriage."

"How did you make it through?" Katie Ann asked.

"We just kept our faith in God and believed he would get us through somehow." Emma stared down at her mug as images of the early years of her marriage swirled through her mind.

Emma pulled two apple pies from the oven, flooding her kitchen with their sweet, warm aroma. She set them on a rack to cool before sticking two more in and setting the timer. Then she started filling plastic storage bags with the cookies she baked earlier, dividing them up by variety. Her goal was to fill her cooler with an assortment of baked goods before taking them to Sally's bake stand tomorrow morning.

It would be winter soon, and she and Sally would have to find other outlets to sell their baking. But she'd have to think about that later.

Once the cookies were packed up, she washed the pans and cookie sheets and then sat down at the kitchen table to make a shopping list. She planned to stop at the market on her way home from Sally's. She had a long list of supplies to buy so she could prepare for the group of tourists she was hosting for supper the following night. As usual, her mother would help. They made a good team.

She glanced at the chair beside her and sighed at the bag of material to sort. She had to start sewing. Her back and neck ached from standing at the counter so long, but she didn't have time to rest. She had to do whatever she could to help Henry with the bills stacked up on the counter beside her favorite cookbook.

She glanced at the clock on the wall above the refrigerator. She had an hour and a half before she needed to start supper. She hurried into the bedroom next to the family room and set to work on a few potholders. This room had become her sewing room shortly after they moved in, but when children came along, she'd put her sewing table and supplies in a corner of their large bedroom.

She'd finished four potholders before realizing it was past time to start making supper. She rushed out to the kitchen and began pulling together supplies. She had to hurry if she was going to have supper on the table by the time Henry arrived home.

An hour later, Emma set baked chicken, rice, and green beans on the table and glanced at the clock. It was six. Henry was normally home by now. Rubbing her tired eyes, she wondered if someone had come into the store at the last minute.

But what if something's happened to him? What if he's been in an accident?

Her heart raced as she pushed away the troubling thoughts and forced positive thoughts in their place. Henry was fine and would be home soon. He was just held up by a customer.

Emma set the food in the oven to keep it warm and then walked to the front of the house. She peered out the window, searching down the street for his horse and buggy. After several minutes, she headed into the sewing room to continue working on her potholders.

When the *clip-clop* of horse hooves wafted into the room, Emma popped up from her sewing table and rushed into the kitchen. The clock on the wall read seven fifteen. Her stomach growled as she retrieved supper from the oven and set it out on the table. She smoothed her hands over her apron and touched her prayer covering as the back door opened and her husband's footfalls sounded through the mudroom.

Henry stepped into the kitchen and her heart warmed at the sight of his handsome face, now sporting a full, light-brown beard. They'd been married a year, and she still relished seeing him when he first returned from work in the evening. But today his blue eyes were dull and his attractive face was clouded with a deep frown.

Her happy mood deflated as she crossed the room and touched his arm. "*Was iss letz?*"

He blew out a deep breath and moved past her to the sink. "I'm exhausted." He washed his hands and glanced toward the table as he dried them on a hand towel. "What's for supper?"

"Chicken, rice, and green beans."

He nodded and then took his usual seat at the head of the table.

Emma sat down next to him. After their silent prayer, she held her breath as he filled his plate and began to eat. His brow was furrowed and his lips formed a thin line. She longed to pull his worries out of him. During the more than two years she'd known him, he'd never been so reticent and despondent. She racked her brain for how to start a conversation that would break down the wall that seemed to separate them.

He looked over at her and raised an eyebrow. "Why aren't you eating?"

"Oh. I was just lost in thought." She shrugged and began filling her plate. "Does everything taste all right?"

He nodded while chewing, then said, "*Ya. Danki.*" He took a sip of water from his glass.

"What kept you at the store so late?"

Henry wiped his beard with a paper napkin. "A customer came in with a big order right at five. Urie couldn't stay late, so I had to help the man load up his truck. Then I decided I needed to work on the books." He shook his head. "I'm sorry. I should have called you to say I'd be late. But if things don't get better soon, I may have to close the store."

The disappointment and frustration in Henry's eyes pierced Emma's soul. Her chest constricted as she took a deep breath.

"We might lose the store?"

"*Ya.*" He rubbed the back of his neck as if massaging stiff muscles. "I suppose we could put this property on the market and go live with my parents. I could work on *mei dat's* dairy farm."

"But that's not your dream." Leaning forward, she took his hand in hers. "Your dream is to run a successful feed store, and you're working toward that."

He withdrew his hand and gestured toward her. "It's my responsibility to take care of you. And I have to take care of any *kinner* we bring into this world. I can't keep a store that doesn't even earn enough to cover my business expenses, let alone our household expenses."

"You can't give up yet." She sat up straight, and her words came out in a rush. "The store has only been open a year, and you're still working on gaining loyal customers. Give it more time."

"How much time can I give it?" he barked, and she winced as if he'd smacked her. "I'm sorry, Emma. That was uncalled for." His expression softened. "I don't mean to take it out on you. I'm just frustrated."

"Give it more time," she said again. She was careful to keep her words measured. "I can feel in my heart that it will get better."

He gestured with his hands. "The bank will give us only so much time before they'll foreclose on this *haus*. Our parents can't help us, so we're on our own."

"We can do it, Henry." Her voice shook as tears threatened to spill. "I believe in you."

"I'm still trying to discover how to best promote the store too. Make my advertising dollars count."

She patted his hand. "You'll get there. And I'm doing what I can to help. I baked nearly all day today, and I'm going to take all the baked goods over to Sally's tomorrow to sell from her stand. I have some potholders and other crafts to sell too. And remember?

I'm hosting a big dinner for tourists tomorrow night with my mother." Tears finally trickled down her cheeks, and she wiped her eyes.

"Please don't cry." A tender expression overtook his face. "I won't give up on the store yet, but if business doesn't pick up soon, our lives might have to change."

"I can adjust, but I don't think you've given the store enough time yet. Maybe we can get more tourists interested in the store."

"What do you mean?" His brow furrowed.

"We know tourists love coming to Lancaster County and buying authentic Amish items. Maybe you need to advertise the store as an authentic tourist stop and sell a few souvenirs." She pointed toward the sewing room. "I can make some crafts to sell. It might help."

He nodded slowly. "That is a *wunderbaar* idea. *Danki*." He pointed his fork toward her plate. "Your supper is getting cold. You should eat."

They ate in silence for several minutes. Although Henry had promised not to give up on the store yet, worry still nipped at her.

"Henry," she said, and he looked up at her. "Promise me, *nee* matter what happens, you won't give up on us."

His eyes showed a fierce emotion. "I'd *never* give up on us, Emma. You are my life."

She smiled as relief enveloped her like a tender hug. "You're mine too."

Chapter 4

So what happened with the store?" Katie Ann's question interrupted Emma's thoughts.

"I had some ideas that worked." Emma fetched a chocolate-chip cookie from the tin. "Henry advertised the store as authentically Amish, and more tourists came. We started selling souvenirs, and the people loved it. He also ran weekly sales for certain items, and that drove more locals to the store. Soon business was booming, and we were able to get ahead on our bills and even start a savings account."

Ephraim picked up a brownie. "That's fantastic. The store is really nice. *Mei dat* shops there all the time."

"*Danki*." Emma lifted her coffee mug. "Henry loved that store. It was a tough decision for him to sell it, to retire."

"I'm so *froh* you persuaded him to keep trying to make the store successful. It would have been a shame if he'd given up," Katie Ann said.

The timer buzzed and Emma got up. She opened the oven door, flooding the kitchen with the perfume of butter and cherries. She set the pan on the stove and turned toward her young friends.

"Looks like they're done," Emma said.

"Oh, I can't wait to try one!" Ephraim rubbed his hands together.

Mandy laughed. "Do you have a tapeworm?"

"I think he does." Katie Ann rolled her eyes, and Emma chuckled.

"They have to cool before I can cut them," Emma said.

Ephraim groaned and folded his arms over his middle.

"You're such a *boppli*," Katie Ann muttered. "We should probably go soon. It's getting late."

"But what about eating the cherry bars?" Ephraim asked.

"You can take some with you. I can't possibly eat them all by myself." Emma searched the cabinet for three containers, ones she rarely used. "As soon as they cool down, I'll divide them among your three households and you can have them tomorrow as a snack." She found the containers she needed on the top shelf and tried to reach for them.

"Let me help you." Wayne appeared behind her.

"*Danki*." Emma took a step back, glad she didn't have to get out her step-stool. Wayne reached up, grabbed the containers, and handed them to her, then stepped aside. "Do you need help with anything else?"

"*Nee*, I've got it. *Danki*." She turned back to the cherry bars. "It really will take a while for these to cool down."

"We should have more *kaffi* then," Ephraim quipped as he crossed the kitchen to the stove. "Would you like me to fill the percolator?"

Katie Ann faced her brother, jamming her hands on her hips. "If you have more *kaffi*, you won't sleep tonight. Besides, you should ask Emma if it's all right to drink more of her *kaffi*, not tell her you're going to!"

"I'm sorry, Emma," he said as he turned to her. She nodded her forgiveness, and he started making the coffee as he replied to his sister. "It's Christmas Eve, Katie Ann. I don't need to sleep."

Ephraim suddenly grinned. "Look at the table. Hank is still sitting there like he's part of the family."

Emma craned her head over her shoulder and found the cat sitting in Henry's chair this time, as if he were expecting something special. She clicked her tongue. "He acts like he belongs here, all right."

The young folks all laughed.

"Should we go sit in the *schtupp* while we wait for the cherry bars to cool?" Mandy suggested.

"That sounds *gut*." Emma pointed to the percolator. "Go on in there, and I'll wait here for the *kaffi* to finish."

"Don't be *gegisch*." Katie Ann touched Emma's arm. "You go sit. I'll bring in the *kaffi*."

Emma raised her eyebrows. "Are you sure?"

Katie Ann gestured toward the doorway. "Go on."

"Just call me when it's done, and I'll help you carry everything we need." Mandy gestured toward the doorway. "Let's go, Emma."

Emma followed her guests into the family room, where she sat in her favorite armchair beside the blue wing chair. Hank suddenly appeared in the doorway. He trotted across the room and jumped up onto Henry's chair, curled into a ball, and closed his eyes.

"You *gegisch* cat," Emma muttered, shaking her head.

Mandy crossed the room and stood in front of Emma's bookshelves. "Have you read all these books?"

The shelves held her favorite gifts from Henry—the Christian novels she so loved to read. Henry often surprised her by stopping at the bookstore near his feed store and picking up one of the latest releases. She kept every book and even wrote the date he purchased it inside the front cover.

"*Ya*, I have." Emma settled back into her chair. "Henry bought them all for me."

"How nice." Mandy turned toward Emma. "May I look at them?"

"Of course."

As Mandy ran her fingers over the spines of the books, tears filled Emma's eyes. She remembered Henry's kind smile as he presented her with those gifts. If only she could see that smile again this side of heaven.

"Did Henry make these?" Wayne asked the question as he stood in front of a shelf filled with woodcarvings, including various birds and farm animals.

"*Ya.*" Emma rested her arms over her apron. "He liked to make them in his spare time. Whittling was sort of a hobby for him. It was something he'd do after a long day at the store. He had an area set up in the barn with a workbench and his tools. I bought him a new tool nearly every year for his birthday or Christmas."

"Wow." Wayne turned toward the shelf again. "He was talented."

"*Ya*, he was." Ephraim pointed to one of the carvings. "Wayne, look at the detail on that eagle. The wings really look like they have feathers on them."

"*Ya.*" A new wave of bereavement swept through Emma. "He was very talented. I once tried to convince him to sell his carvings as souvenirs. You know, people will buy anything that's Amish-made. But he refused to do it. He said he was an amateur and *nee* one would pay *gut* money for his work. Now I'm thankful he didn't sell them. Sometimes I come in here, stare at the carvings, and try to remember when he made them. It's almost like having a piece of him here with me."

"It must be very difficult for you." Mandy gave her a sympathetic smile.

"*Danki.*" Emma cupped her hand to her mouth as a yawn overtook her.

"Are we keeping you up too late?" Mandy asked. "We can leave."

"*Nee, nee.*" Emma waved off the notion. "I'd love to visit for a little bit, at least until the cherry bars cool."

"Great." Wayne sat down on the sofa across from her and nodded toward Henry's chair. "Hank certainly is comfortable."

Mandy grinned. "*Ya*, he is." She sat on the footstool in front of Henry's chair and began scratching the cat's ear. He responded by rolling onto his side as if giving her easier access. "Are you comfortable, Hank?" She laughed and looked over at Emma. "He's purring."

"He purred for me earlier too. He likes having his ears scratched." Emma glanced over at the boys sitting on the sofa and wondered if they were dating the girls. Were Wayne and Katie Ann interested in each other in the way Ephraim and Mandy seemed to be? Her thoughts spun with memories of her youth group. "Are you all in the same youth group?"

"*Ya*," Ephraim responded as he sank back into the sofa cushions beside Wayne. "We all went to school together too."

"I remember *mei freinden* and I visiting some of the older folks in our church district when I was young. We liked to sing to them to cheer them up." Emma leaned over and rubbed the cat's head while Mandy continued to massage his ear. Hank looked up at her, and Emma was almost certain her furry friend smiled.

"Did you meet Henry in youth group?" Mandy asked.

"*Ya*, I did. We met at a combined youth gathering more than forty-six years ago. He was the most handsome man playing volleyball. I thought he wouldn't even notice me, but he came over to ask me to join his team." She told them about their first conversation and how kind and attentive Henry had been to her. "We were married in the fall the following year."

Mandy's smile broadened. "That's a great story. I bet you have a lot of *wunderbaar* memories."

Emma nodded and kept her eyes focused on Hank in hopes of not getting too emotional in front of her guests.

Katie Ann called Mandy to come out to the kitchen for the coffee. A few moments later, the girls returned and distributed filled mugs. Mandy set a tray with a pitcher of cream and bowl of sugar on the coffee table, and they each took turns making their coffee the way they liked it.

"*Danki* for your help," Emma said to Katie Ann and Mandy as she settled back in her chair.

"*Gern gschehne.*" Katie Ann sat down in the rocking chair next to the sofa and looked at the boys. "And before you ask, the cherry bars are still too warm."

Ephraim blew out a frustrated sigh. "We'll check them again in a little bit, right?"

"*Ya.* Just let me drink *mei kaffi* first." Mandy grinned at him as she sat down on the footstool in front of the cat.

"You know you can make Hank get down," Emma told her. "Just shoo him away."

"I'm fine." Mandy rubbed his ear. "He's so comfortable, I don't want to bother him."

"He's a cat," Wayne ground out. "Move him."

"*Nee.*" Mandy stayed the course. "Let him rest."

Katie Ann sipped from her mug and then turned toward the mantel. "The decorations are lovely."

"*Ya.*" Emma placed her mug on the table beside her. "They are."

"What was your first Christmas like in this *haus*?" Katie Ann asked.

"Oh." Emma rubbed the bridge of her nose as she thought back to the early years of their marriage. "We spent our first

Christmas together as man and *fraa* at my parents' *haus* since this *haus* wasn't ready yet. Our first Christmas in this *haus* was the year after we married."

"Do you remember what you gave each other as gifts?" Ephraim asked.

Emma nodded. "*Ya*, I do. I still have the quilt I made for Henry. I'll show it to you if you'd like."

Mandy's smile was wide as she glanced over her shoulder at Emma. "I'd love to see it. *Mei mamm* is a *wunderbaar* quilter, but I don't seem to have inherited that talent from her. I can't even sew a straight line."

Ephraim snickered. "*Nee*, you can't. I saw that lap quilt you were working on for your *dat*."

Mandy gasped. "That's not very nice." Then she chuckled. "But it's true."

Emma chimed in as they all laughed, and her eyes filled with happy tears. Oh, it felt so good to laugh again. "I can show you some helpful techniques if you'd like."

"Oh, you'd be wasting your time." Mandy wiped her eyes with her sleeve. "*Mei mamm* has tried to teach me, and I'm a lost cause. I'm much better at baking than I am at sewing and quilting."

"Don't sell yourself so short." Ephraim grinned. "You're a fantastic baker."

Mandy turned toward Emma. "I'd love to see that quilt if you want to share it with us."

"I'll go get it." Emma stood and Hank jumped off his chair to trot behind her through the hallway. Perhaps he didn't want her to make the journey to her bedroom alone.

As she opened her hope chest and pulled out the quilt she'd made forty-four years ago, another memory surged through Emma's mind. That first Christmas in their own home came into clear focus.

Emma's heart raced as she placed Henry's gifts on the kitchen table. She couldn't wait for him to open them, and she was curious about what he would give her. She stared at the two boxes—one large and one small—and an unexpected pang of disappointment shot through her. Neither gift was much since the store was only now starting to turn around, but worse, neither was the one gift she'd most wanted to give him this year.

Closing her eyes, she heaved a deep, cleansing breath as she reminded herself of how blessed she and Henry were. They had a lovely home and a good, solid marriage. The store was starting to show a little profit. She consistently sold a good number of lap quilts, and she hosted dinners with her mother nearly every week to help with the bills. Their parents were healthy, and loving, supportive friends like Urie and Ella surrounded them. Emma and Henry had a good life together. They would have a child when God saw fit.

Emma refocused on the excitement of Christmas as she placed a platter of pancakes on the table next to the bacon, then filled their mugs with coffee. She had returned to the counter to fetch the sugar and creamer when arms encircled her from behind. Startled, she gasped.

"*Frehlicher Grischtdaag.*" Henry's voice whispered against her ear, sending shivers cascading down her spine.

"Henry!" She spun, smacking him on the chest as his warm laugh filled the kitchen. "You startled me."

"I know." He touched the tip of her nose. "But I startle you when I'm wearing work boots. You never hear me." He pulled her into his strong arms and kissed the top of her head.

Emma rested her cheek on his shoulder as she looped her arms around his neck. She closed her eyes and breathed in the familiar scent of his shampoo.

"Breakfast smells amazing." Henry rested his chin on the scarf covering her hair, then released her from his embrace.

"Why don't we eat before it gets cold?"

"*Ya*, that's a *gut* idea."

Emma found the sugar bowl and creamer and they sat down at the table.

After a silent prayer, they chatted about visiting their parents later in the day, and soon their plates were empty. Emma was nearly bursting with excitement to exchange gifts.

Henry reached down to the floor and lifted two boxes, each wrapped in bright red paper. "I have something for you."

Her pulse raced as she ripped open the paper on the top box. As she lifted the lid, she gasped with delight, pulling out a wooden paper towel holder with hearts on the top and bottom, along with a matching napkin holder. "Did you make these?"

He nodded. "*Ya*. I thought I'd try to make something a little more complicated than a wooden frog."

"I love them!" She lifted the paper towel holder from the box and set it on the table. Then she put the napkin holder beside it. "They are lovely. *Danki*."

"*Gern gschehne*." He pointed to the second box. "There's more."

She unwrapped the second box and found two Christian novels, along with a bottle of cherry-blossom body lotion, her favorite. She flipped open the top of the lotion and breathed in the rich, sweet scent.

Then she opened the books and read the inscriptions in them. Each said *Merry Christmas, Emma. I love you. Always and forever, Henry.*

"These are perfect. *Danki* so much." Reaching across the table, she squeezed his hand. "I can't wait for you to open these." She pushed her two boxes toward him.

Henry lifted an eyebrow as his lips twitched with a teasing grin. "You're eager for me to open these, aren't you?"

She blew out an impatient sigh. "*Ya*, I am. Come on. Please open them."

He opened the smaller box first, revealing a new carving knife. His eyes widened. "This is perfect—*danki*!"

"*Gern gschehne*." She pointed to the larger box. "Please open this one now."

He ripped off the paper and opened the box, his smile fading as he pulled out the queen-size quilt. He ran his fingers over the intricate stitching of a Mariner's Star pattern created in his favorite colors, blue and gray.

"Emma," he whispered, his voice a little rough. "This is so *schee*. I don't even know what to say. I'm overwhelmed by the time and effort you put into this for me. It must have taken you all year."

The emotion in his voice sent warmth curling through her. "I wanted to make you something nice. You complained last winter that the *schtupp* was too cold even with a fire, so I thought I'd make you a quilt to keep you warm while you read the paper."

"This is exquisite." He continued to run his hand over the stitches. "I always knew you were talented, but this is just amazing." He smiled across the table at her. "I love it. *Danki*."

"*Gern gschehne*." Her lips pressed together as her earlier regret invaded her thoughts.

Henry's smile faded. "*Was iss letz?*"

"Nothing." Emma sniffed as tears filled her eyes. "I was just thinking about how *froh* I am this Christmas."

"That's not it at all." He shook his head as he hopped up from his seat, came around the table, and sat down beside her. "I know you well enough to tell when you're holding something back from me. There's something you're not telling me. What is it?"

She tried to clear her throat past a lump, but it continued to swell despite her best effort. "I was hoping to give you something else this year."

"What do you mean?" His eyes seemed to search hers for the truth.

She stared down at her hands to avoid his gaze and drew circles on the tablecloth with her finger. "I was hoping I could wrap a little bootie and tell you we were going to have a *boppli*."

"*Ach*, Emma, look at me."

She kept her gaze focused on the green tablecloth.

"Emma." His voice was more insistent, but she continued to avoid his gaze as a tear escaped her eye and trickled down her hot cheek. "God will bless us with *kinner* when he sees fit. You can't give up hope yet."

Emma sniffed as more tears flowed, streaming down her cheeks and splattering on her apron. "You must be so disappointed in me because I haven't given you a *kind* yet."

He clicked his tongue. "Why would you even think that?"

"Because all our married *freinden* are expecting *kinner*, and we're not." She reached for a napkin and swiped it across her eyes and then her nose. "Their families are growing, and ours isn't. I was certain I was expecting last month, but it turned out I was wrong. It's just not happening. There must be something wrong with me."

"*Ach, mei liewe*." Henry pulled her into his arms. "There is nothing wrong with you. I don't blame you, either. We'll just keep praying. And *nee* matter what, I will always love you. My love for you will always grow, whether we have six *kinner* or we have *nee kinner*. All that matters is that we have each other."

With her lower lip trembling, she glanced up at him, taking in his amazing blue eyes, shining with unshed tears. "Do you mean that?"

Henry gave her a sad smile as he wiped away her tears with the tip of his finger. "Of course I do. *Ich liebe dich*, Emma."

"*Ich liebe dich* too," she echoed, her voice quavering.

He leaned down and kissed her, infusing her with the familiar warmth she cherished. It told her this was the man who would care for her always, completely and deeply.

Chapter 5

Oh, Emma, this quilt is so lovely." Mandy ran her fingers over the stitching when Emma handed her the quilt she'd given to Henry all those years ago. "I'm certain Henry cherished it."

"He did." Emma sat back down in her chair. "It's a bit faded and worn. Not only is it decades old, but he used it right up until the day he passed away. He kept it on his chair during the winter months."

Ephraim touched the quilt. "It's really nice. You do great work." He grinned at Mandy. "It's a shame you can't make something like this."

Mandy rolled her eyes. "You said my gift is baking."

"I'm just teasing you." Ephraim took a sip of his coffee and then looked at Emma. "Do you still make quilts to sell?"

Emma shook her head. "I stopped a few years ago. I thought about going back to it, but when Henry got sick, I became his full-time caregiver."

Katie Ann frowned. "I'm sorry to hear you had to give it up. This is so *schee*."

Emma began folding the quilt so she could put it away. "I'm not sure I have the eyesight for quilting anymore. I'd like to find something else. I don't know what to do with my time now." She carefully set the quilt on her lap.

"I'm going to see if the cherry bars are cool enough to cut." Mandy stood. "It really is getting late." She started toward the kitchen.

"Do you need help checking them?" Ephraim got up and trailed after her.

Emma stood to take the quilt back to her bedroom. "We can eat in the kitchen. I'll be there in a minute."

"I'll get the plates out," Katie Ann said as she and Wayne followed Mandy to the kitchen.

"They're ready to be cut." Ephraim grinned and looked over his shoulder as Emma returned to the kitchen. She offered Katie Ann a knife from the block by the stove, and Katie Ann began cutting the dessert into bars and placing them on a platter Mandy provided.

When she was finished, Katie Ann brought the platter to the table, which Mandy had readied for them. Emma refilled their mugs with coffee from the percolator and they all sat down.

"Oh, Emma," Ephraim gushed. "These are fantastic."

"*Danki*." Emma tilted her head. "Henry always looked forward to eating these on Christmas Eve."

"I need to write down the recipe." Mandy turned toward Ephraim. "I can make them for you."

"That would be *wunderbaar*." Ephraim grinned.

Katie Ann looked over at Wayne, and Emma thought she had a curious look in her eye. "Do you like them?" she asked.

"Oh *ya*." Wayne swiped another bar from the platter. "We need to have these again." Emma noticed Katie Ann nodded her head ever so slightly.

"I'm *froh* you're all enjoying them." Emma lifted her mug and took a long drink. Then she glanced toward the doorway as Hank sauntered across the kitchen, stopping once to stretch each of his legs before continuing his lackadaisical journey to the table. He jumped up next to Emma, on Henry's chair again, and sat erect as he stared at her.

"Do you think he's hungry?" Katie Ann touched Hank's head, but he didn't take his eyes off Emma.

"He shouldn't be." Emma placed her mug on the table. "He ate tuna and bacon earlier."

"Tuna and bacon?" Wayne's eyes were wide. "That's a nice meal."

"*Ya*, it is, but it's all I had to offer him. I'll have to pick up some cat food when I get to the store again. And, oh my, some cat litter too."

As if he and Emma had realized his need at the same time, Hank scooted to the back door and made a pathetic sound. Emma let him out, hoping he wouldn't get lost in the snow. But it wasn't long before he scratched on the door and was let back inside where it was warm. After Emma dried him off, he hopped right back into Henry's kitchen chair.

Emma sat down beside him and rubbed his chin. In response, Hank lifted his head and closed his eyes.

"He likes that." Ephraim chuckled.

"It looks like he enjoys that as much as having his ears scratched," Mandy agreed.

"I think you're right," Emma said.

"What else did Henry like to eat?" Mandy took another cherry bar from the platter.

Emma thought back. "He enjoyed steak and potatoes, of course."

"Every man likes that," Ephraim said, and everyone laughed.

"He also enjoyed my beef stroganoff, hamburger casserole, and chicken and dumplings." Emma smiled as she recalled the times she surprised him with a favorite meal when he came home from work.

Then she remembered something new. "You know, sometimes I even took one of Henry's favorite meals to him at the store, but one of our happiest moments there had nothing to do with food." She stroked Hank's fur as the events of that afternoon came back to her.

Emma rushed through the front doors of Lancaster Farm Supply and came to a stop. Henry was helping a customer at the front counter. She fingered the ties on her prayer covering as excitement bubbled up inside of her. She had news she couldn't wait to tell him.

Her heart thumped in her chest as she took in her husband's bright, intelligent blue eyes and warm, welcoming smile. When the customer took his bags and headed for the exit, Emma rushed over.

"Emma!" Henry came around the counter and pulled her into his arms for a hug. "What a pleasant surprise. What are you doing here?"

"I need to talk to you." She smiled, then pointed toward the back of the store where the office was. "Could you ask Urie to run the front so we can have some privacy?"

"Absolutely." Henry took her hand and guided her toward the back room, where they found Urie unloading a pallet of birdseed. "Urie, I have an important visitor. Could you please run the front for me?"

Urie turned toward them and waved in greeting. "Hi there, Emma. *Wie geht's?*"

"I'm doing well," she responded with a wave. "How are you? How's Ella?"

"Ella is great. *Danki.*" Urie's smile deepened as he walked toward them. "She only has about two months left. I can't believe the *boppli* will be here so soon."

Emma's stomach fluttered. "The time *is* going quickly. I'll have to visit Ella this week."

"You should do that. She'd love to spend time with you." Urie wiped his hands on a rag as he stepped out into the store. "I'll take care of the front. Take your time."

"*Danki.*" Henry steered Emma into his office, where he pulled out a thermos from a cooler on the floor. "Would you like a cold drink?" He opened the thermos and poured water into two Styrofoam cups.

"*Ya, danki.*" She took the cup of water and sat in a chair by the desk. "How is your day going?" She lifted the cup and took a long drink, enjoying the cool liquid on her parched throat.

"It's been a *gut* day. Busy." He pulled a chair over beside her and sat with his leg brushing hers. "I'm more interested in hearing about your day. You rarely come to see me at work, even when you have a driver bring you into town to shop. What prompted this special visit?"

"Well . . ." She stared down at the cup, silently gathering her scattered thoughts. "I have some news."

"What kind of news?"

"Surprising news." She looked up, her eyes locking with his. "I had a doctor's appointment today."

"You had a doctor's appointment?" He tilted his head. "I don't remember you telling me that. I'm sorry I forgot."

"You didn't forget. I didn't tell you." She bit her lower lip as he raised his eyebrows.

"You don't normally keep secrets from me . . . or do you?" He set his cup of water on the desk behind him. "Have there been other secret doctor's appointments?"

"*Nee*, this was the first secret appointment." She chuckled and set her cup beside his. "I don't normally keep secrets from you. In fact, I never have, unless you count birthday and Christmas presents."

"Okay." He smiled, seemingly satisfied with her response. "So why the sudden secrecy?" Then his face suddenly changed, his smile melting into a frown. "Wait. Do you have something bad to tell me? Was this appointment about something serious?" He sat up straight. "Why didn't you ask me to come with you? You know Urie can run the store without me if you ever need me. If you had said the word, I could have gone with you—"

"Slow down." She placed her hand on his. "I didn't invite you to come because I wanted to know for certain before I told you."

Henry's expression flickered with something unreadable before his eyes widened. "Know what for certain?" He leaned toward her, his hands resting on her arms. "Emma, are you ill?"

A laugh burst from deep in her chest. "*Nee, nee, nee.*" She rested her hands on her abdomen. "I'm expecting."

"What?" Henry exclaimed so loudly that Emma jumped with a start. "We're going to have a *boppli*?"

"*Ya!*" She yelped as he lifted her up and swung her around.

He laughed and hugged her before setting her on her feet.

"We've waited so long for this." She held on to him, looping her arms around his shoulders. "I was afraid it would never happen, but now it has."

"Oh, Emma." Henry gazed into her eyes and traced her cheek with his fingertip. "You've made me the happiest man in the world." He kissed her, then rested his forehead against hers. "*Danki.*"

"*Gern gschehne.*" She placed both hands on his chest. "I couldn't wait to tell you, so I asked my driver to bring me here. I thought I might burst with excitement if I had to wait until suppertime."

"I'm *froh* you didn't wait." He kissed her again, making her lips tingle.

"Are you disappointed I didn't tell you about the appointment?"

He shook his head. "*Nee*, not at all. But when are you due?"

"May." She squeezed his hand. "I'm so excited. I've always planned to move my sewing table and supplies into our bedroom so the nursery can be right next to us. Or wait. We should just move my sewing room to one of the bedrooms upstairs. And I have my cradle in the attic. Would you please refinish it? And I think we have your crib. We can clean that up too. And I need to get sewing. We'll have to talk about names. We have so much to do!"

He laughed. "We do have a lot to do. Why don't you go home and make a list? We can talk about it at supper tonight."

"That's a great idea." She hugged him. "*Ich liebe dich*."

"I love you too." He kissed her once more.

"We did talk that night," Emma said after telling the story, minus some of the romantic details. She rubbed Hank's velvety soft ear between her fingers. "We made all sorts of lists, and we started working on the nursery. Henry refinished my cradle from when I was a *boppli*, and he started working on the crib."

She paused for a moment before going on. "But everything changed in the middle of the night when I was in my third month."

Hank rolled over onto his back on the chair, and Emma stroked his middle as she carefully continued the story. She wanted to tell her young friends what happened, but she'd spare them the hardest details.

Emma woke up in the middle of the night and sucked in a deep breath as a sharp, white-hot pain radiated from her lower back to her abdomen.

"Henry." She managed to breathe out his name when the pain subsided. "Henry." She reached over and nudged him. "Wake up. Something's wrong." Tears burned her eyes as the pain flared once again.

"What?" Henry rolled over. "Emma?"

When she gasped, he sat up. "Emma? *Was iss letz?*" He took her hand in his. "Emma? Tell me what's wrong."

"I'm in pain. Can you help me to the bathroom?"

"*Ya, ya.*" He climbed out of bed, rushed around to her side, and helped her stand. "Where does it hurt?" he asked as he led her out of their bedroom.

"My back. My abdomen." She swallowed back a sob when they reached the hallway. "Something is terribly wrong." Tears streamed down her face as fear gripped her. *Please, God. Please protect our* boppli.

"Everything will be fine." The tremor in his voice sent more tears cascading down her cheeks. "I'll take care of you. I promise."

Emma sniffed and wiped away tears as she recalled the next events. When she realized what was happening, she called for Henry through the bathroom door. She was losing an alarming amount of blood, and she asked him to call for an ambulance.

The emergency medical technicians rushed Emma to the hospital, where an exam confirmed the baby was gone. Her womb was empty, and she was no longer going to be a mother. When the doctor told them the devastating news, Emma and Henry sobbed in each other's arms.

The weeks after losing the baby were the most painful of their marriage. In only a couple of hours, they'd gone from preparing to become parents to praying desperately that God would bless them with another child.

But it never happened. Eventually they packed up the nursery. Henry put the cradle and crib back in the attic, where they stayed for years. Emma gave the clothes she'd made to Urie and Ella, who by then were expecting their third child. She couldn't bear to keep them.

"All I ever wanted was to give Henry a *boppli*," Emma whispered as she massaged the feline's side, and Hank gave a little meow as if to comfort her. "God, however, never blessed us with that opportunity. He blessed us in many other ways, but I've always had a longing for a *kind*. After I lost the *boppli*, I blamed myself for a long time. I thought maybe I had done something wrong. For example, if I hadn't spent so much time on my feet cooking or so many hours sewing, maybe the *boppli* would have made it. I said that to Henry once, and he insisted I talk to my doctor about it. He confirmed it wasn't my fault at all. He said sometimes it happens, and there's nothing we can do. But it's still difficult to accept, even though I know it's not my place to question the Lord's plan."

"I'm so sorry." Katie Ann rubbed her arm. "It wasn't your fault."

"*Danki*." Emma grabbed a napkin from the holder in the center of the table and wiped her eyes. "I was *bedauerlich* for a very long time afterward. Sometimes I found myself envious of *mei freinden* and their families, but I knew that was a sin. I had to keep reminding myself of how *wunderbaar* my life with Henry was." More tears escaped her eyes, and she swallowed against a swelling knot of emotion clogging her throat. "But now, without children and without Henry, I'm alone."

"You have us." Mandy touched Emma's hand.

"That's right," Ephraim chimed in.

"We're your *freinden*," Wayne added. "We're here for you."

"*Danki*," Emma said, her voice wobbly, hoping she hadn't embarrassed these young men with her story. But when she looked into their eyes, she saw only compassion. They'd make fine husbands someday.

The cat sat up and purred as he rubbed his head against her arm. She was certain Hank was trying to tell her something.

"You're here for me too, huh?" Emma smiled despite her tears. "Are you telling me I'm your *mamm*?"

Hank looked at her and blinked before curling up beside her, resting one paw on her thigh.

"I suppose that means *ya*." She rubbed the cat's ear one more time. "I used to wonder what it would have been like to be a *mamm*. How many *kinner* Henry and I might have had and what names we would have chosen. I suppose if we'd had a *kind* I might be a *mammi* by now. Now I wonder what that would be like."

Emma clicked her tongue at Hank. "What would Henry say about you? Would he call me *narrisch*? Or maybe he'd say I was *gegisch*." The tabby purred with his eyes closed. "I suppose it doesn't matter, does it?"

Hank opened one eye and then closed it. That, apparently, was his only answer.

She shook her head. "You are a precocious kitty, aren't you?"

"He definitely loves you," Mandy said. "He's a nice kitty. I'm *froh* he found you."

"He did find me." Emma swiped her hand across her wet eyes as Henry's favorite Scripture crossed her mind. It was Romans 15:13: *"May the God of hope fill you with all joy and peace as you trust in him, so that you may overflow with hope by the power of the Holy Spirit."*

As Emma silently recited the verse, she remembered the day Henry brought home a special gift for her. It was just two months after they'd lost the baby.

Emma was putting the finishing touches on a quilt a customer had ordered for her daughter's birthday when she felt as if someone was watching her.

Turning, Emma found Henry standing in the sewing room doorway, and she gasped.

"You startled me!" She gripped her chest and gulped in some air in an effort to catch her breath.

"I'm sorry." He stepped into the room and sat down in a chair beside hers.

She looked at the clock on the wall and cringed. It was after six. She'd been so engrossed in her project she'd forgotten to make supper.

"I'm sorry. I was working on this and lost track of time." She placed the quilt on the sewing table and started to stand.

"Sit." He rested his hand on her arm. "It's okay. We can make grilled cheese or something else that's easy."

"But I promised you beef stroganoff."

He shook his head and smiled. "We can have that another night." He turned his attention to the quilt. "That's the Lone Star pattern you were telling me about at supper last night." He ran his fingers over the pink, purple, and blue stitches. "It's *schee.* You seem to get more talented all the time."

"*Danki.*" She shrugged. "It's one of my better quilts, but it's not perfect."

"I think it is." He met her gaze. "How are you?"

"I'm fine. How are you?"

"Emma." He cupped his hand to her cheek, a gesture she'd come to love. But today she wasn't sure she wanted him probing her emotions.

"I want to know how you're really doing. You're deflecting my questions and my concern about you. I want to know the truth. How are you coping?"

"I don't know." She stared down at her lap and took a deep breath. "Some days are better than others. I try to stay busy so I can't get too lost in my thoughts. That's why I forgot to make supper tonight. I keep wondering if there was something I could've done to save the *boppli*. I feel like I failed both of you." She sniffed and tried to fight back tears.

"Look at me."

She looked up, and the warmth in his eyes touched her deep in her soul. Her mouth dried.

"You know I love you, right?" His expression was hopeful, as if he were trying to convince her he still cared. "We're in this together. What happened was out of our control. You know that, right?"

Emma nodded, even though she wasn't convinced.

"I brought you something." He lifted a bag she hadn't noticed was in his hand. "I thought this might help."

She opened the bag and pulled out a devotional book. "Oh, Henry. It's *schee*."

She opened the cover and read his inscription: *To Emma. May this book bring you comfort whenever you need to feel God close to you. I'll love you always and forever. Henry.*

"*Danki*," she whispered before pulling Henry into a hug.

"My favorite Scripture verse is in there. I marked it for you. Emma, don't ever forget how much I love you." His voice was warm in her ear. "Always and forever, *mei liewe*."

"Oh *nee*," Katie Ann exclaimed, bringing Emma back to the present. "It's really getting late. We'd better get going."

Emma looked at the clock on the mantel. "I'm sorry for keeping you so long, listening to my story."

"Don't apologize," Mandy said. "It's been fun." She paused. "And meaningful."

"We'd better go hitch up the horse." Ephraim tapped Wayne's arm.

The boys put on their coats and boots, took up their lanterns and both of Emma's shovels, and headed outside. The girls insisted on helping Emma clean up while she packed up the cherry bars.

After only a few minutes, Ephraim suddenly called out from the back door.

"We have a problem. We're snowed in!"

Chapter 6

We're snowed in?" Katie Ann spun toward the mudroom. "What do you mean?"

Ephraim chuckled as he came to the doorway separating the kitchen from the mudroom, snow already covering his coat and boots. "I mean the snow is up to our shins."

Wayne appeared beside him. "I don't think we're going anywhere anytime soon."

Emma gasped. "It's come down that much since you arrived?"

"*Ya*, it has." Wayne brushed snow off his sleeves.

"Oh *nee*!" Katie Ann rushed past him. She peered out the window in the back door, but it was too dark to see anything but the shadows of the swaying trees.

Emma and the girls pulled on their coats and boots, and they all stepped onto the porch. Wayne and Ephraim held their lanterns against the wind.

The bitter cold hit Katie Ann's face like a stinging smack, stealing her breath and filling her eyes with tears as she walked to the top of the steps.

"Watch." Wayne held up his lantern and walked down to the bottom step. When he stepped onto the path, his long leg sank into the snow, which really did come up to his shin. "It's deep." He grinned as he faced the porch. "It's like a blizzard out here."

"But look at that." Katie Ann pointed toward the barn. "It's also so *schee*."

Pristine snow sparkled in the light of the lantern as large flakes continued to twirl toward the ground. Katie Ann blew out a deep breath as she took in the beautiful sight.

"It is *schee*." Mandy turned toward Emma, a protective arm still around her shoulders to make sure she didn't fall on the slippery porch. "Have you ever seen snow like this at Christmas?"

"*Nee*, not since I was a *maedel*." Emma hugged her arms to her chest. "It's just breathtaking."

"We're stranded." Ephraim climbed down the steps and stood beside Wayne. "There's *nee* way we can get home safely tonight."

"You can stay here." Emma rubbed her hands over her arms. "You *buwe* can use my phone in the barn to call all your parents and let them know you're going to stay until the roads are plowed."

"*Danki*." Katie Ann turned toward her brother. "You'll call *Mamm* and *Dat*?"

"*Ya*," Ephraim said. "Are you ready, Wayne? We may need to dig out the barn doors. And we'd better check on the horses too."

The young men started toward the barn, armed with both their lanterns and shovels.

"Wait!" Mandy called after them, and they whirled around to face her. "You know my parents' phone number, right?"

"*Ya*, I know it," Ephraim called. "Go inside and get warm."

Katie Ann blinked. Ephraim knew Mandy's phone number? Was that yet another indication that he liked Mandy and she liked him? She looked at Wayne's retreating back, wondering what he knew about those two. Was she the only one in the dark?

Emma touched Katie Ann's and Mandy's arms, pulling Katie Ann from her suspicions. "They'll take care of it. Let's get inside and put on water for hot tea. I think we've had enough chocolate and *kaffi*, but they're going to be freezing when they come in. I have some decaffeinated tea bags too."

Emma steered the girls toward the house but then stopped and pointed at Hank, who was standing on his back legs, peeking through the storm door. His eyes darted around with interest.

"Do you think he wants to come out and play in the snow? Or, uh, just needs to come out again?" Katie Ann asked.

"*Nee*, I think he's wondering why we're out here in the cold while he's inside where it's warm," Mandy retorted with a chuckle.

"Move away from the door." Emma waved her fingers at the cat. "It's cold out here. You need to step back. You don't want to be out in the snow if you don't have to be, Hank. Go on, kitty. Shoo!"

Emma laughed. "Oh, how funny. Earlier today when I first found him sitting on the porch, I tried to shoo him away from *mei haus*. Now I'm trying to keep him inside, where he's warm and safe. Isn't it *narrisch* how my feelings toward this cat have changed since this afternoon?" She tapped on the door. "You've just moved in, haven't you?"

Katie Ann laughed too, enjoying the happiness glowing on Emma's face.

The cat hopped away from the door and trotted through the mudroom toward the kitchen, and Emma entered the house with Katie Ann and Mandy following close behind. They all hung up their coats, took off their boots, and stepped into the kitchen.

"I'll put on the hot water." Mandy grabbed the kettle and started filling it.

"I'll get back to washing the dishes." Katie Ann returned to her soapy water. As she worked, Emma divided the remaining cherry bars into the three containers.

Then Emma laughed again, and Katie Ann glanced down to where Hank walked circles around Emma's legs while rubbing his head against them.

"That cat really loves you." Katie Ann smiled. "He's chosen you as his owner."

Emma leaned down and scratched Hank behind one ear. "He has. And he's already stolen my heart."

The women had the kitchen cleaned by the time they heard Ephraim and Wayne return from the barn. Their hats, coats, gloves, and trousers were all caked in snow, even though Emma was sure they'd shaken off as much as they could on the porch. And the snow had obviously seeped into their boots, soaking their socks and feet.

"Oh dear!" she exclaimed as she hurried toward them. "You must be frozen to the bone! I'll get you towels."

"I'll get them," Mandy offered. "Where are they?"

Emma explained where the linen closet was and Mandy rushed off.

Katie Ann stood in the kitchen doorway as she took in the snow-covered boys. "Is it still snowing that much?"

"*Ya*, it is. It hasn't let up at all." Ephraim shivered. His nose and cheeks were red.

Katie Ann looked out the back door and shook her head. "It's like a winter wonderland out there."

Mandy returned with several towels. "Here you go."

"*Danki*," the boys said, first one and then the other.

"I left a message for your parents," Ephraim told Mandy as he pulled off his boots and socks. "I explained we're going to stay here for the night."

"*Danki*."

"I'll go get you some of Henry's clothes to wear." Emma hurried through the kitchen to the hallway.

"She is so nice," Mandy commented after Emma left. "I'm so glad we came to visit her tonight."

"*Ya*," Katie Ann agreed. "We'll have to come see her again soon."

"I wonder how long we'll be here. It's going to take a while to get the roads cleared tomorrow, especially on Christmas Day," Ephraim said. "This storm is bad."

"I don't remember ever seeing snow get so deep so quickly," Wayne added. "I guess this is what a true snowstorm is like."

When she heard footsteps, Katie Ann whirled toward Emma. "There you are. I'm so glad you have some clothes Ephraim and Wayne can wear."

"*Ya.* I brought thick socks and some trousers. Henry was about your height, but he was very skinny toward the end."

Emma paused and her expression clouded as she handed the clothes to the boys. "I hope these fit well enough. I brought a couple of extra sweaters too. The bathroom is down the hallway to the right. Bring out your wet clothes, and I'll hang them in the laundry room."

Sorrow tugged at Katie Ann's heart. Emma looked so sad.

"*Danki.*" Wayne headed toward the bathroom. "I'll go first."

"Let's make some hot tea for you, Ephraim. That will warm you up." Mandy headed back toward the stove.

Ephraim hugged a towel to his chest and shivered again. "That sounds great."

Mandy made Ephraim a mug of tea and brought it to him in the mudroom.

"*Danki.*" He sank down onto the bench and patted the spot beside him. "Sit with me."

"*Ya*, of course." Mandy's porcelain cheeks flushed bright pink as she sank down beside him.

Emma touched Katie Ann's arm. "Why don't we make four more mugs of tea and take them into the *schtupp*?"

Understanding flashed through Katie Ann's mind. She and Emma needed to give Ephraim and Mandy some time alone. "Oh, *ya*. I'll get the mugs."

Emma and Katie Ann carried the drinks into the family room, where they set them on the coffee table. Emma added another log to the fire.

After both Ephraim and Wayne were dressed, Katie Ann helped Emma hang their wet clothes on the line in the laundry room before they joined the others in the family room. Emma sat in the same chair she'd been in before, and Katie Ann sat in the rocker. Wayne sat beside her on the footstool, and Ephraim sat on the sofa.

"Why don't we sing carols before we turn in?" Mandy suggested as she sat down on the sofa beside Ephraim.

"That's a great idea." Katie Ann rocked back and forth in her chair. "How about 'Silent Night'?"

"Perfect." Mandy cleared her throat. "All right. One, two, three . . ."

The young people sang "Silent Night" in perfect harmony while the fire in the fireplace crackled and popped as if it were their musical accompaniment. Emma started to sing along with them, but then she stopped. Concern filled Katie Ann as she watched Emma's expression falter into yet another frown. Was the music making Emma sad instead of brightening her Christmas? She prayed they were helping Emma cope with the holiday, not making her even sadder.

As they sang, Hank sauntered into the room and stood at Emma's feet. Emma patted the chair beside her, but he leaped into her lap and curled up on her thighs before closing his eyes. Emma stared at Hank for a moment before she began to stroke his head.

"*Frehlicher Grischtdaag!*" Katie Ann said when the song came to an end. "Should we sing another one?"

"How about 'Joy to the World'?" Mandy suggested.

"That sounds *gut*," Ephraim agreed.

For the next thirty minutes, between sips of tea, they sang.

After "Joy to the World," they moved to "O Little Town of Bethlehem," "Hark! the Herald Angels Sing," "The First Noel," and then "O Holy Night." Emma never stopped stroking the cat as she was serenaded.

When they were finished singing, Emma yawned.

"We're keeping you up too late," Katie Ann said. "You should go to bed."

"*Nee*, I'm not ready just yet." Though her tea must have grown cool, Emma lifted her mug from the end table beside her. "You all sound fantastic together. When you visit other older people in the community, do you usually go as a group?"

Mandy nodded as she settled back against the sofa. "We do. We sang for Mary Dienner last week."

"She has cancer, right?" Emma asked.

"That's right." Mandy fingered the arm of the sofa. "She's doing a little better, but the treatments have been difficult."

Emma's smile faded and alarm raced through Katie Ann. One minute Emma seemed fine, and the next she didn't seem fine at all. Yet perhaps, Katie Ann thought, that was the way grief worked for someone who had lost a loved one.

"Are you all right?" Katie Ann reached over and touched Emma's arm. "You look upset."

"Did I say something wrong?" Mandy asked.

"*Nee*, *nee*, it's not you. I was just thinking about Henry. Maybe you didn't know, but he had brain cancer. It was a difficult illness." Emma took another sip from her mug and then set it on the table. "Cancer stole his life. He was so active and funny, and then one day he started to change. He had *nee* energy and he began to forget things. We laughed about it at first, saying we were getting old. But then Urie told Ella and me he noticed it at the store too, and we all started to suspect something was wrong."

"That had to be so heartbreaking for you." Katie Ann's eyes filled with tears.

"It was." Emma gave her a sad smile. "One day Henry forgot his way home, and we knew we had to get help. A scan showed he had a brain tumor, and a biopsy revealed it was malignant."

Emma seemed to forget about Hank for the moment, but Katie Ann noticed him looking up at her, as though he somehow understood his new friend was grieving. Katie Ann wiped away a tear as sadness overcame her.

"It almost felt surreal," Emma went on. "As if I were imagining the entire thing. I almost asked the doctor if he had read the wrong test results, but it made sense. By then Henry had all the symptoms—fatigue, confusion, nausea, dizziness, headaches, and personality changes. It hit me like a smack to the face—I was going to lose him."

"I can't imagine how you felt when you heard the news." Katie Ann's voice held a quaver as she swiped at her eyes with the back of her hand.

"It had to be just devastating," Mandy chimed in. When she sniffed, Ephraim handed her a napkin from the coffee table.

"It was." Emma cleared her throat. "The illness was advanced by the time the doctors found it, so there wasn't much they could do. We tried a couple rounds of treatment, but it didn't help. The treatments were tough on him too. It was difficult to watch his transformation, the slow deterioration. I went from being Henry's partner to being his nurse. I didn't mind taking care of him. After all, he was my husband and my best *freind*. But I missed the man he'd been."

Grief overwhelmed Katie Ann as her heart broke for Emma. Her parents had mentioned Henry's illness before he died, but Katie Ann hadn't realized what Emma and Henry were enduring. She swallowed against the lump swelling in her throat.

"Was it when you got the diagnosis that he decided to retire and sell the store?" Ephraim asked.

"*Ya.*" Now Emma started to rub the cat's chin as she spoke, and Hank's purring grew louder. "He was already too ill to run it. He wanted to stay on and work part-time, but he didn't have the strength. He had to retire. Urie, who'd become a partner in the business by then, bought him out, and he got a *gut*, fair price. It was enough for us to live on and put money in savings for me."

She ran her fingers over Hank's back. "It was tough for him. That store was his dream. It was something he'd wanted since he'd visited his *onkel's* store in Indiana when he was a teenager. He thought he'd work there until he was much older, but it wasn't in God's plan. He also thought he'd leave the store to our *kinner*, but . . ."

"I'm sorry he was so ill." Mandy sniffed and wiped her eyes. "You've been through so much."

"*Danki.*" Emma's lower lip trembled. "The doctors gave him a year, but he lived eighteen months. God gave us a little more time than we'd expected, and I'm thankful for that, though I confess I've often wished we'd had more—even though it was a difficult time." Her voice grew thick. "He was so very ill. I had some assistance with things like bathing, but I had to help him dress, eat . . . He became like an infant, dependent on me for everything."

Tears glistened in Emma's eyes, and soon she was truly crying and covering her face with her hands.

"*Ach*, I'm so sorry." Katie Ann leaned over and rubbed her back. She longed to take away Emma's pain.

"I'm sorry too," Mandy echoed. "I didn't know."

"We should have come to see you then," Katie Ann said softly as guilt seeped in. "I'm sorry we didn't help you through that."

"It's not your fault, and others did help. But *danki.*" Emma sniffed and wiped her face with a tissue from her apron pocket. "I'm sorry for being so emotional."

Emma looked at the cat rubbing against her as if to get her attention. With a chuckle, she leaned down and patted Hank's head. "You *gegisch* cat."

"He can tell when you're upset," Mandy said as she ran her fingers over her mug. "They're *gut* at detecting our emotions."

Ephraim snickered and shook his head. "You and those barn cats."

"What?" Mandy swatted him with her hand. "It's true. I was upset one day, and one of the cats in *mei dat's* barn climbed into my lap."

"He was probably looking for food," Wayne quipped, and Mandy glared at him.

Emma laughed. "*Danki* for coming over and cheering me up. You've really made today easier."

"I'm *froh* to hear that," Katie Ann said, pushing her new curiosity about her brother and Mandy from her mind. "We'd like to visit you more often. Right?" She glanced around the room, and her friends and Ephraim nodded.

"I would like that," Emma said.

An idea came to Katie Ann and she snapped her fingers. "I know what we can do in memory of Henry." She turned toward Emma. "It's sort of a community service project."

"What is it?" Emma asked.

"We could create a community garden here next spring." She pointed toward the back of the house. "I remember from when you hosted church that you have a large garden. We could add on to it and then grow and can vegetables to donate to the homeless shelter. We could even call it 'Henry's Garden.' The food would help our community." She gestured around the room. "We could all take turns planting, weeding, and harvesting the vegetables. Then we could get together to can them. What do you think of that?"

"That would be so fun," Mandy said. "I love the idea."

The boys nodded.

Emma's eyes glistened with renewed tears. "I love that idea, Katie Ann. Henry would have too. He was a caring man. *Danki*."

"Great." Katie Ann rubbed her hands together as more ideas popped into her mind. The four of them could bring happiness to Emma's life and help other people too. "But I plan to visit you plenty of times before we plant the garden."

"I would love that as well," Emma said.

"*Gut*." Katie Ann stifled a yawn with the palm of her hand. "I guess we should do a final cleanup and then try to get some sleep." She stood and grabbed two of the mugs.

Emma gnawed her lower lip as Katie Ann and Mandy cleared the dishes and the boys made sure they were safe from any sparks from what remained of the fire. How could she make her friends comfortable overnight?

"I don't have a guest room anymore. Henry and I were both only *kinner*, and the two bedrooms upstairs are stacked high with furniture and other items we inherited from our parents. We were going to finally sort through it all, but then Henry got sick—"

"That's not a problem, Emma," Ephraim said. "If you have pillows and quilts, Wayne and I can sleep on the floor, and the *maed* can have the sofa and chairs."

"*Ya*," Mandy agreed.

"That will be just fine," Katie Ann agreed. "I'll wash the dishes first."

Mandy stood. "I'll help you get the blankets and pillows while the *buwe* make room for their beds."

"*Danki*." Emma gently nudged Hank off her lap and hurried upstairs to the hall closet where she and Mandy gathered four pillows and pillowcases and some quilts. Then they made a second trip for more quilts.

They made beds on the family room floor and then fixed up the sofa and wing chair.

"Will you be comfortable enough?" Emma asked when the makeshift beds were ready.

"*Ya.*" Ephraim settled onto his pile of quilts on the floor. "This is perfect."

"*Ya*, it's *gut*," Wayne agreed beside him on his quilts.

"We'll be fine," Mandy said from the sofa. "You get some sleep."

"See you in the morning," Katie Ann added from the wing chair. "*Gut nacht.*"

"All right." Emma gave them a little wave and headed to her bedroom.

Hank followed her and jumped up on the bed as she removed her prayer covering and bobby pins. After brushing her hair, she changed into her nightgown and, in her bathrobe, moved to the bathroom, where she washed her face and brushed her teeth. She was going to be much more comfortable than her guests, but there wasn't much more she could do about it.

Back in her bedroom, the cat patiently watched her. "We had a *gut* evening, didn't we, Hank? Sharing my memories was difficult, but afterward I felt better. And we had fun with our new *freinden* too."

The cat blinked before sitting back on his haunches, as if agreeing with her assessment of the evening.

She lowered herself onto the bed beside him and massaged his head. Hank closed his eyes and purred as if drinking in her affection. Emma's gaze went to the devotional on her nightstand. As her thoughts moved to her husband, she smiled.

"*Danki* for the life we had together, Henry," she said softly as she tweaked the cat's ear. "We were blessed to have each other for as long as we did. *Danki* for choosing me and for loving me. I miss you, but I'm so very grateful for the *wunderbaar* life we had together."

Hank rolled onto his side, and Emma laughed. "You are the funniest kitty I have ever known, and I'm *froh* you're my Christmas cat. Maybe you knew I needed company, just like those *freinden* sleeping in my family room did."

Hank opened his eyes and gave a low meow in response.

"Why don't we let you outside one more time and then go check on them?" He jumped off the bed. "I'll take that as a *ya*."

Emma pushed her feet into her slippers, and after Hank's visit outside, she walked quietly into the family room. She stopped in the doorway and took in the sight of the four young people sprawled on the floor, sofa, and chair. The soft glow of the dying fire gave their hair a golden hue.

She felt Hank brush against her leg, and he entered the room. He crossed the floor and stopped to smell Ephraim's hair before moving on to Mandy's. Emma cupped her hand to her mouth to stop a laugh from escaping. Hank turned to look at her as if to say, *I know something you don't.* Then he smelled Wayne's hair and Katie Ann's hair before looking at Emma again, this time with what she imagined was a questioning look.

Don't look at me, Hank, she thought. *I really have little idea what's going on with these four. But, like you, I suppose, I do have suspicions.*

Wondering what in the world she was going to do with such a cat, Emma simply nodded her head. *That's enough, Hank.* He came to sit at her feet.

As she listened to the last crackles of the fire, Emma opened her heart and began to pray.

God, please guide these young people and bless them richly, giving each of them the kind of love Henry and I cherished for so many years.

Hank at her side, Emma padded down the hallway and felt God's embrace like a warm hug. In the morning they would continue celebrating the gift of his Son. She was so grateful that amid her heightened grief and loneliness, he'd sent her not only friends, but a fresh purpose: she was going to help create Henry's Garden.

God had sent her a furry companion too. And to that, Hank seemed to meow a quiet, Christmas amen.

Discussion Questions

1. Emma is grieving the loss of her husband. Have you faced a difficult loss? What Bible verses helped you? Share your answers with the group.
2. Katie Ann, Ephraim, and their friends are like guardian angels to Emma when she's alone for her first Christmas without her husband. Why do you think they feel compelled to continue ministering to Emma even after the Christmas holiday?
3. Emma recalls Henry's favorite verse, Romans 15:13: "May the God of hope fill you with all joy and peace as you trust in him, so that you may overflow with hope by the power of the Holy Spirit." What does this verse mean to you?
4. Katie Ann suggests they plant a community garden in Henry's memory and donate canned vegetables to the local homeless shelter. Have you ever participated in a community project? If so, what was the project? Was it successful?
5. Which character can you identify with the most? Which character seemed to carry the most emotional stake in the story? Was it Emma, Katie Ann, Ephraim, or someone else?
6. Emma lost her husband five months ago, and she has no family. Think of a time when you felt lost and alone. Where did you find your strength? What Bible verses would help during a time like this?

7. What significance did Hank have in the story? How did he help Emma during her first Christmas alone?
8. By the end of the story, Emma realizes these young people have become like her family. Was there ever a time when your friends felt like family members?
9. What did you know about the Amish before reading this book? What did you learn?

Acknowledgments

As always, I'm thankful for my loving family. I'm also grateful for my special Amish friend who patiently answers my endless stream of questions. You're a blessing in my life.

Thank you to my wonderful church family at Morning Star Lutheran in Matthews, North Carolina, for your encouragement, prayers, love, and friendship. You all mean so much to my family and me.

Thank you to Zac Weikal and the fabulous members of my Bakery Bunch! I'm so grateful for your friendship and your excitement about my books. You all are amazing!

To my agent, Natasha Kern—I can't thank you enough for your guidance, advice, and friendship. You are a tremendous blessing in my life.

Thank you to my amazing editor, Becky Monds, for your friendship and guidance. I'm grateful to each and every person at HarperCollins Christian Publishing who helped make this book a reality.

Thank you most of all to God—for giving me the inspiration and the words to glorify You. I'm grateful and humbled You've chosen this path for me.

About the Author

Amy Clipston is the award-winning and bestselling author of the Amish Heirloom series and the Kauffman Amish Bakery series. She has sold more than one million books. Her novels have hit multiple bestseller lists including CBD, CBA, and ECPA. Amy holds a degree in communication from Virginia Wesleyan College and works full time for the City of Charlotte, NC. Amy lives in North Carolina with her husband, two sons, and three spoiled rotten cats.

Visit her online at amyclipston.com
Facebook: AmyClipstonBooks
Twitter: @AmyClipston

Snow Angels

Kelly Irvin

To Tim, the love of my life

Forget the former things;
do not dwell on the past.
See, I am doing a new thing!
Now it springs up; do you not perceive it?

Isaiah 43:18–19

Glossary*

bopli, boplin: baby, babies
bruder: brother
daed: father
dochdee: daughter
Englisch, Englischer: English, non-Amish
fraa: wife
Gmay: church district/community
Gott: God
gut: good
jah: yes
kaffi: coffee
kapp: prayer cap worn by all Amish women
kinner: children
lieb: love
mann: husband
mudder: mother
nee: no
rumspringa: period of running around
schtinkich: stink, stinky
schweschder: sister

*The German dialect spoken by the Amish is not a written language and varies depending on the location and origin of the settlement. These spellings are approximations. Most Amish children learn English after they start school. They also learn high German, which is used in their Sunday services.

Featured Bee County Amish Families

Aaron and Jolene Shrock
Isabella (married to Will Glick)
Matthew
John
James
Molly
Amanda

Levi and Susan Byler
David
Martha (married to Jacob King)
Milo
Rueben
Jason
Ida
Nyla
Liam
Mordecai
Henry

Tobias and Rebekah Byler
Jason
Lupe and Diego (foster children)

Mordecai and Abigail King
Jacob
Caleb (Abigail's son)
Grace (Abigail's daughter)

Chapter 1

The red roan looked like she'd been ridden hard and put up wet. David Byler kept that thought to himself as he paraded the twelve-year-old mare in front of the audience. It was thick with Bee County farmers, housewives, children who wiggled on produce boxes turned upside down, and the occasional curious tourist who'd driven all the way from San Antonio to experience a Plain auction.

Leroy Glick's deep, singsong auctioneer's voice played like sweet music in David's ears. He loved the auction. The clammy November air in the barn plastered his shirt to his back, but he didn't mind. By South Texas standards, autumn had arrived. Cooler weather waited around the year's bend. The stench of manure wafting in from the livestock section mingled with the sweet aroma of the haystacks.

The horse, who might once have been a beauty, tossed her head, making her dark, almost black mane whip. She whinnied, a high, nervous sound like a lady being introduced for the first time at a sewing frolic. He felt for his new equine friend. Reba wouldn't bring much. She had an open sore on her rump, which the owner explained came from something she rubbed against. Her best years might be behind her, but Reba deserved a second chance.

Everybody did.

David smiled as he guided the horse into a second pass while

Leroy upped the ante. "One-fifty, one-sixty, I have one-sixty; who'll give me one-seventy-five? There, one-seventy-five, one-eighty-five. I've got one-eighty-five."

An old geezer in overalls and a train conductor hat held up his number. To David's amazement, a lady with a sunburned face and a pink bandanna covering her red hair countered when Leroy hopped to two hundred. The old geezer tugged at his handlebar mustache, his expression disgusted, and shook his head. He plopped back onto the wooden bleachers, his arms crossed and propped up on his rotund belly.

"Going, going, gone. Sold to number two-twenty-six."

Reba had a new owner. A new start. "Congratulations." David whispered the word like a sweet nothing in the horse's ear. It might sound silly, but he knew how Reba felt. He trotted the horse out the side door into the gray haze of low-hanging clouds that couldn't decide whether to mist or move on. Pink Bandanna followed him out, her flips-flops making a *slap-slap* sound on the hard dirt.

David knew most everyone in the area, but he didn't recognize the lady who waddled toward him. She was shaped like an overweight duck wearing a short-sleeved green-and-pink-flowered housecoat. She carried a woven straw bag on one shoulder and a half-empty water bottle in her hand.

"Poor, sweet thing." She had a high-pitched quack of a voice that served to further David's image of her as a middle-aged, overweight duck. "She'll live out her days safe and sound, giving rides to my grandchildren."

David spent his days training horses. They were beautiful, intelligent creatures. He recognized a fellow horse lover when he saw one. "Sounds like she'll be happy in her new home."

The woman stuffed the water bottle in her straw bag. "I have to call my husband. He'll have to bring up the trailer to fetch Cinnamon."

Cinnamon? "Her name is Reba."

"I like Cinnamon. Where do I pay?"

David turned to point out the booth where all transactions were handled. Molly Shrock walked toward him, her face lit up in her usual shy smile, a gift he still couldn't believe was directed at him on a regular basis. She glanced around, surely checking to see if anyone would notice if she stopped to talk to him. She had the steady stride of a woman who needed no one's approval but welcomed everyone's friendship. Her pale-blue dress and white apron were pristine, her brown hair pulled neatly behind her white *kapp*. Everything about her said *I know who I am and what I want. Gott* willing, she would say yes when he proposed—something he planned to do soon. Very soon.

He handed the reins to the new horse owner. "They'll get you taken care of right there at the booth where you got your number."

Waving off her thanks, he moved toward a row of buggies and wagons lining the space between the Combination Store and the road. The variety, like the open buggy with blue velvet seats or the long glass-covered horse-drawn hearse, never ceased to amaze him. It would be hard for anyone—mostly Molly's *mudder*—to see them between the vehicles angled so they were the first thing buyers saw when they pulled up at the auction.

"Hey."

She had a soft, lilting voice that he'd never heard raised in anger. He swiveled and smiled. "Hey."

"I have to get back to the lunch line, but I saw you there and had to stop. I couldn't resist. Gott forgive me."

Gott would forgive her. Who wouldn't? God treated David far better than he deserved. No one knew that more than he did. His *daed*, his *bruders*, his friends—everyone watched and waited, anxious for him to let go of the past. He had. Molly was his second chance. Perhaps his last chance for a *fraa* and *kinner* and the kind of happiness all Plain men sought. "I'm glad you did, but your mudder will have your hide if she sees you out here talking to me in broad daylight."

"That she will, but she's got her hands full between the meat loaf and the hamburgers. It's a big crowd this time. Gott is *gut*." Her luscious brown-gold eyes squinted against a sun suddenly bursting from a crevice in the clouds, and Molly patted a sorrel gelding tied to the back of a buggy parked next to a weathered two-seater. "We've been seeing each more than a year—I'm sure she's guessed by now. Daed too, but he would never say a word. Her either."

The gentle question behind her statement made his chest tighten. His blood pounded in his ears. "Time flies when you're having fun."

"I'm happy you're having . . . fun." Her hand rested on the wagon, inches from his. "Slow and steady is good, but it can't go on forever."

They'd been moving slowly for more than a year. Life had taught him to tread carefully when it came to affairs of the heart. The loss of David's mother and Daed's grief were forever etched on his memory. But Molly deserved better. Better to take a chance than be alone forever.

He ran his fingers over the back of her hand, sturdy from working in the garden all summer. She smiled up at him, delight spreading across her face. Who could resist that face? "Soon."

Molly chuckled, a sound that warmed him like no other. David's throat no longer felt dry. Everything about her spoke of comfort and warmth and the promise of so much more. "*Soon* covers a great deal of territory. If I didn't know better, I'd think you're giving yourself plenty of wiggle room."

She offered a happiness he didn't deserve. He should snatch it up faster than a horse at full gallop. Molly was everything a Plain man could want. A hard worker. She cooked, she cleaned, she sewed, she did laundry, and she smiled through it all. Her looks made liking her easy, too, with her dark-brown hair and fair skin. She was slim but had curves in the right places.

He ducked his head at the thought and concentrated on a rooster strutting across his pen, looking all high and mighty. "No wiggling. Just working hard these days. Daed's back and legs have been hurting him. Susan has her hands full with another baby and the farm."

"Seeing you settled might give them a happiness that lightens the load."

He let his hand rest on hers, let his fingers tighten. Her skin was warm and soft. "It lightens my load to think of it."

Laughing her high, sweet laugh like a song in his ears, she shook her head. "Will I see you tonight?"

She always let him off the hook. He contemplated her full mouth. Her kisses never ceased to amaze him. The simple, innocent delight she took in exploring, the delight she took in finding her way in an experience new to her.

Not new to him. How he wished she could be his first. That he could be so innocent. That he could respond to her the way he had once responded to another during his *rumspringa*. *Gott, forgive me.* "*Jah.* I can't stay away."

"You sweet talker." She giggled. He loved that sound. Like birds happy that spring had arrived. She grabbed his hand back, squeezed, and let it drop.

The way she returned his touch filled every ragged hole in his heart. He wanted to hang on, yet something in his heart said, *Let go.* Something tucked away behind his breastbone that said, *Be careful. There are no guarantees.* She backed away, not letting her gaze leave his face. "We've had a line at the meat loaf table since eleven o'clock. I have to get back."

He followed after her, not wanting this small encounter to end. Her mother would see and scold her, maybe even send her back to care for the kinner instead of working the lunch table. He looked over her shoulder, watching for Jolene. Or worse, Aaron. Molly's daed was a fierce protector of his daughters. As he should be.

Just beyond Molly stood a woman in a yellow sundress and red cowboy boots, talking to Jacob King, who held the reins to a gorgeous bay put on the auction block by a retiring rancher from down around El Campo.

David's heart resumed an old, almost-forgotten rhythm. In sync with another. As if no time had passed.

It couldn't be her. The blonde hair was different. No long braid. She'd cut it in a blunt style at the shoulders. No cowboy hat covered it. No tight jeans and silver-buckled belt. She glanced at a smartphone in a glittery purple case, then at Jacob.

Gott, don't let it be her.

She looked up, straight at him. Her mouth opened and closed. Those lips, warm and soft and inviting, spoke to him even though she didn't say a word.

"What is it?" Molly two-stepped, turned, and craned her head. "Who's that?"

The Shrocks hadn't lived in Bee County in those days. "No one."

Not no one.

Before him stood the woman he'd promised to love for the rest of his life.

Bobbie McGregor had returned to Bee County.

Chapter 2

A woman didn't need book learning to know when a man lied to her. A sharp, fierce pain like a red-hot fireplace poker pierced Molly's chest in the vicinity of her heart. David had never lied to her before. He lied now. He tried to shutter the look on his face, but naked longing sprawled across it for all Bee County, Texas, to see. Never in the year they'd been courting had she seen that look on his face. Not when he held her and kissed her that first time down by the pond with lips that sought an answer she believed only she could give. David Byler was her whole world, but he had not returned the favor.

This woman in a yellow sundress and red cowboy boots apparently had returned from David's past to the here and now. From David's open mouth and wide green eyes, it was obvious she might have a distinct bearing on his future—and Molly's future—too.

"David!" The woman strode toward them, silver earrings dangling almost to shoulders bare except for the skinny straps of her dress. Didn't she know summer had ended? "It's me."

As if he didn't know. The way his lips twisted said he knew her well.

Molly backed away. Her first instinct was to run. To not be here for this encounter. *Nee, stand and bear it. He's worth it.* "Who's this?"

David's Adam's apple bobbed. His mouth closed. Then opened. Closed yet again.

"Aren't you going to introduce me?" The woman held out a slim hand. Silver bracelets clinked above her wrist. Words like *courage*, *love*, *peace*, and *joy* were inscribed on the simple bands. She wore no makeup. Her face had a clean, scrubbed look. Her eyes were huge and a luminous turquoise color. A dash of pink colored wide, generous lips. "I'm Bobbie McGregor. I used to . . . know David when I lived here. Before I left for college."

She stumbled over the word *know*. A certain pain infused the words that followed. *Before I left for college.*

Molly introduced herself when David didn't. He stood there, arms dangling from his lanky frame, his face red, gazing toward a spot somewhere over Bobbie's right shoulder. Mute in the face of all that prettiness.

In the face of memories? The awkward pause stretched. "Are you buying a horse?" Molly nodded toward the bay. She would grin and bear it if he couldn't. "He's beautiful."

"I'm looking at horses for my daddy—"

"What are you doing back in Bee County?" David's voice had a strange gruffness that bordered on sharp with jagged edges. He ran one hand through his sandy-brown hair. "You haven't finished college in a year and a half, have you?"

"It's Thanksgiving break. I always come home for the holidays." Red spots blossomed on her porcelain cheeks. "I just don't come around *here*."

"Until now."

A question ran through the words spoken with that same gruffness.

"My daddy's looking to replace one of his older horses that needs to be put out to pasture." She lifted her delicately shaped chin. Notes like tambourines emanated from the smartphone in her hand. She didn't look down. "He needed my help since he's not supposed to be exerting himself."

"Is he sick?" David's demeanor softened. "Is he all right?"

"No, he's not. He had a heart attack. They did bypass surgery last week." Her voice trembled. She paused and swallowed. "He's laid up. I came back to oversee the ranch until he gets better. I'm putting my college classes on hold for as long as need be."

Something in the way she spoke the words held a hint of inquiry. Or defiance. Or promise offered. Maybe all three.

Or maybe Molly heard those things because she could never be sure of David. He never quite committed. She was infected by his unspoken doubts, like a low-grade fever that never seemed to dissipate. She saw the doubts in the faces of others. Mother had said to go slow. Wait for him to grow up, even though he'd turned twenty-two in August. Her best friend Rebekah Byler never said much, but she always looked worried when she thought Molly wouldn't notice.

David took a step toward Bobbie. "I'm sorry."

The air between them had its own fragrance of something bittersweet with the spice of a fierce but dampened longing. Or maybe Molly imagined it. She didn't want to think of David with another. Someone so pretty and smart and well spoken.

Molly had a small circle of friends and she liked books better than singings. She preferred the company of mourning doves and mockingbirds early in the morning when dew glistened on the sparse South Texas grass and humidity hung in clouds so low they touched the top of the mesquite.

David never seemed to mind.

Bobbie took a step back and shook her head. "He's home from the hospital now. I'm here to make sure he eats right, takes his medicine, doesn't drive, and doesn't do any heavy lifting until the doc gives him the okay. He's a terrible patient."

"I reckon he would be. He likes his steak and eggs and his flour tortillas. He thrives on hard work."

"And his nightcap."

The tambourines sounded again. "Aren't you going to get that?" Molly wanted Bobbie to get on the phone and get away from David. As silly as it might seem. "Sounds like someone really wants to get ahold of you."

"It's only Daddy. He can't do anything and it's driving him nuts—driving me nuts. He wants me to take him everywhere, but he's the worst passenger-side driver ever. I finally told him he should just text me and I'll get whatever he needs. 'Course now he texts me every five seconds."

David chuckled. Bobbie joined in. Her laugh sounded like a little girl giggling. It held a tiny snort that would make people laugh with her.

They seemed to have forgotten Molly stood there. She watched them like a spectator at a volleyball game, her head swiveling between the two of them, following the verbal ball tossed back and forth with an ease of people who had once played together often and picked up right where they'd left off. They didn't need another player. "I have to get back to the lunch line. Mudder will be looking for me. I'll let you two catch up."

"Nee, wait." David moved. His hand touched her arm. "See you tonight?"

"That's what we said."

Only moments earlier. Now, somehow, in what was not said, everything had changed.

Chapter 3

A best friend was the tonic needed when in the throes of a romantic malady. Molly needed Rebekah's medicine—smart talk, no holds barred. Molly spread flour with a liberal hand across the counter and dumped the piecrust dough on top. Showing Lupe how to make pumpkin pie for Thanksgiving would give Molly's hands something to do while she picked Rebekah's brain about the David-Bobbie thorn in her side. That was how she saw it. David had come by two Saturday nights since the auction, but his mind hadn't arrived with him. He'd claimed to be all hers for buggy rides, but his conversation proved sporadic, his attention wandered, and his kisses had been perfunctory at best.

She wanted to ask about Bobbie, but she didn't. She couldn't, fearing the answer more than not knowing. And David hadn't said a word. Bobbie had been there the entire time, like an invisible third wheel wobbling between them.

Inhaling the sweet scent of baking cookies, she grabbed the rolling pin and began to roll out the crust. "Like this, smooth, smooth, smooth," she told Lupe, who watched, her dark, almond-shaped eyes wide with interest. Rebekah and Tobias's Salvadoran foster children soaked up holiday traditions like flowers soaking up sun in the spring. "Add some flour to the rolling pin if it starts to stick." She handed it to Lupe, who took it as if receiving a precious gift. "You try it. I'll finish mixing the pumpkin filling."

"Like this." Grinning, the fourteen-year-old brandished the rolling pin in a wild motion. "Flat as pancake with rolling pin?"

"Just like that. But gently. We want a light, flaky crust, not one tough as Tobias's Sunday hat."

Lupe chortled and attacked the job with gusto, her skinny wrists and arms whipping the rolling pin back and forth, flour making a dusty cloud around her.

Molly couldn't help smiling. The girl had grown so much in the last year. Molly hadn't been here when Rebekah had discovered her and her brother, Diego, hiding in the shed at the schoolhouse. Half starved, dirty, frightened out of their wits after traveling thousands of miles to the United States from their homeland of El Salvador, seeking a fresh start in a new world. Lupe's dark hair, worn in braids down her back, had a healthy shine to it. No longer waif thin, she'd shot up at least half a foot and filled out her clothes nicely. She wore a blue skirt, white peasant blouse, and black off-brand sneakers with white anklets. Not quite Plain dress, but her own way of showing deference to the people who'd taken her in and worked through the legal system to allow her to stay legally in the United States.

Still smiling at how sweet Lupe looked making the crust for her American pumpkin pie, Molly turned to Rebekah, who stood at the prep table kneading dough for rolls. She'd rubbed her forehead at some point, if the flour decorating it was any indication. Molly ignored it, along with the flour on her gray dress. "Her English is getting so good."

"Isn't it? She's starting to get phrases that aren't easy to understand, like 'flat as a pancake.'" Rebekah flipped the dough and leaned into it with the heels of both palms, in a technique born of much practice. "Teaching her to do things like bake a pie stretches her vocabulary too."

Every time Molly asked Rebekah about David, she hemmed

and hawed as if she didn't know much. Rebekah knew everything about Tobias there was to know, which meant she also knew about David. She'd likely been in the middle of it. But she was no gossip. "Enough small talk. Tell me about Bobbie McGregor."

Rebekah sighed. Her blue eyes were dark against her fair skin. She snagged a frosted sugar cookie from a nearby plate and held it out with a floury hand. "You'll need this. I'll tell you what I know, but only if you promise to let it go afterward. David isn't interested in her."

"Just tell me." Instead of taking the cookie, Molly picked up a measuring spoon and added a teaspoon of cinnamon to the pumpkin in the mixing bowl on the pine table in front of her. She inhaled the scent of nutmeg and ground ginger. The scent of Thanksgiving. She had so much for which to be thankful—Bobbie or not. "I don't know why you didn't tell me before."

"Because Tobias doesn't want me gossiping about his brother or his family."

"It isn't gossip when you're saving the heart of a best friend."

"Also because Bobbie made it clear when she left that she had no intention of pursuing David. She chose to leave." Rebekah rubbed her dress in the vicinity of a pudgy tummy. More flour was deposited. Under chestnut hair straggling from her limp-looking kapp, her pretty face had a green tinge this morning. It appeared another Byler child was in the making. "She thought it best that he stay with his family and his faith. She's a good person."

"She's back now."

"I know, but she didn't come back for David. She came back for her sick dad. Still a nice person."

Rebekah was nothing if not a straight talker. She didn't honey up her words either. And she was right. Bobbie wasn't a person Molly could dislike. Besides, she wouldn't think highly of a man who liked a woman who wasn't nice. David was a nice man.

Which brought her full circle in dizzily short order. "What happened with them?"

"It started innocently enough. Tobias did a custom saddle for her. She had a horse that needed training. Tobias's daed was working on him when the horse spooked and Levi got hurt. That's when all his back and leg troubles started. He was in the hospital in Corpus forever. That's when David and Bobbie spent time together. She felt responsible because it was her horse. Her dad paid all the hospital bills. She and David got close, it seems, according to Tobias."

"What does that mean? Got close?"

"He considered leaving the *Gmay*—leaving everything—for her."

Molly had not been his first love. The thought made her stomach heave. Tiny cracks in her heart appeared and multiplied. "He . . . loved her. He should've told me. Someone should've told me."

"It was in the past. She left and he got over it. It was her choice." Rebekah handed a cookie to Jason, her little one, who dropped it frosting-side down on the wood floor. Her expression distracted, she sighed and handed him another one. She squatted with a grunt, scooped up the fallen cookie, and wiped at the wooden floor with a dishrag. "I know it must've been very hard. That's how I know she's a good person."

"Are you ready for the pumpkin?" Molly went to the counter to inspect Lupe's work. The crust was rolled to perfection. "Time to lay it in the pie tin."

Together, they transferred the thin layer of pastry to the tin and Molly helped Lupe trim the edges. "You do the honors." She handed the delighted girl the bowl of filling. "Don't put in too much. It'll run over in the oven. If there's any that doesn't fit, we can bake it separately. Some folks don't care about the crust. Especially if there's whipped cream."

She turned to Rebekah. "Bobbie chose to leave. He didn't break it off?"

"Bobbie is nice." Lupe looked up from her pie making. "She give me cowboy hat before she leave."

"She is nice." Bobbie's niceness wasn't the issue. "But she isn't Plain."

"I'm not Plain." Lupe wielded a wooden spoon with ease. A splotch of flour decorated her nose. She and Rebekah were a matching set. "I nice person."

"You are." Explaining the problem to someone with limited English proved to be too much for Molly. "When you're older, I'll explain."

"I make pie."

"You make pie."

Rebekah grinned at the exchange, then grimaced. Hand back to her tummy. "True, but he didn't go after her, either."

"You didn't see the way they were looking at each other at the auction."

"You have to trust. Trust David. Trust your feelings. Trust Gott."

Molly did trust Gott. But she also knew His plan didn't always agree with hers. She prayed so hard when her sister, Amanda, was a baby. So hard that she would be miraculously healed. Her parents said Amanda was a gift from Gott just as she was. And indeed she was. Sweet, innocent, loving, kind, happy. Lover of animals and people. She would never grow up, but she would always be all those things. Someone so loving and kind deserved a whole life as a wife and mother, didn't she? Then Daed had his heart attack and their whole world changed again. He spent more time sitting on the porch than working the land. Everyone worked harder to make him feel like nothing had changed.

Then they moved to Bee County and started over close to

friends who could help. And she met David. What was God's plan in that if David loved another? "I don't know what I'd do if David left."

"He won't." Rebekah sounded so sure of herself. "I've seen how he looks at you, all moony eyed and goofy faced."

"We're so different. He's so easygoing, a talker, a social person." She squirmed in her chair. "Everything I'm not. What does he see in me?"

"A kind, sweet, loving, hardworking woman who will make a good fraa. Give him credit for knowing you're more than he deserves."

This was what a girl needed good friends for. "Stop it. So why didn't he bring it up when we went riding?"

"Men hate talking about feelings." Rebekah tugged Jason into her lap and wiped frosting from his chubby cheeks and hands. "There's nothing they hate more. I think they'd rather die than dig into what's going on in their hearts."

"He was distracted—"

"*¡Una carta, una carta!*" Diego dashed into the kitchen, waving a letter in the air. If Lupe had grown half a foot in the time Molly had lived in Bee County, Diego had grown a foot. Same dark-brown hair and eyes fringed by long, dark eyelashes. Ten times the energy. "*Abuela*."

"English, Diego." Rebekah took a swipe at the eight-year-old who danced past her, grinning. "Remember we're practicing."

"Le-ter. Le-ter from Grandma."

Rebekah settled Jason back on the floor, took the letter, and inspected it. An odd expression passed over her face. She turned over the envelope with its blue-and-red-striped edges and the stamped words *Avion Postal* on it.

Molly leaned over the table to get a closer look with Lupe, who wiped flour-encrusted hands on her skirt. "What is it?"

"It's not Ana's handwriting. The return address is different. *Sacerdote.* I think that means 'priest.'" Rebekah handed it to Lupe. "It's addressed to you and Diego together."

"No one else writes us from home. Only Abuela." Lupe grabbed a knife from the counter and slit the envelope with more enthusiasm than care. The parchment-thin paper fell to the table. She handed the knife to Rebekah, picked up the paper, and unfolded it. Her gaze flew across the paper. This time the letter floated to the floor. Her trembling hands covered her face.

"*¿Qué es? ¿Qué dice?*" Diego tugged at his sister's arm. "*Dígame.* Tell me. *¿Que dice abuela?*"

"Not from Abuela." Lupe plopped into a chair. She doubled over, arms around her middle. Tears trickled down her cheeks. She brushed them aside, her dark eyes made darker by searing emotion. "*Abuela se murió.*"

Her shoulders trembled. She began to sob. "She dead."

Chapter 4

David studied Bobbie from afar. Her white cowboy hat hiding her face, she sat behind the wheel of her blue Ford F350, letting the engine idle. If things were different, he could've been driving that truck. He liked trucks. She shouldn't be here, parked outside the corral where he, his daed, and his brothers trained horses, just yards from the saddle shop where Daed and Tobias were working at this very moment.

David fought the urge to race across the uneven, weed-infested ground to the truck, jerk open the door, and demand she say whatever she came to say. The early December wind whipped at his jacket and cooled his burning face. He ripped his gaze from the truck and forced himself to watch Diego, silent, unsmiling, walk the creamy tan buckskin with his flowing black mane and tail. Nice, even pace. The boy had the touch. He was meant to be on a horse, but he was no joyous jumping jack today. He hadn't been since his grandmother's death.

Concentrate on Diego. He needs you.

Let her drive away. Let reason prevail.

Nee. Let her come to me.

Did she like trouble? Did she seek it out? No, she had walked away from trouble a year and a half earlier. So what was she doing here? He'd seen her twice since the auction, both times in town, both times over a quick cup of coffee, both times he said no more and both times she agreed. No matter how painfully obvious their feelings were that day at the auction when she'd stood there in that ridiculous out-of-season sundress talking to Jacob King. Her feelings were plain as the sun in summer. He and Bobbie had come full circle. She gave him up without a fight once. Her presence now, in this place, said she couldn't do it again.

She should leave. She was fishing off someone else's dock, that's what she was doing. He couldn't blame her. Likely his doubts had been plain as lightning on a stormy, rain-drenched night.

He didn't dare make it easy for her. He would stay right here, boots cemented to the hard earth. She would have to decide. Stay or go.

She rolled down the window, stuck her hand out, and made a come-here motion.

He cringed.

"Who is it?" Diego lifted his free hand to his eyes, squinting against the sun. "Lady want you?"

In all things, Bobbie was a lady. And she definitely wanted David. "I have to go see what she wants. Why don't you go for that ride?"

Diego shrugged. His usual ebullience over riding had disappeared in light of the grim reality that he had no living relatives in the world besides Lupe. His experiences traveling between El Salvador and the United States had taught him to trust no one and to be uncertain about how long anyone would be around for him. A sad state of affairs for an eight-year-old. David opened the gate. The horse ambled through, his rider silent and morose.

"See you back here. Don't go too far. Stay off the main road. Jake doesn't like the big trucks."

No answer. David tugged up the collar of his coat to shield his neck from the blustery wind. He lifted his hands to his mouth and blew to warm them as he walked toward the truck. She didn't move. She didn't get out. He still couldn't see her face under that oversize hat.

A George Strait song wafted from the truck. "All My Exes Live in Texas."

Very funny, Gott. This ex lived in Texas. In Bee County. Her home. She shouldn't have to avoid coming home in order to live her life without him. Still, why couldn't she find what she was looking for at that big university in College Station? She had those big lecture classes, parties, clubs, football games. Big football games from what he'd heard. The *Englischers* were always talking and arguing about the Aggies and the Longhorns and the Cowboys and the other teams in an endless discussion that tickled him—it was only a game after all. Couldn't she have found a farmer or a rancher there? After all, Texas A&M was an agricultural college. If life had been different, if he'd gone with her, he might have taken ag classes himself. Book learning didn't interest him much, but he could read as well as the next man.

David stared at her. She glanced in his direction. Tears wet her checks. Her gaze returned front and center. To avoid touching her—he wanted to reach through the window and wipe away her tears with a tender touch—he gripped the doorframe.

The song ended. Neither of them spoke.

Diego passed them, the horse ambling along. He didn't look their way. He wiped at his face with his jacket sleeve.

Bobbie turned off the ignition. She had taught him about real, gut-wrenching, sacrificial love, and she couldn't look at him.

He swiveled and began the long walk back to the corral.

"David."

He stopped, gritted his teeth, and turned. "Are you in the market for another saddle?"

"Why is Diego crying?"

"His grandma died."

"Poor thing. Poor Lupe." Bobbie told him once that her own grandmother had passed when she was fifteen. Her mother left before she was old enough to remember her. She could relate to loss. "I'm so sorry. They must be devastated."

"Seems like she was the only family he and Lupe had left. If there are aunts or uncles or cousins, they don't seem to know them."

Plain families were enormous and close. Nothing came between them. Unless someone did something they felt deserved shunning. Like marrying a non-Plain person. "You got a horse that needs training?"

"Nope."

"Then I can't imagine what you're doing here."

Other than pouring salt into matching wounds.

"Visiting an old friend."

He rubbed at his face with the back of his hand. His fingers were half frozen. "Making my life harder."

She opened the door and stepped out. She wore faded blue jeans and a fleece-lined jean jacket over a purple shirt. Grit crunched under her ostrich-skin boots. Shoving her phone in her back pocket, she walked toward him.

His body stepped back as if controlled by someone else.

She stopped. "My being here only makes your life harder if you still have feelings. You keep saying you don't, but you do."

"My feelings are mixed at best, but I know how to do the right thing. That I know how to do." He forced himself to hold his ground when every muscle in his body quivered with the desire to turn and flee. "So do you. That's one of the things I like about you. You know right from wrong."

"Yet as much as I try to walk away, I can't." She caught up with him.

He turned and they settled into a stride that matched, despite his long legs and her short ones. Everything about them matched. Her scent of flowers—he could never be sure which ones, woodsy and soft and yet spicy—wafted around in the wind. He inhaled, wanting to keep that scent like a memory in a box where he could take it out and enjoy it again when she no longer graced his life.

"I haven't told you how hard I tried. The reason I came looking for you. I could've stayed at the ranch and made it a point not to run into you."

"Why didn't you? What do you mean, you tried?"

"I tried. I dated like crazy. I was a freshman at a huge university where guys are on the hunt, some of them on their own for the first time in their lives. There's booze everywhere, a party every night. I did it all. I dated football players, ROTC guys, farmers, geeks, nerds, techies—you name it, I tried it. I joined clubs. I even joined a sorority. Can you imagine me in a sorority?"

He had no idea what a sorority was. It didn't matter. He was too busy trying not to imagine her on those dates with all those men who wanted her, not because they loved her, but because they wanted to have her. "I don't need to know all this."

"You do need to know. You need to know that I looked for you at the auction because I had no other option. I could only think of you. Being home in Bee County brought it all back, even stronger."

Gott help him, he had done nothing but think about her since that day. Day and night. He shook his head, trying to clear the cobwebs of old feelings that should've been swept away by now. "I plan to ask Molly to marry me."

"She seems nice."

A gargantuan understatement. "She *is* nice."

"Will you be happy with nice?"

Nice. A hard worker. Faithful. Kind. Deserving of his unreserved affection. "I love her."

"You love me."

He could still taste her on his lips. Could a man love two women? "I did."

He changed directions and strode toward the corral. He needed to get to work. He needed solid horseflesh between her and him. The sound of her boots thudding on the ground made it clear she followed. He stopped at the fence and let his hands rest on the knotted wood. A safe place for his hands. No fingers caressing her neck as he lowered his head to kiss her.

"Past tense?" She sounded breathless, as if she, too, remembered the torch that burned through every encounter from the first day they met in the saddle shop. "Feelings like those don't just die. They smolder until they ignite."

Fire. They both felt it as an unquenchable fire. "I would've answered yes to that question before the auction."

"Now?"

"I don't know. Seeing you standing here." His voice had the audacity to choke on him. He slapped at the wood with both hands. "You cut your hair."

"It's only hair. It'll grow out." She turned and leaned backward against the fence. Her hands with those long, thin fingers touched the bobbed strands, tucking them behind thin, delicate ears red with the cold. "I thought it made me look more grown up."

"Plain women don't cut their hair." His hands tightened on the fence. His knuckles turned white.

"I came here to tell you I've never forgotten you or what we had." She took a long, shuddering breath. "We shouldn't have let your family come between us."

"Even though us being together means I lose my family. Forever." His voice rose. He paused, trying to get the traitor under control. "My faith is at stake. Not yours. You lose nothing."

"I know that. I know what you would sacrifice. That's why I left the first time. So it's up to you. It's your call. Your sacrifice. If you think you can be happy here with Molly, so be it. I'll stay far, far away. I can't leave again right now. My daddy needs me. But I won't bother you here anymore."

She straightened and headed toward the truck.

Let her go. Let her go. Let her go.

Say something. Say something. Say something.

Righteousness and longing jousted inside his head, neither willing to give up the fight.

"Bobbie."

She stopped and turned.

"Give me time."

She smiled. His muscles ached at the sight. She gave him a tiny salute. "All the time you need."

"Molly's a good woman. We've courted for a year."

"But you're not married."

"I want to be. She's special to me. I can imagine myself married to her fifty years from now. She has that kind of heart."

"Hers isn't the only heart in jeopardy."

The crux of the matter.

The saddle shop door opened. Tobias Byler strode out into the expanse of brown weed-infested earth that separated the one-story shop with its rusted white siding from the corral. David's older brother had the Byler stamp—green eyes, sandy-brown hair, and broad shoulders. He stopped, his hand to his forehead against the weak sun struggling through gray clouds that looked as if they could start spitting any moment.

"You'd better go."

Her chin went up. The wind whipped hair in her face, but she didn't brush it aside. "I'm not running from Tobias."

"You did once before."

She shook her head. "Don't throw that in my face now. What if I hadn't? Would you have chosen me?"

"I would have." The truth he had never once spoken to another soul. "And never looked back."

"I'm sorry."

"I don't know that I am."

"What's going on?" Tobias halted, legs akimbo, arms crossed, his gaze on Bobbie. "Did you need something?"

"It's not your business." David stepped in front of her. "We're talking."

"It affects everyone." Tobias jerked his head toward the truck, his gaze hard, voice brittle. "You'd best go about *your* business."

No point in flaunting a red cape at the bull. Tobias had David's best interests at heart—or so he believed. Could it be right to let a man marry another woman when the love of his life stood within reach?

A question—a battle—for another day. David turned to her. He touched her sleeve, wishing it were bare skin. He ached for a small touch, a tiny connection. "Tell your dad I'll stop by to see him one of these days. I'm sure he'd love some company."

Her hand landed on top of his. Electricity crackled in the air as if a storm brewed overhead. "I'll tell him."

He waited until the truck disappeared, dust billowing behind it, to face Tobias. "We were only talking. She was leaving."

"Not soon enough." Tobias started toward the shop. "Come inside. I brought a thermos of *kaffi*."

Tobias was like that. A mishmash of commanding and thoughtful. "I have work to do in the barn."

"Talk to me first."

"There's nothing to talk about."

Tobias kicked at dirt with the toe of his worn boot. "You say that, but your face tells a different story. I've been where you are."

"Jah, and you moved halfway across the country to get Serena out of your head and your heart. Now you're married, you're happy, you have kinner." David gritted his teeth, then took a long, slow breath. "I'm still finding my way, but it has to be my way."

"Understood." Tobias stared at the clouds scudding across the sky as if he could find the answers he hunted there. "The wind has changed direction. It feels like winter is coming on."

A change in subject, but somehow it felt like a continuation. "Change is good, they say."

"How did you do with Diego?"

An easier yet still difficult topic. "He smiled a little when he got on Jake, but he was crying when he rode past Bobbie's truck." That Diego's grandmother's days on earth had ended as God planned was small comfort for a child who loved her and had been far, far from her when she passed. "I wish I could do something to make him feel better."

"Just spending time with him helps. If there's more he needs, you'll figure it out." Tobias cleared his throat. "You should be thinking about how Molly would feel about you standing out here talking to Bobbie."

"What do you know about me and Molly?"

"I have eyes in my head. I talk to my fraa and Molly tells her everything."

Full circle. "Would you rather I hide it?"

"Nee. I'd rather you do the right thing and send Bobbie back to College Station and her Aggie football players and ROTC."

The things his brother knew about the *Englisch* world never ceased to amaze David. "It's not my place to send her anywhere. It's up to her."

"Do you want her to stay?"

Nee. Jah. The pounding in his ears had returned. "I don't know."

"Then you'd better tell Molly."

"No announcement has been published."

"Everybody knows you've been courting. This Gmay is too small not to know. We just couldn't figure out what you're waiting for. Now I reckon we know." Tobias headed to the shop, his boots kicking up bits of dirt and twigs as he picked up speed. "You can't have it both ways, neither."

Then why did he want both so much?

Chapter 5

Molly longed for a way to make Lupe and Diego feel better. And herself, truth be told. What could she do to cheer them up—and herself? Some small thing that would let them know she cared.

Lupe sat at the kitchen table, her head drooping over the green beans she snapped. Thinking about her and Diego kept Molly's mind off her own problems. David problems. She could hear Rebekah and her mother talking about it when she walked up to the Byler kitchen door after she and her family arrived for Saturday dinner. Bobbie McGregor had shown up at the shop the day before. David hadn't sent her away until Tobias insisted.

Pausing by the door, she took a quick look around. The women were busy with the spaghetti-and-meatball casserole. She closed her eyes for a second. *Gott, help me. Whatever happens, happens. You have a plan for me. You have a plan for David. Show me the way. If the two paths are to become one, show me the way. Protect David from his desire to wander from his faith. Protect my heart if he chooses to leave it and me.*

Done, the only thing she could do. Pray. And wait. She hated waiting.

Plastering a smile on her face, she moved into the kitchen. Rebekah looked up from slicing a hot loaf of bread. "You're here. Gut. We're arguing over whether to make garlic bread or just leave it plain."

"Not arguing." Rebekah's mother, Abigail King, chuckled. "Who argues over garlic? It's good for the tummy and bad for the breath."

Molly laughed. "No reason not to eat it then, I reckon."

"Not planning to kiss anyone?" Rebekah tapped her shoulder as she walked by, her expression a mixture of sly and kind. Her words drew another chuckle—it could've been a giggle if the woman were younger—from Abigail. "You never know what the evening might bring."

Ignoring the question, Molly cocked her head toward Lupe and sent a questioning look Rebekah's way. Her friend shrugged and shook her head. Little Jason squalled. Rebekah sighed and changed direction toward the playpen in the corner. "I'll feed him, you try."

Molly nodded. She rubbed her hands over the oven, enjoying the heat after the buggy ride in the chilly December air. She took a seat at the table across from Lupe. "How are you doing?"

No response. Lupe snapped the green bean in her hands with more force than necessary. She probably snapped beans and peeled potatoes for her grandma, making vegetable beef stew. Did they eat stew in El Salvador? She probably missed cooking with her abuela. Molly still missed her own grandmother, gone for nearly five years. "Christmas is only three weeks away. Is there anything special you want?"

Lupe shook her head.

"Are you sure? We mostly make our gifts, so we have to have time to do it."

"I wanted Abuela to come here. To stay. To live." She looked up. Tears brightened her coffee-colored eyes. "All of us together. *Familía.*"

"I'm so sorry, Lupe." Molly longed to give the girl a hug, but the news of her grandmother's death had turned her into a prickly nopal. "Do you believe in God?"

"She with God. She in heaven." *Heaven* came out *hea-bin*. Lupe nodded, her expression lighter. "But I no want her to go so soon."

"None of us do, but Gott's plan is Gott's plan."

"*Mi padre* die. Then mi abuela. I no like Gott's plan."

Molly could relate to Lupe's dissatisfaction. Her pain. She didn't like a plan that involved Bobbie returning to Bee County. *Let it go.* She cast about for another subject to take Lupe's mind from her troubles. "What do you do in El Salvador to celebrate Christmas?"

Lupe held a long green bean in the air, pausing, her expression distant and contemplative. She sighed. "We go to *Misa de Gallo*. We have presents at midnight. We put baby Jesus in His bed at midnight. We have *estrellitas*. Fireworks. *Familia y comida*. Turkey, rice, chicken. *Horchata* to drink."

She pronounced *Jesus* with a soft *j*, like *hay-sus*.

Molly looked to Rebekah for help. "She says they go to Mass. *Misa* is 'mass.' I think *gallo* is 'rooster,' but I'm not sure. Family and food. *Horchata* I'll have to look up, but it's something they drink."

Molly nodded, fascinated with the peek into another country's holiday tradition that still had the birth of the baby Jesus at its heart.

Lupe snapped the bean and dropped the pieces in the pan, her expression more animated. "I know what get for Christmas."

"What?" Fireworks weren't entirely out of the question. Lots of folks shot them off for New Year's, so they could be found this time of year.

"*Nieve*." She raised both arms and wiggled her fingers as her hands descended to the table in front of her. She threw her arms around her chest and pretended to shiver. "Brrrr."

"Snow?"

Lupe smiled for the first time since receiving the letter. "You get snow in *Los Estados Unidos*, no?"

In the north, yes. Even in Texas. But in Bee County? Molly had lived in South Texas a little over a year. No snow in that time. Having grown up in a town in Tennessee where it rarely snowed, she understood Lupe's desire for it. As a child, Molly longed for enough snow to have a snowball fight and to make snow angels and snowmen. It never happened. Had it ever snowed in Bee County? She couldn't say. She knew someone who would know and he'd been invited to supper. "I'll get back to you on that, okay?"

Lupe's smile disappeared and she went back to her green beans.

Molly went in search of Rebekah's stepfather, Mordecai King, deacon and man-who-knew-everything. He sat in the rocking chair by the fireplace, a piece of wood in one hand, a red Swiss Army pocketknife in the other. Tobias sat across from his father-in-law, a *Budget* newspaper in his hands. "There's an ad in here for a used trampoline. I was thinking of getting one."

"Jason is too small." Mordecai squinted at the wood. It appeared to be a pig in the making. A Christmas gift for one of his grandchildren most likely. "Or is it for Lupe and Diego?"

Tobias turned the page and shook the newspaper to make it lie flat in his hands. "I'd like to do something to cheer them up."

"Me too," Molly chimed in. "But I don't think I can make it happen."

"Not with that attitude." Mordecai cut a smidgen from the pig's face. A snout began to form. "Anything's possible."

"Lupe wants snow. Has it ever snowed here?"

Mordecai leaned back in his chair and kicked out his long legs so they crossed at his worn, dusty boots. He tugged at a lock of his black hair, now shot through with silver, as his wild mass of curly beard lifted and settled on his broad chest. His knife and chunk of wood rested in his lap as if forgotten. "As a matter of fact . . ." And he was off.

It had been twelve years since the last snow in Bee County. The librarian at the Joe Barnhart Bee County Library located across from the courthouse told him so. That he knew the full name of the library did not surprise Molly. Furthermore, some places in the county received ten inches of snow. It stayed on the ground long enough for some folks to build snowmen.

"So it could happen again."

"Could happen again."

Tobias shifted in his chair. He looked uncomfortable. Unusual for a man so comfortable in his own skin. Molly studied his face. He was itching to say something but not quite sure how to proceed. Unusual indeed. He needed a kick start, so she gave him one. "What do you think, Tobias?"

He wiggled like a man seated on a teeming pile of fire ants. "Not likely. Maybe you should talk to David. He's been trying to think of a way to cheer them up. Two heads are better than one."

A little matchmaking? Nee. Her head would not get close to David's anytime soon. He would have to seek her out first. "I can figure it out myself."

"Might try the library too." Mordecai picked up his knife and squinted with a critical eye at his pig-in-the-making. "They're mighty helpful with research there."

"How could the librarian help with snow?"

Mordecai snapped his pocketknife closed, then open. "Miss Karen is a smart lady. She might even know how to make snow."

The man had enough smarts for three people.

Chapter 6

A brisk wintry wind cooled David's face. It was the coldest winter in Bee County in several years if the farmers he heard chatting over cups of steaming coffee at the donut shop earlier in the day knew what they were talking about.

He tugged his hat down over his head and turned up his collar. Cold or not, he needed to take Molly for a ride. He needed to talk to her. He needed to see her. Somehow he'd gotten off track and now he had to find his way back. What he felt for Bobbie had nothing to do with his heart or his future. If he could catch Molly, talk to her, find his equilibrium in her, he would be right and whole again.

He leaned into the wind, letting it clear the cobwebs from his head, as he guided the buggy down the road that led to Molly's house. At worst, she would tell him to go about his business. At best, she would forgive him for being such a goober these last few weeks. By grace she wouldn't hear about Bobbie's visit to the saddle shop corral. He had let his body overcome his brain, and for that he felt nothing but shame. He was over Bobbie. If he thought it enough times, it would be so. Wouldn't it?

He pulled into the yard that led to the Shrock home. Dusk settled over the landscape as the sun slipped behind the horizon.

Days were short this time of year, and folks tended to go to bed earlier. *Let her be awake.*

"Surprised to see you out after dark."

The gruff voice, not full of the welcome he'd hoped for, emanated from the shadows on the front porch. David cocked his head and squinted. Aaron Shrock sat on a sagging lawn chair situated next to an upside-down bushel basket. He held a coffee mug in his gnarled hands.

"Felt like going for a ride."

"I get a hankering to take off sometimes too, but my fraa doesn't let me off my leash to go gallivanting across the countryside." Aaron chuckled, but the sound held little mirth. "She's afraid I'll keel over in an inconvenient place."

"She's concerned for you."

"Which she points out at every turn." He didn't sound aggravated. He sounded a tad pleased that his fraa cared so much. As well he should. "Come, sit a spell. Keep a bored old man company. Or you could go in the house and visit with my fraa and Isabelle. I don't think you want to do that. Unless you enjoy the cackling of a brood of hens."

Not the company he sought. Still, if Molly was in there . . . No way she could slip away from her mother and her sisters if she was. Better to take his chances with Aaron. Eventually the man would go to bed. So would the others. He could wait around. Take another ride and circle back later. David let the reins drop. Jake would wait patiently. He always did as long as a few slips of grass were nearby to nibble. The horse had no desire to work any harder than necessary.

David trudged up the porch steps and eased into a sad-looking lawn chair with plastic threads that were woven to create a plaid pattern. "Did you have a good Thanksgiving?"

"Always do. Still eating the leftovers. Turkey on toast with gravy. Turkey salad. Turkey sandwiches. Mashed potato patties. Cranberries and more cranberries. Getting fat too." Aaron patted a paunch that tightened the waist of his black pants. "You?"

David stared at the Shrock corral, barn, and other buildings shrouded in dusk. "The pumpkin pie was good as always." Susan and his sister, Martha, and the other women put on a good spread. "Much to be thankful for, as always."

"Molly and Amanda took a walk down the road. I don't like it much when they do that at dark."

Was he trying to tell David something? "It is getting pretty dark."

"You could walk down and see if you spot them. Make sure they get back to the house in one piece. Do an old man a favor?"

David stood, ready to escape the watchful eyes of a man who seemed to know exactly why David had come. Nothing escaped the grapevine in this tiny community. He took the porch steps two at a time.

"David."

He turned. Aaron set his coffee mug on the bushel basket and stood. "My *dochdees* are precious to me. All of them."

"Understood."

"Do you understand?"

"I do."

Aaron leaned into the porch railing, his wrinkled hands tight on the railing. "A daed knows when his kinner are hurting. Sometimes there's nothing he can do. They have to go through life's travails, learn from their mistakes, and grow up to be the people Gott intends them to be."

"My father has told me this too."

"If you are one of those mistakes, I'm asking you to make a clean break. Cut her loose and let her heal so she can move on."

"I'm not a mistake."

"It's mighty hard to tell from this vantage point. My fraa sees things and she knows things. I don't know how and I don't want to know, but she does. She's worried about my girl. If she's worried, so am I, Gott forgive me. He knows what's He's doing. I wonder if you do."

"I'm trying. I'm trying real hard."

"Try harder."

"I will."

With a grunt, Aaron sank back into his chair, his knees cracking.

David turned and hightailed it out of there before the man could say more.

"Don't get lost out there."

Too late.

Ten minutes later he heard the high-pitched giggles of girls on the other side of a thicket of tangled mesquites and live oaks clustered together as if in hopes that sticking together would ensure survival. He sidestepped a nopal hunkered down for the winter months and craned his head. "Molly? Molly, is that you?" It was. No one else had that wind-chime laugh. "Come out here."

She appeared, but the laughter didn't come with her. "What are you doing here?"

"Wandering around in the dark."

In more ways than one.

"Not very smart."

In more ways than one.

He swung his glance to Amanda, who was occupied with a tiny, butterscotch-and-white kitten tucked snugly in the crook of her arm. Amanda, a golden-haired special child who would never grow up, always took care of her babies. She wouldn't understand this conversation—or gossip about it. He turned back to Molly. "I wanted to talk to you."

"A little late for that."

Molly had heard about Bobbie's visit to the corral—her expression left no doubt about it.

Some folks had a lot of gall. Molly didn't know whether to run the other direction or sink into the ground so far she could walk the Great Wall of China. She petted Amanda's kitty, stalling for time. David had no right to show up here. She knew all about the chummy visit to the corral. Tobias told Rebekah everything and Rebekah told Molly.

"Molly, please, I need to talk to you."

"I would think you'd be out of words by now. I reckon you spoke them all to Bobbie McGregor."

"She came to see me. I didn't go looking for her. I mean, I've spoken to her more than once, it's true, but we only talked." David didn't sound all that apologetic. Making excuses. "We only talked."

"I'm a woman, but I'm not stupid."

"Don't be that way."

"Me? Shouldn't I expect my special friend to be special? To only have eyes for me?"

"Jah, you should, but I didn't ask for any of this. I didn't ask for her to come back. I didn't ask for her to come looking for me."

"But she did and it's obvious you still care for her." Molly swallowed against hot, angry tears. *Gott, I'm sorry.* He called her to think of others first and here she stood pushing the man she loved into the arms of an Englisch girl. "If you love her more than me, that's one thing. But do you love her more than Gott? More than your family? We can stop seeing each other, but I'll never stop praying that you make the right choice about your faith."

David kicked at the ground with the toe of his boot. "I know what's at stake. That's why I need you."

"I can't be your anchor. I want to be . . . your fraa. But this is between you and Gott. You have to stand on your own two feet and make a choice. Don't use me as a ball and chain that keeps you from running off to the place you'd really rather be."

"It's not that. I care for you."

"And I *lieb* you." There, she'd said it. She'd said it before he did. Here she was, talking about being a special friend, being a fraa, telling him she loved him. Putting it all out there like a forward, lovesick girl.

She gritted her teeth, breathed. No going back. Too much was at stake. "There's a difference. You can't butter your bread on both sides. Not with me. I reckon Bobbie feels the same way. Leave me out of it. Leave her out of it. Talk to Gott."

"I lieb kitty." Amanda held out her pet. "You want to hold?"

David's gaze stayed on Molly, so she took the kitten, whose plaintive squeak of a meow registered her concern about moving from the safety of Amanda's arms. Molly felt equally defenseless.

David shook his head, his face red, whether from the cold wind or emotion she couldn't hazard a guess. "When did you get so smart?"

He didn't say he loved her back. "It's not smart. It's my heart talking." Shattering and screaming without a sound inside her chest. Kitty meowed again. Molly loosened her hold. "Marriage is between two people. There can be no third party squeezed in between them for an eternity."

"You're right." He held out his hand. "Let me walk you back to the house."

She ignored the hand and turned to Amanda. "I think kitty likes you better."

Grinning, Amanda took her baby back. "He knows me best. I know how to get home."

"I'm sure you do." Molly patted her arm and started down the path. "We don't need a guide, do we?"

"Your daed asked me to find you and bring you back."

"You talked to my daed?" She could only imagine what Daed had said. He hadn't spoken to her, but his intense, troubled gaze often followed her as she set the table or brought him his coffee or helped him take off his boots at night. "He doesn't usually have a lot to say."

"He talked at me pretty good." David's chuckle was dry. "He's a fierce daed."

"He is. He has reason to be." Molly tucked her arm around Amanda's shoulder. "Let's go, *schweschder.* Daed is waiting for us. He won't go to bed until we get home."

She forced a glance at David. "Since we're headed the same direction, you might as well walk with us."

"It would be an honor."

Honor-schmonor.

"I like kitties." Amanda traipsed closest to David. Her expression was sad, a rare thing for her. "I like Simon. He doesn't like me."

Amanda tended to pour out her heart to anyone who would listen.

"Simon likes you." Molly squeezed her sister in a quick hug. Men of all shapes, sizes, and smartness messed up. Simon Glick had stopped coming by because he didn't know what to do next. Men were like that. Even special ones like Simon. "He's just a fraidy-cat."

Her sadness gone as quickly as it had come, Amanda grinned. "Are you a fraidy-cat?"

His face red as a beet, David shrugged. "Let's talk about something else." He shoved back some live oak branches to make way for Molly and Amanda. "How about this? What can we do to cheer up Lupe and Diego?"

Just when she had her heart set on not liking him, David said something like that. He was kind and thoughtful. "I'm working on something."

"Share."

"Lupe and Diego have their hearts set on snow." She explained what Mordecai had told her about making fake snow. "It'll never snow here again, most likely, but I'm thinking we can make enough fake snow to have a snowball fight on Christmas Eve, after the school program. When I was little, I always wanted it to snow in McKenzie, but it never did. We might not make enough for snow angels, but it would be fun for them and for us—for everyone, I mean."

"That's a great idea." David buttoned the top button on his jacket. He rubbed his hands together. "I have another idea. I could get them those globe things. You know, the ones that have snow in them. You shake them up and it snows. It's not as good as your idea—"

"It's sweet." She couldn't help herself. She almost touched his hand, then backed away. "Your heart's in the right place."

"I wish you really believed that."

She glanced at Amanda, who hummed a tuneless song as she picked her way through the weeds and nopales. "I want to, but you've not given me much to wrap my arms around."

"I want to wrap my arms around you." His gaze flashed to Amanda and his voice lowered. "I want to hold you and hug you until you forgive me."

"Make it right. Make it right with Bobbie. Make it right with Gott."

"I'm trying." Pain, as real as any she felt, cracked his voice. "I don't know why it's so hard."

"We often want what we can't have."

"Maybe that's it, I don't know." He breathed out a gusty sigh.

"Bobbie came along when I was new here. I didn't have friends yet. She was there when my daed was hurt and I thought he might die. My mom was already gone. It was a bad time. That made for some strong feelings."

Molly wanted to slap her hands over her ears. She didn't want to hear about what brought the man she loved closer to another woman. Still, her heart ached for what David had been through. She wanted to be the one who was there for him. She hadn't even lived in Bee County in those days. Hadn't known him. Bobbie had.

"I'm sorry it was so hard."

"It was something I had to go through. Bobbie understood. Her mudder left before she was old enough to remember her."

Molly didn't want to know about the other woman's past. Still, her heart opened a little, despite her best attempt to harden it. To grow up without a mother was something she could only imagine. "At least you had good years with your mudder, sweet memories. Something to hang on to."

"It's true."

"You can't fill the void for another person or in another person. A marriage is made of two whole people who come together and become one."

His step quickened. "I'll make it right. You'll see."

"I hope so."

At the corral, she stopped. Daed still sat on the porch, a striped woolen blanket pulled up over his legs, his hat down on his forehead so she couldn't see his eyes. But he saw her. She had no doubt of that. "It's late. You should get home."

"I promise to grow up. To stop chasing memories."

"I'm not going anywhere. I don't tell every man who comes along I love him." She gazed into his green eyes, so dark with emotion. "Even if he can't say it back."

"I—"

"Don't. Come back when you can say it. If you don't come back, I'll know."

She grabbed Amanda's hand and together they walked through the yard, Amanda giggling over the wiggly kitty and Molly counting stars instead of crying.

Chapter 7

Baking soda, white hair conditioner, and silver glitter. Voilà. Snow. Molly grinned to herself as she pushed through the library's glass door and stepped onto Corpus Christi Street. The librarian, Miss Karen, used the word *voilà* and snapped her fingers after showing Molly the video on the computer on something called YouTube. Two little twin girls who made fake snow with two different recipes. Miss Karen had tried both for one of the story-hour activities she did with children who came to the library. She liked the conditioner one better than the other one. It packed better for snowballs, every child's dream in South Texas. Next stop, Walmart for her three ingredients.

Molly shivered. The sun had disappeared behind a thick mat of woolly gray clouds. The wind had turned colder in the half hour she'd been inside the steamy two-story building with its blond brick trimmed in red. She glanced in the floor-to-ceiling glass windows gracing the first floor. She could see herself, her white apron flapping in the breeze in time to the strings on her kapp. Her cheeks were red and her hair flopping loose in the back. Winter had arrived.

"Molly, Molly, wait!"

She'd only heard that voice once before, but it had etched itself on her brain. She breathed in. The cool air made her lungs ache. She turned. "Hey, Bobbie. How are you?"

Bobbie fell in step next to Molly, the heels of her purple cowboy boots pinging against the sidewalk. She wore faded blue jeans and a sheepskin-lined jean jacket. A red plaid flannel shirt peeked from the top of the jacket. "I wasn't sure you'd remember me."

"I remember."

"Yeah, I guess so." She shoved blonde hair from her face and tugged her white cowboy hat tighter on her head. "I can't believe this weather. It's downright nippy."

"It is."

"But you're not interested in talking about the weather with me."

"No."

"Let me buy you a cup of coffee or a hot chocolate."

"No need. I have to go to Walmart." She waved the paper on which Miss Karen had written the snow recipe. "I'm making snow."

"You are? How cool is that." Bobbie laughed and pointed at the sullen clouds overhead. "You might not need fake snow. Listen, it's cold. Let me buy you a cup of coffee at the Coffee Barrel. I'll bring you back to your buggy. I really want to talk to you about David. Please."

How could she say no to a request so politely tendered? Swallowing against the heave of her stomach, Molly nodded and tightened her grip on the tiny drawstring bag that held her meager savings from jam and jelly sales. "But I'd like to buy the coffee."

Bobbie jerked open the door of her huge, gleaming blue pickup truck. "We'll negotiate that when we get there, how about that?"

Warm air filled the cab of the truck. It smelled of pine trees. A sad song about a guy driving his brother's truck filled the air. Bobbie punched a button. The radio quieted. She put the truck in gear, glanced in the side mirror, and pulled out onto Corpus Christi

Street. "You ever had a muffin from the Coffee Barrel? They're really good. So are the kolaches and the breakfast sandwiches."

"I ate breakfast."

"I imagine you did."

The drive was short. Six blocks. Molly counted them silently. What was she doing in this truck with a woman who loved David? "I really don't need coffee."

Bobbie parked in front of a squat red building with overstuffed chairs on its tiny front porch. She shoved the truck in Park and turned the key. The rumbling of the engine died. "Let's get the coffee, then we'll talk. Do you want to come in with me?"

Molly shook her head.

"Milk, sugar?"

She nodded.

Bobbie disappeared and reappeared with two covered Styrofoam cups. She handed one to Molly through the window and then trotted around the truck to climb in on the driver's side. "I like mine black. So does David."

She threw down the gauntlet with ease.

"It's one thing to have coffee in common." Molly set the cup on the dash and stared out the bug and bird poop–splattered windshield. "It's another to have faith and family."

"You're right. I know you're right." Bobbie's voice cracked. Molly glanced her way and back at the windshield. The red on the other woman's face had nothing to do with the cold wind. "But I can't stop thinking about him. I can't stop thinking about us."

"You left once before. Left him."

"But I never forgot him. You have to understand how hard I tried. I knew it was the right thing to do. I dated other guys. I went to football games and tailgate parties. I loaded my schedule with classes so I didn't have to think. I even got a job at some stables in College Station. I studied and partied and worked until

I dropped into bed at night, and I still couldn't sleep for thinking of him."

Not something Molly wanted to know. "Yet here you are."

"Here I am. Through no fault of my own. My dad needs me."

"I understand that." Molly squeezed into the corner of the seat. The seat belt dug into her shoulder. "No one thinks you shouldn't be here for family. And it's not my place to tell you what to do. I'm just a Plain woman who wants . . . to be a fraa . . . a wife and a mudder, a mother."

"That's the thing." Bobbie swiped at her red nose. Even with the tears and the snot, she was still prettier than Molly would ever be. "I never thought of myself as being someone's wife or a mom even. My mom left when I was little. My dad raised me. I don't have any sisters or aunts. My grandma died a long time ago. I've always wanted to be a rancher like my dad. Raise cattle and horses. Then David came along. It's about him. Not about anything he can do for me or we can do together in the traditional sense. It's about us loving each other."

Bobbie's words were like scythes so sharp they sliced through weeds and grass with an effortless flick of the wrist. They sliced through heart and soul. "You think David feels that way about you?"

"I know he does. I can see it in his eyes. I can feel it in the way he holds my hand. The way he kisses . . ." She slammed her hands against the wheel. The horn blared. They both jumped. "Sorry, I don't mean to hurt you. I promise he hasn't been kissing me, not since I came back, not since he met you. You don't have to worry about that."

She did worry. "If he really feels that way, he'll make the decision he needs to make."

"I just wanted to say I'm sorry for causing you pain. I didn't mean for that to happen. I saw him at the auction and I knew—"

"You knew you'd see him at the auction, but you came there anyway. You could buy a horse anywhere. It didn't have to be at our auction."

"I needed to see him."

"You were selfish."

"And you're not? Don't you want him to be happy?"

"I do. Being with family. Staying in the faith into which he was baptized. That's what will make David happy in the long run. Eternally happy." She shoved open the door and hopped down.

"Wait!" Bobbie's voice, high and sharp with emotion, filtered through the window that whirred its way down. "I'll drive you back."

"I'll walk. But thank you."

"It's cold. Take your coffee."

She kept walking. It wasn't nearly as cold on the street as it was in Bobbie's truck where her future alone appeared in the form of a woman in purple cowboy boots and a white hat.

The hat should be black.

Chapter 8

A bad idea indeed. David tugged on the reins and brought the wagon to a halt outside the McGregor house, a long, lean, ranch-style building with a chimney from which a healthy stream of smoke filtered. Their Christmas decorations were hung in full force, the reds and greens bright against the cloudy sky. They had firewood. They didn't need his. *They could always use more*, his heart argued. And Charlie McGregor was in no condition to chop wood. Bobbie had her hands full running the ranch. Calving would be in full swing with stragglers all the way through the spring months.

He hopped from the wagon just as the front door opened. Bobbie strode out, struggling into a fleece-lined jean jacket as she walked. Her face lit up. Because of him. Because she was glad to see him. She wouldn't be glad when he got through saying what he'd come to say. Make a clean break. No more hugging the fence.

Or the girl.

"You're here. I knew you'd come."

"I brought firewood." He stood with his hands dangling at his sides. "And we need to talk."

"You're so sweet and thoughtful." She started toward him. "The only thing we need to talk about is how cute you are when you're embarrassed."

Her dad trudged out the door behind her.

She glanced back. "Daddy, go back inside. I told you, I'll take care of that calf."

"You won't be able to find it."

"Martin told me exactly where it is."

"Roberta Sue, we can't afford to lose any of these calves."

"Don't call me that." Her skin, red from the brisk air, blushed a deep scarlet. "David's here."

Charlie shoved his black cowboy hat back and frowned. "What are you doing here?"

"I brought you a load of firewood. Thought you could use a little extra so you didn't have to chop."

"I can chop my own firewood."

"No, you can't." Bobbie rolled her eyes. She moved closer and tugged at her dad's thick wool sleeve. "Go inside. We'll take a walk down to the corral later when it warms up."

"What is this world coming to when I can't even do my job?" He slapped his glove against the thigh of his faded Levi's. "When a little squirt like you no bigger than my big toe tells me what to do?"

"Because I love you, Daddy." She wrapped her arms around the man and gave him a hearty squeeze. "Now go on, git."

He took three or four steps, then turned. "You know, I talk to Mordecai pretty regular. He's a fountain of information, that man is."

"He is." David squinted, trying to see where the conversation might lead. "Knows something about most things, a little anyways."

"Thanks for taking time from working at the saddle shop to come out here. Your dad likely is missing you now."

Not the subtlest of men.

"I'll skedaddle in a minute. I just wanted to ask Bobbie how her saddle is wearing. Checking up on our work."

The door closed with a brisk *click*.

"My saddle is wearing fine."

"Good."

"Any other questions you want to ask?" She edged closer. So close he could smell her scent. Like lavender. Like spring. So sweet his mouth watered. "I'm all ears."

She was much more than ears. A full mouth, huge blue eyes that hinted of the Gulf of Mexico. Curves that folded in at the waist and flowed back out. David gritted his teeth. "I should go."

Her hand caught his. Warm fingers curled and tightened. "Not yet."

"I shouldn't have come." He should've written a letter. No direct contact. His stomach did that thing like when he had the flu for a week. "I thought we could talk. I could tell you I have to not see you. I can't be with you. I feel like throwing up. That's a bad sign."

"Are you saying I make you want to throw up?"

"The situation does. I can't think straight. When I'm around you, I think of how close we were before. How nice it was. Then I see Molly and I—"

"I don't want to know what you think about another woman." She leaned into him. Her hands raced up his chest and cupped his face. "I can make you forget all about Molly Shrock."

He jerked back and inhaled the cold air. Sweat beaded on his forehead and chilled his neck. "I don't want to forget. I love Molly."

He had been too chicken to tell her, but it was true. He did love her. He loved the way she walked, with her long skirt rustling around her, the way she stared at the sky, thinking, before she made an important point, the way she told him her dreams of having ten children and fifteen chickens and twenty goats—but not in that order.

"But you love me."

He loved the feel of Bobbie's skin under his fingers. He loved how she fit in the crook of his arm. He loved the warmth of her lips on his. He loved the way she slid her arms around his neck and let her bare feet dangle above the ground while she kissed him. "You were sweet to me when Daed was hurt. You made me feel things when I didn't want to feel anything at all. You made me feel things I didn't know I could feel. But it's different. Molly is different. She's like me. She wants the same things I want. We're made for each other."

"Don't say that. You could come with me to College Station. You could study something, anything you want. We could run this ranch together."

"With my family down the road and me never seeing them? Never being able to go to services with them? Knowing Molly is right there and never being able to talk to her again?"

"I could make you happy."

"A different kind of happy, jah. You could." But was it a happiness that would last? Part of him wanted to say yes, but the other part—the part that grew up learning to drive a buggy and make saddles and go to Sunday services with his family—said no. How could two feelings so different, so seemingly right, live inside him?

"Come inside. Have some hot chocolate. We'll talk."

Talk. Just talk. Bobbie tugged, her fingers warm and secure around his. Heat billowed through him. Her simple touch sent it careening from his head to his toes. It couldn't be denied. "For a few minutes."

One more time. Just one more time.

He started toward the door, painted green, with its fir wreath decorated with red ribbons and little Santa Clauses. The workers had strung red and green lights around the door. White lights ran along the eaves of the house and framed each window from one end to the other. Garlands hung from the windowsills. Through one window he could see a tall Christmas tree festooned with all sorts of decorations, little Santas, candy canes, angels, silver bells, and red, gold, green, and silver balls that shimmered in the white lights that flickered on and off, on and off.

Santa Clauses.

As far from a Plain Christmas as a person could get.

He didn't celebrate Christmas with Santa or lights or fancy decorations. He celebrated the birth of Christ with family and friends through prayer and song and simple gifts from the heart.

Bobbie had the door open. She looked back. Her smile died. "You're not coming in, are you?"

"I'll unload the wood and I'll go. I can't stay. Ever. That's what I came to tell you."

"Don't do this. Come in."

"I can't."

She let the door slam.

He whirled around and rushed back to the buggy. Only a tiny remaining sliver of dignity kept him from breaking into a run.

Chapter 9

Dark, persnickety clouds, thick as a triple layer of quilts, hung close to the tops of trees that bent and swayed in an angry wind. Dusk came early in the winter. David tugged his hat down to shield his face from the rain mixed with icy sleet that pelted his face and froze his lips. Despite thick wool gloves, his hands were numb. They weren't used to this kind of weather in Bee County. Neither was Jake, and the horse seemed none too happy to be in the midst of it. At this rate the Christmas play would be over before David arrived at the school. His little brothers and sisters wouldn't be happy with him. They took such pleasure in performing Christmas songs and little skits around the joy of the season of Jesus' birth.

Molly would be there. He would have a chance to talk to her again. To give her the gifts he'd bought for her. He glanced at the seat where the packages lay. A pale lilac shawl his sister helped him pick out for Molly, along with her own snow globe and the snow globes for Lupe and Diego. He'd found them in a Hallmark store in town. Three identical globes with miniature farmhouses, red barns, and decorated fir trees. Countryside that turned white with snow when a person shook the globe. A white Christmas whenever they chose. A forever memory.

He snapped the reins, anxious to get to the program. The wooden buggy wheels slipped and slid on the slick road. The buggy shimmied and careened across the highway's yellow dividing line.

He pulled on the reins. Jake whinnied in distress. "Come on, boy, come on!"

A pickup truck appeared on the horizon, headed toward him on the black ribbon of icy asphalt that separated them. A blue pickup.

Nee. Nee.

He'd made up his mind. He'd chosen his path.

The truck moved fast, too fast.

Slow down, Bobbie, slow down. It's not worth your life.

She didn't obey. The truck picked up speed. David pulled over on the shoulder of the road and stopped. Jake stamped his feet and neighed, neck high and arched.

Still she came.

He waved both arms. *It's me. No need to speed. I'm here.*

She must've seen him. Brakes squealed. The truck swerved left, then right. But instead of slowing, it spun on the icy asphalt. Like an unwieldy, overweight ice-skater, round and round. David jumped from the buggy as if he could somehow stop the inevitable by sheer force of will.

He watched, mouth open, hands in the air, as the truck hit a wooden fence post and broke through. It smashed into the old oak tree that had anchored the Borntrager property for half a century or more. Wheels spinning, it came to a sudden, ferocious stop, engine still running. The smell of oil, gas, and smoke billowed on the furious northern wind.

Heart pounding so hard his chest ached, he darted across the road on legs that didn't want to cooperate. He hit the field at full stride. Black smoke rolled from the crumpled front end. The windshield glass spidered in cracks that went a million directions. "Bobbie? Bobbie!"

She sat slumped behind the huge, ugly air bag, head back, eyes closed. *Gott, no.*

He jerked open the door. A white film covered everything like talcum powder. The smell of an explosion filled the cab. He shoved down the remains of the air bag and reached for her. "Bobbie, talk to me."

She moaned.

Thank You, Gott, for air bags and pickup trucks that are sturdier than tree trunks.

He smoothed back hair flung across her face. Blood trickled from a nasty cut on her forehead. "You're okay, you're fine. You'll be fine."

She moaned again. Her eyelids fluttered. "You're here. I went to look for you and I found you."

"You were driving way too fast." Fury made his voice crack. His whole body shook. Shock made his hands quiver. "You're crazy."

"Crazy for you." She struggled, then sank back. "My chest hurts . . . and my wrists."

"Don't move. Don't talk." The phone. The phone that never left her side. It wasn't on the seat. He scrambled around the truck to the other side. There. There it was. Purple and sparkling against the dark black rubber of the foot well.

His breath caught. He swallowed bitter bile in the back of his throat. His stomach heaved.

Think. Think. 911. 911.

He spoke to the cool, firm voice on the other end of the line. The woman asked questions about the location. He sought answers from a brain scattered across the flatlands of South Texas.

It would take a good fifteen minutes for an ambulance to come out into Bee County. He climbed into the cab and slid across the seat. The cut on her forehead bled profusely. Both arms swelled, bruises already forming along her wrists and forearms where she'd been struck by the force of the air bag. He couldn't complain about that. The air bag protected her from a crushing blow against the wheel or worse. He dug around in the glove compartment, found some Dairy Queen napkins, and applied pressure to the wound. She cried out.

"I'm sorry." He pressed harder. "I want to stop the bleeding."

"You were coming to see me, weren't you?"

Could he lie to a woman who had just slammed her truck into a tree because of him? Should he?

"You need to hire a ranch manager and go back to school."

She shook her head, then groaned and clutched at her face. "You love me. I know you do. Isn't that worth fighting for? Giving up something for?"

"There are many things about you I love, but that's not the same thing. What we have in common is not what a long, happy marriage is made of."

"But we could learn those things. If we had time to get to know each other without everyone and everything bearing down on us." Her head down, she turned toward him.

He couldn't refuse a wounded woman, one who had sought him out first and ended up with her truck wrapped around a tree. He held her against his chest. "You want to run a ranch and make a living. You don't like to cook or sew or bake or go to church. You don't even know if you want children. You wouldn't make me happy. I wouldn't make you happy. I want to be with the woman who loves me for who I am now and not who I might be with time."

"I hurt."

So did he. "I know you do."

"I mean my heart hurts."

So did his. His heart hurt for the pain he'd caused her, but also the pain he had caused Molly. Molly who could make him happy and wanted to make him happy. He was an idiot. "That's the thing about the heart. It heals."

"I hadn't noticed that."

"Stop expecting to get struck by lightning twice. Give another man time to grow on you. Stop running so fast."

Her eyes closed. Her breathing softened.

"Bobbie, don't go to sleep." He shook her gently. "I don't think you're supposed to sleep. You might've hurt your head."

Could an air bag cause a concussion? He had no idea, no experience. "Bobbie?"

She jerked awake. "Molly loves you."

"Yes, she does."

"She'll make you happy."

Gott willing, she'd give him another chance. "And I can do the same for her."

"I want what you have." The words were a mere whisper.

"Stay awake. Stay with me. You'll find it, with time." He rubbed her back and smoothed her hair. She had soft hair. "Help is on the way."

The dispatcher was as good as her word. A few minutes later, sirens blaring, red and blue lights flashing, the ambulance barreled its way down the asphalt road and halted without a hitch at the break in the fence. Within minutes, Bobbie was loaded into the back end. The paramedics assessed her injuries and assured him they didn't appear to be life threatening. She needed stitches, X-rays, and a CT scan. Words that brought back the fear and uncertainty of his father's accident with Bobbie's horse.

He breathed and swallowed. *Don't lose it now.* "Can I come with her?"

"Climb in." The man glanced at Jake. "What about your horse?"

David stamped his feet against the cold and studied Jake. It seemed wrong to leave a horse out in these conditions. He could call the Combination Store and leave a message, but everyone was at the school for the program. Will Glick, who ran the place, wouldn't hear it until tomorrow.

"Don't come." Bobbie raised her head from the gurney. They'd covered her up with sheets and blankets to warm her. Her face was as white as the sheets. "Take care of your horse. I'll be fine."

She had come all the way to Corpus Christi to be with him when his father was thrown by her horse. "I'm not letting you go to the hospital by yourself."

"I'm a big girl. It's not like I'm dying or anything." Her arm, bruised and swollen, crept from under the blankets until her fingers touched the phone the EMT had laid within reach. "I'll call the house. Daddy has a bunch of friends over for Christmas Eve. Louis or Rocky will bring him in. It'll be fine."

"I don't want to abandon you."

A wistful smile whisked across her pale face. "You already did. You just forgot to leave."

No. A man did not leave a friend who was hurt and in trouble. Not a good man. "Not tonight. Tonight, you shouldn't be alone. Ask your dad to send someone for Jake. I don't want him standing out here in the cold all night."

"Are you sure?"

Wetness touched his face. He raised his head to the sky. Sleet. If it got any colder, they might have snow before the night ended. Snow in Bee County. "I'm sure."

Tonight, an old friend needed him. Tomorrow he would find Molly and get his own miracle.

Chapter 10

Molly loved surprises. Not receiving them, necessarily, but arranging for them. Lupe's expectant grin warmed her cold, cold heart. The wind howled outside the Byler house and seeped through the cracks and crevices, creating drafts in the kitchen. Holding her hands precariously close to the wood-burning stove, Molly shivered and inhaled the scent of mesquite mingled with the sweetness of sugar cookies. The aroma warmed her more than the fire. It smelled like Christmas. They weren't used to this kind of cold weather so far south. So close to the Gulf. But it did make it seem like Christmas.

She should be happy to celebrate Christmas Eve with her family and the Bylers, her best friends. David was probably celebrating the holiday with Bobbie. He hadn't made an appearance at the Christmas play at the school. So be it. Tightening her shawl around her shoulders, she turned to Lupe. "You wanted snow for Christmas, so tonight we're making snow."

Lupe's thick, dark eyebrows rose and fell. Her upturned nose wrinkled. She turned to Rebekah, who sat at the table sipping a cup of steaming chamomile tea laced with her stepfather's honey. "Snow no fall from sky?"

Apparently she didn't trust Molly's judgment, which tickled Molly for some reason.

"Hey, I'm not crazy. It doesn't snow around here except once in a blue moon, but that doesn't mean we can't make our own." She offered the girl her best smile. Jesus' birthday deserved a happy, obedient heart. Gott's plan remained, as always, Gott's plan, whether she understood it or not. If Bobbie made David happy, then Molly should wish him the best. "Do you want to help?"

Still looking unconvinced, Lupe climbed into a chair on her knees and looked over the ingredients. Baking soda, hair conditioner, and silver glitter. "Pretty." She touched the tube of glitter. "Snow pretty?"

"It is." She had seen it only a few times. It rained a lot in McKenzie, making the landscape lush and green, but snow that stuck to the ground was a rare event, and there was never enough for a single snowball fight or snow angel, much to her disappointment. "It's prettier to look at than it is to have to get around in."

They weren't used to driving buggies in snow—or the cold it brought with it—and the Englisch folks tended to slide around on the ice in their cars. Not as fun as it sounded.

She handed Lupe a box of baking soda. "Three cups times two. Let's double the recipe so we can make snowballs."

Rebekah edged closer. "I want to make snow too." She sounded like a child who hadn't been invited to play volleyball during recess. "Can I put in something?"

"You can help us mix it up." Molly winked at her friend. "This is Lupe's snow."

A look of fierce concentration on her face, Lupe added the baking soda with such a flourish it billowed over the mixing bowl. She waved her hand and coughed. When the flurry subsided, she poured in a cup of white hair conditioner. Then the glitter. The girl in the video the librarian had shown Molly said it would make the snow sparkle like it did on a starry, moonlit night. "Here we go."

Laughing at Lupe's delighted grin, Molly dug her hands into the goop and together with Rebekah they mixed the ingredients.

It felt cold like snow. The glitter sparkled on their hands. She held them up for Lupe to see. "Get Diego. He'll like this."

Chortling, the girl scurried from the kitchen. A few seconds later, she returned, Diego in tow, the two of them jabbering in Spanish so fast it sounded like gibberish. "He say we no need make snow." Lupe let go of Diego's arm and grabbed Molly's. "He say look outside."

Together, they rushed to the window over the sink. Rebekah lifted the sagging white curtain. Flakes of snow glistened on the outside of the glass.

Molly turned to Rebekah. "It's snowing in Bee County."

Rebekah grinned, threw her hands up, and danced a little jig. "If it can snow here in the land of nopales and mesquite, anything can happen."

Gott's way of telling Molly that miracles were possible? Whatever came next on this unpredictable life journey was bound to be wonderful because God made it so. "Get your coats. We have to get out there before it melts."

Together, rushing, tumbling into each other, they raced for the pegs where coats and shawls hung. They were joined by Tobias, Molly's parents, Amanda, and the other kinner. Molly rushed out behind Lupe and Diego. They deserved to go first. Their first snow. Ever.

A lovely gift from Gott. Molly lifted her face to the sky and let the fat, wet flakes kiss her face. She closed her eyes. *Thank You for giving the children and me this gift of joy during such a hard time. They've been through so much. Heal their hearts. And if You don't mind, heal mine too.*

Something cold and wet zinged her on the nose. "Hey." She opened her eyes.

Diego danced around her. He held the bowl of snow she, Lupe, and Rebekah had made.

"Snow *pelota*. How you say '*pelota*'?"

"Ball." There might not be enough snow on the ground yet for snowballs, but it was falling fast, blanketing the ground around them. The wind blew, making it hard to see through flakes that swirled and danced in the makings of a full-scale blizzard. It wouldn't take long before enough snow accumulated for an all-out snowball fight.

"Ball." Lupe scooped a handful from the bowl and molded it into a perfect ball. "I want to make real snowball."

"There's not enough yet." Molly scooped up a small handful from the ground. It was truly cold, not fake. "But that doesn't mean you can't get someone with it."

She chased after Diego, who dropped the bowl and ran, screeching with joy. Her legs were longer. She tugged at his collar and deposited the snow on his neck. "Cold!" He laughed, a loud, carefree sound that warmed her heart. "Very cold."

"Merry Christmas." She whirled around and around, face to the heavens. "Merry Christmas."

"*Feliz Navidad.*" Lupe and Diego chorused. "Feliz Navidad."

Chapter 11

Driving a buggy in the snow didn't qualify as fun. David lifted his gloved hands to his mouth and blew. His warm breath billowed in clouds. The frigid air made his nose and lungs ache. The snow, ten inches if his daed's guestimation was accurate, glistened in the afternoon sun. Snow was beautiful, even more beautiful on Christmas Day.

Prayers had been said, simple gifts exchanged, and ham, mashed potatoes, gravy, and pecan pie consumed. Not that he ate much. His inability to enjoy Christmas dinner testified to the havoc his nerves were wreaking on his stomach. He had to see Molly. He cared for Bobbie. He couldn't deny that, but he had left the hospital the previous night with a burden lifted from his shoulders. His feelings were wrapped up like a physical blanket that would fray and disintegrate over time. She deserved more than that—they both did. He loved Molly, heart and soul, with a fervor that wouldn't die over time. It would grow and blossom. Theirs would be a love for eternity through good times and bad, woven together by faith, *boplin*, good times, and hard times.

By Gott.

The brown paper–wrapped packages still sat on the seat next to him, along with the snow globes he would deliver later in the day to Lupe and Diego. Their Christmas miracle had come true before he could give them the meager gift of a pretend snowfall.

The two had their real snow now, but the globes would be souvenirs of a Christmas they would never forget.

He pulled the buggy onto the road that led to Molly's house. He'd been down this road a hundred times, but never had the path seemed so fraught with obstacles.

Lord, have mercy on my stupid soul. He squinted against snowflakes brilliant like thousands of glistening stars, each one unique, each one made by a God who left nothing to chance, who saw all and who had a plan . . . a plan to prosper and not harm.

David drew another breath, letting the crisp air calm him. He had no plan. He had a heart so big and bruised his shoulders ached from carrying it. He clucked and snapped the reins. Jake picked up his pace, his breathing noisy in the cold. "Now or never."

Lupe and Diego played with Amanda in the front yard, their woolen coats dark against all the whiteness. Their shrieks of laughter filled the air as they ran through the snow. That meant Rebekah and Tobias were inside, visiting. Which didn't surprise David. The two families were the best of friends. They would share in this special holiday. Likely Abigail and Mordecai were making the rounds as well.

To get to Molly, he'd have to go through Rebekah. She protected her loved ones with a ferocity that bore a resemblance to a brown bear he'd seen up north once. A great quality to have in a fraa and mudder. And friend.

He would start apologizing and keep apologizing until he wore them down. That would be his plan.

A weak plan.

Shivering in the wind, he drew closer. The kinner's chatter wafted through the air, Spanish mixed with Amanda's *Deutsch*. Likely they understood little of each other's prattles, but it didn't matter. They were creating a snowman. Everyone understood that language. Lupe, her long black hair streaming behind her, her nose and cheeks cherry red, bent over, pushing a big snowball, helping it to get bigger. Her kapp hanging crooked, Amanda added to the first ball, which would serve as the base. Diego helped hoist the second ball onto the first. All three clapped with mitten-clad hands and cheered. Amanda danced around and hugged Lupe. The language of love.

Molly was nowhere in sight. David studied the kinner. Another hazy plan formed and reformed. He parked the buggy behind the barn. Breathing hard as if he'd run from his house to Molly's, he marched toward them, his boots sinking into the snow, making it hard to get traction. A man could work up a sweat in the dead of winter. Snow was fine if you didn't have to go anywhere, but if a person actually had to work outside in it, it wasn't so fun.

Amanda saw him first. She waved and clapped. "David, David, help us build the snowman."

"You've already done the hard part, but I'll help if I can."

Lupe snatched up a long carrot from the porch railing. "We have *nariz*. Nose." She waved it in the air. "*Zanahoria*. Molly give us."

"Carrot. Nice nose." He scooped up snow and patted it on the second ball, making it a tad bigger. "Do you have rocks for the buttons? Sticks for the arms?"

Amanda nodded and produced two long sticks. "The rocks are from my collection. Pretty rocks."

"He needs a head. Poor thing."

Lupe laughed. "We make head."

"I'll help." He grabbed enough snow to start the ball. "Is Molly inside?"

Diego nodded. "Rebekah bring her present. Blanket for baby she make. Molly cry. Present no make her happy." He stuck a handful of snow in his mouth. His lips smacked. "Present make me happy. Tobias *y* Rebekah give me saddle."

The boy clomped around, pretending to gallop on an imaginary horse. "Now I need horse."

Someday. David managed to nod and smile. His stomach did ring-around-the-rosy-all-fall-down. She was in there. Rebekah had made a baby blanket, sure Molly would marry soon and need such a gift. Rebekah was the eternal optimist. She'd taken in two children from a foreign country and given them the gift of unconditional love despite long odds for their ability to stay in the country and stay with their adopted Plain family.

He wanted to give that gift of unconditional love to Molly. He would give that gift to Molly, if only she would let him.

They worked quickly, giggling, happy. David threw himself into the project, trying not to think what would happen if Molly walked out on the porch and saw him there. Finally, the snowman smiled at them, snaggletoothed with a nose that would make Pinocchio proud.

"He's quite the looker." David straightened his arms and stood back to survey their handiwork. "Good job."

"You do good job too." Amanda dusted her mittens. "He look good like you."

David chuckled. Plain folks might not care about looks, but Amanda had given him a sweet compliment without realizing it. He motioned for them to come closer. "I need you to do something for me."

Amanda's expression turned serious. Lupe took her friend's hand. Diego crowded closer. "We do job?"

"I'd like you to do me a favor." He chewed his lower lip. "Go in and ask Molly to come out. Tell her you want her to make snow angels with you."

"What this?" Diego frowned. "Snow angel."

He pronounced it with a soft *g*. It sounded even prettier than it did in English.

The snow crunched under his boots, and David knelt, then lay prostrate with his arms over his head. His black Sunday hat flopped onto the ground. Their faces enthralled, the children did the same, Amanda right behind them. They copied his moves as he pushed his arms up and down through the snow. It felt icy on his neck and head. Molly had always wanted to make snow angels as a child. God had given David a way to show her his love. *Soften her heart, Gott. Help her forgive me.*

He sat up, careful not to muss his creation, and stood. "Snow angel."

Crowing, Diego popped up. Lupe and Amanda followed. "Snow angel," they shouted.

"Shhhh." He put a finger to his lips. "We need Molly's angel. Go tell her, but not Rebekah. Not yet. Just Molly. Only Molly comes outside. Rebekah can see later. And whatever you do, don't tell Molly I'm here. It's a surprise. Can you do that?"

They nodded, faces suddenly serious, as if they knew they were in cahoots with a man on a mission. Elbowing, pushing, shoving, giggling, they raced up the steps into the house and let the door slam behind them. Everyone inside would know of their mission. He cranked his head from side to side. His neck popped. Shrugged his shoulders a few times. The cranky goats in his belly wouldn't stop butting each other.

Faith. Have faith. Walk by faith. He studied the snow angels, side by side in descending sizes. Each one perfect in its imperfection. Just as God viewed him in all his imperfection and still saw a man who could be saved.

A man made in His image.

Lord, have mercy on me. Give me a third chance. Your undeserved grace is unending.

The door opened. The children squeezed through, Molly behind them. "Wait, wait!" She laughed, the sound like wind chimes on the brisk winter wind. "I have to get my coat."

"Snow angels." Lupe tugged at one hand.

"Snowman." Diego tugged at the other.

Amanda pushed from behind. "You make an angel, schweschder."

Molly's gaze connected with David's. Her smile died.

She tried to back up. Amanda pushed. "Nee, schweschder. Snow. Snowman. Snow angel."

Molly slowly clomped down the steps. She plowed to a halt, arms crossed, shoes planted, despite Amanda's best efforts to propel her farther. She shifted her gaze over David's left shoulder. "Merry Christmas."

Molly had always been a better person than David. She wanted to do the right thing, say the expected thing, but she couldn't control her heart.

"Merry Christmas." He pointed to the snow angels, then let his finger drift toward the snowman. "We wanted you to see our work."

"What are you doing here?" Her voice trembled. She glanced at the children and her sister, all on pins and needles over her reaction to their creations. "These are great. I like them very much."

She unfolded her arms and patted her sister's shoulder. "You make a pretty snow angel, but you look frozen. Take Lupe and Diego inside for a little bit. Mudder will give you hot chocolate. I'll be right there."

Right there. Nee. Not if he could help it. "Molly."

She shook her head. He waited for them to traipse inside. Lupe paused at the door and looked back. "*Buena suerte.* Good luck."

He didn't believe in luck, but her understanding of his situation boggled the mind. Lupe was a smart girl. He nodded. "*Gracias.*"

The word sounded funny on his lips. She grinned and disappeared into the house.

Silence descended. Molly's gaze seemed fixed on the horizon.

David took a measured step forward. Molly took a step back. He edged forward again. "Could you at least look at me?"

"I can't. All I see when I do is you and Bobbie . . . together. Teacher always said I had a good imagination." The quiver in her voice deepened. "I've made my peace. You don't need to come back here."

"You think I went to be with Bobbie instead of coming to the program last night. You're wrong."

"What else would I think? You never showed up at the program. Tobias said you took firewood to her house the other day. She came to the corral. You've been seeing each other."

"I was on my way to the program to see you when Bobbie came looking for me. Not the other way around."

"You're not helping your cause."

"The road was slick with sleet. She was driving too fast. She hit a tree."

A look of horror on her face, Molly gasped as her hands flew to her cheeks. "I never wished anything bad would happen to her. I only wanted her to go away."

"She wasn't hurt bad. I went with her to the hospital and stayed until her daed could get there. By then it was too late to come find you. I told her that I love you and that I wouldn't be seeing her anymore."

He tugged at her hands. She held them rigid against her face. Her gaze shifted to the snow angels. The pain in her eyes made his chest hurt. "I told her I was on my way to see you."

Finally, her gaze connected with his. Her brown-gold eyes burned through him. She would not let him off the hook easily, as well she shouldn't. It would take an extraordinary act to convince her.

David dropped to his knees in the snow. He stared up at her, squinting against sunlight that created a bright halo around her head. "Can you forgive me for hurting you?"

"Of course I forgive you." The words were tart as freshly squeezed lemonade. Plain people were required to forgive in all matters, so she would forgive. That was Molly. "Stand up. You look silly. Your knees will get cold and wet."

He remained on his knees. Plain men might not do it like this, but he would. She would know how truly sorry he was and how heartfelt his next question was.

"Nee. I have another question for you."

Her hands dropped. The wind whipped the strings of her kapp. Her cheeks turned scarlet with the cold. Her lips parted. She sighed. "What question is that?"

"Will you marry me?"

She ducked her head. "David—"

"If you forgive me, the slate is wiped clean. If you forgive me the way Gott forgives me, you can't keep punishing me. I made a mistake. Don't make me pay for it for the rest of my life. Truly forgive me and let us have the life Gott intended for us to have."

"You're so sure now. You weren't before."

"I was stupid."

"And Bobbie?"

"Going back to school after the new year, I imagine." The image of her tearful face would remain etched on his mind forever. "Her dad will hire a ranch manager to help out."

"She left once before."

"Of her own accord. This time I told her to go."

"Because you knew she would always be a temptation?"

"Because I know she'll be happier. She'll find happiness with someone in her world. Not here in mine."

Tears trickled down Molly's cheeks. Sniffing, she wiped at them with the back of her sleeve.

"If you cry, the tears will freeze."

"I never cry." That sounded more like his Molly. "The cold stings my eyes."

"You haven't answered me."

She tilted her head, gaze on the blue sky, then looked him squarely in the eye. "I will."

His heart soared from his chest. He could barely breathe. He tried to suck in air, but his lungs seemed to have shut down for business. "With no regrets?"

"Not one, so don't give me any."

"I won't. Thank you."

"Don't get all fancy on me. Stand up, you silly man."

He stood. Her arms came around his waist in a fierce hug. Her head burrowed against his chest. No scent of flowers, only the beautiful scent of love. "Took you long enough." Her words were muffled against his coat. "I thought I might have to live out my life alone because the only man I'll ever love couldn't figure out how to love me back."

Gently, he put his hand under her chin and lifted it so he could gaze into her face. "I'm slow, but eventually I figure out the important stuff." He leaned down. Their lips met. All else melted away. In that moment, that kiss became his first. His first as a man committed to one woman and only one woman for all eternity. The kiss deepened until nothing separated them nor ever could separate them.

He straightened. The puffy white clouds of their breaths continued to mingle. She laughed, the chimes climbing higher and quicker. "I lieb you."

"I lieb you too."

The hug this time went on and on, along with the kiss. When they finally broke apart, David's gaze fell on the snow angels. They looked like a family. With one member missing. "You haven't made your angel."

She grinned and held out her hands. "Help me."

He took hold and laid her on the snow with the care one takes with a precious person who cannot be replaced. Her gaze never left his. He let go and her arms fluttered at her sides, up and down, up and down.

"Let me see."

She scrambled to her feet. A perfect angel adorned the snow next to his.

She took his hand in hers. "One day we'll have a family that looks just like that."

She could see a clear, bright future with him, just as he saw one with her. He squeezed her hand. "I have something to show you."

She walked with him to the buggy where he handed her the first present. "Open it."

She removed the paper with care that made him want to laugh. "Rip it."

"Nee, I want to save it."

Finally, the paper fell away and she held the globe in her hand. "It's beautiful." She ran her fingers over the clear glass, then shook it. Snow fell softly on the house, the red barn, and the fir trees. A peaceful country scene that would be their life one day. "It'll remind me forever of this day. Of this Christmas."

He fought the urge to kiss her all over again.

She opened the second package and slipped the shawl around her shoulders, oohing and aahing with delight. "It's perfect." Her smile disappeared. "I don't have anything for you."

"You already gave me my present."

He picked up the gifts for Lupe and Diego. "I have globes for the kinner."

"They'll be so surprised."

They turned toward the porch. There stood Lupe, Diego,

Amanda, and Rebekah, grinning like crazy coyotes. "Make more snow angels," Amanda shouted.

More snow angels. More family. They could never have enough.

Hands clasped, they went to share the news that surely showed on their faces and to celebrate the birth of their Savior with the gift of love.

Discussion Questions

1. Bobbie left Bee County to try to leave her feelings for David behind. Was that a good reason? A good plan of action? Why didn't it work?
2. David has to choose not only between two women, but also between his faith and the outside world. What do you think of the Amish belief that his eternal salvation rests on his baptism and staying in his community's faith for the rest of his life? Do you see value in the Amish people's desire to stay "off the grid" and to keep themselves apart from the world?
3. Molly really hates that she can't dislike Bobbie. She's a nice person. It would be easier if she weren't. Have you ever felt that way about someone? Why?
4. David believes God has given him a second chance at love. What does Scripture say about second chances for people who have hiked off the path of faith? How do you define *grace*?
5. Are there people in your life who are keeping you from a closer relationship with Christ? How do you address that challenge? How do you handle those people?

About the Author

Kelly Irvin is the author of the Amish of Bee County series, which includes *The Beekeeper's Son*, which received a starred review from *Publisher's Weekly*, calling it "a delicately woven masterpiece." She is also the author of the Bliss Creek Amish series and the New Hope Amish series. Kelly's novella *A Christmas Visitor* appears in the anthology *The Amish Christmas Gift*. Her novella *Sweeter than Honey* is included in the anthology *The Amish Market*.

She has written two romantic suspense novels, *A Deadly Wilderness* and *No Child of Mine*.

A former newspaper reporter and retired public relations professional, Kelly lives in Texas with her husband, photographer Tim Irvin. They have two children, two grandchildren, and two cats. In her spare time, she likes to read books by her favorite authors.

Home for Christmas

Ruth Reid

I dedicate Home for Christmas to my Dad, Paul Droste. Dogs have always been an important part of my life, and growing up, I was very blessed to have a dad who I could convince we needed another four-legged family member. Thank you, Dad!

Glossary

aenti: aunt
boppli: baby
bruder: brother
daadihaus: grandfather's house
daed: dad or father
danki: thank you
doktah: doctor
Englisch: English, non-Amish
Englischer: anyone who is not Amish
fraa: wife
geh: go
gut: good
haus: house
hiya: a greeting like "hello"
hund: dog
Ich geh sehe: I go see
Ich: I
jah: yes
kaffi: coffee
kalt: cold
kann: can
Kann Ich spiele mitt Lulu*?:* Can I play with Lulu?
kapp: a prayer covering worn by Amish women

kinner: children
kumm: come
kumm mitt mich: come with me
lumba babba: baby doll
mamm: mother or mom
mei: my
nacht: night
nau: now
nay: no
nett: not
onkel: uncle
Ordnung: the written and unwritten rules of the Amish; the understood behavior by which the Amish are expected to live, passed down from generation to generation. Most Amish know the rules by heart.
Pennsylvania *Deitsch:* the language most commonly used by the Amish*
reddy-up: tidy up
rumschpringe: running-around period when a teenager turns sixteen years old
spielen: play
wilkom: welcome

*Amish children speak Pennsylvania *Deitsch* until they attend school, where they are taught English.

Chapter 1

Ellie Whetstone glanced at the GPS map displayed on the dashboard, then over at her faithful canine companion, Lulu, the standard poodle seated on the passenger side of the RV. "Another five miles, and we should finally be there, girl."

The estimated thirteen-hour drive from Oak, Pennsylvania, to her *aenti's* farm in Posen, Michigan, ended up taking closer to sixteen hours. Lulu didn't seem to mind the drive, even after the grueling weekend she'd spent benched during the National Dog Show. Ellie preferred the show-n-go events where the dogs were not required to remain on their assigned bench, and the handler was not expected to be present to answer spectator questions whenever they weren't in the ring. But Lulu relished the limelight. The standard apricot poodle, wearing her continental clip, loved attention from the photographers too. When she won Best of Breed, Lulu held a slight tipped-up-nose pose for the cameramen, something Ellie hadn't taught the three-year-old.

Ellie yawned. The final few miles of any trip always seemed the longest, and the change of Daylight Saving Time last week hadn't helped either. Ellie still hadn't reprogrammed her brain that in mid-November dusk fell sometime around six. Her headlights flashed over towering pines as the country road took a turn. She glanced at the GPS map again to see if this road in no-man's-land was still taking her the right direction. Maybe she should have told more people about her plan to drop off the grid in northern Michigan for a while—at least until February, which was when Lulu had her next big competition. Lulu had accumulated enough points at the various conformation events throughout the year that she qualified for Westminster without having to compete in Orlando at the Eukanuba National Championship. An incredible accomplishment for a twenty-nine-year-old handler, or so she'd been told. But Ellie was determined not to let it go to her head. Lulu was an exceptional dog.

"In five hundred yards make a right turn," the computerized female voice of her GPS instructed.

Ellie followed the directions, pulling into the long driveway. The vehicle's headlights illuminated several outbuildings as she came to a stop. She let out a long breath and with it some of the road fatigue and overall exhaustion from a demanding show schedule and Lulu's recent competition.

"Destination reached."

"I figured that out, Ms. Atlas." Ellie pressed the button on the GPS to discontinue the journey, then reached over and patted her companion on the head. "We made it, girl."

Lulu yipped, anxious to stretch her legs.

Although Ellie hadn't seen the farm she'd recently inherited, from what she could make out, the exterior resembled the other farms they'd passed along the way. A large barn faced the south side and several outbuildings of various sizes nestled between bare-branched trees. Tomorrow, when she had better light, she would explore the buildings. She turned off the engine to conserve fuel. The gas gauge had dipped low since she turned off the main highway. Ellie popped open the center glove compartment, fished out a flashlight and the keys she'd received in the mail from her mother along with the notice of her *aenti's* death, then climbed out of the RV.

The chilly northern Michigan air sent shivers down Ellie's spine as she let the dog out the passenger's side. She shined the flashlight on the house. It had a nice-sized wraparound porch, a selling point. Wooden chairs. *Aenti* must have spent time sitting on the porch in the summer. She climbed the porch steps while Lulu dallied close by, sniffing the shrubs next to the porch. Ellie tried several keys, but none of them seemed to fit the lock. She considered rummaging through the RV for a bobby pin or something to jimmy the lock, or at least going back for her coat. The weather forecast had predicted snow. Nothing unusual for halfway through November, but her lightweight sweatshirt wasn't enough to keep her teeth from chattering. Ellie wiggled the doorknob, and with a slight bump of her hip, the door opened.

Lulu bounded up the porch steps with renewed energy. She nudged her way past Ellie and began sniffing around the kitchen, then beyond.

Ellie shined the flashlight on the wall next to the door in search of the light switch, then remembered her mother, a former member of the district, talking about how the Amish didn't believe in modern conveniences such as electricity and hot water. She circled the room with the light. The wooden cabinets were plain yet held a polished shine. The counters were well worn and free of clutter. A hand pump at the sink and oversize wood stove gave the place rustic charm.

Lulu's nails tapped the wood floor as she pranced back into the kitchen, a stuffed Amish doll in her mouth. "What did you find, a new toy?" The dog pressed the faceless doll against Ellie's hand. Lulu wanted to play, but all Ellie could think about was crawling into bed. Ellie opened a cabinet next to the sink, removed a drinking glass, then placed it under the pump spigot.

Hmm. Nothing like pioneer living. She inspected the iron contraption, then set the flashlight on the counter and took hold of the cold pump handle. With the first crank on the handle, the flashlight rolled off the counter, hit the floor with a *thud*, then rolled under a kitchen chair. Another hard crank and water gushed to the surface.

"Ta-da!" Ellie lifted the glass to her mouth but then lowered it. For all she knew the water was gunky with a rusty-orange buildup from lack of use. *Aenti* Bonnie had passed away three months ago, and the letter Ellie had received gave little information on how she'd died or how long she'd been ill. As Ellie knelt on the floor to collect the flashlight, Lulu pushed the toy in her face. "Not now, girl."

Heavy footsteps sounded on the porch outside the kitchen door, followed by a garbled muttering of undecipherable words.

Still holding the stuffed toy in her mouth, Lulu's low growl was muffled.

The door opened, bringing a gust of icy northern air into the kitchen. Ellie peered between the legs of the chair and caught a glimpse of knee-high rubber boots.

"Hello?" a man said, lifting the lantern in his hand higher. "Anyone here?"

Ellie tightened her grip on the flashlight, then with her free hand grasped Lulu's collar. For her large size, the poodle wasn't much of a guard dog; she hadn't even dropped the toy to make her growl heard.

As the shadowy figure stepped farther into the room, Ellie jumped up, aiming the flashlight at the bearded intruder. "Who—who are you?"

Ezra Mast lifted his hand to block the bright beam of light aimed at his eyes. He couldn't get a look at the *Englischer*, but judging by her stammering voice, he'd surprised her.

"I'm Ezra Mast."

"Wha-what are you doing here?"

"I live here." He staggered blindly but froze midstep at the sound of a big dog's growl. For some reason, the brazen woman inside his house didn't bother him, but a dog—that was a different story. "Why are you in *mei haus*?"

With a raspy huff, she lowered the light. "Rats!"

"Rats! Where?" he asked, interrupting her rant about some GPS woman misdirecting her. This was the time of year when furry critters started looking for where they would nest for the winter. Of course, they almost always camped in the barn, feeding on spilled grain.

"I'm positive I plugged the correct address in—Where's what?"

"The rats," he repeated sternly.

The dog, chomping down on his daughter's doll, curled its lips, exposing a full set of teeth.

"Lulu, stop." The woman clicked her fingers and the dog sat. "I said *rats* because, well, it's an expression of—You have rats?"

"It's a farm, so yes—sometimes." He drew a breath to keep his patience. "You're in *mei haus*."

The door opened and five-year-old Allison entered. She sidled up beside him, hooking her arm around the back of his leg. A gleam of lantern light flickered in her big blue eyes as she looked up at him. "*Ich kalt*."

When he came out of his furniture shop and noticed the RV parked in front of the house, he'd instructed Allison to stay in the workshop until he checked things out, but seeing her lips trembling, he couldn't reprimand her, even though she'd gone against his instructions.

Ezra placed his hand on her shoulder and guided her behind him. "Don't move," he said to her in Pennsylvania *Deitsch*. Once the woman and dog were gone, he would stoke the stove and reheat the vegetable soup they'd had for lunch.

But his child had a mind of her own. Allison darted over to the dog, pointing her tiny finger at the beast's big mouth. "*Mei lumba babba.*"

Ezra went to pull her away, and the dog flashed its ugly teeth at him again. Retrieving the doll wasn't worth the risk of being bitten, but convincing his daughter to let it be wouldn't be easy. Her mother had hand sewn the toy. Ezra glared at the owner. "Do something about your animal, please."

Without the owner doing anything, the dog dropped the cloth doll, then licked Allison's face.

"That's enough kisses, Lulu." The woman squatted and gave Allison her full attention. "Hi, what's your name?"

"Allison," she said with a giggle, then pointed at the dog. "*Hund.*"

"Her name is Lulu." The woman picked up the rag doll and handed it to Allison. "Is this your doll?"

Allison nodded.

The visitor looked up at Ezra. "Lulu loves kids."

"And I'm supposed to take you at your word after the dog bared its teeth?" He shook his head at the woman, then instructed his daughter to move behind him.

Allison wrapped her arms around the dog's neck and must have squeezed too tight because the dog jerked out of her hold, then immediately showered Allison with more kisses.

"Allison, move away from the dog. *Nau.*" All *kinner* tested their parents' patience, and his daughter was no exception. He added the threat of sending her to bed with his last warning in Pennsylvania *Deitsch*, and that got her attention.

Allison turned, lowered her head, and returned to his side. Ezra picked up his daughter, then set her on the table long enough to light another lantern. He wanted to keep a better eye on that animal. It wasn't that he disliked dogs. They had their place—outside—but this beast practically stood eye-to-eye with Allison. If the dog even bumped into her, it'd knock her down. A shadow on the floor captured his attention and he lowered the lantern. Muddy paw prints. The animal looked as though it had stepped out of a beauty salon with all its puffy balls of fur, and yet the woman thought nothing of letting it walk through the mud or bringing the critter into his home.

"Oh my." The woman cringed. "I didn't realize . . . Please allow me to mop up the mess."

"That's *nett* necessary."

"But I'll be happy to clean it up before I go. I wouldn't want your wife to have to clean up my dog's muddy prints."

"She's gone." He wasn't sure why he'd blurted that to a stranger.

"All the more reason I should take care of it. I wouldn't want to come home to dirty floors, and I'm sure your wife is the same way."

Ezra cleared his throat. "You never mentioned why you're here." He wasn't interested; he merely wanted to help her get on with her journey. He still had supper to make.

The woman blushed. "Obviously, walking into the wrong house embarrasses me. I feel a lot like a real-life Goldilocks and the three bears."

He looked around the room. "You have more than one dog?" Not that her dog's bleached-out tan coat resembled a bear; it didn't. But the twentysomething's long hair pulled back into a ponytail was certainly golden.

She chuckled. "No, just Lulu." The intruder gave the dog a pat on the head. "By the way, I'm Ellie," she said, extending her hand. "I should probably be on my way. Sorry for barging in on you."

Ellie and the dog headed to the door. She reached for the

handle but paused. "Would you by chance know where Bonnie Whetstone's farm is located?"

He swallowed hard. "Why do you want to know?"

"She's my *aenti*."

"She's . . . gone."

Ellie nodded. "I know *Aenti* passed away. I've inherited her place."

"I see." His right shoulder twitched, nothing especially noticeable to anyone but him.

He followed her onto the porch and pointed to the left. "You missed your turn by a few hundred feet. You can take the trail through the pasture to her place. You'll find her *haus* just over the creek."

"I guess that makes us neighbors."

"So it seems." Hopefully she owned a leash for her dog.

"Mind if I turn around by your barn? Backing up an RV can be a little tricky, and I'd hate to run into one of the trees that line your driveway."

He wouldn't bother to explain how the trees helped block the snow in the winter. "Sure."

She let the dog inside the vehicle first, then skirted around to the driver's side and climbed up on the seat and started the engine. The RV was surprisingly quiet, which was why he hadn't heard her pull into the yard over his hammering. Ellie made a hard turn, stopped a few feet from the barn, then backed up, and up, and up.

"Wait!" He jumped off the porch and jogged to the front of the vehicle, flapping his arms. When she didn't notice, he went around to the driver's side and raised his voice. "Ellie, stop."

His warning came too late. One clothesline snapped, the other one somehow hooked itself to a bicycle attached to the back end, and as she drove forward, one aluminum pole uprooted its cemented base and followed her a few feet until she figured out she was dragging something and stopped.

Ellie climbed out of the vehicle. "I was looking for buildings," she explained, inspecting the damage. "I didn't see your clothesline."

"I know." He forced a neighborly smile, then untangled the line from the bike's wheel and frame.

"Sorry." She slapped her fists on her hips. "We're not getting off to a good start, are we?"

Chapter 2

Off to a bad start—that was certainly an understatement. Ellie coasted to a stop at the end of Ezra's driveway, then turned back onto the gravel country road in the same direction she'd come earlier. She drove with one foot on the brake while creeping along the shoulder in search of the entrance to her *aenti's* farm. Ezra said she'd find the turnoff in a hundred yards or so. The headlights flashed over the white fence posts first, then illuminated the rusted iron gate.

"Stay, Lulu." She exited the vehicle. The narrow entrance was overgrown, but the ground felt firm. She worked the latch on the gate, then pushed it open as far as she could. It'd take a tight turn to avoid the ditch, but at least the area was clear of trees. After bringing down the neighbor's clothesline, she was leery of backing up in the dark. The man had tried to hide his irritation behind his press-lipped smile, but the shoulder twitch gave him away. Even if his wife was understanding about the muddy floor, no woman would want to find her clothesline sprawled over the yard.

Ellie climbed back into the driver's seat. With a hard crank of the wheel, she inched forward, then backward, then cranked the wheel more and went forward again. Ellie smiled, pleased with the way she handled the difficult maneuvering. She hadn't owned the RV long. The trust fund left to her by her grandparents had only been accessible since she turned twenty-five.

Clear of the entrance, now all she had to do was follow the cow path to the house. She went forward a few feet before remembering to close the gate. Ellie chuckled. Now she could brag about living in a gated community. Lulu jumped out of the vehicle behind Ellie and immediately sniffed the air. As Ellie closed and secured the gate, she glanced across the field at the glow of lamplight coming from Ezra's windows. Not more than a stone's throw away. No wonder the GPS failed.

"Come on, girl." Ellie motioned to the open door.

Lulu jumped back inside and sniffed at the vents. The fidgety dog whined.

"What do you smell, girl?" Ellie drew in a breath but didn't detect any strange odors. "You've been cooped up in here too long." Usually by now they were parked at an RV camp and she was cooking supper over a fire pit. It'd be nice to spend a few months living in a house, enjoying a large yard, or rather, a large pasture. The vehicle's headlights flashed over something ahead. She squinted as a bridge came into view. The structure was obviously built for a horse and buggy, but would the weathered wood hold the weight of her RV? She pressed the brake pedal. Surely Ezra would have warned her not to cross the bridge if he thought it wasn't safe.

Lulu stood on the passenger seat, then leaned toward the dash and growled.

"It's okay, girl." Ellie's soothing didn't calm her dog. Then she caught sight of the massive beast that had moved into the headlight beams. Ellie leaned into the steering wheel, trying to get a better look through the windshield.

Lulu barked viciously.

"Easy, girl." Ellie patted Lulu's neck. "You can't take on a bull." Nor could they avoid going over the bridge. She wasn't about to be trapped in a pasture with two tons of pure beefsteak approaching the front of the vehicle.

The animal pawed the grass, dipped its head, and snorted.

Oh, Lord, don't let him charge. Ellie braced for impact, closing her eyes with visions of horns puncturing her radiator. Meanwhile, Lulu goaded the bull on with her bark. A few seconds later, Ellie opened her eyes. The massive horned animal had wandered off the direct path and was now on Lulu's side of the vehicle. Ellie lifted her foot off the brake and drove toward the bridge.

The bridge moaned as if in protest as the RV's front tires rolled onto it. Ellie sucked in a breath. Perhaps this was a mistake. This vehicle represented her life savings, a rolling nest egg so to speak. Ellie tightened her grip on the steering wheel. This wasn't the type of adventure she'd hoped to find in northern Michigan.

Oh, Lord, did the bridge just sway? She sucked in a breath, calculated the odds of backing up without going off the edge, and decided against attempting it. Finally, she reached the other side, released the steering wheel, and blew out a breath. Ellie wiggled her arms and shoulders, her muscles relaxing.

The bumpy cow path brought her through a stand of pines and around a cluster of birch saplings before she spotted the clapboard cabin tucked under a canopy of aspens. In the clearing in front of the house, Ellie turned off the engine but left the headlights on to shed light on the front door. She and Lulu climbed out of the RV and up the nice-sized porch, which stretched the entire length of the house. A lone chair sat a few feet from the door. Ellie tried to picture her *aenti* sitting on the porch shucking corn, but her memory wouldn't reach back that far. Ellie hadn't been part of the Amish community since the age of six, not since her father passed away and her mother's conversion to the Amish way couldn't withstand the pressures her *Englisch* parents placed on her to come back home.

She wiped her feet on the worn rug, then picked a key on the ring and tried it in the lock. The door opened. Lulu went in first, nose to the floor.

Inside the house wasn't much warmer than outside. Ellie shined the flashlight around the kitchen and discovered an oil lamp in the center of the table with matches beside it. She set the flashlight down and struck the match, and by leaving the wick long, she found the room filled with light. Ellie could see her breath. She glanced at the massive wood stove, which took up most of the space in the kitchen. A bit intimidating, but she'd started plenty of campfires. A box of kindling, a few logs, and a stack of old newspapers sat off to the side. She opened the side door on the stove and tossed in a few thinner pieces of wood, then bunched up several pages of newspaper. As the paper lit, she slowly added more kindling, but the fire went out almost immediately. She repeated the process, using more paper than wood. Allowing air to reach the flames, Ellie left the door ajar. Logs always took a few minutes to catch on fire. While the fire took off, she picked up the lantern and she and Lulu checked out the rest of the house.

The living room wasn't much larger than the kitchen. A blue area rug took up the center, a desk and chair were against one wall, a lamp table sat between two straight wooden chairs, and on the far side of the room was another cast-iron wood-burning stove and woodbox. She snorted. Her RV offered more amenities, including satellite TV and a state-of-the-art indoor/outdoor stereo system. Still, there was something inviting about the rustic home. A perfect place if one's objective was to disappear from society. Perhaps that could be the selling point, because modern amenities sure wouldn't be.

She opened a door off the living room, her eyes immediately drawn to the beautiful green, black, and white quilt spread over the bed. She didn't know enough about quilts to recognize the pattern, but it was certainly striking. The lantern light flickered, casting strange shadows over the walls. The wick had burned low and the light wasn't bright enough to see beyond a few inches. Inspecting the quilt stitches would have to wait until daylight.

When Ellie was a child, her mother had taught her how to sew by hand; she'd made a few potholders, but as a teenager her interest in sewing faded. It wasn't until she found an old quilt of her mother's packed away in the attic that Ellie's interest was piqued once again. But traveling all year to different dog shows limited her free time.

"Come on, Lulu," she said, coaxing the dog from the area so she could close the door. No sense heating the entire place. Once she checked out the other rooms, she'd pick where they would sleep.

Ellie sniffed. *Smoke.* Thick air filled her lungs and her eyes began to burn. She shot out the front door and, making sure Lulu was with her, ran to the RV. She grabbed the portable fire extinguisher, disregarding her mind's blaring orders not to go back into a burning building. At least she'd kicked up her leg and blocked Lulu from reentering. Her companion didn't like being left outside either. Lulu barked nonstop and scratched at the door.

Pull—Aim—Squeeze—what's the last S*?* Armed with her hand on the trigger, she eased into the kitchen. Nothing. Holding her breath as she ferreted every inch, she came to the quick conclusion that the source of the billowing smoke was the wood stove.

Okay, so building a wood stove fire isn't the same as building a campfire. She needed to remember to close the door so the smoke went up the stovepipe. Campfire smoke just naturally drifted upward—or sideways, when the wind was blowing. Ellie opened the window, stuck her head outside, and coughed. *Sweep*, yes, that was the other *S*. Pull the pin, aim at the base of the fire, squeeze the trigger, and sweep the base of the fire. Not that any of that mattered now. She took a few more breaths of fresh air.

Lulu found her half hanging out the window and began licking her face.

"I'm all right, Lulu. Good girl." Ellie chuckled. If anyone saw her hanging out a window like this, they'd think she'd been hitting the bottle, even though she'd never touched a drop of alcohol in her life. She pulled her head back inside and coughed. The house had been closed up so well it needed a good airing out before Ellie could list it with a real estate agent anyway.

Ellie grabbed the fire extinguisher and stepped outside. On the porch, Lulu jumped up, her front paws landing on Ellie's shoulders, and, whimpering with excitement, lathered her with more kisses. "Okay, okay, I'm safe." She patted the dog's head, and the two of them headed back to the RV where Ellie started the generator and Lulu, like she always did, nosed her way under Ellie's arm to be a part of what was going on. The two of them had been inseparable, spending practically every moment together since Lulu turned eight months old. Ellie clapped her hands to get Lulu's attention. "Are you hungry? Let's eat."

Lulu barked.

Ellie was no longer hungry. The smoke had killed her taste buds. She opened the RV door and stepped into the living quarters. Lulu sat next to her bowl, wagging her tail as Ellie opened a large can of Purina. On show days, Ellie cooked the dog ribeye on the portable grill. She liked to think the treat motivated her furry friend, and Lulu's excitement showed in the ring. And her allotted budget allowed for a little extra spoiling. Lulu ate more prime steak meals and even had more expensive hair-care products than Ellie, but that didn't matter.

Lulu devoured the food, then looked up at Ellie and barked.

"You've had plenty." Usually she hushed Lulu when she barked, but out here in the middle of nowhere, it wasn't like she would bother anyone. *Ah, another selling point—total seclusion.* She ruffled the dog's coat. "Make all the noise you want, Lulu, but sorry, I can't let you ruin your perfect figure."

Ellie sipped herbal tea and read several passages in the Bible as she did each evening before going to bed. Lulu curled up on her doggy bed and fell asleep, something that amazed Ellie since they were tucked in the woods in the middle of nowhere. Shortly after closing the Bible and thanking God for helping them to reach their destination safely, she crawled under the covers, listening to the patter of sleet against the window. Thankfully, she wasn't alone. Although her canine friend was great company, Lulu was, after all, a dog. Conversations were one-sided, and lately, especially since Ellie was turning thirty on New Year's Eve, she longed for human companionship. As a matter of fact, she couldn't remember the last time she'd had a conversation with someone that didn't involve composition scores or who was judging the next round.

She closed her eyes. The lack of human companionship wasn't something she was willing to think about now.

Chapter 3

After a restless night of sleep, Ellie opened her eyes to find Lulu on the bed standing over her. She blinked several times as the dog's image came into focus.

Lulu licked her cheek.

"No, not now, Lulu. Go back to sleep." Ellie tucked the covers up around her neck and rolled over.

The animal persisted, nosing her way under the covers. When Ellie ignored Lulu's attention-seeking kisses, the dog barked.

Ellie cringed at the sharp cry, which echoed off the walls in the small space. Ears ringing, she tossed back the covers and groggily crawled out of bed and walked Lulu to the door. The snow-covered ground sparkled with the pink hues of dawn. Ellie stood at the door, rubbing her arms and shivering as finicky Lulu tiptoed through the fresh snow. The scenery was breathtaking, but the morning's crisp air should have driven the pampered pooch inside. "Anytime, Lulu."

Lulu glanced at Ellie briefly, then continued to scout the new surroundings, sniffing the snowy pine needles until she disappeared into the woods.

Ellie groaned. It wasn't like Lulu to venture off alone. She rose to her tiptoes and searched the area. "Lulu, come."

Top of her class in obedience training, Lulu always came when called. But not this time.

Recalling the bull in the front pasture, Ellie felt her heart beat faster. She shoved her bare feet into her boots, threw her coat on over her lightweight, puppy-print pajamas, and grabbed the first thing she could find to fend off the bull—a broom.

"Lulu!" Ellie scanned the wooded area. No sign. Lulu wasn't even fond of being outside in the winter. Hunting for clues, she spotted paw prints in the snow and tracked them. She ducked under a low pine branch but somehow still managed to knock the snow off the pine needles and onto her head. Coldness trickled down the back of her neck and traveled the length of her spine.

In a short time, Ellie cleared the wooded area and came to a barbed-wire fence. Using the broom handle, she attempted to push down the wire, but the fence didn't have much give, and as she crawled between the wires, her hair became tangled. Ellie attempted to free herself, but every movement made her scalp burn with pain. She let out a frustrated cry.

As Ezra stood outside the barn, he craned to listen for the noise again. He'd never heard an animal howl like that, tamed or wild. Perhaps it was the wind. Leaving his daughter in the house alone while he did the morning chores made him super sensitive. His sister Josephine was due to arrive anytime, but did he dare risk leaving Allison home alone a little longer?

"Help! Someone, please help."

The plea was faint, but clearly it came from a desperate woman and not an animal. "Lord, please watch over Allison." He took off running toward the back pasture, and it wasn't long before he spotted the noisemaker.

Ezra crossed his arms and glared down at the woman who'd let herself into his house last night. He lifted one brow. "Let me guess. Sleepwalking?"

The woman tried to turn her head his direction but was stopped by the wire. "Are you just going to stand there with your arms crossed?"

"You're on private property," he said, but the moment the words spilled from his mouth, his guilty conscience set him straight. Fences were meant for keeping livestock safe, not keeping neighbors out—even neighbors scandalously dressed in pajama bottoms decorated with miscellaneous dog breeds.

He squatted next to the woman, and a flowery scent wafted from her hair. "What kind of pickle did you get yourself into?"

"My hair is caught."

"So I see." He started to untangle the strands, but she wiggled impatiently. "Hold still."

"Can't you just cut it?"

"I won't need to if you relax and give me a moment to fix this mess. I do have some experience getting tangles out. Besides, you don't want a bald spot, do you?" As he held her silky locks between his fingers, he tried not to think about Charlotte and the way his wife's hair had felt in his hands.

"I've been meaning to cut it anyway," she said.

"Why? It's . . . nice."

When she craned her neck to face him, her eyes connected with his. Heat infused his neck and face. He needed to limit his talking to Pennsylvania *Deitsch*. Otherwise, he might blurt out more things he shouldn't.

Her face pinched.

"*Ach*, I'm sorry. I didn't mean to hurt you."

"It's okay. At least I'm not howling anymore."

He smiled. "You did sound like a wounded animal earlier."

"I'm not sure I appreciate being likened to an animal, but I am glad you heard me."

"Let's get you free." He focused on the knotted hair, but the strands he'd already loosened from the wire slipped through his fingers. Ezra pushed her golden strands aside only to have them cascade over the wire again.

"I should have a hair tie in my coat pocket." Ellie shoved her hand into her pocket and fished out a dog biscuit, which she handed to him. "If you'll hold that a minute . . ." Next she produced a whistle, a set of keys, a half-eaten Snickers bar, and lastly, a tube of Chap Stick.

"Must be in the other pocket," she said sheepishly.

Ezra eyed the items he'd been given to hold. Perhaps cutting her hair would have been easier. A bald spot would grow back. Besides, his daughter was at the house alone.

"Got it," she announced.

Ezra set the other things on a nearby stump, then gathered Ellie's loose hair into a ponytail and secured it with the rubber band. Once he isolated the hair still tangled, he was able to free it from the wire without losing too much.

Ellie stood up straight, rubbing her scalp. "Thanks for coming to my rescue." Releasing her hair from the tie, she gave her head a shake, then combed her fingers through her tresses. The falling strands framed her face.

He looked away. "What were you doing crawling through *mei* fence?" *In your pajamas?*

"I'm looking for Lulu. I let her out this morning and she didn't come back."

He helped collect the items she'd handed him. "Dare I ask what you're doing with that broom?"

She shoved her things back into her pockets, then picked up the broom. "This is in case the bull comes at me."

He shook his head and grinned. "You've never been around a bull before, have you?"

"No." Her gaze shifted to the ground and she toed the snow with her boot.

"If you wave that at him, you'll only aggravate him more."

She looked up and smiled, then redirected her gaze to the ground, her eyes scanning the area.

"Are you missing something?"

"Yeah. My dog."

"And you think she's hiding under an inch of snow?" he teased.

"Ha-ha. I was following her paw prints." Ellie took a few steps, paused, then hiked toward his barn.

Ezra wasn't pleased with the direction the tracks were taking them. Some dogs had a tendency to rile livestock. He jogged ahead, his pulse quickening as he noticed the tracks veered away from the barn and went toward the house. He increased his speed.

"Do you see her?"

He glanced over his shoulder. Ellie was tromping clumsily through the snow while holding the broom in one hand and the waistband of her pajama bottoms fisted in her other, something no man in his position should see. Ezra refocused his attention on the large set of prints leading up the porch steps and followed them to the door. Entering the house without taking time to stomp the snow off his boots, he stormed into the sitting room and halted. Lying on the floor in front of the wood stove were Allison and the dog. His daughter, twirling the dog's curly coat around her finger, hadn't acknowledged him.

Ellie entered the sitting room, her snowy boots sliding on the planks. "Lulu, you had me worried out of my mind. I thought the bull might have gotten you."

At the sound of the master's voice, the dog lifted its head momentarily, then laid it back down on Allison's chest.

Ezra snorted. "Your animal is lying on *mei* daughter."

"Isn't that cute how well they've bonded?"

"*Nay*," he said, stiffening his posture. "Tell it to get up. Better yet, take it home."

Ellie jerked back, her eyes widening as though stunned.

"Please, take your dog home," he added in a gentler tone. He wasn't sure he liked the way she was studying him, but he couldn't turn away.

"*Ah*, I get it," she said with a smile. "You must be a cat person."

"Cat person? What are you talking about?"

"You don't like dogs." Her grin widened as she looked around the room. "So where are your cats?"

"*Nett* in the *haus*!" His shoulder twitched. "Would you *please* just take your animal and go home?" The woman had his stomach balled up. *Cat person*.

"Lulu, come." Ellie snapped her fingers.

The dog cracked open one sleepy eye for a moment but otherwise didn't budge. Not surprising. The hunting hounds he had growing up had a mind of their own when they were outside their pen.

"Lulu, come," she said with a stronger tone.

Still the dog didn't move.

Ezra shifted his feet. "Don't you have a leash?"

"Lulu is highly trained and, despite what you think, well mannered. She received her Good Canine Citizen certificate, which if you don't know is a very high obedience achievement. Besides," she said, tipping her chin, "collars tend to rub on her coat and leave a mark. Lulu is a show dog. She's judged, in part, on her appearance."

He stared at her a moment.

Ellie narrowed her eyes at him, then faced the dog loafing on the floor with his daughter. "Lulu, come."

When the dog didn't respond to her command, Ezra left the room. He disappeared into his bedroom and returned with a pair of suspenders. "Here."

Ellie crinkled her brows.

"Please. Use them as a leash."

Ellie fiddled with the suspenders. "I don't know what's gotten into her. Lulu's never been stubborn like this before. Maybe her attitude has something to do with the new environment. She really likes your daughter," she said, making excuses, sounding flustered. Ellie slipped the strap around the dog's neck and gave the command once again with a little tug.

Lulu looked up at her owner, then at Allison, then back to Ellie. Finally, the furry creature shuffled to its feet, though Lulu was still reluctant to move when the *Englischer* tugged on the makeshift leash again.

Allison pushed off the floor and threw her arms around the dog's neck. Only then did the animal look up at Ellie as if for instruction.

Ellie leaned down. "Allison," she said softly. "You and Lulu can play anytime you want."

Allison released her hold on the dog and smiled at Ellie in a way that caused Ezra's throat to tighten. His daughter hadn't always looked people in the eye. Sometimes she refused to acknowledge a person was in the room. At first he thought it had something to do with her mother dying, but when she started staring at him blankly, he suspected something serious.

Allison pointed to the dog prints on Ellie's pajama bottoms. "*Hund*."

"You like Scooby-Doo?" Ellie glanced up at him. Her lips twisted in response to the glare he gave her. "I forgot. You don't own a television."

And I don't approve of parading around in fancy nightclothes in public.

As if reading his mind, she glanced at her inappropriate attire and straightened. "We should be going. I'll bring your suspenders back later." She headed for the door with Lulu in tow but paused, looked over her shoulder, and smiled.

Ezra glanced over at his daughter. Surely the *Englischer's* smile was intended for Allison, but she had already crawled up into the rocking chair and was playing with her doll. He turned back to the woman, but she was gone.

Chapter 4

Ezra stared at the closed door a half second after Ellie and the dog left. He wished his new neighbor hadn't promised his daughter that she could play with that animal again. After a moment, he peered out the window over the sink. The high-strung dog jumped more than it walked, and the scantily clad woman seemed to encourage the frolicsome activity by ruffling the dog's coat and giving it a pat.

He wasn't about to allow Allison to be with the dog, or to be influenced by Ellie for that matter. The *Englisch* woman's ways contradicted their beliefs and practices. And yet she was Bonnie Whetstone's niece. His beloved neighbor had never married or had children of her own, but she'd been like a second mother to him, always baking sweets and helping out with Allison after his wife passed away. The elderly woman had mentioned how she prayed daily for her niece, believing one day Ellie would return to the Amish way.

Ellie glanced over her shoulder, caught him watching, and waved.

Heat trellised Ezra's neck and face. He ducked away from the window. Spying on the neighbor, for heaven's sake, what was he thinking? He needed to set boundaries. Like it or not, they were his new neighbors, and the two-legged one might be as dangerous as her four-legged companion.

Ezra grabbed a pot from the cabinet and filled it with water to make oatmeal. He glanced out the window again, but Ellie and the dog were already out of sight. He set the pot of water on the stove, then measured the dry oats. Waking up to snow this morning had made him hungry for the hot cereal, and while breakfast was a little later than usual, Allison hadn't seemed to notice. He'd tried to keep a consistent schedule. So far, the doctor's suggestion of maintaining a regular routine had helped. His daughter hadn't suffered a seizure in months.

As the water boiled, he looked around the corner at Allison, sitting in the rocking chair and playing with her doll. His gaze caught a shimmer of liquid on the floor. Allison knew the rule of eating and drinking only at the table. He grabbed a rag and marched into the room. Perhaps snow from his boots had melted. He knelt beside the spill, the pungent scent of urine reaching his nostrils. Ezra growled under his breath. The dog had been lying only moments ago in the same spot. He needed something stronger to disinfect the puddle. Ezra pushed off the floor, strode to the kitchen, and prepared a concentrated vinegar solution, then returned to clean up the mess.

He glanced up at his daughter. "Did that *hund* potty on the floor?"

Allison smacked her lips and made deep grunting sounds that Ezra assumed was her mimicking the dog. Until her hand holding the doll flopped over the arm of the rocking chair and her doll fell to the floor.

"Allison?" He dried his hands on the front of his shirt. "Answer me, honey."

Allison's eyes rolled back. One side of her body shook violently, her head thumping against the back of the rocker. His mind shot through the steps he knew to take—ease her onto the floor, move any objects out of the way to prevent harm, gently roll her onto her side. But before he could gather her into his arms, her little body stiffened as though all of her muscles had locked up.

Don't panic. Stay calm. Count. One horse and buggy, two horse and buggy . . . Father, please do something! Shrouded in helplessness, he felt his throat swell with emotion.

The jerking movements started again, this time with more intensity.

Count! The doctor had said to time the convulsions. Ezra resumed counting, stopping at forty-five when the thrashing stopped.

"I have you," he said softly, easing Allison into his arms. Her body went completely limp, sinking into his arms, and unlike with other seizures, the back of her dress was wet. Ezra lowered her onto the floor. Her other seizures hadn't been this violent. The doctor had thought she would outgrow them, and Ezra had hoped the past few months were a sign of that happening. But watching her lie unresponsive, staring at the ceiling without blinking, he had to wonder.

Still dazed a few moments later, Allison sat up, her gaze darting around the room. "Lulu? Lulu!" She repeated the dog's name with more intensity.

"Allison, honey. It's *Daed*. Will you look at me?" Ezra hadn't noticed his sister had arrived until Josephine knelt beside them.

"Did she have another seizure?"

"*Jah*, it just stopped. I don't think she's aware of what happened." He spoke over Allison's panicky cry for the dog.

"Who's Lulu?"

"The new neighbor's dog. Allison, please calm down." Ezra tried to tamp down the panic seeping into his nerves. If Allison didn't relax, she might trigger another seizure.

"You had me running around in my pajamas, making a fool of myself in front of our neighbor, and you're the one sulking?" Ellie sucked in her tummy and zipped up her skinny jeans. Since leaving Ezra's house and returning to the RV, Lulu had lain on her doggy bed and ignored Ellie.

"You're acting like a cat," she grumbled to Lulu. "Here, kitty, kitty, kitty." Usually this teasing provoked a response, but this time, Lulu didn't even bother to perk her ears. Ellie slipped into an old Ferris State sweatshirt, then knelt next to the dog.

"I know you've been cooped up in this RV over the last year and you want to get out and run, but we have to set some boundaries. The little cutie next door might want to be your friend, but her father isn't friendly at all. Not to mention you could get trampled by the bull if you go into the field."

Ellie shoved her foot into a wool sock, then pulled on the other one. "Maybe later we'll take a ride into town. Okay?"

Lulu lifted her head, then plopped it back down with a groan.

Great. She'd been reduced to negotiating with a dog, which underscored how desperately she needed a friend. The year on the road had been equally wearing on her. Ellie slipped on her boots. While it was daylight, she wanted to take a better look at the house and property, maybe start a list of things that needed to be done.

The house still reeked of smoke. Ellie decided to leave the windows open longer and not fiddle with the stove until after she returned from town. She needed gas in the RV, groceries, and some sort of air freshener or scented candle to mask the wood-burning scent. As ideas came up for sprucing the place up so it'd sell more quickly, she jotted down notes. A new rug for the porch, maybe one with the cute Home Sweet Home saying, bright curtains for the windows, and paint. These white, pictureless walls could use a splash of color to offset the oak wood flooring. She made a notation on the paper: yellow paint for the kitchen and living room. In the bedrooms she planned to choose a shade that would bring out the beautiful colors in the quilts. Of course she wouldn't sell the quilts with the house. Those were hers to cherish.

Her list complete, she jingled the house keys and Lulu charged to the door. Maybe if the house had heat she would consider leaving Lulu home alone, but a drafty old house wasn't the place for a grand champion. She couldn't afford for the dog to get sick.

Driving over the bridge wasn't nearly so intimidating in daylight. Off to the far corner of the pasture, the bull nibbled on a patch of brown grass under a large tree where the snow had melted. She stopped in front of the gate and, keeping her eye on the bull, hurried to open it. Then with suspended breath she ran back to the RV, sped through the opening, jumped back out, and closed the gate—all while the bull munched on dead grass.

Ellie drove to Ezra's place first. Only this time, she parked on the road and left Lulu in the vehicle. She hiked up the driveway's small incline. The weather had warmed some now that the sun was up, and her goose-down coat was hot. She knocked on the door.

A woman answered, holding her pregnant belly. "Hello."

"Hi, I, ah . . ." She held up the suspenders dangling between her thumb and index finger. "I wanted to return these to Ezra."

The dark-haired woman's eyes narrowed on the makeshift leash before connecting with Ellie's. "I don't understand."

"I'm sorry, Mrs. Mast. I should have explained first." She motioned to the wooded area beyond the pasture. "I just moved into my *aenti's* house next door and—"

"You're Bonnie's niece, *jah*?" Her expression warmed.

"Yes, I'm Ellie Whetstone." She held out the suspenders and the woman took them. "Your husband was kind enough to let me borrow them. I'm sorry about your clothesline."

The woman's gaze darted beyond Ellie, trouble lines registering across her forehead.

Ellie glanced over her shoulder at the clothesline. "Oh, I see. Ezra must have fixed it." Her neighbor still held the same blank look. "I should probably go." She spun to leave.

"You have a dog named Lulu?"

Ellie stiffened. "Yes, that's right." *I should've mopped the floor.* Ellie turned slowly to face the woman. If Ezra had told his wife about Ellie and Lulu, why did she seem surprised about the clothesline and suspenders? Her thoughts flitted to him untangling her hair . . . while she was wearing pajamas. Heat rose to her cheeks.

"Allison's quite infatuated by your pet."

"Lulu's fond of your daughter too. She's adorable—your daughter, that is."

"*Jah*, I agree. But I'm *nett* Allison's *mamm*. I'm Josephine, Ezra's sister."

Relief washed over Ellie for some reason. It wasn't as though she was interested in Ezra. She didn't believe in love at first sight, and she certainly wasn't so desperate for companionship that she would develop feelings after a few brief encounters. Yet something stirred deep within knowing the pregnant woman wasn't Ezra's wife. Maybe it was just relief knowing she hadn't destroyed this woman's floors and property.

"I've been helping *mei bruder* care for Allison since his wife passed away two years ago from cancer. It's been difficult for both of them."

"Yes, that would be hard." She'd lost her father at a young age and now had only vague memories of him.

"I'll be sure to let him know you returned his suspenders after he gets back from town. He took Allison to the *doktah*."

The child hadn't appeared ill earlier this morning, but then again, that could have been why Ezra seemed overly cautious. "I hope it isn't anything serious."

"I'm afraid it is," Josephine said softly. "We just don't know . . ." Her eyes glossed and she dabbed her fingers at the corner of her eye. "I should let Ezra tell you about her condition."

Ellie had met her new neighbors only yesterday, but tears were filling her eyes as well. The child was sweet, adorable, and poor Ezra had already lost his wife.

Josephine sniffled. "God is in control of everything."

"Yeah." *The good and the bad.*

Chapter 5

Christmas wreaths decorated the main street and blinking lights shone in the storefront windows, giving the small community a festive, old-fashioned feel. Ellie considered driving to Alpena, a larger town, but after weighing the cost of gas to travel forty miles round trip, she decided paying an extra three dollars for each gallon of paint at the mom-and-pop hardware store was worth it. And it supported a local business.

The bearded Amish man lifted his spectacles to view the measuring lines on the battered paint-dispensing machine. The last time Ellie bought paint at a home improvement store, the employee scanned a bar code into a computer and the machine automatically measured the quantity.

"What are you painting?" The man pushed down on the lever and yellow paint splatted into the open flat base can.

She smiled to be polite even though the man didn't look up from studying the book with the specific paint mixture formulas. "The yellow is for the kitchen, living room, and hallway. The green and blue are for the bedrooms."

"Sounds like a big project."

"I'm getting a house ready to sell." She glanced through the big display windows at her parked RV. She had cracked open the windows but still didn't like leaving Lulu alone too long. "Would it be okay if I come back to get the paint? I need to take my dog for a quick walk."

"That's fine," he said without looking up from his task.

"Should I pay before I go?"

He straightened his posture and peered over the rims of his glasses. "You're coming back, *jah*?"

She nodded.

"You can pay when it's ready." He returned his attention to the paint can.

Ellie took a few steps and stopped next to a long wooden bin of different-sized nails. "Would you know where a real estate office is?"

"Clyde Hall's place is two blocks west, then turn right onto Pine Street."

"Thank you." She left the hardware store and returned to the RV. Lulu greeted her at the door, tail wagging. "You want to go for a walk, girl?" She opened a cabinet and removed the nylon collar and lead. The anxious poodle hardly stood still long enough for Ellie to slip the collar on.

Lulu sniffed the buildings, the lampposts, the mailbox, and every crack in the wet sidewalk as if the melted snow had left some mysterious scent. She seemed to enjoy the brisk November air, but the strong wind gave Ellie reason to increase the pace.

Ellie followed the man's directions and turned onto Pine Street. Half a block later, she and Lulu reached their destination. Only she wasn't interested in the two-story white sideboard building with the neon real estate sign in the window, because the horse and buggy parked in front of the brick building next door caught her eye.

Ezra exited the office carrying Ellie in his arms. The child's arms were wrapped around her father's neck, her head against his chest. Allison looked frail. Ellie's heart filled with sadness remembering what Ezra's sister had said about his wife dying of cancer. *Oh, Lord, not the child too.* Ellie turned before he caught her gawking, but Lulu's bark threatened to give them away.

"Hush," she scolded. If she had barked at people or other dogs in the show ring, she'd have been dismissed from the event, but sometime since arriving in Posen, Lulu had picked up the bad habit.

Lulu barked again, then quieted herself to an anxious whimper as footsteps clomped toward them.

"Ellie?"

She turned and faced Ezra with a smile. "I'm not spying on you, really." She motioned to the building. "I was going into the real estate office."

His brow furrowed. "It's closed."

She redirected her attention to the darkened building. The sign on the door read: Gone Hunting (Will reopen after I get my ten-point buck). Ellie crinkled her nose. "You're right."

Allison's hand dropped from Ezra's neck to her side and Lulu nuzzled it. As Ezra shifted his daughter to his other arm, the sunlight filtered down through his straw hat, leaving a strangely familiar polka-dot pattern on his face. The earthy scent of straw and sweat washed over her, not from Ezra, but a distant memory from her childhood. Big calloused hands. Plain clothes. *Daed's* bushy beard that tickled her when he kissed her cheek. Almost breathless, she shook away the surfaced memories she hadn't realized were buried somewhere deep in her mind.

"Why do you need a real estate agent?" he asked, bringing her back to the present. "Are you planning to sell your *aenti's* place already?"

She nodded. "As soon as I get it spruced up."

"This isn't a *gut* time of the year to sell." His lips formed a straight line, a flicker of disappointment in his expression.

"Why is that?"

He shrugged. "*Nett* many folks want to move during the winter. Besides, next week is Thanksgiving, then Christmas, then the New Year. People don't want to move during the holidays."

It wasn't what she wanted to hear, but it made sense. Maybe she'd read more into his nonverbal expression. Ellie opened her mouth to ask how Allison was feeling, then held her question. If the child was sick enough to go to the doctor, she didn't need to press him about what was wrong. "So, how long does hunting season last?"

"Until the end of the month. But bow season starts back up in December."

"And I suppose"—she read the signature on the posted sign—"Mr. Hall also bow hunts."

He shrugged again. "If you need to leave town, I could close up your place for the winter so the pipes don't bust. You could put it on the market *kumm* spring."

"That's awfully kind of you," she said cautiously. He was too eager. From her limited understanding about the Amish, they tended to mind their own business and rarely initiated friendships with outsiders. Why would he offer to help her in this way?

He glanced upward. "Looks like it might snow again."

Ellie inspected the gray clouds moving across the sky. So much for a sunny fall day. The temperature would drop once the sun went behind the clouds.

Allison stirred in his arms. She lifted her head from his shoulder, rubbed her eyes, and yawned.

Lulu's ears perked and she wagged her tail, but thankfully refrained from barking.

Ezra hugged Allison a little tighter. "I need to get her home."

"Of course. I'm sorry. I, ah . . . and I have paint to pick up at the hardware store and grocery shopping to do."

He smiled. "It was nice running into you."

"You too." She tugged the leash and Lulu responded. Ellie took a few steps down the sidewalk, then glanced over her shoulder. His fatherly attentiveness was something to be admired, if only it hadn't triggered a longing for something she might never have—a family, a home without wheels, a sense of belonging. This plus an emptiness from growing up without a father.

Lulu sniffed Ellie's hand, her cold, wet nose jolting her back to reality, and cheerfulness filled her soul. "Yes, I know. Life isn't all bad. I have you, don't I, girl?" She briefly patted her canine friend, then picked up the pace. Surely the hardware man had her paint ready.

"Did you find Clyde?" the gentleman asked as she approached the counter.

She shook her head. "The sign on his door said he was hunting."

"Figured that might be the case." He handed her the paint chips she'd picked out.

The dab of yellow paint in the corner in no way matched. The canary yellow she'd chosen looked more like creamed corn, and the colors she'd selected for the bedrooms were washed-out shades of blue and green. Not what she'd wanted, but she couldn't refuse the order after the man's face lit up showing her the mixes.

"I also need paint tape, rollers, and a good trim brush."

"You got it. Now will this be cash or credit?" He placed the requested supplies on the counter.

"Credit." She removed her Visa card from her wallet.

"Sorry, miss, but I don't take plastic cards. The company charges me every time a customer makes a purchase with one of those things." He hefted a thick leather book from under the counter and thunked it down. "I guess I'm what the *Englischers* might call old school."

"You don't know me, yet you're willing to extend credit?"

"You're driving that RV parked out front so I figured you're Bonnie Whetstone's kin." As if ready for her next question, he added, "News travels fast."

"I guess it does. I only arrived yesterday."

He flipped through the pages, seemingly disinterested in her response.

"I'm her niece." She doubted he was listening.

He jotted something in the book, then turned it around for her to view. "I put your items under your *aenti's* name. Some people pay on the first of the month, some at the end, and others pay off their balance after harvest. I'll leave that up to you." He extended the pen.

Perhaps the town had a nearby ATM machine.

"Is there a problem?"

"My *aenti's* deceased."

"I know. We all miss her. Your father was a *gut* man too." He smiled. "So you have two family members' *gut* names vouching for you."

She swallowed hard. "You knew my father?"

"Best master carpenter in northern Michigan, though he'd never admit it. He built many of the houses and barns around here."

"I didn't know that." She signed the page next to the total, then handed back the pen. "Could you tell me which houses? I'd love to drive by them and take a look, even if it's from the road."

He held up one finger. "Wait here." He disappeared into a back room and returned a few moments later carrying a different leather-bound book. "I retrieved this from the basement." He handed her the ledger. "If I remember correctly, your father had his account separated according to the job he was working on.

Some of the homeowner names have changed, but the addresses didn't."

"May I borrow this?" Her voice quivered.

"You can have it."

"Thank you so much." Over the years, she hadn't garnered much information about her father from her mother, and now she held a piece of her father's past. She thanked the gentleman again, then loaded the paint supplies into the RV and headed home, excited about what bits of information she'd glean.

Chapter 6

The drowsy side effects of the antiseizure medicine had finally worn off, and Allison slowly opened her eyes.

Ezra rested his hand on his daughter's shoulder. "How are you feeling, honey?"

She started, glanced at him, then scanned the sitting room as if unaware of her surroundings. "Where's Lulu?"

At least she remembered the dog. Ezra smiled. "Lulu went home, sweetie. Are you hungry?"

"*Ish geh*," she insisted, sitting up.

Josephine waddled into the room. "She's awake? How is she feeling?"

"*Ish geh*," Allison repeated.

His sister's brows lifted. "Where does she want to go?"

"To see that dog next door." His daughter hadn't been herself since they'd become neighbors with the animal.

"*Mei hund*." Allison tapped her chest. "Mine."

He frowned at his daughter. "She's confused," he explained to Josephine.

"You mentioned the dog and neighbor earlier. Her name's Ellie, right?"

He groaned under his breath. He recognized a fishing-for-information expedition when he heard one. Had Josephine arrived this morning as expected, she would have had the pleasure of meeting Ellie—in her pajamas—at his house. Some things did work together for good. Josephine had a way of unintentionally stirring up a hive, and had she been here, gossip would already be abuzz throughout the district.

"The dog's name is Lulu. And Allison doesn't need to be around the animal—or the *Englischer*."

Allison cried, and when he tried to console her, she turned hysterical. Had she not been sick, he would have disciplined her after such an outburst, but he recognized her tantrum was caused by the medicine. After she'd been weaned off her medicine earlier in the year and seizure-free for months, the doctor had restarted the treatment.

"I think you should make an exception," Josephine said. "Especially if that dog has a calming effect on her."

Despite his better judgment, he had to agree. The doctor wanted her to remain calm, and if being with the dog helped, he didn't have much choice. "Okay." He released a defeated sigh. "I'll take you to see the dog. But only for a few minutes." He turned to his sister. "Do you want to ride along and meet Bonnie's niece?"

"You need a chaperone?"

"*Nay*." He eyed her hard. "I just thought you might want to meet . . . the *Englischer*."

"I already did." She turned toward the kitchen. "Ellie stopped by to return your suspenders."

Ezra motioned to his daughter. "Let's get your coat and boots on," he said in Pennsylvania *Deitsch*.

At times like this he was relieved that his daughter knew only a few Englisch words, because what he had to say to his sister wasn't something her little ears should hear. He stormed into the kitchen. "Why are you trying to make something of loaning my suspenders to Ellie? She needed a way to control her animal. *Mei* neighbor is *Englisch*—enough said."

Josephine wrung out a rag in the sink, then turned to face him. "Bonnie was devoted to petitioning God in prayer for people, and she taught me the importance of making *mei* requests known to God as well. I shared with her how much I wanted to have a *boppli*, and how for the longest time I feared I couldn't conceive. Bonnie prayed with me. She added *mei* name to her prayer journal and kept praying too." His sister patted her belly with a need-I-say-more glow on her face.

His sister's pregnancy hormones had scrambled her brain. "What does all that have to do with Ellie?"

"Bonnie prayed for years for Ellie to *kumm* home."

"And she's here—to sell the farm."

Josephine's shoulders dropped and she frowned for an instant. Then she straightened with purpose. "I'm picking up where Bonnie left off. She was praying *nett* only for Ellie to *kumm* home, but for her to find our Amish way—her way. And . . . I'm praying for you."

Ezra lifted his hands in surrender. "I'm *nett* going to stop you from praying. Just don't include me in connection with the *Englischer* in those prayers."

Once Ellie unloaded the groceries and put them away, she sat down with the ledger and flipped to the first page. Handwritten under the heading "Subject" was "House (1,200 square feet), Minno Zook, 8460 Sunset Ridge." The date, quantity, and itemized description of lumber and building supplies took up the columns. The information meant nothing to Ellie, until she came to the signature at the bottom. She stared at her father's name. David Whetstone. She touched the signature. Her father's hand had written the words. A second glance at the date showed the entry had been made thirty years earlier, just before she was born. She read more entries, then decided to copy the names and addresses onto a sheet of paper so she wouldn't have to lug the old book on her travels and chance something happening to it.

Lulu nudged Ellie's elbow as she did when she needed to go outside. They both could use a break. Besides, she should try to build another fire in the wood stove so they could sleep inside the house instead of the RV tonight. She needed to conserve the RV's generator. In a few days, the prerecorded National Dog Show would air after Macy's Thanksgiving Day Parade. She wanted to watch Lulu's performance and also study the competition for Westminster in February.

Ellie slipped on her boots and coat, then took Lulu outside. She removed her phone from her coat pocket and checked the recent call log. Nothing. Not even a text.

She and Lulu checked out the two-stall barn. The stalls were clean, the grain bins and overhead loft empty. As a girl, she had dreamed of owning a horse, but her mother's allergies to horsehair forbade that possibility. Ellie was grateful her mother let her have a dog. Otherwise, life would have been lonelier moving around a lot. In a way, her mother's multiple marriages, and her not being around much, had prepared Ellie for life on the dog show circuit.

Jangling harness equipment and horse hooves drew Ellie's attention even before she spotted the buggy pulling into the yard. She whistled for Lulu, who had dropped a stick to bark at the visitors. Lulu sat wagging her tail. The chestnut horse tossed its head as Ezra brought it to a stop. Ellie jogged across the lawn and took hold of Lulu's collar.

Ezra climbed out, then reached inside for his daughter.

"Hello, neighbor," Ellie said.

"*Hiya.*" He followed up his greeting with a short nod.

"Lulu!" Allison tapped her father's shoulder. "Please?"

Ezra's gaze bounced from Ellie to Lulu, then back to Ellie.

"You can set her down. Allison will be okay." Didn't he see Lulu's tail wagging? She was excited to have a playmate.

After hesitating briefly, Ezra lowered the child to the ground. "She's been asking to play with your dog." He placed his hand on the girl's shoulder as she gave Lulu a hug. "Don't squeeze the *hund's* neck."

Lulu sat for a moment, then pulled back and ran to fetch the stick. Returning, she dropped the stick at Allison's feet.

When the child didn't seem to know what to do, Ellie reached down and picked it up, then heaved it across the yard toward what looked like her *aenti's* shriveled-up garden, Lulu streaking after it. Allison's eyes lit up. When Lulu came back with the stick, Allison took over the game.

Ezra studied the house. "The windows are open."

"Airing it out." She wasn't about to tell him how smoke had forced them to evacuate.

"Weren't you *kalt* last *nacht*?"

She shook her head. "Snug as a bug."

He shifted his eyes to her, then grinned. "Hard to breathe when the *haus* fills with smoke, *jah*?"

Ellie dug the toe of her boot into the snow, then sheepishly glanced up and cracked a smile. "Yep."

He reached into his buggy, removed a loaf of bread wrapped in cellophane, and handed it to her. "A peace offering, so to speak."

"That's really nice, thank you." *Wow, I can't believe he bakes.* "Wait, why are you bringing me a peace offering when it was my dog that trespassed onto your property?"

"And I was nice enough to untangle your hair too," he added.

"Exactly. What's the catch?"

"*Nay* catch. Just trying to be neighborly." He turned his attention to his daughter playing tug-of-war with Lulu for the stick. "Allison, *kumm* with me. I need to show Ms. Whetstone how to build a fire."

Ellie cleared her throat, determined to defend her campfire building abilities once she had his attention, but the moment his tawny eyes peered over at her, her throat dried. Ellie tapped her neck. "I think I need a drink of water."

"Hope you're *nett* getting sick."

"It's just a tickle." *Ask about Allison.* Ellie followed the child and Lulu with her gaze as they ran in circles in the driveway, laughing. The girl didn't appear sick. Ellie opened her mouth to ask Ezra, but he'd turned his attention on his daughter.

"Allison," Ezra called, and this time both his daughter and Lulu responded.

Ellie smiled. Lulu had found a friend in Allison and vice versa. She opened the door, but Ezra had placed a hand on Allison's shoulder and stopped her from going inside.

"Ask Ms. Whetstone if the dog is allowed indoors."

"It's fine, sweetie," Ellie said, explaining further for Ezra's benefit. "Lulu goes everywhere I do."

Ezra's lips formed a thin line, probably his attempt not to vocalize his ideas about indoor animals.

Once inside, Ellie set the bread on the counter as Lulu and Allison headed into the sitting room, and Ezra zoomed in on the kitchen stove.

"No wonder you smoked up the place. The damper needs to be open when you're starting the fire so the maximum amount of airflow generates flames." He turned the handle on the stovepipe into the vertical position, then knelt beside the stove, opened the firebox, and frowned. "Too much paper creates creosote buildup and can start a fire."

Which is the goal. She pressed a smile.

"A chimney fire isn't *gut*. The roof could easily catch fire too."

She'd made plenty of campfires, but that didn't require knowing anything about damper directions or creosote buildup. Ellie leaned over his shoulder and peered inside the firebox. She needed to know for future reference what creosote looked like.

He turned slightly and must have glimpsed her in his peripheral vision because he jolted. His brow furrowed when she didn't immediately move.

Ellie backed up a tad, and his expression relaxed.

He reached for the small flat-edged shovel and the sooty black bucket next to the woodbox. Ezra scooped several shovelfuls of ashes into the bucket, powdery black soot rising. "Cleaning out the ashes is important too." Next he wiggled out the ash pan from the bottom of the stove.

Ellie shot over to get the door for him, but instead of going straight outside, he stopped at the living room entrance as little-girl giggles carried into the kitchen.

Ellie came up beside Ezra and leaned her shoulder on the wood framing the entry. Allison's arms were around the dog's neck and Lulu was lathering her ear with kisses. Until Ellie saw them playing together, she would have thought Lulu loved being in the show ring more than anything. A twinge of guilt snaked through Ellie. Three-year-old dogs like Lulu were meant to play with little girls like Allison. Ellie gave Ezra a sidelong glance and, noticing his pinched expression, found herself wishing she could read his mind.

He shook his head as if shaking away deep thoughts and turned. "Would you mind getting the door for me?"

Ellie opened the door, then followed him with her gaze as he hiked across the snow-covered lawn over to what looked like her *aenti's* shriveled garden. The black ashes scattered in the wind. Ezra turned away coughing. Inhaling the soot probably dried his throat. She went to the sink and filled a glass with water.

Boots stomped on the porch before the door opened, bringing in a gust of cold air. He returned the ash pan to its place at the bottom of the stove. "You'll need to empty this every two or three days."

Ellie offered him the glass of water. "I heard you coughing."

"*Danki*—thank you." He wiped his dirty hands on the sides of his pants, then took the glass with a polite smile.

"Was that my *aenti's* old garden you dumped the ashes in?"

He nodded.

"I know burning embers shouldn't be tossed close to the house, but those ashes were cold. Is there some reason you emptied the pan in the garden?"

"Hardwood ashes are a good source of calcium and potassium that plants need to thrive. I'm *nett* sure if you plan to put in a garden next spring, but the ashes will help. Just don't dump them in the same spot. Spread them out."

Ellie nodded, although at the moment, staying to plant a garden in the spring seemed highly unlikely. She wasn't sure she would make it through the week, let alone the winter.

Ezra took another drink of water, then set the glass on the counter. He wadded a piece of newspaper and placed it and a few pieces of kindling in the firebox. "You need to start with kindling. Thin, dry slabs."

Ellie nodded stiffly. "Got it."

He lit a match and touched it to the edge of the paper, then blew. Once flames engulfed the bark of the wood, he closed the cast-iron door. "I try to teepee the first few slabs, then add larger logs later."

Exactly how she built a campfire. Ellie motioned to the metal handle he'd turned earlier. "Is this the position I should leave the damper in?"

"Just to get the fire going. Turning the handle on the flue, you'll either increase or decrease the amount of airflow into the firebox. Leaving it open helps to get the fire going, but you'll burn wood much faster and also lose heat. Most of the time, you'll adjust it to be about one-fourth open." He demonstrated. "Then you'll close it more before going to bed or before leaving the house for an extended period. The weather isn't so bad *nau*, but *kumm* winter the pipes might freeze, even break, if you don't have a fire going at all times."

"I'll keep that in mind." Another reason to sell. Leaving in February for the Westminster Championship in New York would pose a problem. She certainly didn't want to deal with busted pipes in the coldest month of the winter.

He lifted his brows. "Have you ever cooked on a wood stove?"

On the road most of the year, she tended to heat things up in the microwave or use her George Foreman to grill. "I've done some campfire cooking." Hot dogs and beans. S'mores.

"The stovetop isn't too hard to figure out. If something is boiling or frying too fast, you can move the pan away from the hot spots. The oven takes a little getting used to," he said with a shrug. "Sometimes things end up unevenly baked."

"Sounds like a good excuse if something doesn't turn out."

He smiled. "I've used that reason one or two times."

"It looks like you've mastered the oven to me," she said, motioning to the loaf of bread on the counter.

"That was *mei* sister's doing. She baked it and sent it with me."

Ellie lifted her brows. "As a peace offering?"

"I said 'so to speak,'" he clarified. "*Mei* sister insisted I bring the loaf, and I can't very well wage war on her. She watches Allison for me." He turned his ear toward the quiet living room, then crossed the room and poked his head around the wall.

Ellie came up beside him and smiled at his little girl curled up with Lulu on the floor. It was nice to have her young neighbor relate to something she'd shared. "Looks like they've worn each other out."

"I suppose you think I'm an overly protective father."

"Understandably so." Ellie wanted to believe her father would have been as protective had he lived long enough to form lasting memories with her. Noticing Ezra's brows lift, she explained, "I'm sure with Allison's health problems you have to watch her closely."

"Josephine told you about *mei* daughter's seizures." He snorted.

"When I stopped to return the suspenders, she mentioned you'd taken Allison to the doctor." *Seizures. How sad.* No wonder he kept a close eye on her.

He motioned to the wood stove in the corner of the living room. "Would you like me to start a fire before we leave?"

"It works the same for the most part, right?"

He nodded.

"Then, thank you, but I'm sure I'll manage." She'd discovered self-reliance the hard way and wasn't one to easily depend on others. Besides, he'd taught her the basic operation. She'd managed harder things on the road.

His gaze traveled around the room in a quiet, reflective manner.

"Did you know my *aenti* very well?"

"Bonnie was like family." His jaw muscles twitched, then his right shoulder.

That stung. It didn't take a genius to figure out what had triggered his muscle tic—not only was Ellie not Amish, but she was the sole heir. "I was surprised when I found out I had inherited her farm."

"It shouldn't surprise you." He smoothed out his tone. "You're a Whetstone. You're Bonnie's only living relative."

Had her father not died, she would have grown up in the

Plain community and had the chance to know her *aenti*. But maybe Ezra could answer a question that had been bugging her.

"Do you know what my *aenti* died from?"

He looked her directly in the eye. "A broken heart."

Chapter 7

Ellie spent half the night scouring her father's charge records in the ledger by lamplight, making sure she had written down each customer's name and address. The other half of the night she spent tossing in bed. Between Ezra's comment about *Aenti* dying of a broken heart, the old house creaking, and the nearby tree branches scratching against the window, she wrestled with sleep most of the night. In time she might get used to the late-night noises, but how could she shake the guilt for not attempting to visit her *aenti* before her death? Ellie found comfort knowing God had blessed her *aenti* with a good neighbor. Ezra was a kind man. Hopefully in time she'd delete the image of his judgmental scowl from her mind. Then again, perhaps his moodiness had something to do with his daughter's seizures. He'd certainly closed that conversation quickly.

Ellie checked the stove first thing. The large pieces of oak had burned down to a glowing bed of embers. After adding another log, she splattered a little water on the stovetop, then set the kettle over the area that sizzled the most. Ezra had been right about moving the pan on or away from hot spots to cook. She fried eggs for herself and Lulu in no time.

Once the breakfast dishes were washed and laid out to dry, she and Lulu headed out to look for houses. Her GPS took them in circles. The first time she passed Ezra's place he was chopping wood, the next time, standing at the mailbox. This time, she couldn't look.

Focused on the fence line, she pressed the gas pedal. After burning half a tank of gas, she turned off the GPS and headed to town to buy a map—what she should have done from the start since the signal on her phone kept dropping and Google Maps wouldn't reboot.

The country market offered dry goods and household items and had a nice selection of potatoes, apples, and squash, but it had only one map of the area and it was a trail guide. The teenaged clerk wasn't familiar with the roads, which wasn't a surprise. She hardly looked up from her cell phone to glance at the list of addresses. Ellie paid for the trail map and a few plastic containers she'd use to pack up her *aenti's* things.

Back in the RV, Ellie studied the map. Hiking trail routes, campground information, animals to see along the way, but nothing about the country roads in the area. Typing *Narrow Pines* into the search engine on her phone brought up nothing. She tried another address, but it, too, yielded no results. She hadn't expected to find all the locations. Several offered no address but instead "*Daadihaus* for E. Yoder," or "*Haus* addition for J. Miller." Still, she should be able to find at least one road. One house that her father had built.

Driving down a back road, she came to a roadside stand. The young Amish women manning the fruit and vegetable stand attempted to help. "Turn at the old mill and follow the road until you reach Kings' . . ." The rest of the directions were a mix of Pennsylvania *Deitsch* and English. Ellie paid for some apples and thanked the women. She attempted to follow the directions but soon found herself driving around in circles again.

Disappointed at not locating any of the houses, Ellie headed home. Maybe tomorrow she'd check the library for local maps, assuming there was a library within fifty miles. Then again, maybe she should focus on getting the house ready to sell. Preoccupied with thoughts of moving furniture in order to paint and packing up her *aenti's* things, she didn't think much about the snow melting until the back tire sank into a patch of soft ground at the front of the pasture. Ellie shifted into reverse, but doing so caused the tires to spin and dig deeper into the ground. After multiple attempts, she resigned her efforts.

"I guess we're walking, Lulu." She grabbed her purse. Her sneaker sank into the soft ground and coldness seeped inside. Following the cow path, Ellie hiked up the small incline, keeping a watchful eye out for the bull. Lulu ran ahead, then darted into the woods at the edge of the pasture.

"Lulu, come." Her authoritative tone didn't work, so she called again in a playful voice. Still, Lulu was nowhere in sight. Ellie groaned under her breath. *Don't let me find you bothering Ezra. He already thinks I have no control of you.*

Lulu barked ferociously.

Ellie cut through the woods, pushing aside branches as she made her way in the direction of Lulu's barking. The dog was growling and clawing at a hollowed-out fallen log. Afraid she'd cornered an innocent bunny, Ellie picked up her pace. She spotted the critter Lulu was after too late. The skunk lifted its tail to Lulu, stopping the dog in her tracks, then scurried away. The scent carried in the breeze, the stench unrelenting. For a moment, Ellie thought she might have been hit.

Lulu lay down and rolled. She rubbed her eyes with her paws and whimpered.

Now Ellie not only had to watch out for bulls, but skunks. "I hope you learned your lesson," she told Lulu as they headed home. Lulu plodded along next to Ellie, no longer resembling the pampered show dog that she was. Burs matted her beautiful apricot coat and her furry pom-poms were covered in mud.

Ellie directed Lulu straight to the bathroom. She wasn't used to cold baths, but there wasn't much Ellie could do about the Amish house not having hot water. As she lathered Lulu with shampoo, someone knocked on the back door.

Chapter 8

Ezra knocked on Ellie's back door and waited. He scanned the clapboard siding, the paint peeling on the porch banister, then glanced at the open kitchen window and shook his head. Apparently the *Englischer* had a stubborn streak and hadn't followed his instructions for operating the wood stove.

He knocked again, waited a half second, then turned to leave. Perhaps he'd worried about nothing. Still, the dog's bark had sounded as if the animal was about to attack. He'd never had problems in the past with hunters trespassing, but he wasn't one to not at least check things out. Especially with the property joining state land and Ellie living in the woods alone. After all, she was Bonnie's niece.

The door opened, and he turned to find Ellie standing in the entry, shirtsleeves rolled up to her elbows, arms covered in suds, and eyes red-rimmed. She craned to look around him. "Where's Allison?"

"She's with *mei* sister."

Ellie invited him inside.

"I didn't mean to disturb you," he said, stomping his boots before entering. "I heard your dog barking and I thought something might be wrong." As he passed her, he caught a whiff of what probably had caused her eyes to water and smiled. "Messed with a skunk, did you?"

"Lulu agitated one." She sniffed her shirtsleeve and wrinkled her nose. "I don't know if I'm smelling me or Lulu."

"Probably both."

She drew back as if offended.

"Skunk spray is incredibly accurate even at ten feet. God's armor of protection." Except against dogs, who were stupid when it came to tangling with wild animals. "I noticed your vehicle in the pasture."

"It's stuck."

"The ground is . . ."

Lulu entered the kitchen, soaking wet and leaving a paw puddle trail. She came in between them and shook, showering them both with her wet dog–skunk scent.

"Lulu!" Ellie pointed to the other room. "I told you to stay." She turned her attention back to him. "I'm sorry. I hope she didn't get you wet."

"It's *nett* a big deal." Half the time he smelled like a horse.

"I considered washing her outside, but I couldn't risk her getting sick." She rolled her eyes. "She's not happy about being bathed in cold water. I was in the process of shampooing her for the third time when you knocked."

"I'm sorry I interrupted you."

"That's okay. I'm not going to get the stink out."

"You need to use tomatoes."

"Tomatoes?" Her nose wrinkled again.

Cute. He glanced away, focusing instead on the dog rolling on the braided rug in front of the sink. *Not so cute.* Dogs belonged outside. Wet or dry.

"I didn't buy tomatoes when I stopped at the grocery store earlier. Does anything else work?"

He shrugged. "*Nett* that I know of. There's something about the acidity that cuts the odor."

She sighed. "It's not likely I'll get back into town with my RV stuck," she muttered under her breath, then twisted her lips as if pondering other possibilities.

"If you're worried about your vehicle . . ." *Don't commit. You're too involved.* "I'll see what I can do to get it out of the mud."

"You've already helped me with the stove. I don't want to impose anymore."

"You're *nett*." He held her gaze a half second, then shifted his attention to the curtains flapping in the cold breeze. "Having problems with the wood stove again?"

She slapped her fisted hands on her hips. "I'll have you know, I built a roaring fire, turned that damper just how you showed me, and—"

"You smoked up the place," he said, glancing back at the curtains. "The open window gave it away."

Ellie dropped her arms to her sides. "I fed the stove too much wood, and it got roasting hot in here."

Ezra chuckled. There was something about this quirky woman. *She's charming, sweet, cares about animals* . . . He sobered. It didn't matter how easy she was to be around or how he hadn't felt this alive in some time. The woman was *Englisch*. He'd be a fool to lose track of that fact.

She moved over to the window, closed and latched it, then gazed outside. "You still think it's going to snow tonight?"

"Probably." He was tempted to join her at the window and view the world from her eyes, but he kept his feet planted on the rug in front of the door.

She pivoted around. "Does paint freeze?"

"*Jah*. Why?"

"I have to remember to take the cans out of the RV, which I bought earlier to spruce up the place."

He furrowed his brow. "What's wrong with the way it looks now?"

"It's . . ." Her gaze traveled over the walls, the ceiling, then back to him. "It's plain."

He nodded. "*Jah*, of course it is."

"Don't you think a little splash of color would brighten up the room? Make it a bit cheerier?"

She didn't appear to be someone who needed cheering up. "Fancy wall colors will do that?" He huffed.

She eyed him with a slight tilt of her head. "Did I say something wrong?"

Ezra needed to remind himself *again*, she wasn't Amish. She certainly didn't have to conform to the rules of the *Ordnung*. "It's your place *nau*. It shouldn't matter what anyone else thinks. But since you asked, I don't see anything wrong with *plain* white walls."

"Oh." Her mouth dropped open and eyes grew large. "Amish are plain people. I didn't put that together until just now. I'm sorry. I didn't mean to offend you."

"You didn't." He walked over to the woodbox and peered inside. "You need more wood."

"I knew I forgot something on my list. I meant to buy firewood while I was out today."

"I thought you were just circling the neighborhood."

Her cheeks turned a rosy glow. "I didn't think you saw me."

"All four times." Watching a sheepish smile light her face, he realized he'd said too much. He cleared his throat. "Were you lost?"

"I was looking for country roads that probably don't exist." She sighed. "I don't suppose this place has a backup furnace?"

He shook his head.

Frown lines webbed her forehead, creasing her smooth, silky skin with lines of worry and defeat.

"I'll check the woodshed." He wasn't sure how much wood Bonnie had left over from last winter. Ezra paused at the door. "By the way, anytime you want to stop for directions, I can point you back to the cow path."

Ellie stood in front of the kitchen window and followed Ezra out to the woodshed with her gaze. He probably thought she was a damsel in distress, unable to take care of herself. He'd accused her of being in a pickle when she'd gotten tangled in the barbed-wire fence. But she wasn't as needy as he thought . . . Was she? Ellie chewed the inside of her cheek. Sure, the RV was buried in mud, she was in the middle of nowhere without a cell signal, which meant she couldn't call a tow truck . . . Yep, she might as well be canned in a pickle jar; she was stuck.

Ezra carried a bundle of wood across the yard.

Ellie hurried to open the door.

"This is it." He lowered the thick slabs into the woodbox. "It'll get you through the *nacht* and most of tomorrow."

She needed to sell. Maybe the real estate agent had shot his buck and was back to work. Something told her he wouldn't reopen until after Thanksgiving. Less than a week to box this place up and paint.

"Don't fret about wood," he said. "I have plenty."

"I'll be happy to buy it from you."

"We'll talk about it later. But as for your vehicle," he said with a sigh, "I don't think there's enough daylight to get it out today."

"That's okay. Whenever you get a chance."

"So you don't plan on driving in any more circles today?"

She liked his sense of humor. "Nope. I have plenty to do here."

Ezra motioned to the window. "I'd keep it closed. The temperature has already dropped." He reached for the door handle. "I think your paint should be okay tonight, but I'll bring it in if you'd like."

"No, that isn't necessary. I'll get it later." He'd already done so much. She couldn't let him think she was incapable of doing anything on her own. "But thank you, for everything. I really appreciate it."

"Just trying to be neighborly," he said, opening the door.

Neighborly. Ezra was much friendlier than she'd expected. Perhaps she'd had the wrong impression of the Amish all these years. Her mother had led her to believe Ellie wouldn't be welcome in the community, that the Amish would actually turn their backs to her if they knew who she was. Obviously her mother had been wrong—just as she'd been wrong about her second and third marriages.

Ellie spotted Lulu rolling on the braided rug and groaned. Now that, too, would smell skunky. She'd have to replace the rugs for sure. Ellie clicked her fingers and Lulu followed her into the other room, though her canine friend offered her paw when she figured out Ellie wanted her to get back into the tub.

A bottle of shampoo later, Lulu didn't smell much better. Ellie toweled her off anyway. It was late, Ellie's stomach was growling, and one more bath wouldn't make a difference. Unless it was her own—and she wasn't about to take a cold bath tonight.

She fed the fire, then Lulu, then herself. The bowl of chicken noodle soup hit the spot. After putting Lulu outside one more time, she settled into bed with a cup of herbal tea. It seemed odd to sleep in *Aenti's* bedroom. Last night she'd slept in the guest bedroom, but the howling wind had pushed the branches of a nearby tree against the window and kept her awake most of the night.

Ellie opened the nightstand drawer. She felt like a snoop, but things needed to be boxed up eventually. The top drawer held a Bible. Ellie lifted the Bible from the drawer and flipped through the gilded pages. Notes were scrawled along some of the margins and other pages were marked with slips of paper. Ellie's own Bible had similar markings. She also underlined Scriptures for future reference, and she, too, had jotted notes in the margins when a particular passage had spoken to her. Ellie closed her eyes.

"Oh, Lord, why did my mother keep me from knowing *Aenti* Bonnie? I should have made a point to find my father's relatives on my own. Now she's gone. I'll never know her."

Ellie read a few of the marked passages, then closed the Bible and returned it to its spot. Curiosity niggling her, she opened the next drawer and found a leather journal. As she opened the flap, a handwritten note slipped out.

To my niece Ellie,

May you discover a wealth of faith and the power of God within these pages. Prayer is a powerful tool. Not everything you ask will be answered immediately, but know God is listening. His Word is without void. So place this passage from Philippians in your heart: "In every situation, by prayer and petition, with thanksgiving, present your requests to God."

I hope you'll see by these entries how meaningful God has been in my life.

Love you, child.
Aenti Bonnie

Ellie read the note again, blinking to clear the sting from her eyes. She turned to the title page: "My Prayers, Petitions, and Praises."

Chapter 9

I go see Lulu?" His daughter's bright eyes pleaded with him first thing the next morning.

Ezra pointed to Allison's breakfast plate. "Eat your eggs." This wasn't the time to go see the dog. He intended to ask the men to help get Ellie's vehicle out of the mud, but he'd planned on Josephine watching Allison.

His sister's buggy pulled into the drive. She tied the horse to the post, then waddled to the house holding her belly. Stepping inside, Josephine removed her cloak. Her face was paler than usual. "Sorry I'm late. *Mei doktah* appointment ran longer than expected."

Allison sprang up from the table and greeted her *aenti* with a big hug, something that filled his heart with gratitude every time he watched their interactions.

"All things work together for good to them that love God . . ." Not always how Ezra wanted, but for the good nonetheless. At least his daughter had a motherly figure in her life.

Allison tugged on Josephine's hand. "Do you want to see *mei* Lulu?"

"Allison, what did I tell you?" He needed to put an end to her possessiveness. The dog wasn't hers.

Her bottom lip puckered. "Eat *mei* eggs."

"That's right." He motioned to her place at the table, and she crawled up on the chair and picked up her fork.

Josephine plopped down on a chair opposite Allison's. "She really loves that dog, doesn't she?"

"It's unhealthy," he grumbled.

Josephine placed her hand on her belly and winced.

His sister had complained of more long-lasting queasiness than Charlotte had when she was pregnant with Allison. But this was something more. Charlotte was never this pale. "Are you feeling okay?"

She smiled. "I'm having twins!"

"That's *wunderbaar* news. Matthew must be excited."

She nodded. "He is."

"But?" He knew his sister too well. She was holding something back.

"It shouldn't be a problem," she said. "I'm *nett* supposed to lift heavy objects, but it'll be fine."

"Unless Allison has a medical emergency and I'm *nett* here to take her into town."

"We're going to pray that she doesn't have more seizures."

He forced a smile and pushed back the racing thoughts about finding another helper for around the house. He had furniture orders yet to complete before Christmas. He turned, went to the cabinet, and removed a glass. His sister had always been good at reading his expression, and he certainly didn't want her probing the selfish thoughts consuming his mind. He filled the glass with water and took a drink. Things would work out—they had to.

"I know what you're thinking," she said. "But please don't worry about your orders. You'll get them done before Christmas. We have plenty of women in our district. If need be, I'll find someone to help." She glanced at Allison and winked. "We'll pray about the matter."

Allison nodded, then lowered her fork. "*Ich geh sehe mei* Lulu *nau*."

"Finish your milk," he said.

"Ezra, why don't you head to the workshop? Allison and I will *reddy-up* the dishes," Josephine said, winking again at Allison.

He glanced down at his smiling daughter, then over to his sister. Ezra opened the bottom cabinet door and removed four quart-sized jars of stewed tomatoes and set them on the counter. "Take these to Ellie when you go." Without waiting for her to ask questions, he went to the door, snatched his hat and coat off the hook, then headed outside to his shop.

Except for responding to Lulu's occasional insistence on going outside, Ellie had been glued to the journal all morning. Reading entries dated over five years ago, she learned a lot about her *aenti*. She was a woman of great faith, and according to the praise report section, many of her prayers were answered. Ellie found herself enthralled by the lives of people she didn't even know. She was fascinated by how her *aenti* involved God in every aspect of her life, including praying about the weather and her garden.

She flipped to the next entry dated May 10, 2012.

> Another beautiful day, Lord. Fifty-six degrees. Trusting we won't have another hard freeze, I planted beans, cabbage, carrots, and beets today. It felt good to work outside and not sink to my ankles in mud, but sometimes I wonder why I should put in such a large garden when I live alone. But, Lord, I trust You will find a purpose for all these vegetables once they are ready to harvest.
>
> Praising You for: healing Alice's sprained ankle, little Jacob's sore throat . . .
>
> Special request: I'm asking for wisdom, Lord. Ezra

and Charlotte have rented the little house in the woods for over a year now, and I'm considering changing houses with them. They are expecting a baby soon and will need more—

Lulu charged at the door, barking. Focused on reading about Ezra, Ellie hadn't heard anyone knock. She pushed aside the curtain and spotted several buggies pulling into the yard. Ellie tucked the journal into the drawer and hurried out to the kitchen to calm Lulu.

"Lulu, sit." Ellie waited for the dog to obey the command before opening the door to the group of Plain-dressed women.

Little Allison squeezed through the crowd. "*Hiya*," she said to Ellie, then shifted her attention to Lulu.

"Lulu doesn't smell good," Ellie said, pinching her nose. "She didn't know not to tangle with a skunk."

"That must be why Ezra sent you these." Josephine handed Ellie a basket of quart jars filled with stewed tomatoes.

"Oh my," Ellie said, clasping her hand over her mouth. One would think she'd been given a dozen roses the way she responded. "He said tomatoes would neutralize the odor, but I didn't expect . . ." Feeling the weight of the women's stares, she blushed. "How unthoughtful I am. Please, come inside and get out of the cold," she said, half expecting a polite decline.

A short, elderly woman surprised Ellie by stepping forward. "I'm Alice Zook. Your *aenti* Bonnie was a dear friend of mine."

"It's nice to meet you, Alice." Ellie recalled the name from the journal. Alice was the bishop's wife, the woman who had sprained her ankle, and a kind soul according to her *aenti*.

As Alice entered the house, another woman introduced herself. "I'm Noreen King."

"And I'm Patty King." She elbowed the other King. "Noreen and I are sisters-in-law. We're very sorry for your loss. Bonnie was a *wunderbaar* friend."

"Thank you, and it's so nice to meet both of you." Guilt pricked Ellie's conscience. Her knowledge of her *aenti* was limited to the journal, her memories of *Aenti* as vague as the ones she held of her father.

Ezra's sister Josephine greeted her next with a warm smile. "It's nice to see you again, Ellie."

"You too," she replied, then turned to the group. "Would any of you like a cup of coffee?" Too bad she didn't have a spice cake or some cookies to offer the women. Next time she went into town she'd be sure to buy snacks.

Alice smiled. "*Kaffi* sounds *gut* if it isn't much trouble."

"It's no trouble at all." Ellie filled the kettle with water, then placed it on the stove.

Allison and Lulu disappeared into the living room, Josephine objecting as she followed them. "You need to ask permission first," Ezra's sister insisted.

Allison returned to the kitchen, her hands folded in front of her and her lips pouty. "*Kann ich spiele mit* Lulu*?*"

Ellie glanced questioningly at Josephine.

"She's asking to play with your *hund*—dog," she explained.

"Absolutely—as long as it's okay with your *aenti*." Ellie turned and grabbed a log from the woodbox, then placed it on the bed of embers.

"You seem to know your way around a cookstove," Alice said.

"The first time I made a fire, I smoked the house up. Then Ezra gave me a quick lesson." When she turned away from the sink, a committee of blank faces stared at her.

"I almost forgot," Josephine said, breaking the tension. "Ezra needs the keys to your vehicle. The men are teaming up the horses to pull it out of the mud."

"He's in the field?" Ellie rummaged through her purse and produced the keys.

"You'd better take them. I think he wants you to start the engine," Josephine said.

Ellie dashed out the door without taking time to put on her coat. She jogged down the driveway and crossed the bridge, her gaze roaming the pasture for the bull. Not seeing the beast, she approached the crowd gathered around her RV. She'd never seen so many men in straw hats. With all the men wearing similar blue or white shirts and suspenders, finding Ezra in the mix wasn't easy. He wasn't one of the workers unloading boards from a wagon, but before she reached the cluster of men who were busy hitching a team of six horses to her bumper, Ezra waved.

He strode to meet her, his boots thick with mud. "If you could put the engine into neutral, I think it'd help."

"Sure." She glanced at the workers positioning boards under the back tires. An Amish AAA roadside service group. Ellie unlocked the door, climbed into the driver's seat, and dropped the gear to neutral. She rolled down the window. "Did you want me to do anything else?"

Ezra shook his head. "We can take it from here."

She climbed out. "You really think the horses can move this motorized beast?"

"We're going to give it a try." He turned his attention to the men hitching the horses.

Ellie stood there a moment, feeling oddly out of place as the only woman. "Well, I should get back to my company."

"*Jah*, okay," Ezra said without taking his eyes off the work in progress.

She turned, took a step, then scanned the field in both directions before cautiously taking another step. That bull was somewhere. Probably snorting and ready to charge.

"Hey, Ellie." Ezra jogged up to her, a dimpled grin splayed

across his face. "If you're looking for Gus, I moved him to the back pasture."

"You think that's why I'm walking around like a chicken with its head cut off?"

He smirked. "I wasn't going to say that . . . exactly."

"Thanks. That bull is rather intimidating." The man's thoughtfulness amazed her.

Ezra glanced over his shoulder at the men. "I think they're ready. I have to go." He turned and hurried to rejoin the others.

Ellie smiled, feeling a bit overwhelmed with everyone's helpfulness. Her mother's leaving the district within a year of her father's death didn't make sense. These people had gone out of their way to be friendly, and Ellie was an outsider. She returned to the house. Opening the back door, she was met by what looked like a mob of angry women.

Chapter 10

"Why do you have a slip of paper with my husband's name and our address on it?"

Ellie eyed the list the bishop's wife held. "I was given my father's old ledger by the man at the hardware store. Apparently my father was a builder, and those are some of the names and addresses I found in the book. I tried to locate a couple of them but wasn't successful. The map I bought didn't include country roads." She scanned the different faces in the crowd and locked on Ezra's sister, the only one smiling. "I hadn't meant to intrude. I only wanted to see something that my father built."

Alice glanced at the list. "Narrow Pines is what everyone called Old Township Road."

"*Jah*, before the acreage was timbered," Patty said.

"And Marsh Landing is *Bruder* Miller's place. The men claim the marsh offers the best hunting in the area."

The women all agreed among themselves.

Though Ellie smiled graciously, the information was useless. Without knowing the people and where they lived, she still wouldn't be able to find the houses her father had built.

Alice handed Ellie back the list. "Your father had a God-given talent when it came to building. If you'd like to *kumm* for a visit, I'll show you the *haus*."

Ellie let out her breath. "Yes, I would love to see it. When? I mean, whenever it's good for you."

Alice smiled. "How about Monday?"

"I'll drive you," Josephine said. "As long as you don't mind Allison coming along."

"No, not at all." The child had a special place in Ellie's heart already.

A small-framed woman with blond hair said, "You can stop by *mei* place afterward. *Mei* husband's name won't be listed in that book since the Glicks were the original owners. But you're *wilkom* to have a look-see at our place too."

"Thank you." Ellie's throat tightened as several of the other women offered to show her their home or *daadihaus*. Ellie had seen in the book the word *daadihaus* but hadn't a clue what that meant. Now, in five days, she would find out.

The women stayed long enough to finish drinking their coffee. Then they filed out of the house and back to their buggies. All except Josephine and Allison.

Josephine poked her head into the sitting room and spoke to her niece in Pennsylvania *Deitsch*.

Lulu and *go* were the only words Ellie could make out.

Allison gave Lulu a final hug, then skipped into the kitchen. She reached for the bottom of Ellie's untucked shirt and gave it a tug. "*Ich kumm* back?"

Ellie squatted down to the child's level. "*Jah*, you're *wilkom* anytime."

"You're picking up some of the language," Josephine said.

"*Nett* many words."

Josephine chuckled. "I'll make a point to teach you a few more."

"I'd like that, thank you."

"*Danki*," she said, adding as she went out the door, "means 'thank you.'"

Ellie waved as Allison and Ezra's sister climbed into the buggy. Meeting some of the women her *aenti* had mentioned in the book had been a special treat. It was as if *Aenti* Bonnie had introduced them herself. At different times during the conversations, Ellie almost blurted out things she'd read in the journal, but she held her tongue. It was best not to share that information with the women. Otherwise, the community might close her off, and she was just getting to know them.

Ellie placed the dirty cups in the sink and debated between reading more of the journal or walking up to the pasture to check on the progress with her RV. She'd never watched draft horses in action, but she also didn't want to be in the way.

She returned to where she'd left off in the journal and read more about *Aenti* possibly switching houses with Ezra and his wife.

> . . . I'm leaving the decision in Your hands, God. Ezra and Charlotte have been real good to me, and I want to help them out . . .

Ellie read several more entries, mostly about the weather and what her aunt had planted in the garden. Had Ellie planned to stay in Posen, her *aenti's* log would come in handy for what to plant when. But she couldn't keep up a house and compete Lulu in dog shows at the same time. And the money in her savings from her grandparents was running low after purchasing the RV.

Lulu paced to the door and back, whining.

"You have to go outside, girl?"

Lulu danced in place, her nails clicking against the wood floor.

Ellie closed the journal. "Give me a minute to get my coat."

Before going outside she leashed Lulu, not wanting to take any chances of her going rogue again. The nippy air sent a chill down to her toes. After a few minutes outside, she couldn't feel her nose, and this wasn't even the heart of winter yet. As she and Lulu cleared the stand of tall pines, the bridge came into view, then the empty pasture. The men, horses, wagon—and her RV—were gone.

Ezra wheeled the axe and split the oak with one swing. He tossed the two pieces into the pile, then readied the next log. His sister was busy hanging clothes on the line while Allison helped by handing Josephine the clothespins. Later, once the clothes were dry, he would take them down, and he and Allison would fold them. Their wash day routine worked for the most part. Though anymore, he longed for change—for a spark of anything but routine—and he'd wrestled with guilt ever since he allowed his mind to wander.

He split more wood, then as he tossed the pieces aside, he glimpsed Ellie and her dog jogging up the driveway, white breath puffs escaping her mouth.

When Allison spotted the pair, she dropped the clothespins and raced to greet them. Ellie stooped to his daughter's level, said something Ezra couldn't hear, then handed Allison Lulu's leash. Leaving them to play, Ellie approached the chopping area.

"Please tell me you moved my RV. It isn't in the field."

He lowered the axe from his shoulder. "Did you leave your key in the ignition?"

She squared her shoulders. "You know I did." Her gaze flitted over the area.

He studied her pinched expression. *The woman certainly clings to her worldly possessions.*

"I moved your vehicle." He motioned to his workshop a few yards away from the livestock barn. "It's behind *mei* furniture shop. It's best if you leave it parked there until we have a hard freeze. Otherwise, you'll only get stuck again."

Ellie exhaled, the fog of air lingering around her mouth. "For a minute there I thought someone had . . . It's just . . . On the road I've stayed in some sketchy areas—not that I think Posen is—"

"You don't need to explain." She was an *Englischer. Ensnared by possessions.* Why was he hoping she was different?

"Did you leave it unlocked? I need to get a few items out."

"If you're talking about the paint and supplies, I put them in my wagon. I was going to bring them to you when I deliver the wood. Unless you need them now?"

"No, I can wait. Thank you. And thank you for moving the RV to solid ground." She glanced over her shoulder at Allison and the dog, then at his sister pinning clothes on the line.

He set another log on the block, picked up the axe, but couldn't swing with her standing so close. Ezra cleared his throat.

"Oh, I'm sorry. I'll leave you alone." She turned, but instead of collecting her dog and leaving, she went to the clothesline and started up a conversation with Josephine.

He swung the axe while at the same time aiming an ear toward the women chattering, then chided himself for eavesdropping. He had work to do in the shop, in the barn, and he wanted to chop enough wood for her to get through tonight and tomorrow since it was Thanksgiving.

Ellie picked up one of Allison's damp dresses from the basket and hung it on the line. Ezra moved to the opposite side of the block. He didn't need any distractions while swinging an axe.

Ellie found a peanut butter cookie recipe in the kitchen drawer and decided to make a batch provided she found the needed ingredients in *Aenti's* cabinets. She had already picked up eggs, butter, and peanut butter the day she stopped at the grocery store. Ellie wanted something to offer Ezra when he delivered the wood. Guilt had pricked her for taking up so much of his time, especially after Josephine mentioned how busy he'd been working to finish a large furniture order due by Christmas.

Ingredients gathered, Ellie mixed the cookie dough, then rolled it into a ball. She hadn't baked in a long time. Christmas cookies for a youth group gift exchange, but that was years ago. Growing up, she and her mother spent many hours in the kitchen cooking and baking together. They made their own bread until *Mamm* went on a carb-restricted diet to shed some extra pounds. Not long after that, her mother remarried, and the two of them no longer spent much time together. Ellie pushed the thoughts aside and concentrated on crisscrossing the cookies with fork marks.

The first batch in the oven, Ellie read more of the journal. She'd left off after a fire destroyed Thomas and Noreen King's house, and having met Noreen when the women paid her a visit, Ellie was curious to learn more. The members of the settlement came to life in the pages like characters in a novel, and Ellie found herself drawn to the people and their plain ways.

The first pan of cookies burned. She opened the window a crack and fanned the smoke with a dish towel. She paid more attention to the second and third batches and the cookies came out golden brown.

Seated at the kitchen table, Ellie looked out the window at a squirrel scurrying up a nearby tree and onto the limb holding a bird feeder. She made a mental note to pick up seed the next time she was in town. It'd be nice to have morning coffee and watch the birds or, more likely, the squirrels.

A flatbed wagon rumbled up to the house. Ezra jumped off the bench, then lifted Allison down.

Ellie stood, but Lulu reached the door first, wagging her tail and whining. At least she wasn't barking.

The sweet scent of cookies rushed Ezra's senses as Ellie opened the door. Josephine and Allison baked cookies, but usually at his sister's house. He hadn't smelled them actually baking in a long time. His mouth watered.

"Hello, neighbor," Ellie said.

Lulu poked her nose outside, and Allison gave the animal a pat on the head. She bolted inside the house the second Ellie opened the door wider.

"I'm sorry. I have to work on her manners." Ezra lowered his head.

"She's okay."

Allison's actions weren't okay, but he'd have a talk with his daughter later.

"Would you like to come in?"

"I, ah . . . I brought you a load of wood and your paint." He motioned to the wagon. "I . . . I'll get it." What had gotten into him, stuttering over every sentence? The scent of cookies had messed with his mind—no, her smile scrambled his thoughts. Ezra grabbed the gallons of paint and bag of supplies. *Avoid her smile . . . and her eyes. Especially her eyes.* He set the paint cans on the floor next to the door and handed her the bag of supplies without making eye contact. He brought several armloads of wood inside and deposited the oak in the box. As he turned around, his gaze found hers. "That should . . . hold you . . ." Looking away, he spotted the open window and frowned.

She darted over to the sink and closed the window.

"Did you get it too hot in here again?"

Ellie shook her head. "Burnt cookies smoked up the place." She shrugged. "I did manage to not ruin them all. Would you like some? I'll make coffee." Tempting his taste buds, she picked up the plate and placed it on the table. "I'll never eat all these by myself. *Aenti's* recipe must have been for a church social. It made six dozen . . ."

Go home. Life is already too complicated. Unable to convince himself to politely decline, he pulled out a chair. "We can't stay long. Tomorrow is Thanksgiving. Allison and I usually spend the day in Oscoda County with *mei bruder*-in-law's family." He wasn't sure why he'd said all that. After Allison's seizure, he'd decided not to go this year. She didn't need the added stimulation being around the other children. Ezra pulled out a chair. "But *kaffi* and cookies does sound *gut*."

"*Gut*." Ellie quirked a smile, then turned to address the whistling kettle.

"You know Pennsylvania *Deitsch*?"

"A few words. *Jah*, *gut*, *kaffi*, *mamm*, *daed*, and a few others. But not enough to carry on a conversation." She poured two mugs of coffee, then brought them to the table. "Do you take cream or sugar?"

"Just black."

"And what about Allison? Would she like milk with her cookies? Oh, I probably should have asked if it's okay for her to have them. I mean, does sugar have anything to do with her seizures?"

"Food doesn't bother her—at least it hasn't so far. And water is fine. I doubt she'll drink store-bought milk."

Ellie filled a small glass with water, then placed two cookies on a paper napkin about the time Allison bounded into the room with Lulu following.

"*Danki*," Allison said, her eyes widening as Ellie handed her the treat.

"Hold on." Ezra stopped her from going back into the sitting room. "Eat it in here," he said in Pennsylvania *Deitsch*.

Allison sat next to him and took a bite. She broke off a piece and fed it to Lulu standing next to her, drooling.

"Oh, wait." Ellie grabbed a ziplock bag from the counter and removed a dog biscuit. She handed it to Allison and pointed to the dog. "A treat for the *hund*." She turned to Ezra and explained, "I don't feed her sweets."

Lulu took her biscuit and ran into the other room.

Allison left her cookie on the napkin and followed.

"Lulu hides them to eat later," Ellie said, rolling her eyes. "I'll probably find it under my pillow. But at least she doesn't smell like a skunk anymore, thanks to you."

"I'm glad the tomatoes worked."

"They tasted good too." She nibbled on a cookie.

"Pardon?"

"I kept enough out to make spaghetti." She blushed sheepishly and shrugged. "I was hungry."

"I'm glad it didn't all go down the drain." He took another bite of the cookie, then washed it down with a sip of coffee.

"If it's not food causing Allison's seizures, do you know what is?"

He shook his head. "The first one happened when she had chicken pox. She developed a high fever and began seizing, but since then, she's had other seizures without being ill or feverish."

"I've heard some children outgrow seizures."

"*Jah*, that's what the *doktah* thought." Ezra lowered his head. He wasn't used to sharing personal matters with *Englischers*. Then again, Ellie seemed different. She was easy to talk to. "The *doktah* had weaned her off the medication and she'd been doing *gut*, but she had another seizure. Worse than her others."

"Is she on medicine again?"

He nodded. "I'm supposed to keep a log of her activities. Anything unusual."

"She's a blessed girl to have you for her father."

Something warmed inside him just hearing her heartfelt words of affirmation. Ezra cleared his throat. "I heard why you were searching for those roads," he said, changing the subject. "You were looking for the houses your *daed* built."

"I didn't even know he was a builder," she said softly.

Ezra wasn't one to brag about anyone, but detecting sadness in her voice, he wanted her to know how good her father was at his trade. "He built a lot of places around here. People hired him in other counties too."

"Several of the women offered to show me through their houses. What's a *daadihaus*?"

He smiled. "A grandparents' *haus*. Usually when a couple is first married they live in the smaller *daadihaus*. When they start having children and need a larger home, the parents swap the larger *haus* for the smaller one and live there until they pass away, then the cycle repeats."

Ellie was silent, staring at her coffee.

"Is something wrong?"

She shook her head. "You said you and *Aenti* were like family," she said without looking up. "I never knew her. At least I don't remember her."

"I shouldn't have said what I did the other day. Bonnie died of congestive heart failure, so in some sense her heart was broken. But I never should have insinuated—"

"I should have known—as her niece," she said.

Ellie was hurting and he was to blame.

"I was five when my father died, and my mother left the faith shortly after, taking me . . ."

He sensed she needed a moment and said nothing. But guilt

chewed his insides. He shouldn't have led her to believe her *aenti's* death had anything to do with being lonely.

"My mother's parents were strong minded. They never wanted her to marry an Amish man in the first place, so when he died, they promised to take care of us financially. Soon after, my mother remarried—a few times. We never stayed in one place long. I often wondered what it would have been like to grow up in one house, one town."

He swallowed hard. "You have this *haus nau.*"

She pressed a smile he suspected was forced, but said nothing. Even without words, he sensed her thoughts. She was selling the house.

He pushed away from the table. "It's getting late. I need to get Allison home."

Ellie stood. "Thanks again for the firewood. Would you like to take some of these cookies home with you?"

"*Nay, danki,*" he said with a smile. "Maybe I'll have another one the next time I bring wood." He went to the sitting room entrance and motioned for Allison, who toddled toward him yawning.

Allison fell asleep in the short time it took to reach the house. He carried her inside, got her into her nightclothes, then tucked her into bed. Only then did he go back outside to tend to Cotton. Once the horse was fed and watered, he trekked back to the house.

Ezra poked his head inside Allison's room. The door creaking open must have startled her because her body started jerking.

Chapter 11

Thanksgiving felt like an ordinary day. Ezra wasn't even sure if Allison remembered it was a holiday. She plodded out to the barn to do morning chores alongside him, not saying a word. They were both tired. The seizure last night lasted twenty seconds, but she was frightened afterward and he spent most of the night rocking her in the chair to get her back to sleep.

He'd kept her up too late going over to Ellie's place. He should have left after the first cup of coffee, but he was enjoying his neighbor's company. He'd shared his frustration about not knowing the cause of Allison's seizures, and she, too, seemed to need someone to talk to—and who wouldn't, hanging out with only a dog every day?

Ezra opened the barn door and waited for Allison to enter. Normally she greeted the livestock and chatted as he milked the cow, but today she sat down on the cold concrete floor and petted the cat. When he'd finished the morning chores, she stood and followed him back to the house. His daughter's sullenness made him wish he hadn't told Josephine and Matthew they wouldn't be joining them. Perhaps Allison needed to be around other children. But his brother-in-law had eight brothers and sisters, and when they all got together with their spouses and children, there was always a lot of commotion—exactly what the doctor wanted Allison to avoid.

Ezra rewarmed the pot of coffee he'd made earlier while Allison went into the sitting room with her doll. A short time later, a knock sounded on the door.

"Surprise," Josephine said, a crock of mashed potatoes in her hands. "We couldn't leave you two alone on Thanksgiving."

His brother-in-law came in behind his sister, carrying a platter of roasted turkey. "Should I put this on the table or counter?"

"Table," his sister replied. "The dressing, beans, rolls, and pies are in the buggy yet."

Ezra took that as his cue to put his boots on. The delicious aroma of turkey had already set his mouth to watering.

Allison skipped into the kitchen, and Josephine put her to work setting the table.

Ezra shot out the door without his coat or hat. He reached into the back of the buggy and removed the crock of beans.

Matthew reached for the dressing and rolls.

"I'm sorry you missed out on spending the day with your family," Ezra said.

His brother-in-law leaned closer and lowered his voice even though no one else was around. "Between us, being around fewer people, having a simpler meal, and not having to travel far is better. I've been worried about Josephine overdoing it."

"I wish she hadn't gone to all the trouble today. Preparing this meal was a lot of work."

"She made the turkey. I made the dressing. Yes," Matthew repeated after Ezra lifted his brows, "I made it by myself. And the pies we bought from The Amish Table, but I don't think Josephine wants anyone to know that, or maybe that was just *mei* family she didn't want knowing." He shrugged.

"The restaurant makes *gut* pies too." He went up the steps but stopped before going inside. "Promise me you'll insist Josephine go home after the meal. I have all day to *reddy-up* the kitchen. I don't want her staying to do the dishes."

"*Jah*, I'll be sure to," Matthew replied.

Ezra placed the container of food on the counter, then went back outside for the pies. As he reached the back of the buggy, he spotted Ellie and Lulu walking up the driveway. "Happy Thanksgiving."

"You too." She motioned to his workshop. "I was going to my RV."

It was none of his business, but he asked anyway. "Going somewhere?"

"Maybe." She shrugged. "Depends if I can get satellite reception where it's parked."

He crinkled his brows, not following anything she just said.

"I shouldn't keep you. Please tell Allison I said Happy Thanksgiving." She turned toward the workshop.

"I see you've started painting," he said.

She glanced down, twisting her body to get a better view of the paint splatters decorating her backside.

"Nice color." He clamped his mouth closed the moment his thoughts slipped out unchecked. *Stop.* These types of thoughts would get him shunned. *Avoid temptation. Do not be unequally yoked.* Biblical warnings blared as he redirected his gaze to the ground.

"I started the kitchen this morning."

He glanced up. "And is the place more cheerful?" She would cheer up any room.

"I like it," she said over her shoulder. "But I'll know more after I'm finished and the real estate agent looks at it."

His shoulders slumped as he trudged up the steps.

Josephine took the pie from his hands. "Did you invite Ellie to eat with us?"

"*Nay.*" He kicked off his boots at the door.

"Why *nett*? There's plenty of food and she's alone."

"She has that dog with her," he grumbled. *And paint on her jeans I shouldn't be looking at.* He tapped his daughter's shoulder and turned her toward the other room. "Go wash up." Once Allison was out of sight, he said, "I've been thinking that dog has something to do with her seizures."

Matthew paused from carving the turkey. "Is that what the *doktah* said?"

"He said to keep an eye on any changes in her routine, and the only change so far has been that dog. She'd gone months without a seizure before that dog arrived, and *nau* it seems whenever the animal is around she has one. Next time I'm in town, I plan to ask the *doktah* what he thinks."

"Maybe you're right," Josephine said. "What a shame. Allison loves that dog and it'll be hard keeping them apart with Ellie living next door."

Ezra huffed. They wouldn't be neighbors long.

The satellite reception wasn't the best. Waves crossed the television screen, distorting the images of the Macy's Thanksgiving Day Parade floats. Ellie would find a better signal in town, but she also might miss the program by the time she drove somewhere and set up. The parade was almost over, which meant the dog show would start soon.

Ellie rummaged through the cabinets for something to eat and found a box of crackers, which were stale, but she'd eat them anyway. Perhaps she'd order a pizza. She smiled, imagining how confused the driver would be delivering to an RV parked behind a workshop on an Amish farm. She wondered if the pizza place would even be open on Thanksgiving Day. She glanced at her phone. Dead. It'd probably take the length of the entire program to charge her phone off the generator. Ordering pizza was out, and so was checking her messages and e-mails. Considering she hadn't had good reception since arriving, she hadn't missed it. Besides, her mother was vacationing in Hawaii, an entirely different time zone.

The dog show began. Ellie turned up the volume using the remote and settled back against the foam-cushioned bench at the table. The two-day event with thousands of dogs performing was video spliced into snippets that highlighted the different dog groups, ending finally with Best in Show. The terrier group was the largest, followed by the working and sporting groups. The hounds were up next.

Someone tapped on the door as the program cut to a Purina commercial. Ellie set the remote on the table and opened the door.

Ezra held out a plate of food in one hand and a glass of milk in the other. "I thought you might be hungry."

She opened the door wider. "Come on in, you look cold."

"I shouldn't." His actions contradicted his words and he entered the small space.

"This looks delicious, thanks." She set the plate and glass on the table.

Ezra scanned the area. "When I drove your vehicle here and parked it, I didn't look inside the living space. This is nice."

"Thanks. This area extends out a few more feet, which I usually don't bother with unless I plan to stay multiple days at the same camp." She glanced at the TV as the program resumed, then continued the tour, motioning to the short hallway and to Lulu perched on the bed. "At the far end are the bedroom, bathroom, and a small hall closet."

He glanced that direction but didn't venture beyond the table. "Looks like everything you need."

She shrugged. Sure, she and Lulu had a comfortable, rewarding life traveling the country, advancing her career, but was it everything Ellie needed? Stifling the thoughts before she slipped and made them known, she picked up the glass of milk and took a sip. "Ah. This is good. I've never had unpasteurized milk before." She took another drink, but set the glass down when he grinned. "What?"

"You have milk"—he grabbed a napkin from the holder on the table and stepped closer—"on your . . ."

Gazing into his eyes—his kind, trusting, tawny eyes—she heard her heartbeat pounding in her ears, making the program announcers' discussion of the characteristics of the basset hound irrelevant. Was he leaning toward her? Her eyes closed automatically.

"Is that gas I smell?"

Her eyes shot open to find him sniffing by the stove. "You're probably smelling the generator. The propane to the stove is shut off." She licked her lips.

He handed her the napkin. "You shouldn't sit in here closed up with a generator running."

"I wasn't going to be . . ." *out here long.*

Ezra went to the window over the sink and opened it, letting in a rush of wintry air.

"I'm leaving after Lulu's group." She glanced at the television as the host announced that the nonsporting group was up next after a short commercial break. "Lulu's judged next," she said.

He looked down the hall to the bedroom, then back at Ellie. "Did you say she's going to be on television?"

Ellie nodded. "The competition was last weekend in Oak, Pennsylvania, but the network doesn't air the show until Thanksgiving Day."

"So you already know who won?"

"The fox terrier stole the show." She turned her attention to the program as the dalmatian entered the arena.

"I wonder how many of those fancy dogs have been sprayed by a skunk," he said.

"Only Lulu." She chuckled. "I doubt any of them, including the hound and sporting groups, have ever seen the woods. And none of them have ever been bathed in tomatoes." She glanced over her shoulder at Lulu asleep on the bed, then redirected her attention to the screen when something was said about the standard apricot poodle. The camera angle offered a glimpse of the judge's neutral expression. Lulu's televised fame lasted less than thirty seconds as Ellie jogged to the end of the arena and back. The judges signaled for the schipperke, who had scored the second highest points in the group.

Ezra moved to the door. "Happy Thanksgiving."

"Thanks again for the food."

"Just being neighborly."

Chapter 12

Ezra spent the two days following Thanksgiving working in his shop. The bedroom set he'd been contracted to build and deliver by Christmas to one of his *Englisch* customers was coming along nicely. The hand-carved, one-of-a-kind furniture took time to build and piece together, and he never wanted to rush any step in the process. Ezra glued the dovetailed drawer joints together, then clamped them in place. He'd let them dry overnight.

As he left the shop, Ezra's gaze drifted across the pasture. Was Ellie painting? Getting the house ready to sell? She should be running low on wood. For sure, the supply he'd brought her the other day wouldn't last until Monday. *Stop making excuses to see her,* he chided. But his thoughts remained focused on her.

Ezra loaded the wagon with chopped firewood. He was hitching Cotton to the buggy when Allison bounded out of the house.

"*Ich geh,*" she said.

Josephine waddled across the yard. "Sorry, I tried to stop her."

His daughter had asked to visit Ellie and Lulu repeatedly over the last couple of days, and now she was climbing up on the wagon bench.

"I should be heading home to start supper anyway," Josephine said.

Ezra nodded.

"I'll see you two at the church meeting tomorrow." Josephine turned toward the house. "Tell Ellie I'll see her on Monday," she said over her shoulder.

Pulling up to Ellie's house, he spotted Ellie sitting on the porch step and Lulu curled up on the doormat behind her. He jumped off the bench. "Everything okay?"

She nodded. "Inhaled too many paint fumes. I needed some fresh air."

Ezra helped Allison down from the buggy and she ran over to Ellie. He went to the back of the buggy and gathered an armload of wood while listening to Ellie's attempt to greet Allison in Pennsylvania *Deitsch*. He smiled. She was trying to fit in.

Ellie was quick to open the door, and after two trips, the woodbox was full. He motioned to the door. "I'll stack the rest of the wood in the shed."

"I really appreciate you bringing more firewood," she said.

"Just being neighborly." He motioned for Allison. "Church meeting starts early tomorrow," he told his daughter. "Tell Ellie and the *hund* good-bye."

Ellie removed the lid on the cookie jar and held it out to him. "Can I offer you a cookie for the road?"

"Sure." He reached inside and selected one for Allison and himself. "*Danki*."

"You're *wilkom*."

Too bad her only interest in the Amish way was learning the language. The yellow kitchen walls were certainly not in accordance with their plain lifestyle.

"Allison, eat so we're *nett* late for service."

Ezra drained his coffee. "Allison?"

His daughter was slow to look up, and when she did, there was a vacancy in her stare.

His pulse quickened. "Honey, are you feeling all right?"

She licked her lips, blinked a few times, then reached for her glass of milk.

"Lord, please," was all he could muster.

Allison picked up her spoon and resumed eating the oatmeal. She didn't eat it all and he wasn't about to encourage her to do so. Not if she wasn't feeling herself. Though who would know? She'd never been able to describe her feelings before or after a seizure. Most of the time she wasn't even aware anything had happened. He'd quizzed her in the past, asking her if her heart was racing or her stomach hurt, but she'd only shrugged at his questions. Allison slipped off the chair and went to the door. She removed her wool cloak from a lower hook and slipped it on.

Ezra put his coat on, then helped Allison with her bonnet, boots, and mittens. *Should we stay home, read the Scriptures, and rest?* He'd always made a point not to miss any church meetings, but certainly God would understand.

"Ready," she said, trying to turn the doorknob with her mittens and not getting a grip.

He shoved his hat on and opened the door.

Allison plodded along, holding her mittened hand out to catch falling snow. Usually on cold days like today, she waited in the house until he hitched the buggy.

Ezra opened the buggy door, placed Allison on the bench, then covered her with the lap quilt he left in the buggy for winter weather. He hurried to the barn and removed Cotton from the stall. As he walked the horse out to the buggy and bent down to buckle the harness, something flashed in his peripheral vision. Lulu, running toward them, dragging her leash.

The dog barked at Allison's door, then circled to where Ezra was squatted down hitching the horse. The dog clamped its mouth over his hand and tugged.

"Lulu, no!"

The dog released his hand, then dashed around the buggy to Allison's side once again. Ellie gasped, a look of horror on her face. "Did she bite you? I'm so sorry. She's never done that before. Are you bleeding?"

"I'm fine, Ellie." He held out his hand. "She didn't bite through the glove." The dog hadn't applied pressure.

"I'm so sorry," Ellie repeated, going to the other side of the buggy where the dog was barking. She took control of the leash. "We were out for a morning walk," Ellie explained. "Lulu's never—"

"She didn't hurt me. Let's forget it." The woman was hard to be mad at. Her dog, on the other hand, was a nuisance.

Ellie nodded. "I know you're on your way to church, so I won't keep you." She turned, took a few steps, then faced him again. "I meant to mention last night that Josephine told me about your furniture order due by Christmas. If you need someone to watch Allison, I'm happy to help."

"*Nay.*" His sister shouldn't have said anything.

Ellie's smile faded. "I just thought I'd mention—Never mind. I understand." She turned and jogged away, the dog keeping stride.

Ezra climbed onto the bench beside his daughter, who was staring straight ahead. "Allison, honey?" As if his voice had pulled her from a trance, she looked at him, only something still wasn't right. He touched her cheek with the back of his gloved hand. Usually when Allison was around Lulu, she wanted to play with the dog. This time, she appeared unfazed. As if she hadn't even been aware of Lulu barking at her buggy door. Was this another type of seizure? "Allison, honey, will you please look at me?"

Chapter 13

The house her father had built was a labor of love. From its high ceilings, wood-trimmed entries, and baseboards to the tongue-in-groove plank floors and original cabinets, her father's workmanship was a masterpiece. Even though she knew little about her father, standing in a house he'd built gave her a sense of closeness. She tried to visualize how tedious the job would have been constructing the home without power tools. "It's beautiful."

"Most floorboards creak with age, but *nett* his work. Even the stairs and second floor are solid," Alice said.

"I noticed." Ellie followed Alice downstairs and rejoined Josephine and Allison, who had chosen to wait downstairs.

"*Nau* let's have *kaffi*." Alice waved them toward the kitchen. "Did you all have a nice Thanksgiving?"

"Matthew and I spent the day with Ezra and Allison," Josephine said.

"Don't you usually go to Matthew's parents' *haus*?"

Josephine nodded. "The *doktah* told Ezra the less stimulation the better for Allison. He knows how rambunctious *mei* husband's nieces and nephews get when they're all together. But we had an enjoyable day."

Alice set a plate of cookies on the table. "What about you, Ellie? Did you have a nice day?"

"Very nice, thank you." She held back from mentioning that

Ezra brought a plate of food to the RV or that they watched a few minutes of the dog show together.

Alice set three mugs of coffee and spoons on the table, then went back for a glass of milk for Allison. Once everyone was served, she sat down. "How are you getting along in your *aenti's haus*?"

"I'm learning how to use the cookstove, and I've finished painting the kitchen and living room." Alice and Josephine exchanged glances, but Ellie wasn't able to decipher if their straight-lined lips meant they were unhappy with her changing things or not. She kept silent about her plans to paint the bedrooms next.

Alice added a spoonful of sugar to her coffee, then passed the container to Ellie. "Is your mother still alive?"

Ellie nodded. "She remarried and is living in Kentucky."

Allison tapped Josephine's hand and said something in Pennsylvania *Deitsch*.

"Excuse us." Josephine and Allison left the room.

Alice continued with more questions. "What does your mother think about you moving to Posen?"

That living among the Amish is foolish. "She thinks I'm here to get it ready to sell."

The bishop's wife frowned. "I see."

Ellie sipped her coffee. "My mother didn't think any of you would . . . speak to me."

"Our way is so different than most people's. Your mother was one of us, but she chose to leave the faith. You, on the other hand, were a child. You had no choice in the matter." Alice reached for Ellie's hand and gave it a squeeze. "Your *aenti* prayed many years that one day you would *kumm* home."

Ellie nodded. She'd found Alice's name written in *Aenti's* journal just that morning. As she read the prayers, her *aenti's* loving thoughts had brought tears to Ellie's eyes.

Allison and Josephine returned, and the conversation shifted to her pregnancy with twins.

"I hope you're feeling up to Second Christmas," Alice said.

"Me too." Josephine turned to Ellie. "On Second Christmas we go *haus* to *haus* visiting and sharing sweets, often by sleigh, which the *kinner* love. It's such a *gut* time for all."

"Sounds like it." Ellie had never ridden in a buggy until today, let alone a horse-drawn sleigh. She found herself wondering what it'd be like sitting next to Ezra.

"If you're finished with your *kaffi*, Ellie, we should probably go," Josephine said. "I promised Irma Pinkham we would stop by The Amish Table. Your father's crew also built the restaurant."

Ellie drank the last of her coffee and stood. "Thank you so much, Alice."

"I'm glad you had the chance to stop over." Alice walked them to the door.

Ellie spent the remainder of the day touring various houses, *daadihauses*, and Amish businesses her father had built. She'd also listened to so many conversations about the Second Christmas menu, she longed to join the fun. Christmas was still a few weeks away; perhaps she would be invited.

Hours later, Josephine stopped the buggy outside Ellie's door, and Allison stretched her neck to look outside the window. She tapped Ellie's hand. "I play with Lulu, *jah*?"

Ellie glanced at Josephine. "Would you like to come inside? We could have a cup of herbal tea while Allison plays with Lulu."

"*Nay*, we better *nett*. Ezra doesn't want Allison around the dog." As if she'd said something she shouldn't, Josephine clamped her mouth closed.

Allison's bottom lip quivered, and she reached for Ellie's hand.

"Maybe another day," Ellie told the child. But if Ezra didn't want her being around the dog, that was unlikely. "Is he afraid Lulu will hurt her?"

Josephine shook her head. "He believes the dog has something to do with her seizures."

Ezra hadn't mentioned anything when he'd told her about the child's seizures over coffee. In fact, he'd said the doctor *didn't* know what caused the seizures. "I've never heard of dogs *causing* someone to seize. I always thought animals were more apt to sense something wrong. In fact, I read an article once about a training facility where dogs were paired with people with certain illnesses or limitations." Ellie's shoulders sagged. "If it's true that Lulu triggered an episode, I'm truly sorry." Ellie smiled down at the child. How sad for them all, including Lulu.

Several inches of snow accumulated over the first week in December. Ezra stopped over to check if the pipes had frozen and to deliver more wood, but each time he came to the house, Allison wasn't with him. He didn't offer a reason for his daughter's absence and Ellie thought it best not to ask. Once the snow let up, she planned to go into town and research the possibility of Lulu causing the child's seizures.

With another tote full of stuff she planned to donate to Goodwill, Ellie sat down with *Aenti's* journal. She read several entries, gleaning insight into her aunt's life and the plain people she wrote about. Flipping the page, she came to a stop.

> Charlotte Mast went to be with the Lord today, a sad time for the entire district. The pain reflected in Ezra's eyes is haunting. Lord, I ask that You will surround him with Your love. Help him through this time of despair, and have

mercy on him and little Allison. Too sad to write more, I'll close for today.

Tears clouded Ellie's vision, blurring the lines on the page. She set the book aside, thinking she could set her thoughts of Ezra aside too, but her heart ached for what he and Allison had gone through. She paced from the kitchen to the living room and back, checked the fire in the stove, and finally, unable to stop thinking about him, picked up the journal again. She had to know how he coped with the loss, how *Aenti* and the others helped and prayed for him. But as she was reopening the journal, someone knocked on the door. Ellie dabbed a tissue at the corner of her eye as she went to answer the caller.

Ezra stood on the porch, his arms loaded with wood. "*Gut* evening."

"Hello." She forced the greeting past the lump in her throat and moved aside so he could enter.

Ezra deposited the wood into the box, then swept bark off his hands. "I have more wood—Is something wrong? Your eyes are red."

She looked at the floor and tried to disguise her sniffles in a cough, but when she glanced up, he was studying her. The longer he stared, the more his eyes pierced her soul.

"These woods can get lonely," he said, rubbing the back of his neck. "Sometimes talking to animals isn't enough."

Her throat constricted even more. He understood loneliness and had probably spent numerous hours talking to his livestock.

"I have more wood in the buggy to unload." Ezra headed outside, returning a few minutes later with another armload. "That should get you through . . ."

She followed his line of vision to the journal.

"That's Bonnie's handwriting," he said.

"It's her prayer journal."

Craning his neck, he inched closer. "Is that why you've been crying?"

Ellie blotted her eyes with the tissue. "It's sad."

"Why are you reading it then?"

She shrugged. "I want to know her—and you—and everyone better."

"Me?" He flipped through the book, his face contorting.

After a moment, Ellie said, "I'm sorry about Charlotte. Losing your wife must have been very difficult."

He closed the book. His face pinched with what looked like a mixture of grief and anger.

"I'm sorry. I shouldn't have—"

"Snooped? *Nay*, you shouldn't have spied into our private lives."

Chapter 14

After a restless night, Ellie and Lulu traipsed across the snowy pasture to Ezra's house. Now that the ground was frozen, she intended to move the RV back to her *aenti's* place—once she returned from town. The totes were already full, mostly with things to give away. The spare room was cleaned out, the first coat of paint was drying, and she needed to arrange for an agent to come out to the house.

Ellie recognized the horse and buggy parked at the fence as Josephine's and headed straight to the RV. Ezra had made his thoughts clear about her reading *Aenti's* journal. He didn't like her spying on him—on his Amish settlement. Josephine would think poorly of her, too, breaking her heart even more.

Smoke billowed from the stovepipe extending from Ezra's workshop. She moved quickly past the shop's windows and was fiddling with the key to unlock the RV when Ezra called her name. She pasted on a smile and turned. "Good morning, Ezra."

"Going for a drive?"

"I need supplies from town." She held back from mentioning her research plans and shoveled a patch of snow with the toe of her boot.

"Drive safely." He returned to the shop.

Ellie climbed into the frigid RV and cranked the engine. The vents blew cold air, and the windshield wipers were frozen. She'd have to wait. *Apologize. You invaded his life.*

"Lord, *Aenti* Bonnie left a note in the journal to me. She must have wanted me to read it, and the more I did, the more I wanted to know about the Amish way. Please help me mend ways with Ezra. He thinks I'm a snoopy *Englischer.*"

Apologize to Ezra.

Ellie groaned under her breath. Her inner voice of reason wouldn't leave her alone. She'd never have peace without at least trying to make things right. Leaving the engine running, Ellie marched into Ezra's workshop. "I'm sorry," she blurted.

He set the sandpaper block on the table and crossed the room.

Not giving him opportunity to speak, she explained. "I didn't read the journal to snoop on you or anyone in the district. I only wanted to know my *aenti* better." As he opened his mouth, she continued, "You don't have to remind me that I'm an outsider. I know I don't belong here."

"Are you done talking?"

She nodded.

"Seeing the journal caught me by surprise," he said. "I always knew Bonnie was praying for Allison and me, but I wasn't ready for all those memories to resurface *nau.*"

"I'm sorry."

"You did nothing wrong. I shouldn't have reacted the way I did. The journal belongs to you."

Then why did she feel so horrible? Ellie reached for the door handle. "I left the engine running." She let her gaze skim the carved bed frame and matching cherrywood dressers. "You do lovely work."

"Thank you."

Silence loomed between them a long moment. Ellie's chest grew heavy. As close as she'd felt to him while reading the journal, she now felt the exact opposite. Reading the journal had driven a wedge between them. *Leave. Don't impose.* "I have to go." Ellie fled the shop before he noticed her tears. She didn't like the uneasiness between them or feeling like the outsider she was. She hopped into the RV and didn't waste time pulling out of his driveway.

Traversing the country roads winding through snow-laden pines that bent under the weight of snow was like viewing a video postcard. Christmas wreaths decorated the sidewalk lampposts, and blinking lights lit the business windows. Disappointed to find the library closed for renovations, she headed to the real estate office.

"I'll Be Home for Christmas" played overhead as she entered the building. An artificial Christmas tree sat in the corner of the room with wrapped packages underneath, tinsel reflecting window light, and an assortment of colored lights blinking in alternating sections.

A man wearing a blue-and-white plaid flannel shirt and jeans stood from behind a desk and extended his hand. "I'm Clyde Hall. How may I help you?"

"I'm Ellie Whetstone and I'm interested in listing my house with you."

"Great, why don't you have a seat." He motioned to the hunter-green upholstered chair positioned in front of his desk.

"Did you get your ten-point?" she asked, removing her gloves.

He turned around a picture frame on his desk to face her. "Eight, but I'm not complaining." He chuckled. "I take it you came by last week and saw the sign."

She nodded, then jumped to the reason for the visit. "How are sales this time of year?"

"Depends. Do you have acreage?"

"Forty, and the house has . . . rustic charm." She'd stolen that description off the home improvement shows she'd watched, but how else would one describe not having electricity or hot water?

"I'm not certain about the property boundaries. I only recently inherited the house."

"That's not a problem. I can search the courthouse records and if we need an updated survey, I can arrange for one."

"I'd like a quick sale," she said.

"Doesn't everyone." He chuckled, poising pen to pad. "Do you know the square footage? How many bedrooms, bathrooms, age of the roof . . . ?"

"Less than a thousand square feet, two bedrooms, one bath. No idea about the roof or the age of the house. There's also a two-stall horse barn and woodshed." She gave him the physical address and explained the pasture gate and bridge.

"Sounds like an ideal hunting cabin."

"But hunting season is over. Does that mean it'll probably sit on the market until next fall?"

"I'll be honest. The closer we get to Christmas, the less likely people will have time to look at property. January, February, and March might be difficult, but I have been known to take potential clients on snowmobile excursions to look at a place. Especially hunting camps. But I'll let you know more after I've seen the house and have pulled comps. Is there a good time later today for me to come over?"

"I'm available anytime—before four." After four the trees blocked the window light, and it'd be difficult to view the house with a lantern. Her mind raced with things still needing attention. She hadn't tackled her *aenti's* bedroom. "Actually, sometime next week works better for me, if you're free."

Fortunately *Aenti* wasn't a hoarder. Otherwise, procrastinating the way she had over the last few days would've left her in a time pinch for meeting with the real estate agent to have the house appraised. As it was, she still had her aunt's bedroom to pack up and paint. Ellie drew a deep breath and entered the bedroom. Other than looking through the nightstand and finding the journal and Bible, Ellie hadn't snooped through any more of her *aenti's* belongings. The dresses hanging from wall pegs caught her attention. *Aenti's* dresses were all dark colors and well worn. She pulled a pretty blue one off a peg and held it against her, the hem touching the floor. *Aenti* was tall. Ellie glanced at her watch. She had a few extra minutes. She slipped the dress on over her shirt and jeans. *No buttons. How on earth did she close the front of the dress?*

Lying on the rug at the foot of the bed, Lulu lifted her head and perked her ears. She trotted to the door, whining, then paced back to the bedroom and barked. She ran back into the kitchen and clawed at the door.

"Hey, stop that. Now I'm going to have to sand and paint it." She reached for the leash dangling from the wall hook. *Don't let it be a skunk.*

Ellie tightened her grip on the leash before opening the door.

Allison looked up, her cheeks and the tip of her nose red. She wrapped her cold arms around Ellie's legs and clung to her. Why wasn't she wearing a coat?

Ellic scanned the area. "Allison, where's your *daed*?" When the girl didn't answer, Ellie picked her up. "Let's go inside and get you warmed up." She carried the child into the house, lowered her onto a kitchen chair, then added another log to the fire. "Are you hungry, sweetie?"

Allison stared blankly, as if in a trance. Lulu sat at the girl's side, watching her, waiting for a signal as she did with Ellie in the ring.

Knowing the girl spoke mostly Pennsylvania *Deitsch*, her not responding was understandable, but the blank stare at Lulu, when she'd obviously come to play, didn't seem normal. She had to get the girl home. Ezra would be out of his mind with worry. Ellie snatched the RV keys from the counter and headed to the door. "Let's the three of us take a ride. Lulu, come."

The dog looked at Ellie, then Allison, then lay down at the girl's feet.

Ellie jingled the keys. Had Lulu forgotten everything since coming up north? Ellie reached for Allison's hand. "Let's find *Daed*."

"Allison's *nett* in the barn, the *washhaus*, or woodshed," Ezra said to his sister, panic threading his veins. His daughter had never run away before.

Josephine's complexion paled. "I searched the *haus*. She's *nett* here." His sister paced the kitchen, tears streaming down her face. "She didn't even put her coat on. Maybe you should recheck the barn. She may have climbed up to the loft."

"I checked there. Stay here in case she comes back." He rushed out the door.

Josephine followed him out. "Where are you going?"

"We need a search team. I'm going for help." He spotted Josephine's horse tethered to the fence post and still hitched to the buggy and jogged toward it. He'd stop at Ellie's first. Hopefully his daughter went to see Lulu. That dog had been nothing but trouble since Ellie moved next door.

Pulling into Ellie's yard, Ezra spotted his daughter and the dog walking to the RV with Ellie trailing behind them—wearing an Amish dress. He blew out a breath as he jumped out of the buggy. "*Danki*, Lord, for keeping Allison safe."

"We were just on our way to your place," Ellie said.

"Allison, get in the buggy." Ezra held his tone even. He'd deal with her running away once they were home. He eyed Ellie.

Had she been wearing a prayer *kapp*, she might actually look Amish. Noticing the shirt and jeans under the unfastened dress, he frowned.

She followed his gaze and pulled at the sides of the dress. "It's one of my *aenti's*."

"I didn't think it was yours." He glanced over his shoulder at Allison, shuffling her feet in the snow. The dog was walking carefully beside her, halting its steps to keep the same pace.

Ellie groaned. "Lulu, come back here. I don't know what's wrong with that dog. She hasn't listened to me since we moved here."

"It'd be better if we keep them apart," he snipped.

"I totally agree." She still didn't believe Lulu was the cause of Allison's seizures, but this wasn't the time to debate it.

The horse's frightened neigh caught Ezra's attention. The gelding tossed its head up and down and pawed at the ground, then attempted to rear up, jerking the buggy forward. Before Ezra registered what was happening, Lulu wedged herself between the horse and Allison just as his daughter dropped on the ground, arms flaying, body convulsing. In the process of hovering over Allison, the horse's hooves struck Lulu. The dog yipped but didn't leave.

Ezra grabbed the reins. "Back," he said, pushing the horse's chest. The seizure had stopped by the time he moved the horse away. Lulu remained at Allison's side. Ezra knelt beside his daughter and the dog. "Allison, are you hurt?"

Her stunned blue eyes locked on his, and she shook her head. "Lulu," she said hoarsely.

Ellie dropped to her knees and placed her hands on the dog's chest, front legs, abdomen, hips. Lulu yipped. "She's hurt. I have to get her to a vet."

Ellie practically pounced on the vet when he entered the exam room, X-ray films in his hand. "How bad is she?"

"She needs surgery," he said, placing the film on the light box.

The dislocated hip and broken leg were obvious to Ellie, but she listened as he explained the planned procedure of using a steel rod and pins to repair her leg. Her stomach clenched and acid coated the back of her throat. "Have you done many of these surgeries?"

"I've worked on worse."

She watched Lulu lying unresponsive on the table. "And afterward the dog had full use of its leg?"

"I've seen it both ways. Complete recovery and amputation. But I need to tell you, Ms. Whetstone, time is a factor. We need to operate now."

Sitting in the vet lobby, Ellie prayed nonstop for Allison and Lulu. It was morning by the time surgery ended. Lulu came through the surgery remarkably according to the vet. Still, she required close monitoring and IV medications, which meant Lulu would need to stay longer at the animal hospital. Ellie had wanted to stay with her but was politely informed that Lulu was heavily sedated, and the vet advised against it the first day. The second day, Ellie spent the majority of the day at the vet clinic. Except for dropping by the real estate office to postpone the appraisal appointment a few more days, Ellie sat next to Lulu's cage and watched her sleep until the clinic closed and she had to leave.

The house was cold. The fire had gone out completely. Feeling exhausted, she didn't want to mess with emptying the pan of ashes in order to start a fire, so she added another quilt to the pile on the bed and hunkered down under the covers for the night.

The following morning the pipes were frozen. Ellie trekked across the field to Ezra's house and knocked on the door.

Josephine ushered her inside. "Look at you shivering—you're half froze."

"I'm cold, but it's my pipes that are frozen."

"Oh goodness. Well, have a seat at the table and I'll pour you a mug of *kaffi*."

"How's Allison? I've been praying for her."

"*Danki*. The *doktah* ordered a brain scan, but we haven't received the results yet. How's Lulu?"

"She had surgery on her leg. The vet wants to keep her a few more days."

"Allison is in her room resting, but I'm sure she'd love to have a visitor." Josephine motioned to the hallway. "Second door on the left."

Ellie nodded, then headed toward the bedroom. She creaked open the door and poked her head inside.

The child's face lit. "Ellie!"

"I wanted to see how you were feeling," she said, sitting on the edge of the mattress.

"Where's Lulu?"

"She's at the *doktah's*, honey." Ellie wished she could tell Allison she would see Lulu soon, but Ellie couldn't give the child false hope. Ezra would never let them play together.

Allison wrapped her arms around Ellie's waist and squeezed.

The door pushed open and Ezra stood in the threshold staring at the two of them.

Ezra's throat dried. Watching the interaction between Allison and Ellie sent a fireball of heat to his stomach. He cleared his throat.

Ellie bounded up from the bed. "I was just checking on Allison," she said.

He swallowed hard. "I understand you have frozen pipes down at your place."

She nodded at him, then turned to Allison. "I'll check on you in a few days, okay?"

His daughter looked over at him, and he repeated what Ellie had said in Pennsylvania *Deitsch*.

"*Jah*, please," Allison said, giving Ellie another hug.

He waited until they were out of the room before asking, "How's Lulu?"

"She had surgery on her leg, but the doctor seems optimistic. I'm hoping she can come home in a few days. I heard Allison had a brain scan. Did the doctor say how long it'd be before you had the results?"

"A few days." He shrugged. "I figure tomorrow I'll make a trip into town. Maybe he'll know something. I hope." Ezra pressed a smile. "I suppose we'd better find out what's going on with your pipes before it gets much colder. Sometimes the insulation around the pipes gets loose or comes off." He put his coat on at the door.

"We'll have *kaffi* another time," Josephine said as she walked Ellie to the door.

"Allison sure liked seeing you," Ezra said as they plodded through the snow toward the little cabin.

"I'm glad she's doing better."

They continued walking silently. No smoke was coming out of the stovepipe; that wasn't a good sign. The inside of the house was frigid, and white clouds of air escaped his mouth. "Your fire is out."

"It was out last night when I got home."

He glanced into the woodbox and groaned under his breath. "You're *nett* out of wood."

"I came home late from the vet and found the fire totally out." She shrugged.

"No wonder the pipes froze. You can't let the fire go out." He softened his lecturing tone and got to work emptying the ash pan, then building a fire. "You must have been *kalt* last *nacht*."

"Felt like the North Pole in here."

He opened the doors of the cabinets under the sink in both the kitchen and bathroom. "Usually it takes a few hours to heat the pipes, but we won't know if the pipes are leaking until they're completely thawed."

Ellie put the kettle on the stove and the cookie jar on the table. Time sped by quickly. They talked about the weather, about her childhood desire to have horses, and about his furniture business. Then somehow they got on the subject of Christmas traditions.

"I don't do much in the way of celebrating," she admitted. "My mother and stepfather are usually wintering in Hawaii. Last year Lulu and I spent the holidays in Florida. There's a big dog show in the middle of December in Orlando . . . and the weather there is nice."

"But this year you decided to spend Christmas in Posen . . . in the snow, with a wood stove you had to keep going so the pipes wouldn't freeze."

"I failed at that, didn't I?"

He shrugged. "They might *nett* have busted—yet. But you still have January, February, and March to get through."

Ellie fell silent.

"But I'll be happy to stop by and feed the wood stove if you need to be away for an extended time. I should have known you would have stayed at the vet's . . ."

"You've had Allison on your mind and rightfully so." She stared at the coffee mug.

Ezra sensed she was holding something back, but he didn't

want anything to spoil their talk. He went to the sink and turned on the tap. Water sputtered. He inspected the pipes under the sink, then checked to make sure the sink in the bathroom was working. With no signs of leakage, he reluctantly made his exit. As he lumbered through the snowy drifts across the field, he couldn't erase the image of Ellie and Allison hugging. His daughter needed a mother.

Two days later, the house wasn't nearly as ready to show as she would have liked. She'd planned to decorate with battery-operated Christmas lights and balsam wreaths with big red bows, but under the circumstances, she was surprised she even remembered the appointment with the agent.

"You have a charming home, Ms. Whetstone."

"Thank you." A heaviness filled her heart. In the few weeks she'd been here, this place had become home. Her home.

"I shouldn't have any problems finding a buyer. Especially with the property bordering state land."

"That's good." She pasted on a smile. The house wasn't even on the market and seller's remorse had pricked her conscience.

"I reviewed the courthouse records and found you own more than forty acres." He handed her the paperwork.

"Two hundred and forty?" Ellie stared at the document in disbelief. "I don't understand."

"That's the description listed in the plat book. Apparently the property was transferred into your name ten years ago."

"Now I'm really confused. I only inherited the house three months ago when my *aenti* passed away." The letter she had received was in the RV. *How was it worded?*

"I've drawn up a listing agreement for you to review and sign.

My fee is six percent due at closing. I advertise locally through the multiple listings catalog as well as over the Internet."

"Can I look the papers over and bring them by your office either later today or tomorrow?"

"Absolutely. But if you don't mind, I'll snap a few pictures before I leave."

"I had planned on giving it a homey feel by putting up a few Christmas decorations. Should we wait with the pictures?"

"I wouldn't if I were you. Christmas is just around the corner, and it'd be better to list it more as a hunting camp anyway."

"Good point. I'll move the totes in the bedroom out of the way." She headed to the bedroom as the man snapped pictures in the kitchen. A few minutes later, Clyde appeared. "You have someone at your door."

"I'll be right back." She headed to the kitchen door and found Ezra standing on her stoop.

He rubbed the back of his head. "May I *kumm* in?"

"Of course." She stepped aside, giving him space to enter. "I was just helping the real estate agent move some totes so they're not in the pictures. Can you give me a few minutes?"

He nodded, though judging by the way he was shuffling his feet, he was either nervous or preparing to bolt.

Clyde returned. "I think I have enough indoor photos. I'll take some of the property on my way out." He shook Ellie's hand. "It was nice seeing you again, and I look forward to talking more with you."

Ellie walked him to the door, then turned to face Ezra. "Have you heard anything about Allison's test results?"

"The test didn't show any lesions. The *doktah* wants to do another scan in three months."

"I'll keep praying for her."

"*Danki*."

He motioned outside the window at the agent's car. "You're selling it?"

"It's for the best. I know you don't want Allison around Lulu and I understand, even though I'm not sure I agree with your idea of Lulu causing the seizures."

"Me either."

"If her seizures start off as a trance-like state, then—Wait, what did you say?"

"I don't think Lulu caused them. I believe she sensed something was wrong, and that's why she refused to listen to you. She was protecting Allison. I relayed to the *doktah* what you told Josephine about therapy dogs, and he believes some dogs don't have to be trained—like Lulu—to be keenly aware of something about to happen."

Ellie smiled. "Lulu's never spent much time around children, and yet she's been very attentive to Allison."

He inched closer. "They have a special connection."

Did she and Ezra share a special connection too? *Stop. Focus on Lulu—on Westminster—on next season.*

"Ellie—"

"Yes."

"That dress you were wearing yesterday . . . It looked *gut* on you."

Ellie swallowed hard. Was that his way of saying she would make an attractive Amish woman? Or he wished she was Amish? *Don't read anything into it.* Becoming Amish was more than putting on a dress and living without modern conveniences. She'd learned about their faith and commitment through *Aenti's* journal, and converting wasn't something someone did without spending time in prayer and following God's direction. "May I ask you a question?"

"*Jah*, anything."

Ellie snatched the paperwork off the table. "Do you know anything about my *aenti* putting her property in my name ten years ago?" She handed him the document. "This says I own two hundred and forty acres."

He studied the forms quietly, then handed them back. "*Jah*, it seems you do."

Chapter 15

Ezra set the block sander down, then grabbed the tack cloth and wiped the fine dust off the mahogany dresser. He hoped Mr. Pergerson's wife was as pleased with the bedroom set as Ezra was with his work. The polyurethane would take a day or two to apply in multiple coats, allowing time for it to fully dry between applications. Then another day to dry before he delivered the furniture. With Christmas eight days away, he should have plenty of time to finish the project.

A heavy pounding sounded on the shop door.

"It's open," he yelled.

Ellie entered, Bonnie's journal in hand. "Why didn't you tell me?"

"Tell you what?"

"The two hundred and forty acres includes your house, the barns, the pastures. According to the courthouse, it's all one piece."

He shrugged.

"That's why you brought me wood. Why you pulled my RV out of the mud. Why you looked after me. You said you were being neighborly when really you didn't want me to sell."

"That's *nett* all true." He tossed the cloth on the dresser and moved closer. "I looked after you because you're Bonnie's niece. I was trying to be neighborly. As for the courthouse papers, I wasn't aware of her putting everything in your name."

She stared at him hard. "And that's all you're going to say?"

He focused on the sawdust floor several seconds before lifting his gaze to meet hers. "It's true, I don't want you to sell the place." He moved closer. "Against everything I believe about . . . separating myself from *Englischers*—from you, Ellie Whetstone—I can't stay away from you. I've tried. So, *nay*, I don't want you to leave."

"You're still not telling me everything."

He moved closer, his willpower weakening. *Lord, stop me if this isn't right.* Ellie leaned closer, her lips slightly parted. His heart pulsed hard against his chest, driving the need to take her into his arms. Capturing her mouth, he found her lips were soft, smooth, and tasted like cherries. He pulled back and gazed into her eyes. Then, feeling a bit off balance with what felt like hummingbirds in his chest, he kissed her again. *Stop. I'm going to be shunned for this. Unequally yoked. Think about the church commitment . . . Allison.* Ezra broke away, this time dropping his hands from around her waist and taking a step back. "I'm sorry. I should have had more self-control."

She blinked a few times, then shook her head as though loosening her thoughts. "You should have told me about the handshake agreement you had with my *aenti*." She set the journal on the worktable, then hurried to the door. "I have to pick Lulu up from the vet."

Ezra stared a long moment at the empty space where she'd stood. He hadn't told her about the agreement because it didn't matter. He couldn't afford to buy the farm. He returned to work, and when he'd finished applying the first coat of polyurethane, he flipped through Bonnie's journal as he waited for it to dry.

His sister had been right about Bonnie praying without ceasing. She'd certainly spent a great deal of time petitioning God for others. He wiped his eyes and his wet face on his shirtsleeve. Recalling Charlotte's battle with cancer wasn't something he wanted to do.

He'd chosen to keep the better days close to heart and focus on her strength and courage. He came to the book marker Ellie must have left in the pages. His handshake arrangement with Bonnie to buy his house and farm. He'd made the monthly payments up until Charlotte was diagnosed, but medical bills left him buried in debt. Bonnie had been understanding. She didn't owe anything on the house, so all she worried about was paying the taxes, and he'd been able to sell enough furniture each year to cover that expense and a little more. But the real estate agent had given Ellie an inflated estimated value to list the place, and Ezra couldn't blame her for deciding to sell. She could live somewhere with electricity and hot water and other modern conveniences.

He'd already talked with Josephine's husband about him and Allison moving into their *daadihaus* until he could get on his feet. Things would work out—if he could rid his thoughts of Ellie. He never should have allowed himself to become smitten. *Englischers* rarely become Amish, and he wasn't leaving the faith.

Ezra read several more journal entries, then forced himself to put it aside and get back to work on the furniture. He applied another coat of polyurethane, taking great care to spread it evenly and not to leave bubbles. After all the pieces were coated a second time, he glanced at the wall clock. Ellie should be home with Lulu by now. He closed the can of polyurethane, cleaned the brush, then took a walk while the furniture dried.

Ellie's RV was parked by her house. He climbed the porch steps and knocked.

She opened the door and stepped aside without saying anything.

"I came to see how Lulu was doing," he said.

"The vet gave her a tranquilizer. She's sleeping." She folded the quilt she was holding and stacked it on the table with some others.

"And her hip and leg?"

Ellie shrugged. "The vet returned the dislocated hip to its socket, but I won't know about her leg until the cast is off."

"I wanted to ask how you go about buying one of those dogs. I thought a dog like Lulu would make a nice Christmas gift for Allison. I'd even let her keep it in the *haus*."

"I didn't think you were a dog person," she said.

"Ellie, I'm sorry I kissed you."

She dropped the quilts into a tote and snapped the lid on the container, then grabbed an Amish dress off the table to fold. "I'm sorry I tempted you," she said, giving the dress a shake. "I hadn't thought I was being . . . flirtatious, but apparently that's what the Amish think about us *Englischers*, isn't it?"

"It was *mei* weakness, *nett* yours."

"Yeah, right." She tossed the dress into an empty tote, then fisted her hands on her hips. "I could have stopped you, but I didn't . . . I didn't want to. One reason I read the journal was to learn about the Amish way. I tried on my *aenti's* dress because I wanted to know what it'd feel like." Her voice cracked. "Spending time in this house, around you and the other members, I felt as though I belonged." Her face pinched. "But I need to ask you something."

"Anything."

"Did the members treat me well for your sake? Because they didn't want me to sell the farm?"

He shook his head. "*Nett* many people know about the arrangement or that I couldn't make the payments. I'm sure the members treated you warmly in honor of Bonnie. They know how much she prayed for you after your mother left the faith and took you away. Bonnie believed God would lead you back here."

"Will you thank the others for me?" She picked up the full tote and went to the door.

Thank them? Ezra followed her to the RV and, noticing

suitcases in the underneath storage compartment, asked, "Are you leaving?"

"I have to take Lulu to Ann Arbor and . . ."

"And what?"

Her eyes welled. "I don't know what's going to happen. I don't know if I'll pick up another dog." She used her shirtsleeve to wipe her eyes.

"You love that dog. How could you get rid of her?" Panic gripped his throat. "Let me take her. You know Allison loves her—she needs Lulu."

Ellie cried harder and ran back into the house.

He took a deep breath. *Lord, help me say the right things.* He walked back to the house and met Ellie standing at the sink. "Will you tell me why you're crying?"

"I can't give you the dog. I'm not Lulu's owner. I'm her handler. After I spoke with the vet about her expected recovery, I found out she most likely won't be able to show at Westminster. I informed the owners and was told to bring her to Ann Arbor immediately. I don't even know if I have a job anymore."

"Do you think the owner will sell her, and if so, will they wait until the twenty-third? I'm delivering the furniture order in a few days and I'll get a check for five thousand dollars." He took a breath and let it out slowly. He'd never spent that much on a horse, and now he was buying a dog.

"Ezra, even if she never competes again, she has breeding potential. A pup with her pedigree will sell easily for twenty to thirty thousand. Average litters are eight to ten, times that by at least four or five litters and—"

He gulped. "Lulu wouldn't have been hurt if Allison hadn't had a seizure." He reached for Ellie's hand and held it. "I'm sorry. This is all *mei* fault."

"No, it isn't." She smiled. "God knows the beginning from

the end. None of this is a surprise to Him, and I choose to trust God."

Ezra's throat swelled. Ellie's strong faith, her trust in God, was something he needed to put into practice. Over the years, he'd allowed the stress and worry of dealing with Allison's condition, and of losing his wife, his farm, to take root in his heart. He knew at that moment, he didn't want to lose Ellie. "Do you have to go?"

She nodded.

"Are you leaving tonight or in the morning?"

"Tonight."

He cleared his throat. "Will you be back for Christmas? Allison and I always go on a sleigh ride, and I'd like you to join us."

She smiled. "I would like that." Her lips quivered and she started to cry again.

Ezra ushered her into his arms. *Lord, please convince her to make this place her home.*

Chapter 16

Ezra stood at the frosted kitchen window, sipping coffee. More snow had fallen since he'd milked the cow this morning, but it still didn't feel like Christmas. He was surprised by how strange and empty he'd felt since Ellie left. How lonely it'd been to check on her house and not see her there. He'd kept the fire going so the pipes wouldn't freeze, all while knowing that if she didn't return by New Year's, he would close up the house until spring—or until it sold.

Allison padded out to the kitchen, smiling. She knew they didn't open presents until later, but she was excited as all *kinner* were about Christmas. He'd carved a wooden horse and a dog out of mahogany and hoped she liked them, even though she'd asked for a new doll, saying the old dolly was Lulu's.

His daughter tugged on his shirt. "*Boppli* Jesus' day, *jah*?"

"That's right." He set the coffee mug down and picked her up, kissing her on her cheek. "We need to get ready for *Aenti* Josephine and *Onkel* Matthew." Last evening, he and Allison had placed candles in the windows in recognition of Jesus' being the light of the world and decorated the table with candles and sprigs of balsam too. Then they spent time making cards out of brown packing paper for the members of the district for Allison to hand out on Second Christmas. He had hoped Ellie would be back to receive her card, but it wasn't looking like she would make it to the celebration after all.

Allison tugged on his arm. "We make cookies *nau*?"

He chuckled. "*Jah*, let's get started." Ezra turned on the tap water and held Allison as she washed her hands, then set her down as he cleaned up. His sister and brother-in-law weren't due to arrive for a few hours, and he'd promised Allison they would make a batch of sugar cookies to surprise his sister.

Allison pushed a chair up to the counter and climbed on it as Ezra gathered the ingredients. Making the cookie dough took longer with Allison in charge of the stirring, but they laughed and had fun together.

Ezra rolled out the dough, and Allison used a canning jar lid to cut out the cookies. Once the first cookie sheet was on the oven rack, he helped Allison wash her hands again. While standing at the sink he noticed a car drive past the window, but with the windows frosted, he couldn't make out the visitor. Ezra grabbed a dish towel and dried his hands as he went to the door.

Ellie? His heart hammered at such a fast pace his breathing turned ragged. The moment she climbed out of the car and flashed her smile at him, he knew there would be no denying his feelings. *Oh, Lord. All those prayers* mei *sister had for Ellie—and me . . . Thank You.*

Ellie waved. "Merry Christmas, Ezra."

He smiled. "Merry Christmas." *Lord, I've missed her so.*

"Can I get your help, please?" Ellie asked.

He glanced over his shoulder at Allison rolling a ball of dough. "I'll be back in a minute." He slipped out the door. "What can I do?"

She pointed to the backseat. "Come see."

He peered into the window. Lulu was lying on the seat, her back leg in a cast and a green bow tied around her neck.

"I'm giving her to Allison," she said, tearing up.

"How did you manage to keep her?"

She opened the car door. "I'll tell you after we get her inside."

Ezra eased Lulu into his arms. His carved wooden dog would pale in comparison to Lulu.

Ellie went ahead and opened the door for Ezra. His heart swelled when Allison squealed.

"*Mei* Lulu." She jumped up and down, clapping her hands, then trailed Ezra into the sitting room.

"Be nice to Lulu. She has a sore leg," he said as Allison sat beside Lulu and patted the dog's head.

Ezra motioned with a head nod to Ellie, and she followed him into the kitchen. "It's *gut* to see you. I missed you."

She smiled. "I missed you too."

"Tell me what happened downstate."

"The owner had an orthopedic vet examine her spine, hips, and legs, and he deemed she would never be show quality again. Another vet determined the accident did damage to her reproductive organs."

"And you sold the RV to pay the bill."

She shook her head. "The owner filed an insurance claim. Apparently she was worth more lame. Once the paperwork and proof were submitted, he told the vet to put her down, but I convinced him to let me have her."

"I can't believe he'd consider putting her down." Ezra shook his head.

"Before he agreed to release her, I had to have her spayed. It was for her own safety. Besides, I didn't think you would want a dozen more Lulus one day."

He chuckled. "One indoor animal is plenty. But why are you giving her to Allison?"

"Just being neighborly." She winked.

He reached for her hands. "So does that mean *mei* neighbor isn't going to sell her *haus* and leave again?"

"That depends." She smiled. "Do you really think I look *gut* in an Amish dress?"

"*Jah*, for sure," he said without hesitation. "Does that mean—?"

"I've *kumm* home? I need to talk with the bishop yet, but *jah*."

Her decision to become Amish was sweet music to his ears.

She sighed. "I wish *Aenti* Bonnie were here to see that her prayers were answered."

"I wish she were here too. I would thank her for praying for all of us and for keeping the journal."

He pulled her into his arms and kissed her. "I've fallen in love with you, Ellie."

"I love you too."

"The Amish way will take a lot of adjustment, but I promise to help you every step of the way."

She leaned back and smiled. "Are you going to teach me how to drive a horse and buggy now that I've sold my RV?"

"Absolutely. We'll start today with the sleigh."

Allison bounded into the kitchen and wrapped her arms around Ellie's legs. "*Danki* for Lulu."

"You're *wilkom*, sweetie."

His daughter's big blue eyes darted between him and Ellie. "*Mei* Ellie."

Ezra chuckled as Allison skipped back into the sitting room. He turned to Ellie. "You know what that means?"

She shook her head.

"Allison claimed Lulu as hers the first day she met the dog, and now she's claiming you."

Ellie smiled. "And what about you?"

Ezra put his arms around Ellie and leaned in so they were forehead to forehead. "I don't think we're going to be neighbors long." As he bent to kiss her, gleeful sounds of Allison and Lulu filled the room. He hadn't felt this alive in years. His heart swelled knowing Ellie loved him enough to walk away from the *Englisch* world. His eyes moistened. Ellie hadn't just *kumm* home for Christmas. She'd *kumm* home to him—home to stay.

Discussion Questions

1. At the National Dog Show, Ellie's fleeting accomplishments of her life's work were captured on air in fifteen seconds. Have you ever worked hard on something only to realize later that in the grand scheme of things it wasn't that big of a deal?
2. Ellie learned about her aunt's faith in God by reading her prayer journal. Do you think that was her aunt's intention in writing it? Have you considered starting a faith journal for your loved ones to read after you're gone?
3. Do you think part of Ellie's attraction to Ezra was because he reminded her of her father? Do you think God sometimes uses unusual ways, such as memories, to draw people together?
4. Ezra was positive the dog had something to do with his daughter's seizures. Do you think he jumped to that conclusion prematurely? Was keeping his daughter away from the dog the right thing to do?

Acknowledgments

I would like to thank my husband, Dan for his love and support. My children, Lexie, Danny, and Sarah, for their help around the house and for being awesome kids.

I would like to thank my agent, Natasha Kern. Thank you for believing in me and for all your help! I owe a great amount of thanks to Becky Monds and Natalie Hanemann for their outstanding work editing this book, Kristen Golden for her marketing expertise, and for everyone at HarperCollins Christian Publishing who has worked diligently to make this book a success! I am truly grateful for all that you do.

About the Author

Ruth Reid is a CBA and ECPA bestselling author of the Heaven on Earth series. She's a full-time pharmacist who lives in Florida with her husband and three children. When attending Ferris State University School of Pharmacy in Big Rapids, Michigan, she lived on the outskirts of an Amish community and had several occasions to visit the Amish farms. Her interest grew into love as she saw the beauty in living a simple life.

Visit Ruth online at ruthreid.com
Facebook: Author-Ruth-Reid
Twitter: @authorruthreid